Tofino Storm

Edie Claire

fifth of the Pacific Horizons novels

Dedication

For my husband,
who makes "happily ever after"
as real as it gets.

Prologue

Peck, Missouri, Spring 1994

Christi Miller leaned over the perpetually sticky, discolored Formica countertop of her rental trailer to peer out her kitchen window. She didn't like the look of the sky. Perhaps the peculiar yellowish cast to the clouds was an artifact of the scratched, cracked glass? There was no wind, nor was there any rain. But she felt uneasy. It had been cloudy all day, but in the last few minutes an oppressive stillness had descended on her home like a shroud.

The toddler beside her shrieked with displeasure and squirmed in her highchair.

"I know, I know, baby," Christi cooed, opening the oven door to check on her latest mommy masterpiece — homemade macaroni and cheese. They might be living in a dump at the moment, but there would be no cheap boxed stuff for her little girl. Christi knew how to make the dish right, with two kinds of real cheese and the perfect speckling of bread crumbs. Unfortunately, the casserole was taking forever to get bubbly and browned, and Laney was hungry. "Just give it another two minutes, okay?" Christi extended a toy. "You want your fuzzy bug?"

Evidently, Laney did not. The 20-month-old's reddened face screwed up into a mask of rage, and she batted the toy away and let loose with another scream just as the phone rang.

"Okay, okay!" the young mother capitulated, grabbing a box of goldfish-shaped crackers from the counter and shaking some onto the highchair tray. "Have an appetizer, then. But you're *going* to eat a good lunch, young lady!"

The child quieted instantly and reached for the crackers. Christi picked up the phone. "Hello?"

"Did you see the tornado watch?" her mother's voice asked worriedly. May Burgdorf was technically her grandmother, but neither made the distinction.

"No, Ma, but I'm not surprised," Christi replied. "What does this make now, three watches this week?"

"Pack up the baby and come over here," May ordered. "I hate you living in that wreck of a trailer. Makes me nervous. It's not safe."

Christi stifled a sigh. It would be easier to argue if she didn't second-guess her own decision on an hourly basis. She had nothing against the stately, yet homey red brick house on Second Street. She'd certainly had a warm and happy childhood there. But Christi had moved on once, and it didn't feel right to go backwards. A married woman with a child should have her own place, even if she had no husband anymore.

She clenched her jaws to stem the pressure that rose behind her eyes. She refused to cry again. Jimbo was gone now, buried three weeks yesterday, and her tears wouldn't bring him back. She and Laney were on their own, and if the rental trailer was all she could afford until her widow's benefits came in from the Army, so be it. Tempting as it was to crawl back into her childhood bed and do nothing but sob, she was a mother now. She could and would stand on her own two feet.

But the damned sky was giving her the creeps. And she didn't believe it was just the glass.

"Okay, Ma, I'll bring her over for her nap. Just let me finish up her lunch first."

"Well, hurry, honey," May replied, sounding relieved. "I'll be waiting for you."

Christi said goodbye and hung up. Laney was beginning to squawk again. The child had eaten only a few crackers before throwing the rest on the floor. "I thought you were hungry!" Christi bemoaned, peering into the oven again. She decided the casserole was brown enough. She grabbed a hot pad, pulled the dish out, and set it on the stovetop to cool. A cracker crunched under her foot. "Teddy?" she called over the child's continuing wails. "Where are you?"

The little terrier mix appeared, his nails clicking on the faded linoleum.

"Aren't you going to eat this?" Christi asked with concern, scooting a cracker in the dog's direction. Since when did any food in her house last more than a few seconds at ground level? The dog practically lived under Laney's highchair.

Teddy moved toward the cracker, sniffed it, and pattered away again. Christi watched as he circled their small living area restlessly. Teddy had always been a hyper sort, but the not-eating thing was strange. He seemed anxious.

Laney continued squawking. Christi spooned some of the mac and cheese onto a plastic toddler plate and began to blow on it. "Just a minute. It's coming," she promised, her eyes still on the dog. He had freaked out before in thunderstorms, but that was because he didn't like thunder. There was no thunder now.

Laney's cries graduated to ear-splitting shrieks. Christi extended one reasonably cool spoonful of the cheesy noodles, but the toddler showed no interest. Her little hands clamped on the edges of her tray and she arched her back, trying to slip down through the hole to freedom.

"Oh, all right, all right!" Christi agreed, removing the tray and unbuckling the child's seatbelt. "We'll eat something at Gran's."

Laney slipped down out of the chair and was toddling off after the dog when Christi heard it. The high, mournful wail of the city storm siren. The tornado watch had turned into a warning. Her muscles tensed, but she was more annoyed than frightened. How she hated that sound! It had plagued her since childhood, sending her and her classmates to crouch beside concrete walls with their hands over their heads, driving her family into their little downstairs bathroom — sometimes for hours at a time. The little half bath had always smelled of sewer gas no matter how well May cleaned it, and now the unpleasant smell and the ominous wail of the storm siren were forever linked in Christi's mind.

She groused to herself as she fetched plastic storage containers from the cabinet. Tornado warnings in the spring were part and parcel of living in Peck, a town of roughly three hundred people situated on the flat plains north of the Missouri Bootheel. But this spring had been worse than usual. The warnings seemed to get more frequent every year, stirring everybody up over what almost always turned out to be nothing. She understood the terms: a watch meant that a tornado might happen, whereas a warning meant that somebody somewhere *thought* they saw a funnel cloud. But as many times as the siren had gone off, a real tornado hadn't hit Peck in nearly a hundred years.

"Laney, honey, can you find your shoes?" she called. "We're going to run over to your grandma's real quick, okay?"

Teddy barked. Christi looked up from spooning hot macaroni and cheese to see the little dog running in tight circles in the living room. The toddler followed him around and around, laughing. "Teddy?"

A sudden noise sent a cold chill down her spine. The wind had picked up. It had picked up considerably. Just minutes ago, there had been nothing. She whirled back to the window to see tree limbs bowing, some of their newly emerged leaves ripping from their still-green stems and flying away.

Perhaps they wouldn't go to the house on Second Street. It was only a five-minute drive, but...

"Dog dog," the toddler babbled, the light laughter no longer in her voice. "Go!"

Christi didn't need to look to know that the dog was now racing from one end of the aged two-bedroom trailer to the other with the toddler in full pursuit. She could feel the vibration of the floor beneath her feet. She grabbed the plastic containers and the still-hot casserole dish and shoved them all into the refrigerator.

Something hit the side of the house with a bang, making Christi jump. Was that a stick? A tree branch? Her adrenaline spiked. Maybe this warning did mean something.

"Laney!" she called again, thinking hard. What should she do? She couldn't take her daughter out in the car now. Not in this wind, with everything blowing around! They'd have to take cover in the bathroom. They could get into the tub, put a mattress over their heads...

"Dog," Laney cried again, distressed. "Dog, Mommy!" The terrier was in the kitchen again, running rings around the empty highchair.

"He's okay, honey," Christi soothed as she worked her way around the crazed dog. "Hey, I know! You want to play hide and seek? Teddy can play with us! We'll all go hide in the bathtub. Okay?"

The wind had gotten louder. The trailer began to creak and groan as if giant hands were squeezing it between them. Christi's ears popped. They had to hurry! She had to get the mattress. But no, she couldn't, could she? The new one Jimbo had gotten her for Christmas was queen-sized, and it weighed a ton. Even if she could move it, it would as likely suffocate them as protect them.

The dog moved to the kitchen door. He jumped up and down, scratching at it frantically. The toddler teared up in distress. "Doggie wannow!"

Christi paused for a fraction of a second, her brain dutifully registering the significance of what could possibly have been her baby's first sentence. But she had no time to dwell on it. "No, he's fine. We're all going to play hide and seek!" Pellets of hail assaulted the metal roof and siding. *Hurry!* She decided to settle for the crib mattress. "Go and get in the tub right now!" she ordered, giving the toddler a push toward the little bathroom that was — at most — eight feet away. "I'll be right there!"

She scrambled into the nursery, pulled up the mattress, and stashed it under one arm. She was turning back toward the doorway when she heard a train approaching. It was rumbling across town at a crazy speed, vibrating, shaking everything in its path, coming on louder and louder still, bearing down...

Christi moved as fast as she could back into the living room — it was only a few feet! — but she stumbled; her legs felt like lead. "Laney!" she yelled, but she could barely hear herself. Her ears were pounding; her whole body felt as if it were submerged in some mysterious liquid. "Laney!"

The toddler wasn't in the living room. She must be in the tub already. *Good girl!* Christi fought to cover the last few feet to the bathroom, but a wet wind struck her face, blew her backward, ripped the mattress from her arms. She looked with horror to see her kitchen exposed to the outside, the thin metal door banging furiously on its hinges.

A fiery heat of determination surged through her veins. She pushed back against the strange pressure that surrounded her and forced her way toward the bathroom and her daughter. She had lost the mattress, but no matter. She still had her own, well-padded body...

The tiny room was empty.

Laney wasn't there.

Christi screamed. A loud, shrill, bloodcurdling scream. She whirled around, looked through the doorway to the other bedroom. *Empty.* The train hadn't stopped. It was only getting louder. Stronger. Closer...

She scrambled back into the living room. The walls of the trailer were groaning, heaving, straining... the kitchen door was gone.

Doggie want out.

Christi stared into the void. Debris flew past horizontally.

Doggie want out.

No.

No, no, no, no...

Christi lunged toward the open doorway, but wound up with her feet straight out in front of her and her back pressed against a wall. Where she could see grass before, tree branches waved.

She remembered nothing else.

Chapter 1

Jason Buchanan shot a glance at the nautical clock that adorned the far wall of his office, which was also the lobby of the Pacific Rim Surfing Lodge. He blew out a breath of frustration. Ordinarily, he enjoyed his time here. He had paneled the interior by hand with reclaimed barnwood and decorated it with a personally pleasing mixture of nature photographs and surfing paraphernalia, and its giant picture window offered an amazing view of the Pacific crashing against the west coast of Vancouver Island. But his last guest of the day was now officially overdue. The surfing lodge was known for its casual atmosphere and self-serve mojo, but he still had to check new people in, and he'd been hoping this one would be early. A storm was coming in tonight, and he wanted to catch a late afternoon wave before conditions deteriorated.

He turned his gaze to the vista outside, and a satisfied smile chased away his frown lines. Being able to lay his hands on a piece of property fronting Chesterman Beach had been the coup of a lifetime, and he appreciated it hourly. Never mind that the parcel in question had been a pie-shaped wedge littered with the debris of a collapsed shack and tainted by rumors of drainage and septic issues. Jason was good with his hands, and he knew people. He'd lived in British Columbia since he was ten and had been a fixture of the Tofino surf scene ever since he'd gotten permission to drive his grandfather's truck down from Port McNeil. He'd been patient, he'd watched, and he'd waited. And when the right property surfaced, he'd jumped on it. Now, barely in his thirties, he was the sole proprietor of a one-of-a-kind hostel that provided fellow surfers around the globe with a comfortable, budget-friendly home base from which to explore the cold rush of the Canadian Pacific.

Jason Buchanan loved his life. He loved Tofino, he loved his surf lodge, he loved women, and he loved his job — with the exception of moments like this one, when customers tested his sunny good nature by violating one of his few but clearly stated rules. Everyone knew that if you wanted a bed at his hostel, you'd better pick up your key during the designated window. Arrive after the stated hour, and catching up with the proprietor was your problem. It got dark early in January, and Jason had his own surfing and barhopping to do. It was simple common courtesy.

He gazed out at the sky, which was rapidly darkening with heavy, fast-moving clouds. The waves were kicking up nicely, but unfortunately, so was the wind. *Forget it, dude.* There would be no more sweet rides today.

He fired up his laptop. If he was stuck here awhile, he might as well catch up on his bookkeeping. As tempted as he was to put out his "no vacancy" sign and leave his tardy check-in to her own devices, he couldn't bring himself to do it. If one of his regulars were messing with him, he'd have taken off half an hour ago. But the woman on the phone had sounded so clueless he felt sorry for her. She wasn't a surfer and didn't even know what a hostel was; she'd just been desperate for someplace inexpensive to stay. Fortunately for her, he'd had a single room open, and offering safe digs for women traveling solo was a point of pride for him. Besides, she'd said she was taking the ferry over from Vancouver, which meant she could have been delayed any number of legitimate ways.

He was deep into accounting mode when the door to the lobby quietly opened and shut, followed by steps that were nearly noiseless except for the squeak of a wet sneaker on the floorboards. He clicked on save and rerouted his attention.

The woman before him looked like a drowned kitten. Her puffy parka was soaked through, its useless faux-fur trimmed hood dangling down her back beneath wet, stringy clumps of blond hair. Her well-worn jeans were darkened with rainwater and her squishy shoes had left puddles in her wake. Jason had been so intent he hadn't even noticed it was pouring outside. Still, there was no way the amount of liquid she was packing had fallen on her between the parking lot and his door.

He couldn't help but grin. She looked so adorably... well, pathetic. She was of average height and build for a woman, but being soaked to the skin did lend her a certain childlike quality, as did the plastered strands of hair that obscured the majority of her face. "Oh, my," he said playfully. "Looks like you got caught in it."

The woman stepped up to the counter. She centered her dripping coat over the floor mat but made no attempt to pull her soggy bangs off her face. "You still have a room?"

Jason raised an eyebrow. Her tone wasn't quite rude, but it was definitely all business, with virtually no inflection and absolutely no humor. Some of its flatness might be due to the midwestern American accent he'd picked up on the phone, but his casual levity was clearly not appreciated.

He could have wiped the sympathetic grin off his face, but that wasn't the way he rolled. "We absolutely do," he said cheerfully, reaching under the counter. "Provided you are..." he trailed off, prompting her to supply the name on the reservation. He'd gotten burned by posers before.

"Laney Miller," she replied. "Sorry I'm late. The bus broke down."

Jason raised both eyebrows. "The bus?" he said incredulously. Nobody took the bus, at least not in January. The free shuttle around town only ran in the summer; winter visitors were pretty much stranded without wheels of their own. Besides which, the nearest bus stop was a good twenty-minute walk away. No wonder she wasn't feeling it.

He studied her further. She wasn't supermodel material, but she was probably pretty cute without all the hair stuck to her face. What he could see of her eyes was certainly intriguing. They were large, beautifully shaped, and of a vibrant, cerulean blue. Jason cleared his throat, then served up his most charming smile. "Well, that explains a lot. Sorry for the lousy welcome to Tofino!

If I'd known you were hoofing it, I'd have come out and picked you up myself."

The wet woman made no response. Her pretty eyes flickered over him with disinterest and focused on the picture window beyond.

Ouch. So much for the charm offensive.

"Can you see the ocean from here?" she asked, with the first detectable hint of pleasure he'd heard. Ordinarily it would be a stupid question, since only a few hundred feet separated the lodge from the powerful waves that buffeted the black rocks and brown sand of the coast. But at the moment, little was visible to her besides fat drops of rain streaking across the glass.

"You sure can," he said proudly. "This view's as good for storm watching as any of the pricier resorts." He reached under the counter and produced her key, which he delivered with his usual check-in spiel. She took the key from his hand with a nod, but appeared to be only half-listening. Her gaze remained locked on the window, her expression pensive. "So, what brings you to Tofino?" he finished pleasantly, attempting to break her trance.

She turned back to him, her manner all business again. "Do you know where I can rent a car?" she asked, ignoring his question. "Not a regular place — I mean something local, and super cheap. I don't care if it's a wreck as long as it runs."

"I... might," Jason said uncertainly. In fact, he did. He had an extra car himself. But he wanted to know a little more about her first. "If you give me until tomorrow, I can ask around."

"Okay." Her blue eyes surveyed him critically, as if every word from his mouth was suspect.

If he were not in fact half-lying, he could be offended. But he didn't offend easily. He smiled at her instead. "So, I'm guessing you're a storm watcher?"

The pupils within her blue eyes widened, as if she were surprised by the question. Then she averted her gaze and stepped away from the counter, back toward the entrance. Only then did he notice her luggage, and the reason she was soaking wet in the first place. She did have a rain jacket — she'd just chosen to wrap it around her suitcase instead of herself. "I'm here to see the ocean," she surprised him by answering as she tugged her suitcase toward the door to the common room. "It will be a first for me."

"First time seeing the Pacific?" he asked gaily, excited on her behalf.

"Any ocean," she replied, turning her back to him.

"*Any* ocean?" Jason repeated with amazement. "Like, ever? Really?"

But he was doomed to wonder. Before she could reply — assuming she even would have — the outside door swung open wide, admitting a very tall man wearing a comparatively expert-looking waterproof jacket, backpack, and boots. Laney threw the newcomer only a passing glance, then disappeared through the doorway without another word.

Jason stifled his disappointment as he turned to his other guest. "Hey there," he greeted. "I hope you're not looking for a room tonight, because we're all—" He stopped himself. He'd never met the man before, but he'd seen a picture or two. The visitor was in his early thirties, with ginger hair and a friendly, mischievous sort of smile. "Ben Parker?" Jason guessed.

The man's smile widened. "Afraid so!" he replied, extending his hand. The men exchanged a fist bump, followed by a hearty shake. "And you must be Jason. Great to meet you finally."

"Likewise," Jason agreed. He and Ben had been conversing by email for well over a year now, after having been put in touch by a combination of mutual friends and family. Ben had been trying to decide whether to pursue his doctorate in oceanography at the University of Victoria or elsewhere, and since Jason had graduated with a bachelor's from the relevant department, he'd been able to supply an insider's scoop. Through the process they'd discovered much in common, and once Ben's decision was made they'd hatched plans for him to come up and surf sometime. Today's visit had been expected... just not today.

"I know I'm early," Ben apologized. "Don't worry about putting me up tonight. Sorry — impulse thing. Haley wanted to spend a few extra days with her sister and the kids in Newport Beach, and I had to get back to school. But Victoria's deadly boring without her."

Jason chuckled. He'd never met anyone who talked more frequently and glowingly about his wife, with the exception of his brother Thane, of course. But at least Thane was a newlywed. Ben and Haley had been married for years already! How they kept from getting deadly bored with each other, he had no idea.

"I wasn't putting you up here at the lodge anyway," Jason explained. "You can crash at my place. Makes it easier to get an early start. Assuming the storm's blown over by then..."

The men fell into an enthusiastic discussion of weather and waves as Jason shut down his laptop and prepared to lock up the office. The rain abated as they talked, but the wind had kicked up another notch.

Jason finished what he needed to do and was about to suggest they leave when he noticed an unexpected look of concern on Ben's face. "What?" Jason asked, following the other man's gaze out the window. "Nobody's trying to surf in this mess, are they?"

Ben shook his head. "No," he said in a low voice, pointing not at the surfing beach, but toward the jumble of boulders at the nearby point. "It's that woman. Look. She's making me nervous. She looks like she's thinking about climbing up on those rocks."

Jason located the figure in question and sucked in a breath. He knew that crimson-colored raincoat. He'd seen it not ten minutes ago. "That's Laney."

"Does she know what she's doing? I mean—"

"Hell, no. She just told me she's never been to the ocean before!"

Their eyes met with shared alarm. When they looked back out, the distant figure was placing two hands and a sneaker up the side of a boulder.

Both men uttered expletives and lunged for the door. They collided shoulder to shoulder in the process, after which Jason took the lead, heading outside and around the building, then sprinting down the slope and onto the sand. "Laney!" he yelled. "Laney Miller! STOP!"

But his cries were useless against the howling wind, which stole the words from his mouth and tumbled them off over his shoulders. His waving arms were equally useless, since she was looking the opposite direction. By the time the men reached the base of the rocky outcropping, she was already on top of the large boulder closest to the water, standing with her face to the open ocean. From where they stood on the sand, she could neither see nor hear them.

Jason turned to Ben, gesturing in case his words were lost, even at this close distance. "I'll go up," he shouted. "You stay underneath."

Ben nodded, and the two exchanged another look — this one of sheer determination. What Laney didn't understand was that bracing oneself against the wind, particularly on wet rock, was one thing. Doing so while perched at the edge of an angry Pacific was another. She obviously had no knowledge of waves — how dramatically they could change in size and reach, coming from nowhere to pound heights that were previously untouched. Accidental drownings were more common in places like Hawaii, where the waves could get truly immense, but even in British Columbia, unsuspecting rock climbers were regularly swept to their deaths. The spot where Laney stood now might not appear dangerous, but even a modestly above-average wave could knock her off her feet. And with any slip, her body would strike the jagged rocks below even before she plunged into the frigid whitewater.

Jason scrambled up the side of the rocky outcropping, uncertain of his best plan of attack. He needed to reach her as quickly as possible, but he also had to avoid startling her, and the latter would be difficult when the only way he could approach her was from behind. He could see Ben moving into the surf below, wading out as far as he could to try and place himself in her peripheral vision. If Laney would turn her head even a fraction, he might succeed. But the woman remained standing still as a statue, looking not at the roiling surf below but *up* — facing straight into the wind, staring at the clouds overhead.

Jason had no time to ponder what in hell might be wrong with her. He chose his footing carefully and picked his way across the boulders in order to approach her from the far side. That way, if he did startle her, she would at least tend to fall toward where Ben — who had given up on catching her attention — should by now be waiting below.

He skirted the black rocks behind and around her exposed perch. Then he began inching forward over the large boulder itself, careful to place his feet in grooves and crags where he had some hope of maintaining traction in a wave. Eventually, he made his way far enough out to see the side of her face.

Laney's wet blond hair blew back in the wind, exposing high cheek bones flared with color and a small, pert nose. Wrapped in the oversized crimson raincoat, at first glance she again gave the impression of a vulnerable, defenseless child. But when he made out the grim expression on her face and the intensity of her gaze, he was struck with an unexpected sense of awe.

She was not appreciating the power of nature as an ordinary storm-watching tourist might. She was not reveling in it, worshipping it, or seeking inspiration from it. Nor — he was certain now — was she surrendering to it, as would someone who was suicidal. No, this small, inconsequential woman was freakin' *daring* it. She was standing alone on a rock at the edge of the most powerful, most deadly ocean on earth, staring into an infinite wind that could at any moment crush her like a bug, and her overriding attitude toward the storm she faced appeared to be... well, for lack of a better description... *Eff You.*

With an effort, he snapped himself back into action. "Laney!" he shouted, having little confidence that she could hear him, even now, when he stood mere feet away.

As expected, his voice dissolved into the wind, buffered by the constant crashing of the surf, and she made no response. Jason cast another glance out over the ocean and tensed. A taller than usual wave set was closing in. He double-checked his footing, then waved an arm as far out to her side as he could reach. "Laney!"

On the third sweep of his arm, her head swung round. Thankfully, her feet didn't follow. Her bold eyes fixed on him with a clear look of surprise, mingled with an appropriate degree of alarm. "What are you doing here?" she demanded.

Jason was reading her lips as much as he could hear her. He stretched one foot out onto a more vulnerable position on the rock and extended his arms. The taller waves would strike any second. If he moved any closer to where she stood now, they would both be toppled. "It's not safe!" he called, gesturing urgently for her to move toward him. "Come this way!"

The emotions on her face were easy to read — at least for him, since reading women was a skill he took some pride in. She was thinking that his sudden, unsolicited appearance here in her private space was an intrusion, and she resented it. She was perfectly fine, she thought, and didn't need his assistance. In assuming that she did, he was acting like every other patronizing, patriarchal, overbearing, egotistical, *yada, yada, yada...*

"There's no time!" he begged. "Come on!"

She looked over her shoulder. She must have registered the height of the wave currently bearing down on them, because when she turned back around, her face was ashen. This time, she did slide her feet, and as Jason feared, the wet rock was unforgiving. She might have regained her balance in time if she had reached out for him, but to his dismay, she opted to go it alone, throwing her arms out to her sides as ballast. Whether it would have worked or not they would never know, because in the next instant the wave broke and swept over the surface of the boulder, striking her lower legs with a blast of chilly seawater.

Forced to step back to hold his own position, Jason felt frustratingly helpless as he watched her footing become unmoored. But as he'd hoped, the wave swept her toward him involuntarily, and he was able to grasp one flailing wrist just as her body flipped horizontally and slipped beneath the foam. Her arm went disturbingly limp, and as the wave began to recede it tugged her unresisting form away from him again and out toward the edge of the boulder. Jason held on fast, swinging her weight in an arc to keep her from slipping over. As the wash that held her aloft began to stream away he quickly reeled her in, fighting to keep her head out of the water. At last, her whole body was within his control.

A barely audible voice shouted something to Jason from out of sight, and he looked over the edge of the boulder to see Ben standing in waist-high water, poised with his arms up, ready for a handoff. How the man managed to be standing there when three seconds ago he would have been underwater, Jason didn't know and didn't ask. He merely gripped Laney's still-limp form by the armpits and lowered her down.

"Got her!" Ben announced. Settling Laney over one shoulder like a sack of potatoes, he immediately began moving up the beach, only to be struck from behind by the next crashing wave. Fortunately, the second peak lacked the height of its predecessor, and Ben kept his feet easily and continued to move. Jason lost sight of them as he picked his way back over the boulders, but when he reached the sand he could see that Ben was well up the hill already.

Jason broke into a run and joined them just as Ben laid Laney down flat on the floor of the lobby and bent over her, running through a quick CPR check. "Her pulse is good," he proclaimed. Then, after a tense second or two, "And she's breathing."

Both men exhaled heavily. Jason grabbed his cell phone off the counter, then sank down on the floor. "I think she hit her head," he said miserably.

As he dialed 911, Ben gently put a hand to her wet blond hair and felt around to the back of her skull. When he pulled his hand back, his fingers were laced with blood.

Jason's heart sank in his chest. "We need an ambulance," he answered the dispatcher. "And quick."

Chapter 2

Laney couldn't help but chuckle to herself as she looked out over the barbed wire fence at the stagnant pond. It was surrounded by pasture on three sides and a county road on the fourth, and she could see nothing in the vicinity besides fence posts, a few scraggly trees, and six cows resting languidly in the shade of the latter. She shook her head in amusement. It wasn't funny, really. It would cost somebody significant money. But she still couldn't keep herself from smiling.

She walked back to the truck and checked for a cell signal. She was in luck. She found the number and dialed. "Hey, Dr. Jarvis," she greeted. "It's Laney. I think I found it."

"Awesome!" the older female voice on the other end of the line replied. "What kind of shape is it in?"

Laney cleared her throat. "I'm guessing not great, since it's submerged in about six feet of water. And, uh... cow manure."

There was a pause, followed by a random sampling of that uniquely colorful vocabulary for which the venerated professor was famous. "Are you serious?" she finished finally. "Where?"

"Pretty much right where we expected, based on the coordinates," Laney replied. "They're pointing to a cow pond. I can't be sure, because I can't see to the bottom of it. But I know I'm in the right spot, and if it was lying anywhere else around here, I would see it."

Dr. Jarvis swore again. "Well, take some pictures of the area and come on back, then. We'll just have to manage with the others for a while. I still can't believe it took off like that — damn things are supposed to be more stable. That's what they're made for!"

Laney surveyed the central Oklahoma landscape, which

extended in every direction as flat as a pancake with no other visible bodies of water. "Sheer bad luck, I guess," she commiserated. The weather pods were designed to withstand storms, but not to swim.

She looked at the trees under which the cows were lying and noted the recent wind damage. Some leaves still remained in the center of the trees, but the outer areas had been stripped bare and many distal limbs had been snapped off altogether. She wondered that any tree managed to survive to maturity in this area. Nearby Norman, Oklahoma was home to the National Weather Center — and the University of Oklahoma School of Meteorology — for a reason. It sat squarely in the middle of one of the most active zones of tornado activity in the world.

"At least that pod was one of the old ones," Laney continued, trying to soothe her mentor. "This wasn't its first direct hit from an EF4." *Not that EF3s couldn't do enough damage,* she thought absently, the tornado that tipped her mother's trailer never far from her mind. In the nearly twenty-five years since that fateful spring day, she had personally witnessed a dozen or more tornados and studied accounts of countless others that were far worse. Still, despite her best efforts at objectivity, the Peck tornado of 1994 would always play an outsized role in her psyche. At least she no longer suffered its emotional effects, those having been neatly suffocated by the weight of dispassionate scientific analysis required by her profession.

Dr. Jarvis made a sound halfway between a sigh and a growl. "Yeah, the base was already cracked. I noticed that when we set it out. God only knows how that happened."

Laney, who knew exactly how it had happened, squelched a smirk. The weather pods were designed to measure wind velocity, air pressure, and temperature under the most severe of conditions. But tumbling off the back of a moving pickup irresponsibly loaded by a team of hungover first-year grad students could cause a crack in just about anything. The guilty students had dutifully reported the event to their supervisor. But even he wasn't brave enough to pass that info on to Jarvis.

"I suspect we may find the base somewhere else, eventually," Laney suggested. "But the business end has had it."

Jarvis swore a little more, then released her — reportedly favorite — doctoral candidate to her duties. Laney snapped some pictures of the area as requested, then climbed back into the university's truck. She had just dropped her phone onto the empty passenger seat when it rang with a "yoo-hoo," the ringtone she'd assigned her mother.

"Hey, Mom," she greeted, picking up. "I'm out in the field right now — signal's touch and go. What's up?"

"This isn't your mother," a gravelly voice proclaimed. "I have her phone."

A unpleasant feeling rose up in Laney's middle. Her great-grandmother couldn't operate a smartphone. She had a hard enough time with a wireless portable. "Gran? Is something wrong?"

"Yes, honey," the voice answered with a croak. "Your mom's dying."

Laney's heart skipped a beat. But no, it couldn't be. Her mother had been perfectly fine yesterday! She drew in a long, slow breath and regrouped. The person to worry about wasn't her mother; it was Gran. May's mind had been slipping for a while now. She'd been repeating herself in conversation for years, cracking jokes about senior moments, misplacing things. But during Laney's last visit home to Missouri at Christmas, Gran had seemed noticeably worse. She couldn't add numbers in her head anymore, a talent she had always been proud of. She hadn't done any of her usual holiday baking, and she seemed reluctant to leave the house, even for a shopping trip to Poplar Bluff. Laney had expressed her worries to her mother at the time, but Christi believed it was merely old age. May was nearing ninety, after all.

"Gran?" Laney asked in as calm a voice as she could manage. "What do you mean exactly? I just talked to Mom yesterday. She was fine."

"No, she wasn't," the gravelly voice argued. Gran didn't

sound like herself at all. Having smoked cigarettes half her life, she'd never had the voice — or the demeanor — of an angel. But the tone Laney was used to was steady and tolerant, not sharp and agitated. "We're at the doctor's."

Laney's pulse quickened. Her mother *had* said something about a doctor's appointment today, but she hadn't sounded concerned. "What did the doctor say?"

"She's got cancer," May barked. "It's bad, honey. Real bad. She—" There was a gulp. Then Laney could hear her mother's voice in the background, indistinct and muffled, followed by a scuffling sound.

"Laney, don't you listen to her," Christi's voice came through, strong and angry. "She doesn't know what she's saying." The next phrase was slightly muffled again, and evidently not directed at Laney. "I can't believe you took my phone!"

"Mom," Laney broke in. "What's going on?"

After a pause, her mother answered. "Your Gran is just a little upset, that's all. She's overreacted to something the doctor said."

"Which was?" Laney demanded.

"Nothing!" Christi insisted. "I just went in for a checkup over some minor thing, and then they wanted to do these tests, but it's nothing to worry about!"

The hand that held Laney's phone began to tremble. She knew her mother too well to take such a blithe analysis at face value. Christi had always hated going to the doctor. Being generally healthy, she'd skated through life with relatively few medical intrusions and no complaints. Laney should have been more suspicious when her mother mentioned an appointment yesterday, considering that she'd mentioned nothing of the sort in years. "Mom, please tell me the truth," she begged. "What did the tests show?"

There was another long pause, during which Laney was certain she heard a sniffle. "I just need surgery," Christi replied, her voice suddenly thin. "And maybe some chemo. That's all."

In the background, Laney heard a hoarse, keening sound that chilled her. Her grandmother — the pride of Peck, the famously strong woman who comforted others but never shed tears herself, not even when she'd lost her husband of 49 years — was sobbing.

"Mom," Laney said firmly. "Hang in there. I'm coming home."

Chapter 3

Jason rose to his feet as a familiar man in a white lab coat stepped into the waiting room of Tofino's ten-bed hospital. "Hey, Jason," the doctor greeted solemnly. "They told me you were out here."

The men shook hands, and Jason quickly introduced Ben, who had been sitting next to him for the last hour. After Laney was taken away in the ambulance, the two of them had dropped by Jason's place in town just long enough to change out of their dripping clothes before following her here. "So how bad is it, Steve? Is she going to be okay?" Jason asked anxiously. He knew the doctor well; he had taught both the man's sons how to surf.

The doctor drew in a breath. "She's still unconscious, I'm afraid. Is it true that you don't know anything about her? She hadn't stayed at the lodge before?"

"No. I only just met her when she checked in."

"I was afraid of that," the doctor replied, sounding disconcerted. "And there was no one with her?"

"No." Jason was feeling increasingly disconcerted himself. "The paramedic got her wallet; have you reached her next of kin?"

The doctor scratched his chin. "Not yet, I'm afraid."

Jason frowned. Nobody should be alone in the hospital, particularly in another country. "She's going to be okay, isn't she? I mean, I can't help feeling responsible for her. She..." He stopped talking when he realized he had nothing rational to say. He'd talked to the woman for all of five minutes and knew virtually nothing about her.

"I'm sure you don't need to feel responsible," Steve assured, misunderstanding.

Jason shook his head. He didn't blame himself for Laney's injuries. He knew that he and Ben had done everything they could to prevent a worse catastrophe. But Jason did feel responsible *to* her. She might be ignorant of basic ocean safety, but five minutes was all he'd needed to know that she was a strong, self-sufficient person who would find her current state of helplessness mortifying. She might not have taken to him personally; doubtless she would have preferred he mind his own business rather than try so hard to be friendly. But she'd walked into his establishment healthy and vital and she'd left it on a stretcher. He was not okay with that.

"You really can't locate her family?" he pressed.

The doctor's thin lips smiled sadly. He seemed to come to a decision. "I'm afraid that right now, the two of you are all this woman has got. Her wallet had her driver's license and a student ID, and we did reach the university she attended. They said she wasn't currently enrolled, but they were willing to pass on her emergency contact information. We tried both names, her mother and her great-grandmother, but every number was disconnected. So the staff did a little digging online. It turns out that the patient's mother died less than a month ago, and the home address listed for both of them is up for sale."

Jason felt a sudden weight on his chest. He'd felt sorry enough for Laney before. He stole a glance beside him. Ben hadn't said a word, but in his eyes Jason saw the same, involuntary empathy — and irrational sense of responsibility — that he himself was feeling.

"Do you have any idea what brought her to Tofino?" the doctor asked. "Did she mention knowing anyone here? Meeting friends?"

"No. She only said she was here to see the ocean." Jason replayed everything he could remember from their brief conversation. "She said she'd never seen it before. But she did ask about renting a car, and she'd booked the room for a full week, so she must have had something specific in mind. Something besides surfing."

The doctor's brow furrowed. Then he let out a sigh. "Well, Jason, I can tell you this much. She has a cut on her scalp and some nasty bruises, but her main problem is concussion and the fact that she's been unconscious so long. We've got a neurologist in Victoria managing her case remotely, and he's advised monitoring her here, at least for now. As long as she shows some improvement over the next twenty-four hours, which he seems optimistic that she will, she should be all right. Hopefully she'll wake up soon and tell us all we need to know herself."

"Hopefully," Jason repeated. But hope had never been enough for him. Action was always preferable. "When she does wake up, will you let me know? She's bound to be confused, finding herself in a strange place. Maybe seeing my face and being able to go over what happened will help. Call me, day or night. I can be here in fifteen minutes."

The doctor smiled. He leaned in and shook Jason's hand again. "Will do."

Jason turned his master key in the lock of room number eight, opened the door, and slipped inside. Whether what he was about to do was technically legal, he didn't know. He didn't particularly care.

He took a look around the small but functional hostel unit that held a single twin bed, a dresser, a built-in closet, and a small sink. Laney couldn't have spent more than a few minutes here before heading out to see the ocean, but she had apparently used her time well. She'd hung her wet coat on the peg near the heater and scattered the soggy contents of her backpack across the floor to dry. Then presumably she'd put on the rain jacket, slipped her thin wallet and room key into a pocket, and taken off.

Jason surveyed what she had been carrying in the lightweight backpack. She had evidently expected the contents to get wet, because she'd stuffed it with nothing but wadded up clothes and toiletries. He surmised that anything she didn't want to get soaked, she had packed in the suitcase protected by her raincoat.

He glanced at the sorry, mud-spattered roller bag that sat beside the bed. It was still standing upright, fully zipped. Unless Laney had taken her phone to the beach and then lost it in the fall, it should be inside. Her phone and, with luck, some evidence of where she was headed.

Jason didn't hesitate. He lifted the bag up onto the bed and unzipped the main compartment. If she was protecting any electronics, she would have buried them deep. He pushed aside an assortment of cotton sweatpants, heavy sweaters, and thick socks with a smile and a shake of the head. *Americans.* They thought of Canada as nothing but snow and pine trees. Never mind that even in January, the coldest month of the year, the temperature in Tofino rarely dropped much below freezing. If Laney had done her research, she would have left the bulky stuff at home in favor of some quick-dry, insulating layers and a good pair of wellington boots.

He paused a moment, wondering if she had, in fact, done any research before boarding a plane — or a bus? — and heading someplace as offbeat and out of the way as Vancouver Island. Or had she packed up and taken off in a hurry, desperate to put both time and space between herself and her recent tragedy?

The corner of what appeared to be a laptop case peeked out from behind a pair of mittens, and Jason quickly unearthed it. He pulled out the computer, set it on the bed beside him, and booted it up. While it chugged and whirred to life, he dug a bit deeper and discovered her phone. He clicked the button, expecting to be stymied by her password but hoping for some clue from her home screen.

The picture that popped up filled him with unexpected sadness. It was a selfie of Laney with a middle-aged woman, both smiling broadly for the camera against the background of a family Christmas tree. An open, natural smile lit up Laney's face, displaying good cheer and a loving nature — neither of which Jason had had the pleasure of witnessing before.

The other woman in the picture had to be Laney's mother. Their comfortable posture with each other betrayed a tight bond, and the older woman's illness was painfully obvious. She was bone thin, her skin sallow and splotchy, her bald head partially covered by a Santa hat. But her smile, like her daughter's, was defiantly cheerful.

Saddened all over again, Jason blew out a breath and returned the phone to the suitcase. If Laney's great-grandmother was still alive, he intended to find her. The hospital had tried, but probably hadn't dug all that deeply. The medical staff had other duties, after all.

The laptop chimed, announcing its reawakening. Jason turned to it, but all he could see was a password prompt on a stock image of blue swirls. He shut the computer down again and closed it with a snap. Then he rifled through the remaining compartments of Laney's suitcase. She must have been carrying something helpful that wasn't password protected. Trip maps? A physical calendar? A note pad? At last, inside a separate zippered section, he hit pay dirt. A vinyl pocket folder.

He pulled it out and laid it across a knee. The folder was the same crimson color as her raincoat and was emblazoned with an intertwined O and U. Ohio? Oklahoma? He wasn't much into U.S. college sports; he would look it up in a minute. First, he would look inside.

The first thing that met his eyes was the distinctive dark blue cover and shiny gold eagle of an American passport. Behind it were a few other items, the first of which was a yellowed piece of newspaper, folded and encased in a loose-leaf sheet protector.

Jason looked at the passport first. Laney looked younger in the mugshot; her blond hair was longer and her cheeks a bit more round. Which made sense, given that the passport had been issued nearly seven years ago. Laney Carole Miller had been born in the state of Missouri in September, 1992. She was now twenty-seven years old. As far as he could tell from the lack of visas or stamps on the pages following, this was her first trip out of the country.

He set the passport aside. Then he drew in a breath and unfolded the fragile section of newsprint. It was the front page of a paper called the *Daily Republic*, from the city of Poplar Bluff, Missouri, dated May 14, 1994. The headline was bold and stark.

Peck Tornado Claims 3 Lives, 1 Still Missing

Ten minutes before noon yesterday, the National Weather Service reported that a funnel cloud had been sighted approximately one mile southeast of the city of Peck. Within fifteen minutes, a powerful tornado touched down in a field near a bend of the St. Francis River and then plowed its way across the train tracks and Highway 51, tracking up along the east side of the city and a stretch of Highway 60 before disappearing over fields to the northeast. As of press time, three people have been reported killed and one individual is still missing.

The tornado, tentatively designated as an F3 by the National Weather Service, was estimated to have been packing winds of 160-200 mph. An unidentified couple, apparently traveling on Highway 60 in a sedan with Tennessee license plates, were found deceased several hours after the storm. Their bodies were discovered in a field some distance from the highway, while their vehicle was flung off the road and was severely damaged. A third storm-related death occurred when Chuck Weimer, a 76-year-old Peck resident, suffered a heart attack and died while taking shelter with his son Adam in a first-floor closet of the family home on Third Street. A fourth resident, thirty-seven-year-old Trixie Davis, is considered missing. Anyone knowing her whereabouts at any time after nine AM yesterday is asked to immediately contact the Butler County Sheriff's Department.

Residents stated that although the storm siren sounded a few minutes before noon, they had little time to react before the

dangerous winds bore down. Vehicles were
tossed into nearby structures, utility
poles were toppled, and over a dozen homes,
including that of the missing woman, had
significant roof or structural damage.
Trees lost leaves and branches and many
were felled. Several residents received
minor injuries from fallen and flying
debris.

In one miraculous story, a young mother
faced near-disaster when the mobile home
in which she resided with her 20-month-old
daughter on the northeast side of the town
was tipped onto its side and its front door
blown off. Twenty-five-year-old Christi
Miller emerged from the wreckage of her
home to find her daughter missing, and a
search was immediately undertaken by
friends and neighbors. Four and a half
hours later, the child was found wandering
in a field nearly a mile away. Both mother
and daughter were taken by ambulance to
Lucy Lee Hospital in Poplar Bluff, but
witnesses reported that neither appeared
to have suffered major injury.

Currently, all 354 residents of Peck are
without power, as are approximately 23
people in the surrounding...

The hand holding the news article dropped onto Jason's lap.
He sat in a daze. For a long moment, all he could see was an
image of Laney standing on the bare face of the boulder, her hair
streaming behind her as she faced the wind.

Door blown off... found wandering in a field nearly a mile away...

He shook his head in amazement. Was what the news story
implied even possible? How could a small child be lifted up into
a funnel cloud... carried some distance... and lowered down
again... only to "wander" away? Uninjured?

It couldn't be possible.

He gave himself another shake. Fascinated as he was by the
information, he was still no closer to finding a living relative of

Laney's. He refolded the article and placed it back in its sheet protector, only to notice several other, similar articles behind it.

First things first, he lectured himself, pulling out his phone and clicking to the internet search bar. He typed in the name of Christi's mother and "Missouri" and within seconds had found what he sought: an obituary. Christi May Miller had died on December 17th at the age of fifty, from causes undisclosed. She was survived by her daughter, Laney Carole Miller, of Norman, Oklahoma, and her grandmother, May Burgdorf, of Peck, Missouri.

Jason quickly began a new search on May. He wondered if the hospital had already done so, and if he were about to hit the same dead end. He'd tried a simple search on "Laney Miller" earlier and come up empty-handed. He would have recognized her in an image, but she had zero social media presence, and there were too many Laney Millers in the U.S. for him to pin her down, at least with what little information he'd had before. He could do better now.

The results from his search on Laney's great-grandmother flickered to life, but were disappointing. The only hits were the obituary he'd already read and a bunch of scammy background-check sites, which were useless aside from offering the address of the house in Peck where the family no longer lived. He scrolled around to see if any other relatives were named, but only Laney and her mother Christi popped up.

No matter. He had plenty to go on now. Using the address, he looked up the real estate listing and placed a call to the agent.

One ring. Two rings. Voicemail.

Dammit. He left a message that made it sound like he wanted to buy the house. Then he took a breath and returned to the newspaper articles in Laney's folder. The second was another front page spread of the same newspaper, dated one day later, two days after the tornado. He unfolded it carefully and began to read.

Missing Woman Found Safe After Peck Tornado, But Death Toll Rises to Four

The F3 tornado which struck the town of Peck just before noon on Monday has claimed a fourth life. Officials were made aware Tuesday morning by relatives of deceased motorists Elizabeth and Carl Macdonald that the couple was traveling with an infant when they left their home in Nashville, TN en route to Branson, MO. The infant is missing and presumed deceased. The bodies of the couple were found separately in a field adjacent to Highway 60, while their vehicle was thrown several hundred yards from the highway. Officials confirmed late yesterday that an empty child safety seat was present in the vehicle, which was severely crushed on impact.

The fourth casualty of the storm was Chuck Weimer, a 76-year-old resident who suffered a heart attack while sheltering. Trixie Davis, previously reported missing after the tornado ripped off the garage roof from her home on Dale Street, was found safe early Tuesday morning. She had been visiting a friend in Dexter and was not at home when the damage occurred. Christi Miller and her young daughter Laney, who were injured when their mobile home tipped onto its side, were released from Lucy Lee Hospital in Poplar Bluff yesterday morning and are reportedly in good condition. All other injuries were reported to be minor and no one else was hospitalized.

County officials estimate the total cost of damage from the storm to be...

Jason skimmed the remainder of the article, but found nothing else specific about Laney or her family. He moved on. The next article Laney had saved was from several days later — a lengthy spread inside the Sunday edition. He sucked in a breath at the poignant, black-and-white picture of a younger, healthier version of Laney's mother standing in front of an overturned mobile home. A gaping hole where a door had once been pointed toward the sky. One whole corner of the trailer had buckled and collapsed, revealing a framework of thin studs and loose insulation. The yard was littered with debris. At the woman's feet, a small wiry-haired dog sniffed at what appeared to be an overturned highchair. In her hands, the woman held a toy plastic barn. She looked not at the camera, but off at a distant sky, her expression conveying bewilderment.

"MIRACLE BABY" SURVIVES SPIN INSIDE PECK TORNADO
Funnel Cloud Sets Toddler Down Alive Over a Half Mile From Home

When twenty-five-year-old Christi Miller's rental trailer was flipped on its side by Monday's F3 tornado, she was in the process of shepherding both her 20-month-old daughter, Laney, and their dog, Teddy, toward shelter in the bathroom tub. The next thing the young mother knew, there was a hole above her head where the kitchen door used to be, and both her daughter and her dog were gone.

"I don't know what I was thinking," Christi relates five days later as, for the first time, she revisits the scene. "Honestly, it's a blur. I just remember crawling out between the studs and looking around and screaming for Laney. I couldn't see her anywhere. I couldn't understand what was happening, where she had gone."

What happened, according to Poplar Bluff Fire Chief Leonard Rosen, is that both the dog and the toddler were likely sucked out of the trailer by the powerful tornado and lifted aloft. "These tornados can pick up bicycles, grills, cars," states Rosen. "They can pick up people and animals too. The miracle here is that the girl wasn't

more injured." Rosen noted that the child
could easily have suffered fatal injury,
either from being hit by other debris
circling in the twister or from the fall
when she was released.

Dick and Terri Turner, the neighbors who
found Laney on their farm just over half a
mile away, reported that they did not
notice the child until a full four and a
half hours after the tornado touched down.
Terri spotted the toddler moving slowly
through the field behind their barn,
appearing dazed. She was cold and
shivering, and was bleeding from a few
minor cuts, but was otherwise uninjured.
She was wearing a shirt, but no pants or
diaper, and her feet were bare. "The wind
can tear the clothes right off of you,"
Rosen explained. "Considering where they
found her, I think there's a good chance
she landed on a hay bale. To have no broken
bones... it's just hard to see how else
that could have happened."

Christi Miller doesn't seem concerned with
the particulars. "My baby girl is alive,"
she states. "She's back with me and she's
safe, praise God. That's all I need to
know." When asked how the toddler is doing,
Miller tears up. "She's scared still.
Whatever happened, it shook her up really
bad. And me too. But we're alive. And we'll
get through it."

Also alive, amazingly, is Miller's dog,
Teddy. "I remember that I was walking
around shouting for Laney, and at some
point he was just there," Miller explains.
"I didn't see where he came from. I only
remember picking him up and carrying him
with me — I didn't even think about it,
then. How he'd survived it, too."

"Physically, to go through what those two
did and just walk away afterwards... I've
never seen anything like it," Rosen states.
He points out that there are other verified

reports of people and animals having been
lifted up into tornados and transported
some distance. But most, like the Macdonald
family who encountered the Peck tornado
while driving north of town on Highway 60,
do not survive the ordeal.

Reporters and well-wishers have been
steady at the door of the house in Peck
where Christi and Laney Miller are now
residing with family. But while Christi
Miller appreciates the support, she asks
that people refrain from personal visits
for the time being. "Laney really needs her
life to get back to normal," Miller
explains, her eyes tearing up again. "She
just lost her daddy a month ago, and she's
moved twice since. I think we all just need
a little peace and quiet."

Miller affirms that neither she nor her
daughter suffered any significant physical
injury. But the emotional scars from such
an experience could take longer to heal.
"Now psychologically, that's something
else altogether," Chief Rosen adds. "What
that little girl must have gone through...
Well, I'd imagine she'd have nightmares for
a long time to come."

Jason sat numbly for a moment before refolding the article.
Tornados were rare in Canada, and he knew very little about
them. The events described in the clippings were beyond his
imagination. He also knew nothing about child psychology.
Would Laney remember something that happened before she
was two years old? Would such trauma have an effect on her
psyche, even if she didn't consciously remember it?

He returned the article to the folder. Laney wouldn't thank
him for poking into her private history. He was here to find
contact information for her great-grandmother, and that was it.

He thumbed through the rest of the folder's contents and was
disappointed to find nothing else but photographs. Envisioning
an irate Laney in his mind, he didn't peruse them other than to

check that none had relevant contact info on the back.

He returned the folder to her suitcase, which he quickly confirmed held nothing else of use. Then he returned all of Laney's belongings to where he had found them, relocked her room, and sank down onto the chair in his office.

One more time, he pulled up the search engine on his phone, searching on every conceivable combination of names and initials for Laney, her mother, and her great-grandmother. Aside from a few hits for Laney in the byline of some academic papers, he found nothing. May Burgdorf's current whereabouts remained a mystery.

As did Laney herself. What had possessed this "miracle baby" to devote her professional career to the physical phenomenon that had so nearly killed her? Every professional paper she'd contributed to had something to do with tornados. Was it simple morbid fascination, or had she found her life's purpose in trying to spare others from her fate?

In his mind he saw her again, standing exposed and vulnerable on the rocky outcropping, her blue eyes wide open and her cute little chin held high. Whatever she might have felt as a toddler, Laney Miller wasn't afraid anymore. She'd been standing up to the wind, meeting it, facing it down, freakin' *daring* it.

He felt his lips crack into a smile. A fellow adrenaline junkie, eh? She'd probably make a damn good surfer.

He rose from his desk, locked up his office, and headed out toward his apartment and his nearly forgotten houseguest. He would find Laney's great-grandmother, somehow. In the meantime, he would make sure the hospital took good care of their patient. No way was this fierce fighter of a female going to survive a killer Midwestern tornado only to succumb to a slightly above-average British Columbian wave.

Chapter 4

Never in her life could Laney remember being more tired. Every muscle in her body ached, protesting at even the smallest of movements. Worse still, her brain was tired. She felt as if her gray matter had been removed, wrung out like a dishrag, and stuffed back in. She couldn't remember the last time she'd slept soundly. Or digested a full meal. After the last of the guests had departed from the funeral reception yesterday, her aunt had sat her down at an actual table for her first real supper in a week. But it had all come back up again later.

Now it was daybreak again. Lying in her childhood bed staring at a fresh water stain on the ceiling, she steeled herself to face another day. She was alert, as she had been all night, for the sound of her great-grandmother stirring in the room next to her. For weeks now, Gran had risen at all hours, always looking for someone or something. She would wander the house opening drawers and cabinets, and if not intercepted, she would eventually put on her coat — or not — and head outside into the cold. Laney had lost count of how often Gran had been up last night, but she was certain it marked a new record. Most alarmingly, the eighty-seven-year-old had once made it all the way out into the street before Laney caught up with her. She felt terrible about that — she should have woken up long before the front door slammed. She had obviously been less alert than she'd thought she was.

Laney knew that she had to get Gran to a doctor. She also knew, without anyone speaking of it specifically, that there wasn't going to be much a doctor could do. The dementia had been coming on gradually for years, but Christi's illness and death seemed to have accelerated the process. Whether the instability Laney was seeing now was a temporary exacerbation or a new normal, she didn't know. All she knew was that without Christi here, Gran couldn't continue living in the big brick house where she'd spent most of her adult life. The thought of Gran having to move somewhere else was dreadfully sad. As was pretty much every other thought torturing Laney's sleep-deprived brain.

"Christi?" Gran's hoarse voice croaked from the other side of the wall. "Do you have my medicine?"

Laney forced her limbs into motion. "Coming, Gran," she called back, glancing at her phone as she swung her legs over the edge of the bed. It was nearly nine. How had that happened? She could swear it was only six-thirty the last time she looked! Gran should have had her morning meds at eight.

Fail. Laney shrugged on the plush robe her mother had insisted she buy herself as an early Christmas present and hurried down to the kitchen. She noted that the house looked cleaner and less chaotic than usual, even after the reception yesterday, and she mouthed a silent prayer of thanks to her aunt and cousin for pitching in. She truly didn't know what she would have done without them. Handling Gran was a full-time job, never mind everything that had to be done for the funeral. Friends and neighbors had pitched in too, but... some things would always be left to family. Such as putting Gran in the shower in the middle of the reception because she had inexplicably soaked her slacks with floor cleaner.

Laney grabbed the morning meds from the carefully labeled pill minder she'd been trying to convince Gran to use — *Why, I've put my meds in the candy dish for years and I know exactly what's there and when to take them!* — and jogged back up the stairs.

"Here, Gran," she said as cheerfully as she could fake. "I have your medicine." She poured a cup of water from the pitcher she'd set out on a special table, along with an assortment of snacks. She'd hoped the handy food would forestall extra trips to the kitchen in the middle of the night, but Gran wasn't used to the table being there and never seemed to notice it.

May, who was sitting up in bed, stared at Laney uncertainly but took the pills and the cup and swallowed the medicine without complaint. Her eyes were red and puffy; she had obviously been crying again. "I'm so worried about my baby," she said morosely.

Laney wasn't sure which baby she was talking about. More than once she had forgotten that Christi had died, only to become upset all over again when reality dawned. But lately, her daughter Carol, Christi's mother, had also been on May's mind.

Carol had been August and May Burgdorf's only child, born in the early fifties and ready to raise all hell by the end of the sixties. Throughout Laney's childhood, Gran had never mentioned her daughter in anything more than passing, but of course Laney knew the story. Carol had been the prototypical wild child chafing at the constraints of life with a conservative family in a small midwestern town. As the daughter of a respected funeral home proprietor, she led a life of relative privilege. But Carol's discontent — or perhaps, Laney suspected, something more organic — led her into substance abuse at an early age. Pregnant at fourteen, she gave birth to Christi at fifteen, then promptly disappeared. She returned occasionally over the next few years, usually in need of funding, and then would leave again. The circumstances surrounding her drug-related death, at age twenty, were never clear. Her body was found alone in a St. Louis motel; she was buried in the cemetery of her parents' church.

"What's bothering you, Gran?" Laney said gently, sitting down on the edge of the stout four-poster antique bed.

Gran's face was ashen, her expression bleak. "They're in hell now," she pronounced. "Both of them."

Laney allowed herself a tired sigh. May's talk of sin and hell had increased dramatically in the last few weeks. Her religious views had never been secret; she believed in hell and the devil and everything they implied. But prior to Christi's illness, May had never spoken in such blunt terms about the fate of people she knew. "Nobody's in hell," Laney soothed, perhaps too glibly.

May's piercing dark eyes fixed on her great-granddaughter with disapproval. "If you sin and don't repent, you go to hell," she said more clearly. "Lying's a sin, and so is stealing. She did both, and she was never sorry, and even my good sweet Jesus can't forgive her for that now."

Laney was at a loss. Should she probe May's feelings more deeply? Bag it and go with distraction? She couldn't talk May into feeling better unless she understood where the angst was coming from. But even if she did understand, there might be nothing helpful she could say. Worse yet, there could be nothing coherent to understand in the first place. "Are you hungry?" Laney asked brightly. "You want me to scramble you an egg?"

May's sharp gaze didn't waver. Her voice was unusually clear. "There's nothing any of us can do, now. My Christi's gone to meet Jesus, and that sin is on her soul." She reached out and took Laney's hands in hers. "We can only pray he'll understand why she did it and take pity. Lord knows that's what I did. I knew it was wrong, but I didn't stop her. I could have, but I didn't. And that sin is on my soul, too!"

May appeared so earnest, so guilty, and so horribly fearful. "You are *not* going to hell, Gran," Laney insisted. "And neither is my mother. She was a wonderful, warm-hearted, and good person, through and through. And so are you!"

May closed her eyes and shook her head. Her bony fingers clenched tight around Laney's. "You don't know, child. You don't know! I wanted her to tell you. I tried to save her, I swear to you. I told her to tell you the truth before she died. I warned her she'd go to hell—"

"Gran, please," Laney begged as blue veins began to bulge in May's neck and forehead. She was confusing Laney with Christi, and Christi with Carol. It would not be the first time. "Please don't talk this way!"

A rapping on the door below startled them both. Laney rose and looked out the bay window. A familiar green Corolla was parked in the street out front. "It's Aunt June," she announced. "I'll just go let her in, okay?"

"June's a good girl," May replied. The angst on her face receded. She seemed thoughtful now, almost dreamy.

Laney would take it. She hurried down the stairs and opened the door to June, who was actually May's niece by marriage, the daughter of Laney's great-grandfather's brother. What that made her to Laney she had no idea, but "aunt" had always worked fine. "Hi," she greeted, noting that she sounded every bit as flustered as she felt. She looked over June's shoulder to see her "cousin" Amy, June's daughter, waiting outside also. "Come in. Please." Laney opened the door wide and stepped back. "Gran's had a bad night... and morning. And I... I don't know what to do for her."

June Burgdorf, who was somewhere in her mid-sixties, was the sort of woman for whom the term "motherly hug" was invented. She drew Laney into her arms and held her in a tender, pleasantly padded embrace, complete with a deep, rumbled murmur of empathy and understanding. "Oh, honey, of course you don't," she soothed. "It's a big old problem, but you know you don't have to handle this alone."

Unbidden tears flooded Laney's eyes. Embarrassed, she drew back and blotted them with the collar of the plush robe.

"Aunt May has something called delirium," Amy said in a hushed tone. "It's not uncommon when someone with dementia goes through a major life upset like this. She's been declining slowly for years and been able to hold it together, but since Christi got sick she's been in a tailspin." Amy spoke with authority, which was typical. In her early forties with two teenagers, she was a no-nonsense woman who worked as a nurse at the veterans' center in Sikeston, not quite an hour away.

Laney nodded vigorously. "That makes sense," she agreed with a gulp. "I... I guess I didn't know how bad she was before."

"Christi was covering for her," Amy said more gently. "It's what the closest relative often does."

A series of recognizable creaks sounded overhead. Gran had gotten out of bed and was now in the bathroom. Laney sucked in a breath and composed herself.

"We came over here to talk to you, honey," June said quietly. "Can we sit a minute? I suspect your Gran will be in the bathroom a while."

Laney nodded. They moved to the eat-in kitchen table.

"I'll start some coffee," June offered as Laney and her cousin sat down.

Amy focused her keen eyes on Laney, speaking in a firm whisper. "Here's the thing," she began. "You know that May can't live here anymore. Not by herself."

Laney nodded once more. She was beginning to feel like a bobble head, but it was easier than talking.

"Nobody expects you to take care of her by yourself, either," Amy stated with emphasis. "Even if you could move back to Peck right now, you couldn't care take of her here, in this house, by yourself. It just isn't possible. Not with her getting up at all hours of the night and wandering out the door."

Laney swallowed. She hadn't said anything to anyone about Gran's wandering. But she wasn't surprised that June and Amy knew. They were familiar with the neighbors, and the neighbors knew everything.

June moved closer to Laney's ear. "And don't you even *think* about quitting school to come back here and try!" she ordered. "You know that your mother wouldn't want that, and neither would your Gran, when she was in her right mind. She was always so proud of what you've accomplished. We all are. So you're going to get that doctorate and you're going to save lives from tornados just like you always said you would. And that's that!"

Some inner part of Laney nearly crumpled in relief, even as another part felt guilty. In the midst of her grief over her mother's passing, the possibility of having to leave school permanently had always lurked in the back of her mind. But it was too disturbing to contemplate.

"We know you're overwhelmed right now," Amy continued. "You might not even have had time to think about all this yet, which is why we didn't want to say anything until after the funeral."

Laney remained silent. She had been thinking about it, just not coherently.

"What Aunt May needs is a specialized kind of assisted living, called memory care," Amy explained. "There's a facility in Sikeston now that's designed just for people with dementia. I have friends who work there. It's a lovely place, with private studio suites. Aunt May can bring her own furniture and we'll fix it up nice and cozy with things that are familiar to her. She'll be safe there, with people watching over her twenty-four seven. No more wandering down the street, knocking on doors at four o'clock in the morning in her sock feet."

Or barefoot, Laney thought with chagrin.

The toilet upstairs flushed. June sat down beside Laney and put a hand on her arm. "The best part, honey, is that the center's less than ten minutes from me. I can go and see your Gran every day. And believe me, if anybody there isn't treating her right, I'll be having something to say about it!"

"They'll treat her very well," Amy insisted. "Three meals a day, medical care, and a daily program of activities to keep her active and socially engaged." Her voice lowered as May's steps began to creak on the stairs. "We understand that the final decision is yours, Laney. But honestly, there's no reason to wait. They have an opening now, and I have it tentatively reserved. There's just no point in Aunt May getting into a new routine here, without Christi, and then having to uproot again. She might as well make the move now, so she can get settled into a permanent place as soon as possible. Believe me, it'll be better for her that way."

Laney felt herself nodding slowly. What her relatives were suggesting made sense. May had always been close to her niece. Both women loved her dearly, even if they weren't blood relatives.

She began to feel a dull sort of hope — the first glimpse of light in a future that for months now, she'd been unable to envision at all. She also felt a deep sense of relief, even as she felt guilty for abdicating her duty as next of kin. But her feeling guilty didn't mean that following her family's advice still wasn't the right thing to do. If she took her great-grandmother back to Oklahoma with her, May would have to uproot again when Laney graduated and with every move thereafter. In Sikeston, May could stay put indefinitely with three generations of family by her side. "You're right, and thank you," Laney agreed.

May's footsteps creaked on the stairs. After a moment she appeared in the doorway wearing a winter coat over her nightgown. "Who all are you people?" she barked, her eyes narrowed with suspicion.

Laney's heart sank. Gran's recognition of people had never been this bad.

"It's your niece June, Aunt May," June said brightly, springing up from her chair. "My daughter Amy and I came over to have some breakfast with you and Laney." She put a hand on May's arm and smiled at her. "You remember me now, don't you?"

"Of course I do," May said readily, patting her hand. She nodded at Amy. "And how are you, honey?"

"I'm just fine, Aunt May," Amy answered with a smile. "Can I get you a fresh cup of coffee?"

May didn't answer the question. Her gaze swung toward Laney. As their eyes met, the older woman's face fell. "And you," she said dully.

"It's Laney, Aunt May," June jumped in quickly. "You remember Laney, your girl Christi's daughter?"

May's dark eyes continued staring. Seeing, yet unseeing. "I remember Laney," she said clearly. "But you're not her."

Laney's chin trembled. She had known that this would happen. But it was still hard.

"Why, sure she is!" June chirped. "She's just grown a lot since you saw her last, I bet!"

But May was having none of it. Her face hardened, and her tired, red eyes flashed with anger. "Laney died," May said clearly. "Died up in that tornado. She never came back."

All three woman froze in stunned silence. "Now... what on

earth are you on about?" June said finally, wrapping an arm around May's frail shoulders. "Of course our Laney survived that tornado! You know she did. Why, she's right there in front of you! See!"

"I see her," May repeated. "But she's not our Laney." The dark look disappeared. Her eyes filled with tears. "She's the other one."

Chapter 5

The expected storm struck with its full fury just as Jason set out from the lodge to return home. Cold rain fell in torrents onto the windshield of his aged Civic, and his wipers worked so hard to keep up that the whole car rocked with their motion. The storm came with neither thunder nor lightning, which was typical for the island coast, but it packed violent waves and strong, wet winds. Jason made slow progress up the two-lane Pacific Rim Highway, having to dodge several fallen tree branches along the way. He then maneuvered through the grid of streets in town, splashing through a maze of standing puddles until at last he reached his duplex. He parked on the driveway — his truck occupying his garage — and made a dash for the door. Getting his street clothes wet wasn't ordinarily a big deal, but getting them completely soaked twice in one day was galling for a man who spent half his waking time in a wetsuit.

He threw open his unlocked front door, but had to fight the stubborn wind to get it closed again. "Geez, it's nasty out there," he complained as he kicked off his shoes. "Do you want to—"

He stopped short at the entrance to his kitchen. He sniffed. He had dropped Ben off to unwind and settle in during his own quick spy run back to the lodge. The last thing he'd expected was for the oceanographer to *cook*. But here Ben was, rattling around Jason's afterthought of a kitchen, putting its hodgepodge of pots and pans to actual use creating an aroma that was freakin' fabulous. It was evening already, and Jason had barely had any lunch; suddenly he was starving.

"Dude," he said with reverence. "Whatever you charge, you're hired. What is this?"

"Secret family recipe," Ben replied. "It's called whatever-the-hell-you've-got spaghetti."

"I had spaghetti?"

"It takes creativity."

Jason chuckled and dropped down on a bar stool. "You didn't have to cook. I was going to order a pizza or something. Make somebody else go out in the rain." He looked around his living room, and his brow furrowed. He was pretty sure he'd left a load of finished laundry dumped on the couch. "You cleaned up, too?" he asked with amazement.

Ben grinned. "I am an excellent house guest. Makes for repeat invites."

Jason laughed again.

"Enjoy," Ben proclaimed, spooning his pasta concoction onto a plate and sliding it across the counter to his host. "Did you find out anything?"

Jason took a bite before answering, closing his eyes with appreciation. Who'd have guessed that a combination of elbow pasta, bacon, and canned corn and tomatoes could taste so good? "Nothing helpful so far as locating Laney's next of kin," he said finally. "But I did learn some things."

"Oh?" Ben settled onto another stool, and Jason summarized his findings as the two men ate.

"That's incredible," Ben agreed. "I've never been around tornados either, but... wow. Do you think—"

Jason's phone rang. He didn't recognize the number and was about to ignore it when he remembered the voice mail he'd left. "I think this might be Laney's real estate agent," he told Ben as he picked up. "Hello?"

There was a brief pause before a woman's voice answered. "Hello. Is this Jason Buchanan? This is Karen Rhodes. From Hess-Foulk Realty. You called about a listing in Peck?" The caller sounded middle-aged, and although she was trying to sound professional, highly uncertain.

Jason smiled to himself. No doubt it would seem suspicious for someone interested in a house in rural Missouri to have a Canadian area code. "Yes," he answered smoothly, "I'm calling on behalf of Laney Miller, actually. I was hoping you could help her out. I own a hostel here in Tofino, and she checked in earlier today, but then she was in a bit of an accident. We've been trying to reach her next of kin, May Burgdorf, but we don't have a current number. We were hoping you might know how we can reach her."

Another pause. "An accident? Where'd you say Laney was?" the woman asked. She sounded upset; her flat American accent had gone even flatter. "Tof— What?"

"Tofino," Jason repeated. "British Columbia."

More silence.

"In Canada," Jason tried again. "On the Pacific Coast."

"Well, what in the world is she doing up there?" the woman demanded.

Jason's shoulders slumped a bit. Clearly, the agent was not a close confidant. "We don't know, I'm afraid. But we would like to find her great-grandmother."

"Is Laney okay?"

Jason rubbed his forehead. He didn't want to give out too much personal information, but he didn't want to cause a panic among Laney's friends, either. "We're hoping she'll be fine," he said evasively. "But she listed her mother and great-grandmother as emergency contacts—"

"Her momma died not a month ago. Oh, Lord, this is terrible!"

Jason agreed. "Do you have a number for May I could pass on to the hospital?"

"Won't do you no good, hun," Karen replied, all trace of professionalism gone now. "Laney's grandma's got Alzheimer's. That's why they're selling the house, you know. She's in a care home now, I think in Sikeston? I can't remember."

Jason's hopes fell. Even if they could reach May, it didn't sound like she would be in a position to travel to or make medical decisions for Laney. Besides which, the last thing the poor woman herself probably needed after losing one relative was to hear that another had been hospitalized!

"Laney does have some other family around," Karen continued. "You want me to try and get their numbers? I can't remember how they're related exactly..."

Jason considered. Locating the people Laney had specifically listed on an emergency contact form was one thing, but involving random relatives in her affairs was another. "No," he answered. "That won't be necessary. At least not right now. But thank you." He launched into a delicate schmoozing operation aimed at convincing the realtor to keep her mouth shut about the situation — theoretically until Laney herself gave permission. Then he hung up the phone with a sigh.

"Smooth," Ben commented with a smirk as he finished off his plate. "I do believe that poor realtor thinks you're in love with her."

Jason chuckled sadly. "I just wish my stint as a private investigator had actually accomplished something."

His phone rang again.

"Maybe she'll ask you out," Ben teased.

Jason raised an eyebrow. Laney wasn't really his type; besides which it seemed crass to talk about her when she was injured.

Ben's grin broadened. "I, uh... was talking about the realtor."

Jason rolled his eyes and looked at his phone. He read the name and swiftly answered. "Steve? What's up?"

"She's awake," the doctor replied heartily. "She's a little disoriented, but overall the signs are very encouraging."

Jason blew out a breath of relief. He smiled at Ben and passed on the news. "Should I come down now?" he asked the doctor.

"At some point, yes," Steve replied. "Seeing and talking to you again might jog her memory."

"She has amnesia?"

"Not like you're probably thinking, no," the doctor assured. "She knows who she is. But a little bit of confusion and short-term memory loss are common with concussion, especially when there's been a prolonged loss of consciousness. She can remember her mother passing away a few weeks ago; she's just fuzzy on more recent events, which is typical. And usually temporary."

"Does she remember coming to Tofino?" Jason asked.

"No, nor does she have any idea why she made the trip," the doctor answered. "Which is upsetting to her, as you can imagine. Odds are that it will all come back to her soon. But it's possible that talking to you could speed up the process."

"Got it," Jason replied, picking up his keys. "I'm on my way." He thanked the doctor, hung up, and relayed the news to Ben while moving toward the door.

Ben moved with him. "Okay. You're going back to lodge first though, right?"

"No," Jason answered. "Why would I?"

"To get her stuff."

Jason shook his head. "It's way out of the way. Besides, they have gowns and toothpaste and everything there."

Ben raised his palms in the air. "Look, you can do whatever you want, but take it from an old married man who grew up with four sisters — any woman who wakes up in a strange hospital bed after traveling all day and then getting accidently dunked in the ocean is *going* to want her stuff. Her own clothes, her deo, whatever the hell she uses on her face, not to mention her phone. Show up with it first and you'll make a friend for life." His eyes sparkled with humor. "Trust me, man. I know these things."

Jason, who considered himself highly knowledgeable on all issues female, gave a noncommittal nod. Then he made another run through the rain to his car, drove back to the main highway, and turned toward the lodge.

Chapter 6

Laney stared out the window beside her bed, her eyes narrowed with concentration. It was dark, and it was raining, and all she could see outside by the light in the parking lot were two cars and a line of pine trees.

British Columbia. *Canada!* This was insane. What the hell was she doing so far away from home? Her first reaction had been that she must have been kidnapped. It was a crazy thought, yet no other explanation seemed any less ridiculous.

If what the staff kept telling her was true — and why would they lie? — she'd come to Tofino of her own free will. Alone.

It was unbelievable. She'd never even heard of Tofino.

She desperately wanted to talk to her Gran, to make sure that she was all right and not worried about Laney's absence, but Gran wasn't at home anymore. Laney seemed to know that, even before the staff told her that the landline was disconnected. But where was she? Laney had a horrible feeling that she had lost her. That Gran was out there, somewhere, wandering and confused. Her Aunt June had to be told, but Laney didn't have her cell phone and didn't know the number. Her mushy brain couldn't even produce June's last name! Hell, she could barely remember her own. Wait... what was it, again? Oh, dear God, surely she— *Miller!* She practically teared up with relief. At least she could remember that!

A tentative knock sounded on the door, and the freckle-faced doctor returned. Behind him came another man carrying an object that made her heart sing.

"My suitcase!" she heard herself exclaim, sitting upright in bed as she did so. A bolt of pain shot through her skull and the room began to swim, but Laney held out both arms anyway. "Oh, thank God!" she cried, and this time her eyes did tear up. "I've never been so glad to see an inanimate object in my life!"

She was telling the truth. There was something profoundly comforting about the familiar blue and purple patterned roller bag. It was a piece of home, a piece of her old self, a piece of flippin' *sanity*. She moved her legs to one side and the man obliged by lifting the bag and setting it at the foot of the bed.

"Ms. Miller," said the doctor. "This is Jason Buchanan. He owns the hostel where you made reservations for the week. You chatted with him briefly when you checked in."

Laney fumbled with the zippers until she had the top open. One look flooded her with comfort. Her own clothes! Her stuff!

"Ms. Miller?" the doctor said again.

Suddenly aware of her lack of awareness, Laney looked up from the bag. She did remember being told something about a hostel. It was yet another unreal aspect to the story. She had zero experience with such places; she'd always thought they were a European backpacker thing. But if she had to imagine the proprietor of such a business, she certainly would not envision the individual standing next to the doctor. This man was not much older than herself, and he was exceptionally good looking. Tall and lean, with the wide shoulders and narrow hips of a swimmer — or at least that's what image came to her mind, having been a competitive swimmer herself as an undergrad. He had light-brown curly hair, a sexy scruff of beard over the kind of bone structure that graced cologne advertisements, and unusual gray-green eyes. She didn't need a second look to know that he was also the kind of man who was never, ever lonely.

And he had apparently saved her life. Somehow.

"It sounds like I owe you a lot," she offered sincerely. "Thank you. I don't completely understand what happened, but whatever you did for me, I appreciate it."

The man whose name she had already forgotten shrugged at her with a smile. An amazing smile. It came with straight white teeth, a twinkle of the eyes, and whatever mysterious, indescribable quality for which the phrase "lit up the room" was coined. "It was nothing," he replied in a smooth baritone that completed the package. "My friend Ben was the one who spotted you. And carried you in from the beach. We're both just glad you're okay."

"Well, thanks to both of you, then," Laney insisted, feeling awkward. The thought of having some other man she didn't know carrying her unconscious body anywhere was disconcerting. Having this one stand here, looking at her like he wanted something, was even more unsettling. What on earth could he want? Perhaps he was just jazzed about being a hero and wanted additional props. She could do that. "I'm still not sure what could have happened to me," she admitted. "I'm usually a very good swimmer." *I actually set a college record in the women's breaststroke,* she added mentally, *which makes this whole situation even more mortifying.*

Mr. Hostel Owner responded with such a high-voltage, flirty smile that she nearly looked behind her to see who else he could be aiming the thing at. God knew she looked like roadkill. Did he turn on this much charm with every female he met?

Evidently.

"Well, you never really had a chance to swim," he explained. "When the wave hit, you lost your footing, and when you fell you hit your head."

"A wave knocked me over?" Laney asked curiously. "But how? Why didn't I see it coming?"

"You had climbed up onto some rocks that jutted out into the water," he continued. "It's a common mistake people make when they're not familiar with the ocean. You look at where the waves are breaking now, and you assume you're out of range. But wave heights can change quickly. You didn't see the larger waves coming because at the time you were looking up... at the sky."

There was a question in his voice. For a brief moment Laney could feel a strong wind buffeting her cheeks, tangling her hair. She could see gray clouds swirling overhead, hear the whining, incessant roar of an atmosphere in motion. But she was remembering other times, other storms. In her memory, there were no waves. As much as she had studied ocean weather patterns and the physics of tides, her practical knowledge of ocean safety was admittedly zero. Her experience of oceans was zero, period.

She felt self-conscious as his remarkable eyes studied her. What could he possibly find so fascinating? Perhaps he just thought she was weird. Well, *that* she was used to. "I guess I should explain. I look at the sky because I'm a meteorologist. Storms are what I do."

"Well, this all makes perfect sense, then!" the doctor proclaimed. "No wonder you came to Tofino! People come from all over the world to storm-watch at our beaches."

Laney made no response. Having never heard of this place, she was almost certain that wasn't the reason. Still, it made the most sensible explanation so far.

"I asked Jason to come by to see if your talking to him again could jog your memory a bit," the doctor continued. "I'm guessing it hasn't. But don't worry. I've spoken with the neurologist and he's confident you'll make steady progress. We just have to be patient and let nature take its course."

Laney nodded, but she was sure her frustration showed. She was not a patient person. When a problem presented itself, she researched and she took action. And not always in that order.

"Looking through your bag might help, too," Mr. Hostel Owner suggested. "Your phone and your laptop are in there, as well as some papers."

Now *that* sounded like a good idea, Laney thought. Evidently his pretty head contained a brain.

"I should confess that I did take a look in there," he apologized. "We were trying to locate your next of kin when you were unconscious, and I thought you might have packed something that would help. Sorry if I shouldn't have."

Laney shrugged. All her important stuff was password protected. She didn't give a hoot who saw her underwear, at least not when she wasn't wearing it. "That's okay," she replied, managing a smile. "I would have done the same, I'm sure. Thanks for making the effort." She turned her attention back to

her bag. After a moment's digging, she unearthed the holy grail.
My phone!

She wasn't sure how she looked as she pulled out the device,
but whatever her expression, it made both men laugh out loud.
She looked up at them with a thankful smile, anxious to get to
work. "I'm sorry," she said to the cute guy, "but I don't
remember your name."

"Jason," he answered, flashing another Hollywood grin.
"Jason Buchanan."

"Well, thank you, Jason, for not letting me drown in a fit of
my own stupidity," she offered. "And thank you, Doctor," she
couldn't remember his name either, dammit, "for being so
encouraging. I hope to be out of all your hair as soon as
possible." She clamped her phone to her chest, waiting.

"I'm afraid you're going to have to be very careful with that
phone," the doctor warned. "I understand you're anxious to
reconnect, but overstimulating your eyes and therefore your
brain could have some very unpleasant consequences. We'll have
to monitor your responses very closely. I'd say no more than five
minutes on the phone, to start."

"I'll be careful," Laney insisted.

The doctor didn't look convinced, and Laney didn't blame
him. She had things to figure out, and she was going to take care
of business, come what may. He threw her a skeptical look, then
turned to the door and gestured for Jason to join him. "I'll send
someone in to check on you in a few minutes."

"Just so you know," Jason added cheerfully, "if they spring
you before the week's out, you still have a room at the lodge.
You have a few things left there — wet things drying out, mostly.
If you want me to bring any of them here, just give me a call.
Here's my card."

He sounded so earnest; his tone so legitimately friendly. Were
all Canadians so hospitable? Laney didn't know. But unless this
one was perversely into hospital gowns and brain damage, his
playful flirtatiousness must be a default setting. She took the
card, said a polite goodbye to both men, waited for the door to

close behind them, then lay back on her pillows and turned on the phone.

As her screen sprang to life, showing the last picture she'd ever taken with her mother, a noxious wave of emotion overwhelmed her. She was a horrible daughter; she was *forgetting something!* Something important, something she should know. It was painful, horrible, unbearable. And it was waiting there, just beyond her reach...

A bolt of pain shot across her skull, and she groaned and shut her eyes. What the hell was going on? Were these feelings real, or just another symptom of her injury?

She focused on breathing slowly, and in a few seconds the pain faded. *Oh, Aunt June. I need to talk to you!*

Her phone battery was very low, but it would have to do. She pulled up her aunt's name in her contact list and pushed call. The tone rang for a frighteningly long time before a warm, beautifully familiar voice met Laney's ear.

"Oh, honey!" June said with enthusiasm. "What on earth is up with you, darlin'? Where did you go in such a hurry?"

Laney blinked. "You... you don't know where I went?"

There was a pause. When her aunt spoke again her voice was slower, almost cautious. "Well, no. I asked you, but you didn't seem to want to explain."

Hot tears welled up behind Laney's eyes. What was *wrong* with her? "I had a little accident, Aunt June," she said, embarrassed by the tremor in her voice. "I'm fine now, except I have a concussion, and I can't remember what happened the last few days..." She told the story in as coherent a fashion as she could manage.

June was understandably horrified, and Laney spent the next several minutes turning down offers for various relatives, friends, and complete strangers to travel up to Canada to fetch her immediately.

"I really am okay staying here, for now," Laney insisted. "Everybody at the hospital keeps telling me I'll get better faster if I rest and try to relax. At least for a week. Apparently I'd planned to stay here that long anyway. Is Gran okay? Where is she?"

June assured her that May was doing as well as could be expected in her new home, and as soon as the memory care center was mentioned, Laney found she could envision it. But still, her anxiety didn't abate. "Are you sure I didn't give you or Amy *any* clue why I would want to go to Canada?"

"You didn't say a word about where you were going to either of us," June insisted. "We just knew that something had really upset you. It must have happened when you stopped in to see your Gran that last time, because I'd talked to you on the phone earlier, and you seemed fine then. But that night you were so upset... you just looked awful, honey. I think your Gran must have said something to you, but you wouldn't say what."

Another wave of foreboding arose in Laney's gut. So, something *had* happened. Something horrible.

"She'd been getting you confused with your mother a lot, and sometimes she didn't seem to know you at all, which I know upset you. But I could tell it was more. She's gotten pretty doggone mean with me once or twice lately — maybe that was it, that she got a little ugly with you? Lord knows she gave me and Amy both an earful this morning!"

Laney swallowed. "Maybe. I... I really don't know."

"Well, honey, all I can tell you is that night you wasn't hardly yourself. You just looked like a ghost. You said you needed to go on a road trip somewhere and you'd be gone for a while — maybe a couple weeks. I asked where you were headed and why, but you just kept saying it was a personal matter, and that you were sorry but you really had to go."

"So I drove," Laney murmured. If she had driven herself to British Columbia, then her car must be here! Comforted by the thought, she sat up and rooted around in the suitcase for her keys, but couldn't find them. She had probably left them in her backpack. Hadn't Jason mentioned some stuff left in her room? She needed her stuff back. She needed her life back.

"Aunt June," she pleaded as a new, duller pain crept into the back of her skull. Moving her head was not a good idea. "Is there anything else I said that could explain why I would drive all this way? Did I say anything about wanting to see the ocean?"

"Not that I heard, honey," June replied. "But if that's all you wanted, don't you think you'd have gone down to Biloxi or Gulf Shores? Who on earth drives all the way up to Canada just to see the ocean? In the middle of winter?"

"Nobody," Laney agreed. It was enough of an undertaking just getting to the Gulf of Mexico. She knew because she'd spent half her life wanting to do it, but could never quite afford to make it happen.

"Now, you did ask me a couple of questions I thought were odd," June added.

"Like what?"

"Like asking me what I remembered about the tornado. But of course I couldn't tell you anything you didn't already know about that. And then you asked me about your daddy, how often we'd gotten to visit with him when he was alive. What we did for holidays and such."

Laney felt like crying again. "Why on earth would I ask any of that?"

"I wish I knew," June replied with frustration.

"Is Gran really all right? I mean, now?"

"She's doing a little better every day," June said firmly. "She's even got a friend already. Woman just down the hall named Hazel. Don't you worry about your Gran, honey. You worry about getting yourself better. You hear me?"

Gulping through another irritating bout of tears, Laney made all sorts of promises to her aunt with regard to her own health, safety, welfare, and future communications before saying goodbye. She barely managed to hang up before her phone died completely. She gazed out the window into the dark and the soaking rain. No wonder it had taken June so long to answer. In Missouri, it must be the middle of the night.

Her head ached abominably. She rolled onto her side and closed her eyes. She hadn't come to Tofino just to see the ocean, stormy weather or no. There was something else. Some other reason. Something so awful it terrified her. Oh, why could she not remember!

The tears kept coming, squeezing out through her tightly clamped lids.

Perhaps she didn't *want* to remember.

Chapter 7

Laney surveyed the papers spread out across her great-grandparents' antique dining table. The big old house was unnervingly quiet. Although Laney had grown up inside these walls, before this week she could count on one hand the number of times she had slept here alone. Last night made two in a row, but on neither occasion had she noticed the silence. She had been far too exhausted to feel anything except anticipation for sweet oblivion. Now, as the sun rose while she savored a very dark cup of coffee, the quiet seemed deafening. The resonant tick-tock of her Gran's family clock, which had sat on the fireplace mantel since May herself was a child, was as much a part of the house as its brick walls, high ceilings, and wainscoting, and its absence left the space feeling wholly alien. There were no creaks from human footfalls, no hum of the toilet running in the upstairs hall, no fresh bacon crackling on the stove. Laney was alone.

Two days ago, Aunt June had taken May back to her house for a "short visit." Amy's whole family had then descended upon the big house, helping Laney to sort through May's most precious belongings, hauling the curated collection to the memory care center, and then moving it into May's new space, where they had tried to recreate the familiar right down to the arrangement of pictures on her walls. The undertaking had been both daunting and sorrowful, but two nights of quality sleep had at least managed to refresh Laney's brain enough for her to tackle the mountain of financial and legal chores that had piled up over the last month.

Unfortunately, getting everything laid out in a logical and organized manner had succeeded only in making the tasks ahead loom larger. Gran's financial situation was not good. Grandpa

Auggie, whom Laney remembered as a big, strapping man with a large belly and a laugh like Santa Claus, had been a bedrock of his community and a well-loved local businessman. The funeral home he had inherited from his father had served the town of Peck and much of the surrounding countryside for generations, but as the larger neighboring towns grew, competition had increased, as had his costs for overhead and upkeep. Never as skilled at bookkeeping as he was at charming people, Auggie eventually wound up underwater, and by the time a heart attack compelled him to sell the business, he and May had no cushion on which to retire. Laney was aware that, after his death over a decade ago, Christi herself had bought the family home from her mother. What Laney hadn't realized was that if not for Christi's good credit and largesse, May would have had to reverse-mortgage the house just to get herself out of debt. The only funds May had now to put toward assisted living were social security and her veterans' widow's benefits, which would not be enough to cover her monthly costs.

Laney rubbed her face in her hands. She would likely inherit some money from her mother eventually; Christi had worked as a bank teller for decades and did have a life insurance policy and some meager savings. But after Laney paid the family's still-accumulating bills, her best guess was that the sum remaining could support May for at most three years. After that, without additional funding coming from somewhere, Gran's only option could be a Medicaid-approved nursing home.

The house has to be sold as soon as possible, Laney announced to herself. There was little else she could do to change the financial calculus except finish her doctorate and pray for a good job.

She lifted her chin and set about reordering the paperwork. The thought of returning to school in Oklahoma gave her a dull sense of despair, but she ignored it. Her feelings about the various institutions she attended didn't matter and never had. She went wherever she could get the degree she needed while accruing the least amount of student debt. Full stop.

She dove into the tasks at hand. Unfortunately, addressing

even the most immediate among them required an entire morning of phone calls and forwarded documentation. At noon she forced down some reception leftovers and headed back to Sikeston. The plan had been for June and Amy to move Gran into her new room first thing this morning. Laney was to arrive mid-afternoon and then stay with May through bedtime.

By seven PM, Laney was exhausted all over again. The staff assured her that Gran's reaction to the move was typical, but that didn't make all of May's tears, confusion, and remonstrations any more easy to handle. Laney did her best not to take the attacks personally, and in this she was aided somewhat by the fact that Gran continued to mistake her for her mother. In between the pleas to go home and the crying jags associated with her newfound fear of hell, May did occasionally coo over the fine furnishings, lovely outdoor courtyard, and — of all things — the old-fashioned popcorn popper in the day room. All things considered, Laney was pleased with the staff and facility and was confident that May would be well cared for. Even so, she couldn't shake a crippling sense of sadness. And when, just before her scheduled departure time, May's dark eyes fixed on her with fresh hostility, it took all Laney's strength not to collapse into tears herself.

"I told her it was wrong," May barked coolly. "I told her she had to make it right. But she wouldn't listen to me."

Laney made no reply. Her Gran had been spouting off equally unintelligible statements for days now. Laney merely smiled as they sat in Gran's favorite armchairs, which Amy's sons had managed to stuff against the wall opposite the bed. The family clock sat on a credenza between them, its sound magnified tenfold within the confines of the small studio apartment.

"I understand why she did it," May continued dully. "She'd just lost Jimbo, and that was all the hurt her heart could take. She couldn't lose you, too."

Laney tuned in. Jimbo, aka James Robert Miller, was her own late father, an Army corporal who had been killed during a training exercise shortly before the tornado. At least May seemed to know who Laney was at the moment. "She didn't lose me, Gran."

"Oh, but she did," May retorted, her chin beginning to quiver. "The tornado took you away, and you never came back."

Not this again, Laney thought uncharitably. With all the actual loss May had endured, Laney had diminishing patience for her lamentations over something that never happened. "I survived the tornado, Gran," she said again. "It was a miracle, but I did. It was in the paper, remember? I was famous for a while." She tried to smile again, but her effort was poor.

"They never found her body," May pronounced.

Laney raised an eyebrow. This was a new one. "Whose body?"

"Our little Laney's," May insisted. "It was just gone with the wind, I guess. Maybe blown into the river. We'll never know, now."

"Gran," Laney replied, trying and failing to remove the frustration from her voice. "Terri Turner found me in the field behind their barn, remember? Everybody was out looking for me, and they found me. And they called Mom and she came racing over, and it was happiest moment of her life. Remember what she always used to say? That God gave her a miracle?"

To Laney's surprise, May scoffed. "Oh, it was a miracle all right," she said derisively. "For somebody else." She looked straight at Laney. "You had the cutest blond hair, curly like your daddy's. And those big old, baby-blue eyes."

Laney made an attempt at levity. "Yeah, I was cute as all get out. Still am, don't you think?"

"I think that's what did it, you know," May continued, seeming not to hear her. "The blond hair and blue eyes. You were smaller than our Laney, but so much like her. I looked at you and my heart just dropped into my shoes, but my Christi, she didn't bat an eyelash. Just stood there stock still for a second, then gathered you right up in her arms. 'My God,' she said. I can remember it like it was yesterday. 'My God, it's my baby. *You're* my baby.' And after that very moment, you were, you know."

Laney's blood went cold.

You're the other one, Gran had said before.

"Are you saying..." Laney lost the thought and tried again. "I don't understand, Gran. I *am* your Laney. Yours and Christi's. Look at me!"

Gran expression didn't waver. She had been staring at Laney the whole time. "No, honey," she said softly, compassionately. "Our Laney died. But we loved you just the same."

Laney's legs jerked her to her feet. She shouldn't be listening to this. May was delirious. She could be saying anything, making up anything... to assume there was anything to it would be lunacy. If the real Laney Miller had died, who the hell was she? Had Christi adopted her somehow?

Impossible. Laney had read the newspaper articles a million times. The whole affair had happened within hours!

"I think you're tired, Gran," she pronounced. "And so am I. But I'll come back to see you tomorrow, okay?"

But now May was crying. "She didn't mean any harm. Truly, she didn't. The other parents were dead, both of them. And she had so very much love to give! It wasn't fair; it just wasn't. She was only trying to make things right. She didn't mean to hurt anybody. Oh, sweet Jesus, He's simply got to understand!"

Laney froze. *The other parents were dead.* Images flashed through her mind of yellowing newspaper and blobby Courier print. A whole family of out-of-towners had died in the Peck tornado. A young couple and a baby.

Of course! she thought with relief. There *was* one body that was never found, true, but it had only been that of a little baby! That was why no one was particularly surprised when it didn't turn up. Debris of all sizes had scattered for miles; several missing animals had never showed up again, either. Her Gran must be getting the old stories confused!

"It was a *baby* who died in the tornado, Gran," she insisted. "Not me. I was nearly two years old, remember? I was walking around! Maybe you're thinking of another tornado?" She let out a nervous breath. Of course, that would be it. May's mental timeline was nonexistent; she could be remembering any tornado.

May's tears continued to fall. Her mouth formed a grim line. "No one else knew what you looked like, not really. Christi said that you were her Laney and who was going to argue? You did look like her. Blond hair and the bluest eyes! Our Laney was bigger, but you were a smart little thing. So smart! You were already talking as good as she was. Nobody knew. Nobody questioned. Babies change every day, people know that. And my poor Christi, I swear she didn't even know herself! Not after. She wasn't in her right mind, she wasn't. It should be me going to hell, not her, for letting her keep pretending. My best little angel, she didn't deserve to suffer like that! She had so much love to give! I couldn't say anything. I couldn't. And I didn't say a word, and I never will! If hell's the price I pay for it, then so be it, and may God have mercy on us both!"

The room around Laney was spinning. She wanted to comfort her great-grandmother, but no words would come. She couldn't move; she wasn't sure she was even still breathing. But she did know that Gran's pain was real. May *couldn't* be making up everything she was saying!

"You'd best be getting ready for bed now, Ms. Burgdorf," the merry aide who entered the room announced in a sing-song. "You ready to try out your new shower? The controls might look kind of strange, but come on now and I'll help you figure them out, all right?"

May's countenance changed in an instant. "Is it time to go home?"

"It's shower time," the aide repeated. "Then we're all going to have a special late-night snack. What's your favorite flavor, Ms. Burgdorf? You like chocolate or vanilla?"

May rose. "Vanilla," she said decisively.

"Ooh, that's my favorite, too!" the aide chuckled, even as she caught Laney's eyes and gestured her surreptitiously toward the door. "Some people think it's bland, but I just love vanilla icing, or vanilla pudding either one. You like those vanilla wafers? You know, the little round cookies you get in a box?"

Laney backed her way to the door and slipped out into the hall. As May's response about preferring Fig Newtons echoed into the corridor, she felt her feet moving her toward the exit. Her heart pounded. Her mouth was dry.

Not possible, she assured herself.

It's just not possible.

Chapter 8

Jason jogged up onto the beach, his split-toed surf boots making their usual weird, hooflike prints in the wet brown sand. The sky was blue this morning, the waves were awesome, and Ben was having a blast. Though the oceanographer/boat captain was every bit as lousy a surfer as he said he was, he clearly enjoyed being out in the ocean — as opposed to sitting inside a building studying it — and his childlike joy was infectious. Jason didn't often get the opportunity to instruct a bona fide resident of Hawaii on the art of surfing, even one as unaccomplished as Ben. But he'd been having a rather excellent time himself, particularly after Ben offered to return his hospitality with an open invitation to stay at the couple's condo on Maui — which apparently was sitting empty while they spent the academic year in Victoria.

Yet even as Jason's head filled with giddy thoughts of surfing a warm ocean in nothing but board shorts, he could not stop thinking about Laney. He'd heard nothing about or from her since last night, and he couldn't help wondering whether he should deliver the rest of her stuff whether she called him or not.

He pulled off his gloves, reached into the bag he'd left on the beach, and pulled out his phone. He had several texts, as he usually did after he'd been out on the water awhile. Two were from women he'd met only recently, both fishing for meetups. The first, a surfer from Australia who'd rented some equipment from him, was a definite maybe. She was in town for two weeks and appeared to be the sort of fun-loving free spirit whose company he most enjoyed. The other, a new resident who'd just taken a job at the Tofino municipal center, was a definite no. Never mind that she was smart, funny, and by far the more attractive of the two. He could tell she was looking for a long-term relationship, and that was a nonstarter. "Forever girls" might make wonderful mates for other men, but if they fell for him they'd get hurt, and he didn't do that kind of drama.

He hesitated over the text from the Aussie, then decided to answer her later. His third, unopened text seemed more compelling, despite its coming from an unknown number. He clicked to open it.

> Hi, this is Laney Miller, of near-death fame. I hate to put you out again, but the next time you're in the area, if you could bring my backpack, I'd appreciate it. Thanks.

A broad smile spread over Jason's face. He looked out over the ocean, wondering if Ben was ready to take a break. The men exchanged a series of gestures, and Ben rode the next wave towards shore. Then Jason popped off his hood and called one of the backups who covered his front desk. Within half an hour, he was on his way.

Laney stared with annoyance at the built-in hospital cabinet where her phone and laptop were stored. They hadn't technically been confiscated; she could get them if she wanted. But she didn't really want them. Not if she also wanted a head that didn't pound with pain.

Light, as it turned out, was a highly undesirable thing for brain tissue that had just been violently slammed against the inside of one's skull. She had been introduced to this fact while trying to use her phone last night, reintroduced to it when the sun rose this morning, and then whopped upside the head with it when she had tried using her laptop a couple hours later. The sad fact was that until her headaches were under control, the sun was barred from her window and any and all screens would remain powered off.

Naturally, she was bored to tears. She was also consumed with anxiety, which was unlike her. The doctor had assured her after her exam this morning that all signs were positive and that most likely her memory would return to normal within a day or two. She was improving all the time; as of this morning she had no more trouble remembering things that happened after she'd come to the hospital or recalling particular data bytes like her own last name. But she still didn't know why she was in Canada.

She reached up and touched a hand to the staples in her tender scalp, grateful that at least her hair was clean now. She'd insisted on getting a shower and shampoo the first minute the staff would allow it. She might not give a rat's behind how she looked, but she hated the feel of greasy hair. Her blond locks fell limp and straight as a stick even when—

She broke off the thought as a wave of horror swamped her consciousness and unsettled her stomach. She dropped her hand from her hair and stared at the tent in the blanket created by her toes. Her heart beat fast, every muscle tensed. Had something happened? What was wrong? Why didn't she know?

Her mind searched for some explanation. She'd heard of panic attacks, but never experienced one. Most likely, the strange feeling was just another fun symptom of concussion. Anyhow, it was already fading.

You're fine.

A knock sounded on the door.

"Come in!" she practically ordered, not caring who it was. If the visitor could distract her from both her boredom and the bizarre panic she would happily welcome any and all salesmen, marketing surveyors, cult missionaries...

It was the hottie who owned the hostel.

"Hi there. I'm Jason Buchanan," he explained, seeming unsure whether she would remember him. From the way he was squinting, she supposed he couldn't see her well in the darkness. The light in the hallway was blindingly bright in comparison to her room, a fact that resulted in another zing of pain behind her eyes. "I brought your backpack," he added cheerfully.

"Oh, I'm so glad!" she said sincerely. "Do me a favor, close that door and don't turn on the light, okay? Can you see well enough to sit down?" She had texted him earlier — or rather, a friendly housekeeper had done so for her — but she hadn't really expected him to show up. At least not this fast.

He shut the door behind him as requested, felt his way to the chair by the window, and sat down. "I'm guessing the light hurts your head," he said sympathetically. "Which probably means no screens either. Bummer. You bored?"

"Beyond all endurance. Thanks for coming so quickly. You really didn't have to."

He shrugged. Then he set the backpack beside her.

She was trying to face him as a polite person would do, but the narrow sun streaks that stole in around the blinds behind his chair were enough to set off the eye-arrows again. She gave up, closed her lids, and concentrated on the backpack. She felt around, found the small front pocket and pulled out her keyring. "Wait," she exclaimed, fingering it. "My car keys are gone!"

"You told me you came on the bus," Jason said. "You asked me about renting a car."

"Renting a car?" Laney repeated, confused.

"Sorry," the voice said sympathetically. "But I can only tell you what you told me, which wasn't much." He described the conversations they'd apparently had both over the phone and when she arrived at his hostel. But other than the part about her not having much money to spend — which was always the case — nothing he reported made any sense.

"I'm sure I was driving, at least when I left Missouri," she insisted.

"Was it an old car? If you had a breakdown somewhere and had to leave it in a shop, that would explain the missing keys."

Laney contemplated a moment, then huffed out a laugh. "It's a 2003 Malibu, and now that you mention it, it would be a miracle if it *did* make it all the way up here." She braved opening her eyes. Her alleged lifesaver was relaxing in his chair, looking perfectly at ease in a dim hospital room with a crazy person.

"It must be frustrating," he said mildly. "Not being able to remember something from your own past."

"Frustrating is a word," she said glibly, wondering why he was still here. A man who looked like he did was bound to have better things to do on a sunny afternoon. She waited for him to make his excuse and leave.

"Have you reached any other relatives yet?" he asked. "Or friends, or whoever?"

"Yes," she replied. "I spoke with my aunt last night. Everything's fine at home."

He smiled. "Well, that's a relief."

An explanation for his solicitousness suddenly occurred to her. "I hope you're not sitting here listening to me whine because you're afraid I'm going to sue or something," she said bluntly. "The accident was my own stupid fault. End of story."

"Oh, I'm not worried about that," he said with humor. "Canadian courts don't do windfalls for pain and suffering like American courts do. Besides which, you weren't technically on my land when you fell."

"Ah," Laney replied. "So why are you sitting here listening to me whine?"

He regarded her for a moment, his expression inscrutable. Then he stood up and ran a hand through his hair. When he began to pace near the foot of the bed, Laney was glad. Away from the window she could look at him more comfortably, and he was very nice to look at.

"I've been concerned about you," he answered finally. "I do feel responsible that you got hurt while staying at my lodge. But there's something else."

Laney waited. The man got more interesting all the time.

"I told you I opened your suitcase," he confessed, sounding guilty. "I really was looking for something that would help the hospital locate your great-grandmother. But what I found was your newspaper articles... and I couldn't help but read them. It was such an amazing story. I couldn't read something like that and not be curious about you."

Laney blinked. "What are you talking about? What newspaper articles?"

He blinked back at her. "The ones about the tornado."

The tornado.

She drew in a sharp breath as the damnable black feeling suffused her again. Her muscles stiffened and her heart raced. *The tornado. No, no...* The thought was diffuse. Unformed. But it was very, very bad...

"I've seen lots of tornados," she heard herself say. "Which one are you talking about?" Her voice was weird. Way too cheerful.

"The tornado in Peck, Missouri," he answered. He was looking at her oddly, which was understandable. She felt odd. "The one when you were a toddler."

"Oh, *that!*" the ninny voice replied. She even heard herself giggle. She *never* giggled. "Yeah, I was kind of famous for a while."

Her desire to change the subject was overwhelming.

"I'm curious how you came to be a meteorologist," he continued. "After experiencing something like that... What drove you to want to study tornados?"

Stop saying that word!

"I've always been fascinated with weather," she said evasively. "That's all."

He was standing still now, looking at her. Thank goodness the light was so dim. She could feel beads of sweat breaking out all over her body.

Change the subject! "What I really need to do right now," she said earnestly, "is figure out why I came to Canada."

Jason considered. "Have you looked at the folder you brought with you?" he suggested. "In your suitcase?"

Laney remembered no folder in her suitcase. "Show me what you're talking about."

She directed Jason to the cabinet, where he found her bag and extracted a report folder from the zippered pouch in the top which, in her previous searches for underwear and sleep pants, she had overlooked. He set the folder in her hands, and even in the darkness she could make out the University of Oklahoma logo on its cover. She remembered having put some of her class notes in it before she rushed home to see her mother last spring. But when she opened it, she found none of those documents. What she found was her passport, some original newspaper clippings about the Peck tornado, and a bunch of loose photographs. She had spent enough time staring at the newspaper articles to identify them without looking closely, but the photographs were harder to make out. She tried holding one up closer to the window, but was immediately rewarded with a sharp shaft of pain in her temple.

"Ouch," she said involuntarily, dropping her hands to her lap and closing her eyes. "Bad idea." The anxiety was creeping up on her again, but the sensation seemed less acute now, and she decided to try and push through it. Maybe if she—

"You want me to tell you what I see?" Jason offered.

Laney had nearly forgotten that he was there. She bit her lip with indecision. The staff at the hospital were all very nice, but taking the time to help her work through her personal problems was not in any of their job descriptions. Jason must have better things to do as well, but at least he was offering. And she was just selfish enough to let him. She held out the picture, her eyes still closed. "Please," she asked. "And thanks."

He took the photograph from her hands, and she felt the folder being lifted from her lap as well. A series of creaks told her he had settled back in the chair.

"Keep your eyes closed," he suggested. "I'm going to lift the blind a little."

Laney complied. He was quiet for a moment.

"They're pictures of a little girl," he said finally. "Pictures of you, obviously."

Her brow furrowed, which hurt. She raised a hand and massaged her forehead. "Of me?" she exclaimed, baffled.

"Well, it's clearly you in this one with a little dog. You're only a toddler, but your nose and chin are pretty distinctive, as well as your eyes."

"What's so distinctive about my—" Laney shut herself up. It

felt weird to know that he was studying her face so closely and
noticing such details... particularly when the pain was so bad she
couldn't look at him at all. But it didn't matter. "Go on."

"There are several with your mom," he continued. "One with
an older woman I'm assuming is your great-grandmother.
Another with her and an older gentleman both. And this one's
from a birthday party. I'd say you look two or three, maybe? I'm
not good with kids' ages."

Laney recognized his descriptions. They were all photographs
she could remember leafing through in the family album on the
shelf in the living room. Pictures that Christi had taken before
digital cameras became a thing, back when she still bothered to
make print copies. "Are they all pictures of me?" she asked.
"Aren't there any of just other people?"

"No," he answered. "You're in every picture."

They sat quietly for a moment. Then Laney felt suddenly,
inexplicably angry. "This is ridiculous," she barked. "Who does
that? What egotistical moron carries around their own baby
pictures?"

She thought she heard him chuckle. But his next words held
no trace of levity.

"I'm sure you had a good reason."

"I'm not sure of that at all," Laney argued. "As far as I can
tell, I lost my mind even before I hit my head. Tell me honestly,
when we first met, did I seem crazy to you?"

He waited entirely too long to answer. "No, you didn't seem
crazy. You did seem... well, preoccupied. Focused. Like you were
on some sort of mission, and my friendly chit-chat was an
annoyance to you."

Laney raised an eyebrow at his tone, which held a tiny, yet
definite hint of affront. If "friendly chit-chat" meant idle flirting,
then he was probably right about her reaction. She'd never been
into wasting energy on men she wasn't interested in, particularly
narcissistic types who craved constant attention and flattery. But
she *did* try to be polite about it, so if he'd come away wounded,
she'd either been majorly distracted, in the bitchiest mood of her

life, or he simply wasn't used to rejection.

She cautiously peeled open one eye. *Oh, yeah. It was the third one.* When a guy that gorgeous graced a woman with his attention — whether he was actually interested in her or not — he would expect her to simper like an idiot.

Laney moved on. "Well, I think I was losing it," she admitted. "My aunt told me I seemed messed up. She says I took off without telling anyone where I was going, much less why."

The blackness crept up again. Her stomach heaved.

"I mean, who does that?" she continued irritably, talking more to herself than she was to him. She was frustrated, she was scared, and she was angry about both those things. "Who drives north in the middle of January, for God's sake? Carting around their own freakin' *baby pictures?*" Her voice choked on the words. Tears threatened, but her pride helped her hold it together. "I'm sorry," she apologized. "You really don't have to listen to this. It's okay if you leave now. I'll be fine."

His voice, when it came, didn't acknowledge her offer. "There's no question you came to Tofino with a specific goal in mind," he said gently. "So what if your motive isn't easy to reconstruct from your suitcase? There's no reason it should be. Nothing about any of this makes you crazy."

Laney sucked in a breath. He did make a point. "You're right," she said more calmly. "And thank you. Maybe I wasn't out of my mind then. Now's another matter."

He chuckled. "You're not crazy, Laney." The sound of her name on his lips was oddly pleasing. "It's just going to take some time, that's all. You did have a major head injury. I'll be happy to help if you want me to. Just say the word."

She was confused again. His motive for being so helpful still escaped her. "I really can't believe you don't have someplace better to be," she reiterated, opening her eyes just long enough to catch him in a shrug.

"I don't have all day," he admitted. "But I could spare you another half hour. What do you need?"

The offer caught her off guard. What did she need? "I, uh... I don't even know."

"Well, I have a suggestion," he offered. He stood up again and crossed to the cabinet. "Which, for the record, you would think of yourself if your brain wasn't inflamed."

Laney smiled. His glib acknowledgment that she couldn't think straight was paradoxically comforting.

He sat down again, and she could hear her laptop booting up. "You may not be able to look at screens, but I can. There must be something on here that explains why you came to Tofino. Just tell me what you'd like to look up, and I'll read it to you."

Laney felt stupid, but only for a moment. He was right. She would have thought of it herself if she wasn't brain-damaged. Self-recrimination was pointless.

"My email, maybe?" she suggested. "I checked my inbox on my phone, but then my eyes started to explode and I didn't get a chance to look at much else. Anyway, any mail important enough to save would be stored in the folders on my computer."

"Gotcha."

She talked him through the process of reaching her email folders, but after twenty frustrating minutes, they had uncovered nothing helpful. Laney didn't save much personal email, as a rule, and in the last awful month, she'd been on her computer only sporadically.

"I bet we'll find more in the search history on your browser," Jason suggested. "You must have researched your route, looked up places to stay. Unless you do that on your phone?"

Laney shook her head. Doing so hurt, but the sound of her own voice bouncing around in her skull hurt nearly as much. "No, my phone is crap. It's so old it freezes up on websites; it can barely handle email. I use the laptop to go online. But as you can see, it's a piece of crap too. I have the app set to delete my search history and cookies and everything on exit, otherwise it gets too slow."

"Oh." Jason blew out a breath. "Well, that does make things harder."

Laney felt like her brain was rebelling against her. It didn't want to think anymore — it wanted to take a nap. But Jason was here now, and he wouldn't be coming back. She had to take advantage while she could. Who knew when she'd be able to use screens again?

"I usually make doc files," she explained, talking as quickly as her head would allow. His thirty minutes had to be up soon. "I don't write things out on paper too much. Maybe if you search by date, look for any new documents?"

"Good idea." Jason clicked some keys and waited. And waited, and waited. Laney gritted her teeth. She'd hoped to get a new laptop last fall, but when she'd had to take a leave from grad school, she'd lost her stipend, too.

"Here we go," he announced finally. "You've created seven files since the first of December."

"Read the names." That sounded rude. Geez, her head was killing her.

"FuneralPlan. Obit. DementiaResources."

"No," she murmured.

"Stuff2Move?" His voice had gotten softer.

She shook her head slightly.

A beat passed. "Are you sure you're up to this right now?" he asked.

"Please just finish."

"Finances. Tremblay."

The pounding in Laney's head was almost unbearable. Worse still, the panic was returning. *Something bad... so bad!* "What the heck is a tremblay?"

"It's a surname," Jason said with surprise.

"Never heard of it." Her heartrate accelerated. She could feel the vessels in her temple pulsing.

"It's a very common name," Jason practically whispered. "At least in Canada."

"Open it!" Laney squeaked. Her hands felt clammy. *Stop! Don't do this!*

Jason sighed. "Laney, it's obvious you're in pain. We can pick this up again later, when you're feeling better."

She let out an involuntary groan. "No! I have to figure this out!"

"And you will," Jason assured. "But it doesn't have to happen right this second. I'll stop back in again later, okay? If your head's stopped hurting and the doc says it's all right, I'll read you anything you want."

Laney wished she could argue. She wanted to demand answers, to scream and to shout and to rage — not just against the annoyance of the delay, but at this *thing* that gripped her insides, begging her, pleading with her to STOP THIS NOW before everything she was afraid of burst its bounds and exploded, just like the pulsing mass of fire in her skull.

"I'm going to send a nurse in," the soothing voice continued, this time from a distance. "I'll be back later, I swear."

I swear I never meant to hurt you, Christi had cried near the end. *I love you so much, honey. I never meant to hurt anybody, I swear.*

I swear!

Laney rolled herself into a ball and buried her face in her pillow.

She could make no coherent reply.

Chapter 9

Laney sat on the stiff-backed couch in what had been her great-grandparents formal living room, staring through the darkness at the built-in bookcases on the far wall. She'd been doing the same thing for at least an hour. She kept telling herself that she should either finish what she came for or go back to bed... yet neither thing happened. She remained where she was, motionless, as the quiet night hours stretched toward dawn.

Our Laney died.

Her Gran's words swirled endlessly in her mind, and try as she might, Laney couldn't distill the confused jumble into reason. She wanted to settle on an explanation, be done with it, and move forward. But two distinctly different visions of reality warred in her mind.

The first seemed simpler, and saner. May was eighty-seven years old and she had moderate dementia exacerbated to the point of delirium by both the trauma of losing a loved one and the upheaval of relocation. That should be enough. Laney should give herself a shake, throw her shoulders back, and forget every single thing May had babbled while not in control of her faculties. The approach was practical, reasoned, and involved no unnecessary drama... just like Laney herself.

If only she could leave it there. If so she would be warm in bed right now, snoring away under a pile of the Burgdorf family quilts. Instead she was wide awake, laying sideways on an uncomfortable Ethan Allen reproduction with her bare feet exposed and her eyes staring at the shelves of photograph albums across the room.

The second possibility for May's words was ridiculous. Ludicrous. Preposterous. Laney's no-nonsense brain cells refused to go there. Such craziness didn't justify the effort of research! There was no reason for her to reexamine the photo albums. Had they not always been on the shelf where anyone could look at them? She wouldn't find a single scrap of evidence to bolster such an inane theory. She should go back to bed.

Laney didn't move.

Her toes felt like ice.

Go back to bed!

Your baby pictures are in the pink book, the one right there.

Don't be stupid. You're being stupid.

What you are, Laney Miller, is afraid!

She jerked herself to a sitting position and slammed her numb feet onto the floor. To hell with it. She was *not* afraid. She would prove this was all about nothing if for no other reason than to avoid getting frostbite!

She stumbled across the room, grabbed the pink album off the shelf, and settled into an equally uncomfortable armchair with her feet tucked underneath her. She switched on a light and opened the book.

It began with her baby pictures from the hospital. There were Christi and Jimbo, beaming with pride as they held their nondescript little bundle of responsibility. To Laney's eye they looked like teenagers, even though Christi had been twenty-three at the time, and Jimbo twenty-four. The wrinkled face that peeped out from under the knit cap could have been any newborn, and Laney flipped forward dispassionately, looking for a more recognizable image of her face.

There were plenty of pictures, and as she grew, her features became more distinctive. She'd been bald as a cue ball, but her eyes were the same cornflower blue, large for her face, and she had her mother's high cheekbones and damnable button nose. As a baby she'd had a more rounded face with a broader chin... but of course she had. She was a baby!

Laney turned another page. *Yes!* There, looking back at her with a stuffed cat in her hands and a delighted smile on her face, was absolutely, definitely, incontrovertibly *herself.*

She laughed out loud, releasing a long pent-up breath. The

eyes, the chin, the cheeks, the nose, and the impish little grin were all there. Her hair had come in, finally, and it too was clearly recognizable. More of a childish platinum than her current honey blond, but limp and straight as a stick, not a curl in sight—

Laney's breath caught in her throat. Her body went still even as her heart thudded.

Her hair. Where had it come from? She flipped back to the previous page. In the last picture, she'd been bald. She was sitting on a blanket with toys spread around, looking far too little to walk. Yet on the very next page, she was a toddler.

Laney flipped through the next few pages. Then she flipped back again. There was a gap. Where was her first birthday?

Didn't I have a birthday party? a small voice echoed in her mind. Laney had always had a party. As an only child, her birthdays had been a family festivity second only to Christmas and Easter.

Of course you did, honey! her mother's voice had answered. *The photo place lost that roll of film, that's all.*

Laney's middle rolled with nausea. She remembered now; she remembered plain as day. The pictures had always been missing. She'd never thought about how *many* pictures, but now she could see how much time had lapsed. The last baby picture showed a child less than a year old — maybe as young as six months. In the next picture, she was almost two.

The next picture was after the tornado.

The album slid off her lap and fell to the floor.

This proves nothing! she told herself quickly. *It only fails to disprove it!* Rolls of film that required sending off somewhere for developing and printing were an antiquated concept to Laney, but she could easily believe that such materials could get lost. And if they did, there would be no other copies.

She got up from the chair and stumbled back to the bookcase. Shelved alongside her mother's albums was a scrapbook of her own. In it she had carefully preserved all the original newspaper clippings about the Peck tornado, as well as several others that had hit nearby afterwards, including the EF5 that had destroyed the town of Joplin on the day of her high school graduation. She

grabbed the book, dropped down onto the rug, and pulled out
the article she wanted. She had read it so many times she knew
exactly where on the page to look for the words she sought.

"Right here!" she proclaimed out loud, poking at the printed
words with a trembling finger. "It says 'an infant.' I knew it did!"
The child who had died was *an infant in a car seat. Ha!*

Laney sat a moment. She should feel better now. She should
be able to put the albums away and go back to bed confident that
her great-grandmother's rambling fantasy had been disproved.
But she wasn't confident. And she knew why. The article said
specifically that the missing body was that of an infant. But it
also said that old Mr. Weimer had been sheltering with his son
in his house on Third Street, when everybody knew he'd been
with his daughter and son-in-law in their place over on Maple.

Newspapers made mistakes. All the time.

Damnation. It wasn't enough! Laney needed more. If she
couldn't find it, she might never sleep again.

She reread the article from the beginning, attempting to do so
with fresh eyes, focusing on the family who had died. *Elizabeth
and Carl Macdonald.* They had been traveling from their home in
Nashville, Tennessee en route to Branson, Missouri. Country
music lovers, perhaps? Laney skipped ahead to reread the
subsequent articles. There was no further information about the
couple or their infant, which was not hugely surprising. Local
papers cared about local people.

She replaced the scrapbook on the shelf and shuffled through
the cold, dark hallway to the kitchen, where she'd left her laptop
charging on the table. She plopped down in a chair and turned it
on, then waited impatiently while the aged electronic chugged
back to life. Still sitting in the dark, she pulled up the search
engine, found the name of the primary newspaper in Nashville,
and clicked through to its archives. Unfortunately, the listings
she wanted weren't public, requiring her to sign up for a free trial
subscription. But after creating yet another login ID and
password and then searching for several more minutes, she
located the information she sought. It had appeared in an interior

page of the paper's Sunday edition, dated May 15th, 1994.

Local Family Perishes in Missouri Tornado

Three of the four fatalities caused by the
F3 tornado which struck the town of Peck,
Missouri just before noon on Friday have
been confirmed as local residents.
According to family members, Carl A.
Macdonald, 32, of Belle Meade, and his wife
Elizabeth, 28, were traveling through the
area with their sixteen-month-old daughter
Jessica Nicole on Highway 60 en route to
Branson, Missouri when the funnel cloud
struck. The remains of the couple were
found separately in an adjacent field late
Friday afternoon; the remains of their
young daughter have not been located as of
press time. Authorities are uncertain
whether the family attempted to remain in
their vehicle or...

The newsprint swam before Laney's eyes. Sixteen months?
Sixteen months was not an infant! She skipped over details of
the tornado, looking for more personal information.

Carl and Elizabeth Macdonald, originally
from Toronto, Ontario, are Canadian
citizens. The couple relocated to Belle
Meade in August of last year when Carl took
a position as Senior Managing Director of
the newly opened Nashville office of
Whitney Mayer, a Toronto-based investment
banking firm. Funeral services for the
family are expected to be held in Toronto;
no local services are scheduled.

Laney stared at the blobby typeface until the serifs blurred.
She wouldn't, couldn't absorb its meaning. By itself it proved
nothing; it meant nothing. If she kept digging she was bound to
find some proof that would satisfy her.

She dove back into the newspaper archive and searched for
further hits on the couple's names. They must have had proper
obituaries somewhere. After much frustration, pursuit of useless

bunny trails, and another sign-up for a free trial that she would have to remember to cancel, she at last found what she was looking for in a daily paper from Toronto, Ontario. The article was dated May 27th, 1994.

Expat Family Laid to Rest After Perishing in US Tornado

Services will be held tomorrow at 1:00PM at the Mission Funeral Home for Toronto natives Carl A. Macdonald, 32, Elizabeth Tremblay Macdonald, 28, and their daughter Jessica Nicole Macdonald, 1, all of whom perished in a tornado that struck the town of Peck, Missouri on May 13th as they were motoring through the area.

Carl A. Macdonald, son of the late Reginald C. Macdonald and Sarah Alvin, of Ottawa, had relocated his family last year to Nashville, TN where he was employed by Whitney-Mayer, the locally based investment banking firm for which his father-in-law, Gordon Tremblay, currently serves as President and CEO. Elizabeth is survived by her parents Gordon and Joan Tremblay as well as by her brother, Richard G. Tremblay, all of Toronto.

Visitation will be held at...

Laney's gaze fell to her lap. There were no pictures. No descriptions. The names on the page were just that... names. The article told her nothing, really.

Yet her heart pounded against her ribs, and her stomach roiled. The names did mean something. Carl, Elizabeth, Jessica, and herself... they were all ordinary human beings who had been minding their own business one second and were swept off the ground by 160-plus mile per hour winds the next. Had the four of them all swirled around in the funnel cloud together? Had Laney seen, with her own frightened toddler's eyes, the doomed Macdonald family spinning and flailing and screaming right alongside of her? Was the memory of that nightmare locked inside her still, impossible to access, yet impossible to purge?

How could she ever know? How could anyone?

Two little girls had gone up in that tornado. Only one had come down alive.

Only one.

An imagined scene sprang to life behind her eyes: a small, pink granite headstone iced with a thick layer of Canadian snowfall. *In memory of our beloved,* it said. *Jessica Nicole Macdonald.* But in the frozen ground beneath, there was nothing. No coffin, no remains. Three faceless grandparents and an uncle stood nearby, mourning a life cut pitifully short, disquieted by the knowledge that the tiny, delicate bones would forever lay elsewhere, unacknowledged, on foreign soil.

Laney's hands shook above her keyboard.

Where *was* Jessica Nicole Macdonald?

"She's dead," Laney whispered hoarsely, assuring herself. The conclusion was practical and reasonable. It made more sense than any possible alternative. There was no clear evidence to the contrary. It was almost certainly true.

Was that good enough?

Laney tried hard to think straight. She would like to believe that she could let it all go — be satisfied with the lack of evidence on hand, move on, and eventually forget. But she knew herself too well. The nightmarish "memories" playing out in Gran's addled mind might have almost no chance of being true. But what chance could Laney justify ignoring, when the lives of other people besides herself could be affected? One in a thousand? One in ten thousand? One in a hundred?

She blew out a breath of resignation.

None. There was no chance she could accept. The issue would be settled only after she had proved conclusively that she *was*, indeed, Laney Carole Miller. And — thank God for modern technology — the means of doing so was within her grasp.

She launched into another computer search, collected the information she needed, and set to work. An hour later, she had a parcel sealed and ready to mail to the laboratory. It contained the necessary paperwork, a cotton swab from her own cheek, and several strands of hair carefully selected from the copious quantities still lingering in her mother's hairbrush. It would take about three weeks, the company claimed. Then she would receive an email, and the nightmare would be over. Whatever nonsense her Gran came up with afterwards Laney could easily, safely, and happily ignore.

As she set the package down by her purse, she surprised herself with a genuine smile. Then she wolfed down a stale piece of pumpkin bread, headed upstairs, and took a very long, very hot shower.

Chapter 10

After an equally awesome afternoon session of surfing at Chesterman Beach, Jason dropped off his houseguest at Tofino's premier whale-watching establishment, then drove on to the hospital. The boat tours didn't run this time off year, but Ben had already connected with the owner and wanted to talk marine mammals, so he and Jason had split up with plans to reconnect for dinner later in the evening.

Jason was anxious to check on Laney again. He had been thinking about her all afternoon, wondering how she was doing. And every time he caught himself thinking about her, he wondered why. There was something about the woman that fascinated him, even beyond his curiosity over her mysterious past. Was it her brash midwestern accent? Her utter lack of social pretense? Her reckless defiance of wind and weather? All were new to him, and all intrigued. He could explain himself no better than that.

He approached her room fearing that she might still be alone in the dark, wincing and bored. He was surprised to discover her door standing open and tense voices echoing into the hall. He stopped at the doorway and looked in to see her fully dressed in jeans and a sweater, transferring items between the suitcase and backpack that were laid out on her bed. "I have no choice!" she said flatly.

The senior staff nurse on the opposite side of the bed sighed with frustration. "I wish you would at least wait until the doctor can come speak with you. We have procedures for—"

"I'm sorry," Laney interrupted firmly, zipping up her suitcase. "But I have to leave. Now." She hoisted her backpack onto her thin shoulders and turned around. She started at the sight of

Jason.

He tried not to do the same. She looked awful. Or rather, he could tell that she felt awful. Her brow was furrowed, her eyes were squinted with pain, and her complexion was practically green.

"Jason," she said absently. "I forgot you were coming. But I'm glad you're here. Could you possibly give me a ride to that room I rented?"

The nurse blew out another breath and pushed past him. "See if you can talk sense into her," she muttered as she exited. "I've got to call the doctor again."

"Don't bother," Laney said to one of them. Possibly both.

Jason stepped inside the room. Laney was clearly in no shape to be hauling luggage around. She seemed unsteady even with the modest weight of the backpack on her shoulders. "Of course I can give you a ride. But what's the rush?"

She backed up to lean against the bed. "I had a visitor just now," she said dryly. "They call them 'Patient Financial Counselors.' Her job was to inform me that as a non-Canadian, I am entitled to receive emergency health services in British Columbia. I am also obligated to pay every damn cent out of my own pocket."

"Oh," Jason said awkwardly. Foreign tourists often assumed that since Canada had a national health service, emergency care, at least, would be free to anyone who got injured here. It wasn't unusual for unwitting foreign nationals to run up huge bills in the provincial hospitals.

"They're talking to me about payment plans," Laney muttered. "It will take me forever to work off what I already owe, and they want me to stay another night? Well, I don't have that kind of money. I've got to take care of Gran."

She rose to her feet again, swaying a little in the process. Jason readied himself for a save, but tried not to show it. He had enough experience with women to distinguish those who appreciated having doors opened for them from those who would smack your hand off the knob, and Laney was definitely one of the latter. "Are you sure you—"

"Yes," she said tiredly. "Can we go now? I have to get out before the doctor comes back or they'll charge me for another consult."

Jason grabbed the handle of her suitcase before she could reach it. "May I?" he asked politely, genuinely afraid she would pass out if she attempted it herself.

Her uncomfortably forced "thank you" confirmed her feelings about male chivalry. He let her lead the way outside, but followed close enough to catch her. "Take a right at the end of the hall," he instructed. She couldn't possibly know the way to the parking lot, but he suspected she'd rather wing it than ask. He continued to give unsolicited directions as they made their exit through a gantlet of disapproving glances, many of which were directed at Jason.

"Thanks for that," she said dully as she settled into the passenger seat of his Civic. Jason watched to make sure she could shut her own door, then loaded her bag in the trunk and got behind the wheel. "Hope I didn't get you into trouble, too," she said.

"No problem," he insisted. It might indeed be a problem, since Steve was a good friend and one of the medical assistants was on his A-list for an uncomplicated night on the town. But his sympathies lay with Laney. He was fairly certain that whatever bills she racked up, she would indeed pay, no matter how long it took her. Given that the doctor *had* said that what she mainly needed was rest, her self-discharge didn't seem unreasonable to him.

He pulled out of the hospital parking lot and headed through town back to the highway. The winter sun had just set, and the town's lights began to twinkle as his fellow merchants prepared for happy hour and the dinner rush. He stole frequent glances at Laney, amused by her obvious interest in her surroundings. Her eyes were still only half open, but she took in the various gift shops, surf shops, bars, restaurants, tour offices, and museums as if there would be a quiz later.

"I'd think a beach town like this would be completely dead in the winter," she commented.

Jason chuckled. "If you saw it in the middle of July, you'd think this *was* dead. Summers are absolutely insane by comparison. But for the surfers and the storm watchers — and some hikers, too — winter in Tofino is pure magic."

As they headed out of town and onto the tree-lined highway, she leaned forward to look up at the sky. The lingering colors of sunset glinted through the trees on the west side of the road, even as the moon began to rise overhead. "I think I'd prefer the winter myself," she said thoughtfully, her eyes opened fully now. "I've never experienced an oceanic climate. Everywhere I've lived has been humid subtropical. Meaning hot and humid in the summer, bitterly cold in the winter, and swinging wildly everywhere in between."

Jason said nothing. He liked listening to her voice. Much of the time she'd spoken before, she'd been in pain. Now she sounded almost happy. The further they drove into the forest, the more animated she became, practically pressing her cute little nose against the window.

"I can't wait to see these trees in the daylight," she mused. "I always thought of the Pacific Northwest as being nothing but *gray*... gray clouds, rain, and cold water. But I underestimated the evergreens. I bet it's more colorful here now than it is in Missouri or Oklahoma. All we've got this time of year are naked branches."

"But you have snow, right?" Jason interjected. "A little white must liven things up."

"Missouri usually has a fair amount of snowfall. But lately it hasn't materialized. It's been warmer than it should be on average, but at the same time, we've had more unusually frigid cold snaps." She glanced over at him, briefly, then returned her gaze to the trees. "Don't get me started on climate change. You don't have that kind of time."

Jason chuckled. As a surfer and lifelong outdoorsman, he had a fair amount to say on that subject himself. "Maybe later."

"How much longer till we get to the ocean?" she asked excitedly. "Is the hostel very far from the beach?"

His smile broadened. "The Pacific Rim Surfing Lodge is *on* the beach."

Her head snapped around. "I can't afford that!"

He laughed. "Give your pre-concussion self some credit, will you? You did your research. For a single traveler, my lodge is the most affordable accommodation in the area."

"How can it be?"

He smirked. "Exceptional management? The lodge is my pride and joy, you know. We book months ahead year round. You were lucky I had a cancellation or you wouldn't have gotten the room you did. I also rent surf equipment and teach lessons, if you're interested. When you're better, of course." She was turned sideways looking at him, and he wished he could study her face. But the truck in front of him was braking erratically, and he preferred not to give his passenger a second concussion.

"That's impressive," she replied. "I'm anxious to see it."

The truck pulled off the road, and Jason turned his head. She was smiling, looking very much like the joyful, carefree child in her pictures. "I've looked forward to seeing the ocean for so long," she said wistfully. "I can't believe it happened yesterday and I don't remember it!"

"I'm sure it will all come back to you soon," he assured.

Her smile disappeared. "I might remember everything up until then, but my understanding is that the last few hours — or at least minutes — before the head slam tend to get obliterated for good."

"Well then, a redo is definitely in order," Jason said encouragingly. "As for the rest of the hour before, don't sweat it. From what I understand, you spent most of that time either sitting on a bus or walking in a downpour."

"I've walked in downpours many times," she said absently.

Jason turned onto his access road. He wished she would smile again. "I hope you like the lodge. It's pretty rustic inside, but the beach access can't be beat. If all you need to regain your memory is a little rest and relaxation, it should definitely fit the bill."

"I'm not sure what it will take," Laney answered grimly. "I keep getting the feeling that a part of me doesn't want to remember."

Jason's brow furrowed. "Why do you think that is?"

Laney wouldn't meet his gaze, but continued staring out the window. "Because every time I feel like I'm getting close to remembering, I get this sense of panic. It's weird. I've never felt anything like it before."

Jason sat quietly, thinking. He was warmed by her candor, and he wanted to say something comforting, something helpful. But nothing came to mind. It was all he could do not to pepper her with questions to satisfy his own, inexplicable curiosity. But he didn't have the chance to do either. In the next beat, she squared her shoulders and forcibly cast off her melancholy.

"Never mind," she proclaimed. "I'll figure it out. It's just a matter of pushing through it."

He admired her chutzpah. As if it wasn't enough to be injured, clueless, recently orphaned, alone in a strange place, *and* financially strapped, she had to contend with some mysterious, unknown fear as well? "Well, if you need any help at all, just ask," he offered as he steered the car into his parking spot. "You want to take your stuff in first, or would you rather—"

Her car door was already open. "Ocean," she interrupted. "That way?" she pointed around the near edge of the building.

He nodded and opened his own door. "Hey, take it easy!" he couldn't resist calling as she slammed her door with a bang and started off with a visible wobble in her step. He locked up the car and hurried after her.

Laney couldn't believe the moment had finally come. She'd taken an insane detour to get here, and everything else in her life right now might be one giant, swirling nightmare, but... *the Pacific Ocean!*

She had to restrain herself from running. There was a trail

through the trees around the building, but the light of dusk was dim, the ground was uneven, and bushes and tree branches encroached from every direction. She'd never seen a temperate rainforest in the daylight, and she couldn't wait until morning to explore this one. But first... oh, she could hear it!

Her foot hit something. She lost her balance and nearly went down, but sheer determination kept her moving. Her head started aching again, but she didn't care. The sound was amazing. "I'm fine," she yelled over her shoulder in response to whatever Jason had said. She didn't want him to think she needed coddling; she owed him way too many favors already.

She rounded the far corner of the lodge and stopped to catch her breath. There it was. The ground under her feet sloped from the dark silhouette of the tree line down past bushes and rocks and tumbled logs till it met the great, dark, water that stretched as far as her eyes could see. The sun had set a good half hour ago, but flame colors lingered in the western sky, illuminating a distant cloudscape and highlighting the whitecaps below.

Her feet began to move again, carrying her closer and closer to where the churning liquid crashed upon the sand. The sight and the sound... all the video in the world couldn't capture the richness of even those two senses! And yet, there was more. A breeze lifted the hair from her neck, and she breathed in deeply of the strange scent that filled her nostrils. She'd never understood how air could smell salty... but it did! Salty spray, a hint of fishiness, wetness, earthiness, and... was that seaweed? She didn't know. But she would soon figure it out!

She kept walking closer, stopping only when the sand before her shone with recent moisture. If the air hitting her cheeks wasn't quite so cold, she'd be tempted to kick off her shoes and wade, but... well, she did have some common sense left. She raised her chin and fixed her gaze on the horizon, mesmerized by the endless movement, the continually changing, complex patterns of the waves. Those crashing on the giant boulders and jumbled rocks made one sound; those folding in on themselves before splashing upon the sand made another. Far out to sea, infinitely more waves rolled and rocked, each to its own rhythm, based on the tides and the wind and the currents beneath and the waves to the right and the left. Such an enormous volume of water! Even contemplating the physical power it contained was beyond her grasp. But absorbing the sheer, raw beauty of it... she felt she could stare for a lifetime and never take it in.

She lifted her hands to grasp the arm of the man next to her, but stopped herself in time. Some primitive impulse to share the magic of the moment, no doubt. If only her mother were here. Or her Gran. Or any of her friends.

Her eyes welled with hot liquid, but the emotion wasn't sadness. The ocean was too beautiful for that. Her mom and Gran would be happy for her. Her friends would be, too. She could be alone and still feel joyous. And she did.

She stood perfectly still, basking in it all, for quite some time.

"Is it everything you thought it would be?" Jason asked her finally.

Laney nodded with a smile. She would say that when she reached for him, she'd forgotten who he was, but she'd be lying. Her animal subconscious was acutely aware of his presence. He had been watching her this whole time, experiencing her joy vicariously. And her animal subconscious liked it.

Thank God she had a brain.

He gestured down the beach to where the land curved and a jumble of boulders jutted out into the water. The waves crashed around its base with an exciting hum, and as she watched, she could imagine herself standing barefoot upon it, feeling the power of the ocean resonate through the rocks. "Look inviting?" he asked.

She took a step in that direction.

He stopped her with a gentle hand upon her arm, his deep voice rumbling with laughter. "I wasn't serious! That's where you—"

"Well, how am I supposed to know?" Laney shot back, embarrassed. An unexpected warmth crept from his hand through her sweater and up her arm. It had been a long time since... *Never mind.* She shook him off, then let out an unladylike snort of laughter. He was right, it was pretty funny. Or at least it would be if it'd happened to some other idiot. "Fine. Yuck it up. Then can we pretend my little adventure on the rocks never happened, please?"

He continued to chuckle. "Sure."

"Thank you."

"Would you like to see your room now?" he offered. "It's uh... kind of cold to be out here without a coat."

Laney hadn't noticed. She drew in another breath of the fascinating sea aroma. "I'll be back," she promised the ocean. Then she turned around.

The surfing lodge perched on the slope ahead of her was a single story building of modest construction, in contrast to the expensive private homes to its south and the sprawling resort to its north. Though tightly wedged in between its neighbors, it was separated from them by clusters of trees, creating the feel of a private retreat. A giant picture window faced the ocean, and a door opened onto a wooden staircase that led down the slope, first to a spacious deck and then to a circle of logs and a fire pit on the beach.

"It looks very nice, for the price," Laney complimented. Even as she spoke, a small group of people emerged, talking and laughing, and descended toward the deck. They appeared to be carrying plates. "You serve meals, too?"

Jason chuckled. "Oh, no. I provide a full kitchen and — for an additional fee — private mini-fridges. Most people buy groceries and cook their own. Restaurant meals are crazy expensive here."

"I see," Laney replied. She was annoyingly short of breath all of a sudden, and she stopped a moment, calculating whether it would be easier to take the stairs or to ascend the steep path she'd just come down. When a wave of nausea threatened, she opted for the route with a handrail.

She began walking again, and noticed that Jason fell into step behind her, rather than beside her. How interesting. If he had picked up on her sudden lightheadedness, he was more perceptive than he seemed.

"So what's the career path one takes to run a surf lodge?" she asked, slowing her steps to catch up on her breathing. "Do you get a degree in business, or do you just surf until you win the lottery?"

"Neither," he replied. "In my case, you get an interdisciplinary major in physics and ocean science, blow your life savings rehabbing a scumbag hostel no one else will buy, bust your butt turning a profit, and then eventually reinvest in a new building."

Laney stopped climbing stairs and turned around. Damn, her legs felt weak. She was also confused. "You majored in physics and what?"

"Ocean science," he answered. "You know, surfing stuff."

She couldn't see his face clearly, but from the hint of humor in his voice, it was clear he was messing with her — probably for assuming he wasn't smart enough to major in something like physics. Well, that was fair. She *was* surprised. Surfers were supposed to be mental lightweights.

She turned back around and continued the climb. The slower she got, the closer he followed. *Hmm.* The man was indeed smarter than he looked.

They climbed the rest of the stairs in silence, with the exception of the few words Jason exchanged with his guests on the deck, all of whom seemed to know him well. The woman in the group was clearly flirting with him, which Laney supposed most women did. But he kept pace immediately behind her, a fact for which she was secretly grateful, since her knees nearly buckled three times. When at last they reached the building, Laney opened the door for herself and stepped inside.

"This is the common room," Jason explained, moving around her and pointing as he talked. "You've got your kitchen, your rental fridges, and your coin-operated laundry. There's a table for eating meals, but no lounge furniture. Alcohol and smokes stay strictly outside. So does the partying. I rent space for people to sleep and eat, and I make sure everyone can do that comfortably.

The idea—" His phone rang, and he frowned as he pulled it out to check the number. Then he declined the call and repocketed the phone.

Laney watched him as he moved. Even without the ridiculously handsome face, the man radiated sex appeal. His lean, strong, and well-proportioned form was destined to draw the female eye, and she was not immune. Her gaze was still fixed on the play of muscles beneath his tight-fitting shirt when he spoke again.

"Why don't I take you to your room, and then I'll bring your bags in," he suggested, his eyes glinting with amusement as Laney — a beat too late — returned her attention to his face.

"Fine," she said curtly, annoyed with herself. He'd been very nice and was proving inordinately useful, but besides being out of her league on the attraction index, the man was obviously a player. The glimpse she'd gotten of his phone had showed a whole screenful of text notifications in addition to the calls, most of which, she was sure, were from women.

He led her through the common room and down a hallway, then turned a corner. "Half-baths and showers are staggered with the rooms. They're all shared, but each is separate with its own door, and everything's gender neutral."

Laney nodded, impressed with the layout. It seemed like a place she could be comfortable staying alone.

He led her to a numbered door, opened it with a key, and stepped aside. "Home sweet home," he said with a smile.

Laney stepped in to see her puffy winter coat hanging on a peg.

"I took everything else to the hospital, but your coat was still a bit damp," he explained. "Do you know what happened to your room key? The paramedics found it in your pocket, but I don't know what—"

"It's in my backpack," Laney replied, admiring the setup. The room was tiny, but it had everything one needed for a comfortable night's sleep. It even had a screened window that opened, with thick shrubbery and a pull-down blind for privacy.

She smiled. "This is great. Did you come up with the design yourself?"

Jason's gray-green eyes flickered with pleasure, but before he could answer, his phone rang again. He frowned and checked the number. He silenced the call, but whoever it was had distracted him enough to forget her question. "Listen," he began, "I know you probably just want to kick back and rest right now, but the fact is, there's no food here. Are you hungry?"

Laney hadn't thought about it, but since she'd barely touched either breakfast or lunch, the mere mention of food made her stomach growl. Loudly. "I'd say that's a yes."

He grinned. "Tell you what. I'm meeting a friend in town for dinner — why don't you join us? You've met him before actually, it's the guy who carried you in from the beach yesterday. He's an oceanographer working on his doctorate — great guy, really interesting to talk to. Then afterwards I'll take you to the co-op and you can stock up on groceries for the week. What do you say? If you're not too tired, that is?"

Laney hesitated. She didn't want to feel any more beholden to Jason. But she probably did owe her second rescuer a personal thanks, and there was no way around her immediate need for inexpensive food. Besides, eating out with the guys sounded like fun. The majority of her colleagues were male; she was used to being the only woman at a table.

"Sounds great," she agreed.

Chapter 11

Laney stepped out of the small brick bungalow that served as the Peck post office and looked up. It was just past noon, and the clouds that had dimmed the cold January light all morning had finally decided to scatter. The sky was mostly clear now, with a cheerful blue hue.

The day hadn't been going so badly after all, even if she was operating on near zero sleep. Her package for the laboratory had been successfully sent on its way, as had the majority of a morning's worth of paid bills and completed paperwork. She had even managed, by sheer luck of online searching, to engage a highly motivated real estate agent who had driven out from Poplar Bluff immediately, taken pictures of the house, and promised to get it listed ASAP. She had not promised to *sell* it ASAP, but that fact spoke well of her honesty. Much as Laney loved the old house, it was an oversized, antiquated relic in an economically depressed town, and she could afford to turn down no offer, reasonable or otherwise.

Rays of cool sun bathed Laney's face, and she found herself smiling. Why not walk the long way home? One could circumnavigate the entirety of Peck without much commitment, but any exercise would be good for her. She'd been sedentary for weeks now; it was time she built her strength up and began looking forward.

Gradually, her smile faded. Try as she might, she seemed unable to muster any real joy about her future. Her academic motivation, too, was lagging. She knew she was grieving the loss of her mother, as well as that of the great-grandmother she knew, but still, she couldn't shake the belief that her malaise went deeper than it should. That it had started, truly, even before her mother's illness. Inertia in any form had never been in her nature, and her inability to "snap out of it" now seemed like a personal failure.

She didn't even know where she would go from here — where she would live, what she would do. The timing of her mother's death had resulted in missed deadlines for her reenrollment in the spring semester, and though she could get a waiver for late registration, reinstating her fellowship funds was another matter. Barring an administrative miracle, she wouldn't be able to return to graduate school until June, at the earliest. And though it might make sense financially for her to stay put until the house was sold, the idea of living in Peck without her mom and Gran filled her with sorrow.

A brisk wind kicked up, swirling dead leaves and paper trash around her ankles. She stuffed her hands in her pockets, hugged her coat more tightly around her, and pressed on. The sidewalks under her feet were cracked and broken, as was much of the rest of the town's humble infrastructure. The whole area had suffered greatly from the opioid crisis, and its fortunes had dwindled even since Laney left it. Though many of the houses around her were still cared for as meticulously as they had been in her childhood, others had become dilapidated, and a few were boarded up and abandoned. Everyone knew someone who was affected by addiction. Virtually no family had been left untouched, and entirely too many children were in foster care. Christi had been training to become a foster mother when she got her diagnosis.

Laney blew out a breath and tried to regroup. She did have good memories here. Peck was a friendly place, and her childhood had been a warm and happy one. She had grown up knowing all the neighbors and having all the neighbors know her.

See, that's another thing! Wouldn't the neighbors have noticed you were a different kid?

She wished she could stop the doubting, the constant internal debate. She'd promised herself that once her package was mailed, she would put the issue out of her mind. But apparently, it wasn't that easy.

Yes, of course they would have noticed. Forget about it.

She walked by the square, yellow-brick church building that had once housed her preschool. Her memories of it were largely pleasant, except for the one that stood out starkest, even after all these years. She'd once punched a classmate. It was the first and last time she'd ever engaged in physical fighting, but she had been wholly unrepentant. The little brat had had it coming.

"Laney's got no Da-ad! Laney's got no Da-d!" She could hear his taunting singsong as if it were yesterday. But the words he actually said were not the heart of the conflict. There was no shame in having a father who had died with military honors. What the obnoxious little boy had taunted her over was the lack of photographs on her shoddily drawn family tree. Everyone else in the class had pictures of relatives on both their mothers' and their fathers' sides. Laney's tree was grossly lopsided.

She stopped and stared at the basement windows. The child — whose name she had long since forgotten — probably was an insufferable brat. But it would be safe to say that preschool Laney had been overly sensitive on the issue. As well-loved as she had always felt in Peck, being cut off from Jimbo's family was a pill she'd found bitter to swallow.

Why weren't you allowed to see them?

Laney started walking again, her pace unnaturally brisk. She had to stop this. It was crazy. Her mother had good reason for keeping the Millers at bay during her childhood. Jimbo's long-divorced parents were both alcoholics and had neglected Jimbo as a baby, which is why he — like Christi — had been raised by his grandmother. Jimbo had cut ties with both of his parents the day he'd turned eighteen, and he had reportedly never looked back, even after his grandmother died. Of course, as a child, Laney couldn't grasp such complexities. Instead she had fantasized about her mystery grandparents and blamed her mother for their absence.

Because his family would have known you weren't the same kid.

Laney gritted her teeth and kept walking. Christi had made the right decision about the Millers. Laney herself had proven that point when, at the tender and impossible age of thirteen, she had played detective and acquired her grandmother's phone number. Remembering the brief, traumatic call spurred a surge of acid in her gut, even now. Not only did Jimbo's mother blame his young widow for encouraging his enlistment and thus his death — she'd had the gall to deny that Christi's daughter was actually his child. Over the phone. To that child herself.

Laney's steps halted abruptly. *Dear God, no.*

She drew in a breath and held it, her mind searching frantically for the exact words Jimbo's mother had spoken.

Had she known? Is that why she hated her daughter-in-law so? Is that why they wanted nothing to do with me? Think, Laney. Think!

It had all happened so very long ago... and she had tried so hard, for so long, to forget it! But the scratchy, slurred voice *was* still etched in her memory. The hurtful words had practically carved themselves on her soul.

Your momma ain't nothing but a two-bit whore, I tell you what! She packed him off to the Army so's she could run around on him, she did, cheatin' on him! You better believe ain't nobody know who that baby's daddy was—

Laney stopped the internal recording abruptly. There was no need to recall the rest of it. Jimbo's mother had been a sick woman, and she was dead now anyway. Her hateful words meant nothing and deserved to be forgotten.

She inhaled deeply of the cold air, then stopped for a moment and looked around. She'd paid no attention to where she was going; in Peck it wasn't possible to get lost. But somehow or other, her feet had brought her here. To the end of the street, at the east edge of town. Her eyes rested on a well-kept modular home with a small plastic wishing well and a flock of metal flamingos in its yard. The house had not always been here. Twenty-six years ago, a rental trailer had stood in its place.

The wind picked up again, and Laney pulled her hood over her tingling ears. This is where it had happened. Where she had — presumably — opened the door to let her little dog out, then followed him. Where the tornado had picked her up and carried

her away, tipping the trailer and knocking her mother
unconscious. No one had ever figured out where the dog went.
Had he turned around and scuttled back underneath the trailer,
finding shelter there? Or had he also been lifted up and spirited
away, only to find his own way back by instinct?

Laney remained motionless, still staring. She could remember
none of it. Never had, and never would.

"Laney, love! Is that you, darlin'?"

She swung round to see a familiar face. It was Nan Kennedy,
her third grade teacher. Nan had lived in the little bungalow from
which she now emerged longer than Laney had been alive. "It is
me," Laney replied cheerfully, grateful for the interruption.
"How are you doing, Mrs. Kennedy?"

"Call me Nan, honey. You're a big girl now!" the woman
replied, meeting Laney on the sidewalk and enfolding her in a
motherly hug. Nan Kennedy was a fixture of the town: honest,
hard-working, and good-hearted. She was a widow now, long
since retired and getting frail, but one of her grown sons had
recently moved back in with her, and everyone said she seemed
content. "I'm all right now, honey, but I just feel terrible about
missing your momma's service. Darn flu had me flat on my back
for nearly two weeks. I'm so sorry."

"Please don't apologize," Laney said quickly. "I know you
would have made it if you could. I'm glad you're better now."

Nan's warm eyes swam with compassion. "And how are you
doing? That's the question. I heard about your Gran moving to
the home in Sikeston. I know it's hard, but I think the same as
everyone else — in a situation like this, it's for the best."

Laney nodded gratefully. She had worried that the family's
decision to move May out of Peck would be criticized. But it was
clear that Gran's friends were aware of how dangerous her
wandering had become. "It is for the best," Laney agreed.

"You thinking about the tornado?" Nan asked matter-of-
factly.

Laney was taken aback. But her thoughts must be obvious,
given what she'd been staring at. "Yes, I suppose I was."

Nan smiled and patted her arm. "Only natural. You'll always be our little miracle baby, you know."

A hopeful thought arose in Laney's mind. Hadn't Nan lived next door at the time? "Do you remember when my mom and I moved into the trailer?" she asked. "We weren't here very long before the tornado, right?"

"Oh, no. You'd only just moved in."

"A couple weeks?"

"Oh, I'd say days, more like."

Laney pressed on. "But you were here when we moved in? You saw me, and the dog, and... everything?"

Nan cocked her head quizzically. "Well, I can't say I remember your moving in. I was teaching then, you know, so I wasn't home during the day. I do remember baking your momma one of my strawberry rhubarb pies as a welcome to the neighborhood, and I felt bad I never got it to her. It was still sitting in my kitchen after the tornado, and I remember just looking at it and worrying so much about you both."

Ask her. "But you did see me... I mean, you visited with me and my mom at some point before the tornado hit, right?"

Nan's brow furrowed.

Laney fumbled on. "I was just wondering about... how my mom handled the move and everything. So soon after my father died."

Nan shook her head sadly. "Oh, we all felt just awful for her, losing her husband like that, so young. It was a pity his funeral was so far away. I would have liked to have gone, just to support your momma. She was one of my very first students, you know."

Laney nodded, her mind racing. Her father's funeral wasn't here? People hadn't seen her then, either? She had visited the cemetery in Dade County where her father was buried alongside his grandparents, but with her Grandpa Auggie being in the business, she'd always assumed her father's funeral had been in Peck. Of course it wouldn't have been. He and Christi had met at Three Rivers Community College in Poplar Bluff; they'd never lived here. His funeral must have been held either at Fort

Leonard Wood, where they were living at the time, or back in
Dade County, where his own friends and family could attend.

Did anyone in Peck ever even see me before the tornado?

"So, um... when we moved to Peck, you hadn't seen either
one of us for a while?" Laney asked.

Nan waved a hand. "Oh, I can't recall, honey. It's all been so
long ago. But the day of the tornado... now, that's a day none of
us will ever forget."

Laney wanted to let it go. Desperately. But she couldn't. "I'd
love to hear what you remember," she said, trying to keep her
voice light. "About that day. About what happened when I was
missing, and... how my mom got me back."

Nan smiled at the invitation. She had always loved telling
stories. "Well now, that's a sad tale with a happy ending, for sure.
I was up at the school; we were just getting ready to go to lunch
when the siren sounded. As often as that happened, the kids
weren't too scared usually. But that day was different. You could
feel a kind of tension outside. One little boy looked out the
window and said to me, 'Mrs. Kennedy, the sky's colored wrong!'
and I knew just what he meant."

A troubled look passed over her face. "I hustled the kids out
of there, and we hunkered down in the hallway. I started them
singing to take the edge off, but soon enough the wind got so
loud I couldn't hear myself. It sounded like a jet engine taking
off, right over our heads." She paused in thought. "I've had
tornados pass nearby before... but I've never heard anything like
that. You could feel it, a pressure like, straight down to your
bones. Thank God the school was sound. We lost a couple
windows, but nobody got hurt. Soon as it was over, parents
started trickling in. So many worried hugs! They all wanted to
take their kids home right then. It was a while before we heard
about you being missing, but once we did, that's all anyone could
talk about. We couldn't hardly believe it — it just seemed too
cruel."

She turned to Laney. "I was so upset for your momma. I
remember someone telling me that they'd checked my house and

I only had some shingles missing... and I remember thinking, 'Oh, that's right! I'm next door!' Honest to God, honey, I forgot all about my own place. All I could think about was how horrible it would be if your momma lost you so soon after losing your daddy."

Laney put an arm around the older woman's shoulders, though she felt less than steady herself. "Did you join the search?"

Nan nodded. "It was hours before I could leave the school, but after all the kids had been picked up, I walked back home and took a look. It was a horrible sight. That trailer on its side, all banged up and falling apart, with toys and clothes scattered everywhere... it was awful. Made you sick inside. People were roaming around the whole town like ants, calling your name, looking under anything bigger than a breadbox. I didn't know where to look either, but I put on my boots and headed out that way." She waved an arm.

Laney looked. The fields bordering the edge of town, long since harvested of their corn, stretched before her eyes monotonous and uniformly brown. Unlike some other parts of town, this particular scene had changed little in twenty-five years.

"The corn was about knee-high, then," Nan continued. "You'd *think* you could see a good ways, but those green stalks could fool you. I remember—" She broke off thoughtfully. "You know, it must have been a while since I'd seen you, come to think of it, because I remember not being sure how big you were. I was worried you could be curled up somewhere and I'd look right past you. We were all scared to death; by then we'd heard about the two people found dead by the highway. It was so awful."

Nan's gray eyes misted over, but then she smiled. "Finally I heard some yelling, and it was Mr. Barwick coming through to tell everybody that you'd been found, and that you were all right." She patted Laney's hand on her arm. "I do believe those were the most amazing words I ever heard. We were all hoping for the best, but I don't think a one of us expected it."

Laney released a breath she hadn't realized she was holding. "What did the Turners do when they found me, do you know? Did they call the police?"

Nan seemed surprised by the question. "Oh, I wouldn't know about that. I expect they were focused on getting you back to your momma. Terri said she brought you inside and covered you with a blanket and just sat there and held you until your momma arrived. I remember her saying you didn't cry. You just seemed shell-shocked. Pale as a ghost and shivering something awful. The wind took off most of your clothes, you know."

Nan's voice turned cheery. "I do wish I could have been a fly on the wall for that reunion! Terri said your momma was nearly as pale and shocky as you were when she walked in... I don't think your momma believed it was true until she saw you there with her own two eyes. Terri said she just swept you up in her arms saying 'my baby, my baby!' and that she wouldn't let you go, not for anything. Your grandpa wanted to take you both to the hospital right away and Terri said they couldn't hardly get your momma to let go of you long enough to strap you in the car seat! Of course, nobody blamed her a bit."

Laney's arm dropped back to her side.

"Are you okay, honey?" Nan asked with concern. "You don't look so good. You don't remember any of this, do you?"

Laney ordered herself to breathe. She'd heard the reunion story a million times before. Was Nan telling it differently, or was she only hearing it that way? "No," she answered hoarsely. "I don't remember any of it." She collected herself and steadied her voice. "I was just wondering... do you know how I reacted? Was I as excited to see my mom as she was to see me?"

"Well, I wasn't there, of course," Nan answered. "But I expect you were in shock, still. You had a pretty bad time afterwards, you know. Your momma took you to back to her folks' house, and Mary Agnes next door said you cried and cried. For days. She thought you were never going to stop crying. It was so pitiful, honey. We all just felt terrible for you both."

Laney drew in a ragged breath, willing the excruciating drip,

drip of inconsequential pieces of circumstantial evidence to cease.

"But the crying stopped eventually, and before long, you were happy as a clam, running around and talking up a storm!" Nan continued with chuckle. "So, no lasting effects, thank the Lord. We were all so happy to see you out and about after. You were such a cute little thing. Looked just like your momma. Everybody said so."

Laney's hands had begun to tremble. She shoved them deep in her pockets.

"Bright, too," Nan praised. Her gray eyes twinkled as she leaned closer. "Just between you, me, and the fencepost, I'd say you were my brightest student *ever*."

Laney tried hard to smile. "Thank you. And you were my favorite teacher." It was a lie, but a well-intentioned one. Nan was trying her best to be helpful; she could have no idea how her honest recollections had just chilled her audience to the bone.

"Aw, thanks honey. You want to come in for a cup of hot coffee? It's too cold to stand out here talking all day."

Laney felt horribly guilty as she noticed the bright red flush on Nan's aged nose and ears. Her frequent failure to dress appropriately for the weather was an endless source of amusement to her fellow meteorologists. But it wasn't funny to Laney when her obliviousness affected other people. "Thank you, but no, I've got some more walking to do. I've been trapped indoors for so long; it'll do me good. You go on inside, though, please. I don't want you relapsing."

The women exchanged another hug and a round of goodbyes, and Laney set off. But as soon as Nan disappeared into her house, Laney cut between two yards and headed off into the fields.

She had no specific plan. All she could think to do was to keep moving, to push herself physically until the disturbing doubts were purged from her mind. Her ankles twisted as she plowed through the rows of cut, dried husks, her sneakers less than ideal for traversing the uneven, frozen ground. She could hear the traffic from Highway 60 in the distance. The highway where the Macdonald family died.

She kept walking. She was vaguely aware that both her hands and feet were numb, but she couldn't rally herself to care. She needed to prove... something.

Her steps slowed only when she approached what used to be the Turners' farm. Terri and Dick had passed away years ago, and their fields had been annexed to an adjacent farm. Laney didn't know who lived in the house now, and she was in no mood to meet them. She remained at the edge of the yard, standing and staring.

Just past the now-unused and crumbling barn on the other side of the house lay the field where she had been discovered. Laney had heard the story from several different sources, including Terri Turner herself. As a child, she hadn't liked hearing the part about her bleeding cuts and state of semi-nudity, focusing instead on the fanciful idea that she had been making her own way home when intercepted. Wanting to make herself the hero of her own story, she'd insisted that she hadn't needed "rescuing" at all.

She grinned weakly at the memory. Such an egotistical little twerp!

The highway was close enough now that she could see the traffic zipping by. She imagined the path of the storm, which she had researched before. The funnel cloud had brushed the east side of town, ripping off roofs, lifting cars, and toppling the trailer. The place she stood now was northwest of where the tornado had hit the nearby highway. The bodies of Elizabeth and Carl, and their damaged car, had been found in fields between the two points. The tornado had tracked north along the highway until it passed the Turner farm, then veered off to the northeast.

Laney bit her lip. Everyone had always assumed that she had been lifted from her own yard, spun aloft, and held in the air until she was inexplicably deposited onto some relatively soft landing place on the Turners' property. It was fantastic, but it was plausible. When the tornado changed direction, shifts in its currents could very well have ejected her from the funnel. "Soft landings" had been reported before.

And Jessica? Everyone assumed that the lightweight "baby" must have been lifted higher and carried farther. The tornado's path to the northeast was sparsely populated and included stands of trees and a river. No one was shocked when the little body couldn't be found.

Laney felt a sharp pain in her lip, accompanied by the tang of blood. She turned with a huff and started back home again. She had learned nothing. It could all have happened exactly as everyone thought it had.

She walked faster, slamming her sneakers on the ground until a painful tingling indicated a return of blood flow.

It could have happened the other way, too, the scientist in her admitted. The difference in weight was negligible. Either toddler could have landed at the Turners' farm. An argument could be made that Jessica's shorter path and lesser time aloft would be more consistent with survival.

Laney stomped harder.

Don't be stupid, she chastised herself. *Possible isn't probable.*

Her mind was chasing shadows, and she knew it.

Still, she couldn't stop.

Chapter 12

Tofino, British Columbia, Present Day

Jason smiled at Natalie, who had unfortunately been assigned to wait their table, and tried hard to be polite as he parried her inane questions about the group of semi-pro Brazilian surfers who were currently staying at his lodge. He was never rude to a woman he'd been involved with, but there had been nothing between them for years now, she *had* a boyfriend, and she was acting flirtier than normal for no apparent reason. He would gladly give her twice her normal tip, in advance, if only she would leave him alone.

Another burst of merry laughter from Laney made his jaws clench. Ben had only arrived ten minutes ago, and already the two were acting like old friends. Jason cast a glance across the booth — where they sat side by side — and saw Laney's ordinarily pale cheeks flushed with rose. She looked so relaxed, so comfortable. Why the hell did she act so easygoing with Ben, when around him she was so tense?

"I said, did you want a refill on your drink?"

As Natalie's voice broke through the clamor in his brain, he realized he must have tuned the waitress out entirely. He looked down to find his glass barely touched. "No thanks," he replied, attempting to smile at her again. Natalie was a beautiful woman: tall and willowy with long dark hair, almond-shaped eyes, near-perfect bone structure, and an expertly augmented set of curves. But she was also a drama queen with a well-deserved reputation for trash talk, and he avoided her when he could.

After another painful moment of chit-chat, Natalie at last departed the table. Jason returned his attention to Laney, only to hear his damn phone ringing again. He shut off the ringer and tossed it onto the bench beside him out of sight. But not before

Laney's eyes flickered conspicuously in the ringing phone's direction.

He stifled a sigh, wondering what impression she must have of him. Whatever it was, it must make her nervous. Unlike the *married* boat captain across the table, who in a matter of minutes had her snorting with laughter.

"What about you, Jason?" Ben asked in a laudable attempt to reengage him in the conversation. "Ever lose any hair to a nesting seagull?"

Jason had not. But since a spiny fish had once gotten so snarled in his curls he'd had to extract it with a pocket knife, he told that story instead. His mood improved with Laney's continued laughter, and he wondered if — aside from Ben's charms — she was feeling better in general. She'd had no alcohol, per doctor's orders, but being out of the hospital and away from her troubles had definitely sparked new light behind her eyes.

As he watched her blossom back into what must be her normal personality, he felt a welcome sense of relief, along with a certain sense of accomplishment. She could easily have died yesterday, but she was going to be all right. He and Ben both had seen to that. With a little help from his friend Dr. Steve, of course.

He continued to watch her as she talked, her blue eyes sparkling on either side of her enchanting little nose. He still couldn't figure out why she intrigued him so. She wasn't what you'd call beautiful. Any number of other women in the restaurant now were prettier than her, sexier than her. But there was nothing amiss with Laney, either. He was sure that under her shapeless clothes lay a hot little bod that was both muscular and athletic. Her naturally blond hair had looked so soft and free blowing in the ocean breeze that his fingers had itched to brush it from her face. And her face... well, it was perfect just the way it was. Cute and fierce. Sparkling with intelligence and — as he was only just now beginning to appreciate — a wicked sense of humor. So what if she didn't do makeup, much less cosmetic

surgery? Laney Miller was a natural. She was herself. She was real.
And she's not for you, dude. So cut it the hell out.

Jason gave his head a shake. Laney wasn't in his swim lane. A woman like her wouldn't dip one toe in his pool.

"What does your wife do?" she was asking Ben. Honest to God, did she have to look at the man like that?
No "forever girls." Full stop.

"She's an attorney," Ben answered proudly. "Right now she's working with an environmental group. Fighting the good fight against ocean pollution, among other things."

So if Ben had such an awesome woman at home, Jason thought uncharitably, why was he trying so hard to attract this one? Not that it mattered who Laney was attracted to. She was an interesting new acquaintance, nothing more, and he was totally cool with that. He had lots of platonic female friends.
Sure you do. And every one of them is married. Ever notice that?

"My brother works for Fish and Game in Alaska," Jason interjected, trying to distract himself. "Plastic on the beaches makes him crazy." As he launched into an amusing anecdote Thane had shared on the phone last week, he made a point of acting relaxed and casual. Why shouldn't he? Male or female, they were just three new friends, chilling over some burgers.

There was nothing unusual about that.

Laney was feeling so much better, she could almost pretend that her entire hospital stay had been a bad dream. Imagining that she'd taken an impromptu road trip to see the ocean and just happened to run into two seriously great guys in the process was *so* tempting. Ben and Jason were two of the sharpest, most interesting, and most fun-to-be-with men she'd ever met, and she couldn't remember the last time she'd laughed so hard. Besides which, who knew that something as simple as a hot, drippy burger could make her feel like a whole, functional person again?

She felt silly, in retrospect, not realizing how little she'd eaten lately. The "bacon" the hospital had served for breakfast was too thick and practically raw, and by noon her head had hurt so bad she couldn't even think about food. Last night she'd been offered nothing but crackers and Jell-O, and God only knew if she'd eaten anything on the bus or ferry earlier in the day. No wonder she felt debilitated!

Now, as they waited for their checks to arrive, she felt blissfully sated. The prices in the bistro Jason had suggested were frighteningly high, even after the conversion to US dollars, but she couldn't begrudge the restaurant its due. With her eyes still sensitive to light, the comfy four-season patio area with its wooden candlelit booths, scattered gas-log firepits, and a heater at every table fit her mood perfectly. The whole local vibe, which seemed to consist of surfing, socializing, and enjoying good food, was a welcome change to her system. She'd enjoyed every offering on the sampler appetizer they'd shared — including the fried squid — and the apple and miso slaw on her burger was to die for. The evening would cost more than she could afford, but not a penny more than it was worth.

She dug in her purse hoping to find enough cash for a tip at least, but stopped when she remembered she had no Canadian dollars. She would have to use the credit card. Concerned, she made a mental note to check her balance as soon as she got back on her computer. She hated to think how much she had charged on this trip already. But under no circumstances was anyone else paying her way. She'd made that clear when she'd requested separate checks.

Her phone caught her eye, and she noticed she'd received a voice mail. As Ben and Jason launched into a semi-scientific debate over whether coldwater or warmwater fish were more likely to nibble on humans, she put the phone to her ear and played the message. It was several hours old; she wasn't sure how she had missed it.

Hello, uh... this is Dave at Kuntz Motors. I'm afraid it's like we thought... Laney only half understood the gearhead jargon that followed, but as she got the gist, her heart sank. Wordlessly, she returned the phone to her purse.

"Something wrong?" Jason asked immediately.

Laney nodded. And to think she'd actually been having fun for a while. "You were right about my car. It broke down someplace in Vancouver. Apparently I left it at a shop, hoping they could get it running again before I started home. Well, they couldn't. They say the transmission's shot, and the car isn't worth fixing. Basically, it's scrap."

"Tough break," Jason commiserated. "I'm sorry."

"Are they offering you anything for it?" Ben asked. "I hope they're not trying to rip you off."

Laney snorted out a laugh. "Good luck to them if they are. That wreck has been running on borrowed time for months now. I'm surprised it made it as far as it did, since it barely got me back from Oklahoma. Oh, well." She raised her water glass to the defunct. "Maybe now I can save some money on duct tape."

The men laughed, and she laughed with them, even as newfound worries gnawed at her insides. Her joke reminded her of her mother's car, which she did still have and which was newer and more reliable than her own. But a couple months ago her Gran had backed it into a utility pole, and its rear fender was, quite literally, attached with duct tape. It could be fixed, for a price, but if Laney had no car *here*, how would she get home? Stringing bus routes together would be a lengthy misery. Flying would mean more stress on the credit card, and she had no idea how long it would take for her mother's will to get through probate.

Ben began telling a car story that was probably funny, but Laney was unable to focus. Jason appeared to be listening, but more than once she caught his unusually observant eyes on her. She had enjoyed his company immensely today, and it would be easy to mistake his natural empathy for something more. But Laney knew better. Jason Buchanan was a man of many, *many* women. Even without the calls and texts he got constantly, she would know from the reactions of those around him. If obliged to guess, she'd say he'd been involved with at least one woman on staff at the hospital, the surfer on the lodge deck, the driver who'd just honked at him in the crosswalk, and — please, how obvious! — their current server.

Still, she was certain that the eyes that watched her did so with genuine concern. Player or not, she believed that his efforts to be helpful were sincere. And since she wasn't in the business of judging other people, why should his record of conquests matter? There was no reason they couldn't be friends, so long as she kept her own lust in check. He wasn't considering her for his all-star lineup anyway. She was more like a stray puppy he brought in from the rain.

"Here you go," the Barbie-doll waitress chirped, handing each of them a slip of paper in a tray. "I can take that whenever you're ready." She stretched out one perfectly polished nail, stroked a leisurely trail along Jason's scruffy jawline, then winked at him as she turned away.

Ben, who had been in mid-swallow at the time, let out a queer gurgling sound. Jason frowned and shot a glance at Laney.

She directed her attention to her bill.

Chapter 13

Laney was standing in the kitchen with her coat on and her purse slung over her shoulder when her cell phone rang. She checked the caller and answered immediately. "Aunt June? Is everything okay?"

"Your Gran's fine, honey," June answered, her tone belying her words. "She's just got herself a little upset about something."

Laney dropped into a chair. Last she'd heard from the memory care center, Gran's first day of limited family contact was going well. The plan had been for June to check on her briefly in the morning, and Laney in the late afternoon. She was on her way now. "Upset about what?"

"Oh," June replied, her frustration evident. "It's that teddy bear again. You know the—"

"I know the one," Laney interrupted, her head drooping. She would never forget it, either. As one of her more prominent adult failures, it would likely haunt her the rest of her life. Christi's requests for her own funeral had been modest and undemanding, the most specific being her choice of items with which to be buried. The first was a small, misshapen baby pillow, sewed for her by her mother in a ninth-grade home economics class. The second was the bear.

"She's upset it wasn't in the coffin," June explained miserably. "I don't know why she's remembered that all of a sudden, but she has. And it's more than that, even. She wants the thing herself. She made me promise I would look for it and bring it straight over to her. I told her I would, figuring she'd forget about it, but they called me back just now and said she's been going on about it nonstop. Wandering all over the building, looking under the furniture and crying. They almost had to give her a sedative, she was so upset. She keeps saying Christi will never forgive her."

Laney closed her eyes. "What she means is we'll never forgive ourselves. I know I won't."

The teddy bear had been a gift to Christi from Jimbo on the couple's first Valentine's Day. Its deep brown fur was made of a super soft, extra fine plush, its plastic eyes sweet and adoring. In its paws, it held a red silk heart. Laney had admired "Jimbo Bear" from afar throughout her childhood, but he had always belonged to her mother. During the day, he sat with the lopsided pillow at the head of Christi's bed. At night, both moved to her bedside table.

"Now, don't you start that nonsense again," June said firmly. "Your momma told me and Amy both what she wanted, and we forgot right along with everyone else. We're only human."

But it hadn't just been a matter of forgetting, Laney thought ruefully. Christi's final days had been cruelly prolonged, lengthening the interval between her requests and her funeral, and rendering her caretakers both physically and mentally exhausted by the latter. Laney *had* managed to remember the task by the morning of the service, at which point they still had time to get both items to their final resting place. But when she went to fetch them, they had disappeared.

"I hate to ask you this, honey," June continued. "But do you think you could look for it one more time before you head out? They're doing their best to reassure her, but she can't seem to let it go. She's worried someone's going to steal it or something."

Laney sighed. It was her Gran's paranoia that had set the sad sequence of events in motion. Over the past year or so, the more precious an item was to her, the more likely she was to "protect" it by squirreling it away. A good portion of Gran's waking time was consumed with looking for things that been misplaced, none of which she remembered hiding. Her wallet would appear behind the toaster; her favorite broach in her sewing basket. The morning of the funeral, Laney had found Christi's pillow wedged between some sheets in the linen closet. But despite an all-out effort by everyone present, Jimbo Bear could not be found.

"I have no idea where else I can look," Laney said with despair. "We went through all Gran's things again before the move. There's no way we could have missed it twice."

"It wouldn't have to be with your Gran's things," June insisted. "I found her glasses in the ice cube tray once. And your momma told me one time she opened up the fireplace flue and a checkbook fell out! That teddy bear could be anywhere. Next time I get over there I'll scour the house myself — I just thought I'd call and see if maybe you could get lucky. Maybe if you put some thought into it... last time, you know, we were all in such a tizzy we were just running around like chickens with our heads cut off."

"That is true," Laney agreed, remembering the chaos. "I'll try to put myself in Gran's head, see if it helps."

June thanked her for her efforts, wished her good luck, and hung up. Laney set down her purse and removed her coat. "Okay, Gran," she said out loud. "What were you thinking?" She walked up the stairs to her mother's room. Steeling herself against the grief that still spiked every time she saw its emptiness, she stood over the bed, imagining herself to be Gran. If she wanted to keep a small pillow and a medium-sized plush toy safe, where would she put them? Laney pulled both regular pillows from the bed and took them with her. Who knew... maybe the physical props could be useful. She turned and walked out into the hall.

Voila. Gran's first thoughts were easy to recreate, since the linen cabinet was directly across from Christi's room. Laney opened the door and stuffed the first pillow onto a shelf. The bear wasn't in the same closet — she had eliminated that possibility earlier. It wouldn't be quite as easy to hide, since it was bulkier.

She closed the closet and looked down the hall. The bear had definitely not been in Gran's bedroom, nor was it in her own or Christi's. She moved into the much smaller guest room, which was used mainly for sewing and storage. She had already searched it, as had several others. But the floor was cluttered with stacks of fabrics, crafts, and garments waiting to be ironed, and the closet was stuffed to bursting. It would not be that difficult to overlook something.

She held the pillow in her arms and pictured the teddy bear. Keeping its size in mind, she dissected any pile of loose items large enough to conceal it. *Nothing.* She opened the door of the closet. The jumbled mess on the floor could be sifted with one foot. *No bear.* The top shelf seemed unlikely. It was packed tight with boxes from end to end, and Gran wasn't nearly tall enough to open and stuff a bear in any of them, even if they weren't already full. Laney turned to the hanging bar, which resembled a vintage clothing shop. Her great-grandfather's army uniform hung here, as did as his old tuxedo. Two generations of prom gowns. Christi's wedding dress, which she had wanted Laney to wear someday. A whole bunch of Gran's old formal dresses and coats, none worn in decades.

Laney reached out her free hand to unzip the hanging bag that was jammed into the closet's left corner. She was pretty sure she'd felt around its bottom before, but she tried it again just in case. As a child, she had refused to touch its contents on moral grounds. Gran used the vinyl bag to store her fur coats, none of which she had worn in Laney's lifetime, but all of which she refused to part with. The musty smell and disintegrating skins still made Laney's own skin crawl, and she withdrew her hand as quickly as possible.

A flash of red struck her eye. She dropped the pillow and dove back into the furs with both hands, spreading the hangers apart. *Unbelievable.* How diabolically clever could May Burgdorf be? There was Jimbo Bear and his red silk heart, practically at her Gran's eye level, wedged into the triangle of a plastic hanger, nestled within a collar of fur nearly the same color as he was.

"Gotcha!" Laney muttered, pulling the bear from his perch. She would feel triumphant if she didn't feel so stupid. Why hadn't she found him the first time? If she had, all this upset could have been avoided! *I'm sorry, Mom.*

She replaced the pillows where they belonged and carried the bear downstairs. He smelled musty too now, and seemed stiffer than she remembered. But Gran would doubtless be relieved to see him. Laney was pulling her coat back on when she noticed the bear had a thread trailing. She grabbed the string and gave it a tug, but it held fast. When she inspected its source, she frowned. Several inches of the bear's bottom seam had been resewn. The stitches were of a slightly different color than his fur, and they looked as uneven and amateurish as if Laney herself had done them.

She hadn't. Nor could she imagine the bear needing repair, when no child had ever played with him. She gave him a squeeze and noticed the unusual stiffness again.

Someone's put something inside.

She didn't stop to think who. Or why. She just fetched a pair of scissors and cut open the seam. Her fingers dug into the polyester fiberfill, working upward toward the bear's center until she touched something firm. The object was about the width of a ruler, stiff, but flexible. Her fingertips grasped its edge and pulled it out.

She stared. Multiple strips of plastic, bound with a rubber band. Black and brown semitransparent plastic.

Photographic negatives.

She slid out one of the strips and held it up to the light over the table. It had individual sections. Each one was a picture, but the light parts were dark and the dark parts light. She stared some more.

Mom. No doubt about it, despite the reversal of color. Christi was standing over the same table at which Laney sat now. She was holding a cake on a plate. A single, lit candle shone at its center.

Laney gulped in a breath. There was a child in a highchair. With a little bit of hair. But the face was too small... she couldn't see! She dropped the negative onto the table and pulled another from the back of the stack. A quick perusal showed several photographs of a toddler; she zoned in on the biggest closeup.

The reverse colors were maddening. Still, she could see the rounded face. The broad chin. The same, recognizable features she'd seen on the earlier baby pictures. With one clearly notable difference. This older toddler had hair. Unruly, wispy, *curly* hair.

You had the cutest blond hair, Gran had told her last night. *Curly like your daddy's.*

Laney's hair was straight. The very first picture in the family album that showed any hair at all had showed straight hair. Every picture after the time gap had absolutely, definitely, been a photo of Laney. Every picture before the tornado had been—

Laney choked on the lump in her throat. *This girl.*

The hand that held the negative shook so violently she couldn't focus. This girl was the baby. The baby was this girl.

You're the other one.

A moan escaped Laney's throat. She dropped the negative. Her body went limp, and she slipped off the chair and onto the floor.

It was true.

She could explain everything else away, add up all the little pieces and dismiss them wholesale. But *this*... this could not be explained. Christi hadn't lost any pictures. She had taken them out of the album, selectively, and hidden them away. The prints she might have destroyed, but the negatives... well, how could she? They were the last pictures ever taken of her *real* daughter, hers and Jimbo's, a child that she herself had consigned to death without a grave!

Huge, racking sobs consumed Laney as the pieces of the puzzle continued to fall, with painful precision, into place.

Laney, honey, Christi had said mere weeks before she died, *I want you to do something for me.* She couldn't let anyone — especially Laney — find the negatives. It had been dangerous enough for her to keep them in the house while she was alive. Yet she couldn't destroy them. So what could she do? *I want the pillow and Jimbo Bear buried with me, okay? I know it sounds stupid, but I do.*

Of course, Mom, Laney had assured her. *It's not stupid at all. I'll take care of it.*

I've already asked your Gran to do it, Christi had said quickly. *I think it will be better that way... it will give her something useful to do, when the time comes. I just need you to be sure she remembers. Can you promise me that?*

Of course Christi had wanted Gran to do it. If Laney handled the bear, she might notice the new stitches — sewn by Christi's own, then unsteady hand. But Gran couldn't be trusted to remember, so there were backups. Laney. June. Amy. All had been appropriately advised.

But Gran had protected the items too well. And now, today, some part of her mind had remembered that urgency. Yet she hadn't asked Laney to look for the bear; she'd asked June to do it. Gran's damaged brain still registered the need to keep the damning evidence out of Laney's reach — never mind that Gran had already, unwittingly, divulged the truth. Gran had been keeping Christi's secret for twenty-five years. Grandpa Auggie must have kept it too.

The sobs kept coming. Laney lay curled on the floor, hugging her knees.

Did June know the truth? Maybe, maybe not. She had been busy with her own family at the time, and Christi and Jimbo had lived hours away on the other side of the state. Certainly June knew nothing of the negatives, or she would never have asked Laney to search for the bear...

But she could still have known. And Amy too. And Nan and the Turners... did all of Peck know? Had they been laughing at her all along? Throughout her whole, fraudulent, completely unreal life?

Laney's cheek was pressed against the cold, hard kitchen tile. It felt dusty and dirty.

She didn't care.

She would never care about anything, ever again.

Two toddlers swirled in circles in her mind. One flew into a haystack. The other, into oblivion. Yet somewhere, way to the north, in Canada, a stone marker stood atop a tiny, empty grave.

She should be in it.

She wasn't Laney Carole Miller. She never had been. She never would be.

She was *Jessica Nicole Macdonald.*

Chapter 14

Laney unloaded her groceries into the rented mini-fridge, then closed the door of the cabinet enclosing it and removed the key from the lock. "Do people steal food if you don't use the lock?" she asked.

"Steal is a strong word," Jason replied good-naturedly. "But mistakes happen, and I like to minimize conflicts between my guests. We don't do drama, here. Not if I can help it, anyway."

Laney rose to her feet with a smile. She had to admit, she liked everything about the surf lodge, including the price. Jason was a gifted entrepreneur. "What's the cost for the rental?"

"It's nominal," he said dismissively. "I can put it on your tab."

Something in his tone told Laney that was unlikely to happen. She'd have to make sure they settled up fairly when she checked out. But her leaving Tofino was one of several things she didn't want to think about right now. She'd just had an absolutely wonderful evening in the company of two sharp, funny, objectively good-looking men. She had a supply of groceries, a kitchen, and a safe place to sleep. And tomorrow morning, the sun would rise to show off the full glory of the Pacific Ocean — right outside her doorstep.

"Before I head out, I wanted to ask you," Jason began somewhat hesitantly. "We never finished searching your computer. I'd be happy to help you with that again, if you're having trouble looking at the screen."

Laney's happy mood crashed instantly. She didn't want to think about what might be on her computer. Not now. The black cloud of fear that had assaulted her earlier hadn't disappeared; it was merely waiting, lurking just beyond her conscious reach. Could she not remain happily oblivious for a little while longer?

"I'm sorry," Jason said, looking chagrined. "I knew I

shouldn't have brought it up."

Laney was surprised. She thought she'd concealed her angst. Jason was indeed good at reading people; she would have to remember that.

"No," she insisted, trying harder. "I appreciate the offer. But I'm sure I can manage the laptop by myself now."

It was another lie. She'd answered a text from Amy in the car and had thought her skull would split. Since she'd left the hospital, the pain in her head had subsided to an occasional dull ache that was mild enough to ignore. But looking at screens still produced the dagger-in-the-eyes effect, and until that stopped, blue light wasn't happening.

"So," she said cheerfully. "Where are you guys going surfing tomorrow? I'd love to watch."

She wasn't so bad at reading faces herself. Jason was delighted.

"Probably right out here, at Chesterman," he answered. "If the doc hadn't said 'no physical exertion,' I'd bring an extra wetsuit and you could give it a go yourself."

Laney laughed. She couldn't imagine herself on a surfboard. "I don't think so. Doctor's orders or not."

"Why not?" Jason demanded. "You said you were a good swimmer."

"In a pool!" she clarified. "With lanes and rules and a defibrillator. I don't do riptides and sharks."

"We don't have shark attacks up here," he boasted.

"No sharks?"

He smirked. "I didn't say that."

"No thanks," she said with a laugh. "I'll stick to watching from the beach."

He didn't reply immediately. He just stood there studying her, his gray-green eyes sparkling so intently she had to avert her gaze. No wonder the guy had women all over him. A girl could lose herself in those eyes. He was like a friggin' cobra.

"You wouldn't last an hour just sitting," he pronounced finally. "I saw the way you looked, standing up on that rock, facing the wind. You're a thrill seeker at heart; don't deny it. I know a fellow adrenaline junkie when I meet one."

Laney's mouth dropped open. And she'd thought he was perceptive! "You're crazy! I'm about as far from a thrill-seeker as you can get. I'm the most boring, do-nothing academic on the planet."

Jason grinned. "Says you."

If he'd been one of her grad school buds, Laney would have delivered a playful smack to his shoulder and changed the subject. But she had no intention of touching Jason, playfully or otherwise. The man was too dangerous. Too handsome, too sweet, too attentive. Too easy to fall for. He would make an amusing guy friend. But she would not be any cobra's midnight snack.

"Well, we'll just have to see," she replied, quashing the subject. "Thanks again for the chauffeur service. Looks like I'm good now, so I think I'll turn in. Despite the whole coma thing, I feel like I didn't sleep a wink in the hospital. I'm pretty beat."

"Of course you are," he agreed. "Ben and I will probably hit the beach early tomorrow — swell's supposed to fade by noon. We'll keep an eye out for you."

"Likewise," Laney promised. "Thanks again."

He shrugged off her thanks, bade her farewell, and exited through the door to his office.

Laney remained in the common room a moment, staring after him, before turning towards her own room. She shook her head in puzzlement as she walked. If she didn't know better, she'd think the man was interested in her. But she did know better.

She opened the door to her room, stepped inside, and locked it behind her. The lodge was supposedly full tonight, but no one else was around. The others were probably out enjoying the bars and would stumble in loudly later. No matter. As tired as she felt, they couldn't wake her if they tried.

A smile crept over her face as she remembered Jason's words. An adrenaline junkie. *Her.* Ha! This insane road trip to Canada was probably the most adventurous thing she'd ever done. Aside

from getting up close and personal with tornados, of course —
but that was a part of her job.

She would have loved to travel more. She had always longed
to see the ocean, stroll through the forests of the Smoky
Mountains, hike to the bottom of the Grand Canyon. Hell, if
someone else was paying for it, she'd go just about anywhere, do
anything. But no one else *was* paying for it, and what little money
she had had always been spoken for. There was a difference
between what she wanted to do and what she needed to do, and
the latter came first. It was called adulting.

She threw on her sleep clothes and crawled into bed. It was a
comfy mattress for the price, and she caught herself smiling
again. She really was looking forward to watching the guys surf
tomorrow. Ben's wife Haley was a very lucky woman. If only
Jason—

Well, he's not. So never mind. She closed her eyes and drew up
the covers.

Sleep wouldn't come. Her mind preferred to replay her
pleasant evening. A handsome face. A deadly smile.

She groaned and rolled over. It had been far too long since
she'd had a boyfriend... or anything else. But her past
relationships had been uninspiring. She'd hardly dated at all in
high school, partly because of slim pickings, but mostly because
of her own immaturity. In college she'd rectified both those
issues, but two long-term relationships had ended with two
painful breakups. She'd tried again while working on her
master's, but the result was the same.

She didn't blame the guys — they were who they were, after
all. All three had been steady, responsible, good-hearted, and
family-approved. They wanted the same things out of life that
she did: a happy marriage, a good job, a stable future. She had
genuinely cared for all of them and had thought they might work
out. Whether she had loved any of them, she didn't know. All
she knew was that when the marriage talk started, everything else
fell apart. It wasn't that she didn't want to be married someday.
She thought she did. The problem was that the thought of

spending *the rest of her life* with any of the three of them made her
want to bust out the door and keep on running.

She had tried to explain herself, to let them down gently, but
her best intentions had failed. She'd hurt them all, and she wasn't
proud of that. Nor was she anxious to repeat the experience.

She figured she must be missing a gene. She didn't doubt the
existence of the kind of love that lasts a lifetime; she'd seen it in
action herself. But acquiring it was more elusive, and she worried
that she was incapable. She was destined to be a spinster nerd,
eating lunch alone in her cubicle at the Storm Prediction Center,
crawling into bed at eight o'clock with her five cats.

She flipped over with another groan.

"Looks good for tomorrow morning," Jason told Ben as he
grabbed a handful of popcorn from the bowl on the coffee table,
then leaned back into his sectional couch. "Mostly clear, glassy.
Waist to shoulder."

"Just my speed," Ben replied. "Don't feel like you need to
babysit me all morning, though, if you'd rather be with the big
kids at Cox Bay."

Jason shook his head. "Chesterman's fine. I'm used to
teaching there; it's my biz. Besides, Laney said she wanted to
watch us in action tomorrow." He grabbed another handful of
popcorn. "This is awesome. What'd you put on it?"

Ben smirked. "Sorry. Family secret. You want a repeat, you'll
have to invite me back."

"Dude," Jason said with appreciation, "anybody who cooks
likes you *and* cleans up has a standing invite. Besides which, the
more you stay with me, the more cred I'll build toward that Maui
condo offer."

Ben chuckled. "No need. You can cash in anytime. And it's
not me Laney wants to watch in action."

Jason shook his head. "Hate to downgrade my own rep, but
I don't think she's interested."

"Oh, no?" Ben replied. "That wasn't my impression."

Jason refused to take the bait. "Laney's great, but like I said before, she's not my type. I can see us being friends, though."

"Can you?" Ben asked. "You have a lot of female friends?"

"Sure," Jason answered immediately. He searched for an example. "I get along great with my sister-in-law, Mei Lin. And her sister Ri, of course."

Ben nodded. Ri, a marine biologist in Alaska who'd done an internship on Maui, was the mutual friend who had introduced them. "They're both married. I'm talking about single women."

Now Jason smirked. "Well, you met Natalie earlier. She was pretty friendly."

"Single women who aren't exes," Ben clarified.

Jason thought a moment and came up empty. Hell, there had to be someone. "The woman who manages my equipment rental—"

"Is old enough to be your mother," Ben interrupted.

Jason frowned. "Is there a point to this?"

Ben laughed. "Sorry. Just saying it isn't easy to manage a friendship with someone you're attracted to when you're both single. I should know. I tried hard enough."

"So what happened?"

"I married her."

Jason harrumphed. He heard enough blabbering about wedded bliss from his brother. "Well, I'm not marrying anyone. And Laney *is* the marrying kind, so that's that. Is this all the popcorn?"

"No, there's more. What's so bad about marriage?"

"Nothing," Jason said, growing frustrated. "I just like my life the way it is."

Ben grabbed the empty bowl and rose. "Well, that makes two of us," he said cheerfully. "Aside from all the other reasons I like being married to Haley, it makes it easier to have female friends. Whenever I meet an interesting woman, I throw my marital status out there, first thing. Taking sex off the table makes people act differently, you know. They're more themselves."

Ben headed into the kitchen, and Jason stared after him. Was that why Laney had seemed so comfortable with Ben so fast? Interesting.

But hardly relevant for his own life. He couldn't very well walk up to Laney and say, "Hey, you're cute and all, but due to differing life philosophies I'm not interested in sleeping with you, so will you relax already?" He chuckled at the thought. He had enough experience with women to know how *that* would go over. It didn't matter if it was true; it wouldn't even matter if she specifically didn't want to be pursued. He'd still get some handy object upside the face. Women liked to feel they were attractive to a man.

Men liked that too, of course. He got his fair share of female attention, and he enjoyed it. He frowned suddenly, remembering his first introduction to Laney, pre-concussion. She had gone out of her way to show *dis*interest. Why?

He wondered, for the first time, if she might have a guy back where she came from. A guy she no longer remembered. His frown deepened. If she did have somebody, and the guy wasn't concerned enough about her whereabouts to track her down and get his ass up here, he didn't deserve her.

Jason ground his teeth for several seconds before realizing that scenario wasn't possible. Laney remembered everything up to the last few days — she could hardly have acquired a boyfriend in that amount of time. No, if she wasn't interested in Jason, she had another reason.

His brow furrowed. And what might that reason be, anyway? She did seem to enjoy his company. He wasn't marriage material, but she didn't know that. Not yet, anyway. So what was her problem?

"Damn, you look serious," Ben said lightly, reentering with a fresh bowl of popcorn. "Something I said?"

"No," Jason replied, scooping up another handful before the bowl hit the table. "Just thinking about an accounting issue at the lodge." He crunched a mouthful of kernels. Laney must not be looking for any kind of relationship, with anybody. Well, that was fair. He just needed to make clear — somehow — that he was perfectly capable of enjoying the company of a single woman without sleeping with her. Then they could be friends.

He did want to get to know her better. He wanted to know what had been going through her head when she stood out on that rock, and why she was so wrongly convinced she wasn't a thrill seeker. He wanted to see the sheer, ecstatic joy on her face when he finally got her up on a surfboard — and she realized that he'd been right.

He smiled to himself. He couldn't wait for her to see the ocean in the daylight tomorrow. As far as he could tell, the woman had always lived inland and hadn't traveled much of anywhere. There was so much he wanted to show her, help her experience for the first time. Those amazing blue eyes of hers would really light up once he—

"Dude, you must really love accounting."

Jason looked up to find Ben smirking at him.

He flicked a piece of popcorn at his houseguest's head and told him to shut up.

Chapter 15

Laney had no idea how long she'd lain on the kitchen floor. How long she'd cried. Or even what she'd been thinking. At some point, she simply got up. Her mind felt drained and empty. She walked upstairs to the bathroom and took another hot shower. She emerged and got dressed, her actions mechanical and unplanned. She returned to the kitchen and ate something, despite having no appetite. Then she grabbed her sewing supplies and stitched closed the seam on Jimbo Bear's bottom. She took the negatives and stuffed them between the pages of the photo album where they should have been all along. Then she returned to the kitchen table, sat down, and stared at the purse and keys she'd set out a lifetime ago.

Gran. She had promised to see Gran this afternoon. She needed to go.

Her limbs didn't move. That surprised her.

She had always been driven by obligation, by a clear sense of duty, by a strong compulsion to do what was practical, what was right.

She didn't know what *right* was anymore.

She felt deceived, and she was angry. She was angry that the people she loved most had knowingly put her in this hellish limbo. Yet at the same time, she couldn't blame any of them. She knew her mother well, and she understood her. Christi had only wanted to love her; she hadn't meant to hurt anyone. She would never have taken a child from living parents, of that Laney was sure. And whatever repercussions might be had, in this life or the next, Christi had been determined to bear that burden alone. No deathbed confessions to soothe her soul... not if it would hurt Laney. Gran and Grandpa must have made a similar calculation.

They couldn't have told the truth without putting both Christi and Laney at risk. And what purpose would the truth serve, once the damage had been done?

It was a victimless crime. Except for Laney herself.

Or was it? She inhaled sharply. It was true that the other parents were dead, that they would never miss their daughter, never mourn her. But Jessica Macdonald had other family, did she not? Other relatives who knew and loved her?

She turned with a jerk towards her laptop. She booted it up. As it slowly flickered to life, she cursed herself for not copying the information she'd dug up earlier. There had been grandparents... three of them. And an uncle, too.

Were they all still alive? Had the grandparents been close to their grown son and daughter? Spent time with their baby granddaughter? Had Jessica had little cousins to play with?

The computer started up, but for Laney it could not move fast enough. These people... *they* were the victims. Maybe they didn't care. Maybe they never had. Perhaps it would be better for everyone if they didn't. The past could stay buried, nothing would change, and Laney could go on with her life.

She found the Canadian obituary she'd located before. *Sarah Alvin, of Ottawa.* Jessica's grandmother — Carl's mother. Carl's father had died before he did. Laney took the woman's name from the obituary and ran a search. It took only seconds before an unexpected stab of grief pierced her.

Died June 7th, 2015.

Laney bit her lip, hard. The obituary mentioned Sarah's predeceased son. But where such articles normally mentioned surviving relatives, this one said nothing. Nor was there any mention of a spouse, current or former, living or dead.

Laney swallowed her sadness and closed the reference. Whatever Sarah might have felt when she lost her granddaughter, she wasn't hurting anymore.

Was anyone? Laney switched to Jessica's mother's side of the family. *Gordon and Joan Tremblay, of Toronto.* Her heart began to race as the hits on Gordon stacked up. He was mentioned in a variety of Canadian news articles, all having to do with his banking job. She skimmed through the details. Was the man alive or wasn't he?

He had retired. No surprise there. He was on the board of something or other. Laney didn't care about his business career; she kept scrolling. There was no obituary. The last mention of him came from a Toronto paper a little over three years ago. She started a new search on Joan Tremblay, holding her breath as she did so. What exactly was she hoping for?

Again, no obituary.

Laney released the breath with a surge of relief. Jessica's mother Elizabeth's parents were still alive. Both of them. But where? She dove into the sites that mined street addresses and came up with several in Toronto. But when she searched on the most recent one, she pulled up real estate listings. The house had been sold less than a year ago.

Undaunted, Laney kept digging until she located one site with a different address. It was on the other side of the country, in the city of Ucluelet, British Columbia. She ran an additional check on related real estate listings, but could find none.

Gordon had retired, Laney told herself. Perhaps they'd moved to a better climate? She ran a new search on Ucluelet and determined that it was indeed a tourist town. People in the middle of Canada probably retired to their western coast like Chicagoans retired to Florida.

She ran one more search, this time on Jessica's uncle, and found him likely still living in Toronto. A newspaper article mentioned his name, Richard Tremblay, in conjunction with an art gallery, but gave no personal details. Another article from a regional magazine described him as a "visual artist," and referred to a husband whose work was on display in the same gallery.

Laney stared at the picture of a slim, unassuming-looking man in his late fifties, but felt no particular emotion. His coloring was dark, his features unfamiliar. From what she could tell, Jessica's uncle had no children.

She clicked back to a map of Ucluelet. It was right on the

ocean. On Vancouver Island. It appeared to be a long way from the city of Victoria, where most of the island's population was concentrated. Why had Gordon and Joan moved so far from the beaten path after a lifetime in the city? Did they appreciate the quiet? Did they own a boat, maybe? Did they like to fish?

The wheels in her brain chugged to a slow, grinding halt.

Did they miss their granddaughter?

Jessica Macdonald was the only grandchild the couple had ever had. Barring a late-in-life adoption on their son Richard's part, she was the only one they ever would have.

But *did they miss her?*

Laney's eyes could produce no further tears. But the new emotion inside her made them burn with dry heat. What if she were in their position? They had raised a boy and a girl, watched them grow up and get married. Their little girl had had a baby girl of her own. And then — the worst possible tragedy. Their daughter, son-in-law, and granddaughter were all dead. Gone forever in the blink of an eye. Decades later the couple is facing old age with one middle-aged son and a son-in-law. No grandchildren to spoil; no great-grandchildren to even hope for. But if the granddaughter they'd thought they lost was actually a healthy twenty-seven-year-old woman... would they want to know? Would Laney want to know if she were them?

Of course she would.

A wrong had been done to these people. Was it not her responsibility to right it?

Still, she hesitated. Their Jessica had died twenty-five years ago... their emotional wounds should have healed. What if hearing the truth now caused them more pain than it spared? They could never get their toddler back, after all. That little girl didn't exist anymore.

No, she didn't, Laney confirmed to herself. Besides which, there could be harm in exposing the truth. Before she did anything, that harm had to be weighed against the good.

She took a moment to consider what the harm might be.

Christi's name would be besmirched forever, for starters. If the full truth were known, she would be labeled a kidnapper. If she were alive, she could face criminal charges. Even if Laney did her best to keep the details quiet, she might not be successful. Any journalist running across such facts would see an irresistible human interest story. The sensational headline would be everywhere. *Toddlers Switched in Funnel Cloud; Surviving Mother Steals Dead Mother's Child.*

No. That couldn't happen. The publicity would devastate June and her family, whether they had known of Christi's crime back then or not. And if Gran were to hear one word of it, she'd go right back to obsessing over hell and damnation.

No, Laney repeated to herself. If she admitted the truth to anyone in authority, there could be problems beyond her understanding. If the child Laney Miller was officially declared deceased, what would happen to her social security number? Her birth certificate? Her whole legal identity? Would she still be Christi's beneficiary? Could she access the money to care for Gran? Would she even still be Gran's legal guardian?

She closed her eyes and dropped her head in her hands. Without her identity, she had nothing. The legal mess she'd be left in was so monumental it would take an army of lawyers to untangle it — lawyers she could not afford. Could she even go back to school? Reclaim the fellowship she'd won under false pretenses?

A sudden thought struck her with horror. Carl and Elizabeth had been Canadian citizens. Their daughter had been born while they were still living in Toronto.

Jessica Macdonald was not even an American citizen!

Forget school. Forget absolutely everything you'd ever planned for yourself. Laney felt numb.

Exposing the truth was completely unthinkable.

So where did that leave her?

She sat at the kitchen table, staring at nothing, for a long time. Very gradually, her thoughts began to coalesce. The best thing to do, almost certainly, was nothing at all. If she said nothing, no one would ever know. Her Gran's babbling would not be taken seriously, even by June — assuming June didn't know already, which Laney strongly suspected she did not. If the photo negatives were destroyed for good, everyone's life could proceed as normal. Except for one thing.

Laney would feel guilty. She might not bear any culpability for the crime already committed; but from this point on she would. She would be knowingly keeping grandparents from their granddaughter, an uncle from his niece. They could be nice people. They could care very much. For her to assume how they would feel, what they would want... how could she, when she didn't even know them?

You have to know. You have to be sure they're all right the way they are. That it's better this way. For everybody. Not just you.

Laney gave her chin a sharp nod. Her silence could be justified, and her conscience cleared, only after she obtained all the necessary information. She had to meet these people, figure out who they were and how they felt about family. How she would accomplish this while concealing her true purpose, she had no idea. But she would make no final decision until it was done.

She copied the most recent addresses of Jessica's grandparents and uncle into a file and saved it. Then she pulled up a map program. The uncle in Toronto was closer, but Jessica's grandparents were a higher priority. She typed in her location and the destination in Ucluelet, then looked at the suggested path with a grimace. Iowa, Nebraska, South Dakota, Montana, Idaho... she'd have to drive 2500 miles through the Northern Plains in the dead of winter!

Well, so be it, she thought with determination. Flying wasn't an affordable solution, not when neither Peck nor Ucluelet were anywhere near a real airport and she'd wind up having to rent a car, too. She had enough financial woes without blowing another grand. She'd just have to prepare herself for blizzard conditions and hope to hell her car was up to the task.

She would leave first thing tomorrow.

She shut down her computer and grabbed her keys. She

would have to research her route carefully, find cheap places to stay. And she'd need to pack like it was a freakin' polar expedition... food, emergency blankets, warm clothes. But she could do all that later tonight. Right now she was overdue for her promised visit to Gran.

And Laney Miller always kept her promises.

Chapter 16

Tofino, British Columbia, Present Day

Laney donned her knit cap, mittens, and the five dollar sunglasses she'd bought at the co-op and headed out the door of the common room. She'd awakened after nearly twelve hours of sleep with a dull ache pounding in her head, but some acetaminophen and a quick bowl of granola had coaxed it mostly into submission. With blue sky showing through the skylight in the ceiling and the sound of chirping birds and crashing waves echoing through the walls, she was going outside regardless.

She smiled as the cool, clean air washed over her cheeks and filled her lungs. *Beautiful.* Everything was beautiful! She pushed her sunglasses up onto her head, willing to endure a little pain for the sake of full color. The trees around the building were tall and deeply green, their graceful boughs trailing with feathery, light-green moss. The steps she descended carried her through a wonderland carpeted with billowing bushes, hardy ferns, and tumbled gray stone, and as she looked up into the treetops, she saw a mix of evergreen and bare deciduous trees, the latter of which had added a colorful layer of red-brown leaves to the forest floor.

"Hallow," a friendly voice called from the deck as she passed. Laney smiled in greeting and waved back, but didn't attempt conversation. The half-dozen lodgers enjoying a late breakfast *al fresco* had been speaking in a foreign language she had no hope of identifying; she could barely understand the heavily accented greeting. She finished her descent of the stairs, stepped off onto the sandy ground, and moved toward the water.

A yellow and white signpost caught her attention. *Caution* it said in bold print. *You Are in Wolf Country.* Laney stepped closer. An outline of a wolf, straight out of Little Red Riding Hood, was placed in a yellow warning triangle. Below it was a list of instructions, each ominously illustrated with unfortunate stick figures. *Group Together. Scare Don't Stare. Don't Run! Back Away Slowly. Fight Back!*

Laney swallowed. They had to be kidding. This wasn't some backcountry wilderness... it was a tourist beach! On a freakin' island!

Keep Dogs on Leash.

The sign had to be a joke. Scaring gullible international tourists must give Jason some kind of thrill. Wolves, indeed!

She moved on, drawing another invigorating breath of the cool, moist air. She knew, intellectually, that an oceanic climate, even in the far north, could be warmer in January than inland plains farther south. Still, when she thought of how she'd nearly gotten frostbite just walking around Peck...

Her steps halted abruptly, and her body swayed. *Peck. The horrible thing.* A swell of new memories dumped into her brain with a whoosh. She was wandering around town, and she was cold. She saw her preschool and remembered the obnoxious kid. She'd seen Nan... Nan had been sick and missed the funeral... she wanted Nan to help her but the teacher had only made her feel worse. She'd walked across the fields — why on earth would she do that? She'd been thinking about the tornado—

Stop! Laney gave her limbs a shake; inhaled and exhaled deeply. She wanted to remember everything... but not right now. Right now, this morning, she had more pleasurable things to do. Would it be so wrong if she dealt with the horrible thing this afternoon?

She faced the water, doubled her pace, and filled her senses with the glorious present. An arc of soft brown sand spread out before her feet, angling wide in either direction. At its near edge lay grassy slopes, tumbled logs, and rocky ledges from which tall green trees sprang. A few houses were visible on the higher ridges, peeking out between the trees to display their oversized windows, just like the lodge behind her. But the most amazing view lay straight ahead, where the mighty Pacific finished its tumultuous journey from the far beyond by coalescing into powerful, wide swells that moved like an advancing army — only to turn to frothy whitewater as they smashed upon the shallows. Some were forced to divert around the low, rocky islands that dotted portions of her view. But in the center of the arc, nothing stood in their way. She could look straight up from her own two feet and draw a line to the horizon that crossed nothing but endless, moving water.

Breathe. Even the magnificence of the ocean couldn't completely shake the sense of foreboding brought on by the rush of memories. But she would keep trying.

She turned her attention to the humans in the equation. She counted nearly a dozen surfers, either out on the water or resting with their boards on the beach. Other visitors walked along the shore, and several dogs chased both sticks and each other in and out of the water, making wide circles of tracks in the sand. She walked to a convenient log, sat down, and pulled her sunglasses back down over her eyes.

Okay. So which one was he? Her brow furrowed as she surveyed the surfers, all of which looked nearly identical in their dark, full-body wetsuits. Even their hair was covered by their hoods, and most of the time, all she could see out on the water were bobbing torsos. But each time one of them stood up to catch a wave, their skin-tight suits showed off their physiques. Laney's gaze quickly narrowed on two likely suspects, and after a few moments, one of them waved at her.

She smiled broadly. *Jason.* She was sure of it. He and Ben were similarly well-proportioned, but Ben was slightly taller and lankier. After a gesture passed between the men, the second surfer also waved, then made a show of pointing up at the trees. Laney looked up, saw a large, brown and white mottled bird perched at the top of a nearby pine, and laughed. *Ben.* Definitely. He had promised to show her a bald eagle before he left. The hunched-over lump didn't look like an eagle to her, but whatever. She would take the naturalist's word for it. She returned a thumbs up.

She sat on the log watching them for nearly an hour, marveling at the art of a sport she'd never given much thought to. Riding the swells successfully required a well-choreographed dance of wave selection, timing, smoothly quick movements, and — of course — excellent balance. Ben could manage the basics all right, but he struggled with the latter skill. He kept falling off his board in unpredictable and dramatic fashion, appearing as if he enjoyed a good dunking. Jason, she realized quickly, was a master. He rode the flowing mountains as if he and his board were a part of them, making the whole process look both fun and ridiculously easy. While Ben and many of the others held their balance in a crouch, Jason stood tall and straight, chin up and arms relaxed, as if the feat took no effort at all.

When he executed a particularly dramatic switchback maneuver, basically cutting a Z on the moving face of a wave, Laney felt moved to applaud. Her hands quickly stilled when she realized that two other women, sitting together on a log about thirty feet away, were also applauding. "Woohoo!" one of them hooted, rising in her enthusiasm. "Nice one, Jason!"

As Laney watched him respond with a friendly wave, her good spirits took a nosedive. Then she got annoyed. With herself.

She'd had Jason's number thirty seconds after meeting him, and she knew damn well that developing romantic feelings for a guy like him was about as smart as walking into a brick wall. How her defenses had gotten so weak she wasn't sure; she could only hope she'd caught the childish emotion early enough to squelch it.

She stood up and began to wander, turning her attention from the surfers to the sand. The beach was crisscrossed with interesting tracks, both human and animal. She saw signs of sandals and sneakers, big dogs and small dogs, one barefoot human (seriously?), and some strange V-shaped scratches she guessed were bird's feet. Equally intriguing was the bizarre seaweed deposited by the last high tide. Some clumps were colorful and leafy, reminiscent of a gourmet salad, while other species looked more like medieval weapons. One specimen resembled a long pole with a heavy round bulb at its tip, decorated with a spray of green-brown streamers. Noting that the bulb looked hollow, Laney lifted a foot and stamped on it. A puff of cloudy gas shot out, making her jump.

"Bull kelp," said an older man strolling nearby. "It makes a nice salad, believe it or not."

Laney did not. "Interesting," she replied with a smile.

"Is this your first time to Tofino?" the older woman with him asked politely.

"Yes, it is," she answered. "It's all very foreign to a Missourian."

The couple laughed. "I'm sure it would be," the man said. "We've got nothing like bull kelp in Montana either. But we love the ocean, and compared to home, this is nice and warm, right?"

Montana. The images crowded into Laney's consciousness, unbidden, unrelenting. Everything around her was white. Falling snow, drifting snow, blowing snow. Where was the freakin' road? She had followed a truck for hours, staring at its dirty bumper, praying the driver could see landmarks she couldn't. She was running low on gas, so she'd turned off the heater. It was hard to steer with mittens, but no harder than with numb hands. Why the hell was she even doing this? Because she had to see them—

Laney blinked at the friendly white-haired couple before her, confused. She had come here to see them? No... another couple. A couple she didn't know. A couple who could ruin her life—

Stop it! She fought to return her thoughts to the present. She was supposed to answer something, but she had no idea what. "Do you come here often?" she asked instead.

"Nearly every winter," the woman answered cheerfully. "The cold gets harder to take every year, you know. I say we should just move to Texas. Galveston is nice."

"You don't want to move to Texas," the man returned crossly, indicating a debate of longstanding. He nodded to Laney. "Well, you have a good vacation, young lady."

She agreed, wished them the same, and moved on, at which

point her thoughts shot straight back to drifting snow. *Stop!* The memories seemed clearer now, closer. If she tried to remember more, she believed that she could. But she didn't want to.

The snow delay would cost her extra. She had to get to Ucluelet. The sooner she got there, the sooner she could leave. The horrible thing—

Not yet! Not now!

She stopped walking and looked out over the water again, finding Jason. Thinking about him was problematic too, but it was an infinitely more pleasant problem. She threw him a gratuitous wave, along with her best smile. He waved back.

"Hey, Jason!" a female voice called out cheerfully from nearby. Laney turned to see a ridiculously buxom woman just pulling the hood of her figure-revealing wetsuit over a head of chestnut curls. The woman grabbed her surfboard from the sand, tucked it under an arm, and headed off into the waves toward him.

Laney groaned. She didn't even know which of them Jason had waved at! She was desperate for distraction, yes, but she could only go so low before losing all self-respect.

Brisk exercise, perhaps? She increased her pace and began a determined march to nowhere. She had progressed all of ten paces when she passed a family with two little kids. The girl was wearing mittens with a big red heart on the back of each hand.

So miserably sad...

She felt a chilling wave of desperation. Was she going insane? What was there about a simple, innocent red heart that could fill her with such wrenching sorrow?

She was hunting for something in her Gran's linen closet. She had a pillow—

Laney clapped her hands to her temples. She could stop it, yes. But for how long? A feeling of despair swamped her as she realized that she might as well be fighting the tide. Her memory had already recovered itself. The horrible thing *was* coming back, whether she liked it or not. It was only a matter of time.

"Laney!" She heard Jason's voice and turned. He was riding

into the beach, waving in her direction. Ben was splashing through the whitewater after him. They were both coming in.

Thank God. Maybe she'd get a little reprieve.

She was lying on the floor of the kitchen, crying. Her cheek was pressed against the cold tile. Her heart was in pieces, ripped, ragged, torn, empty—

She broke into a run.

Jason wasn't sure what had brought on Laney's bout of rampant enthusiasm, but he liked it. She seemed eager to see him — or maybe them — and he was delighted that she'd seemed to really enjoy watching him — or them — surf. But the closer her jogging feet brought her, the more he questioned why she was hurrying at all.

She didn't seem right. She looked less than fashionable in her dowdy sweats, winter coat and hat, and cheap sunglasses, but he was used to that. What wasn't right was her expression. She was too pale, too tense. And as she drew up to them and pulled back her sunglasses, he could see that her eyes were strangely bright.

Clearly, she was upset about something.

"Are you okay?" he asked.

"Of course," she replied shortly. "And how are you two? Is it tiring to surf for so long?"

"Tiring? Never," he insisted. "Sheer ecstasy."

"Speak for yourself, Buchanan," Ben laughed, pulling off his hood. His wavy reddish hair responded by sticking out from his head in all directions. "I'm exhausted."

Laney looked like she was fighting a snicker.

Ben reached up a hand to tame his tresses. "I have serial-killer hair again, don't I?"

She cracked up. "It's cute."

Jason pulled his own hood back. His curls could get pretty wild, too. But she didn't seem to notice. She seemed only half present, despite her attentions to Ben. "Let's get something to drink," he suggested, moving toward their stashed cooler.

"Yesss," Ben said with appreciation, beating him to the cooler and promptly pulling out a water bottle.

Laney tagged along with them. She was practically prancing with nervousness... or something. Jason wondered if she'd accidentally ingested a six-pack of Red Bull.

"I really enjoyed watching you guys," she chattered uncharacteristically. "It was fascinating. I've never thought about the mechanics of surfing before, but now I can see it's fairly complicated. Were those typically sized waves for here? How does the wind play into it? And also I was thinking, doesn't the direction the waves are coming from affect where the best spots are?"

Jason smiled with inward satisfaction as he pulled off his gloves. Whatever she'd been smoking, it did have some desirable effects. Usually after a woman watched him surf, she complimented his skill. Only Laney would use the occasion to prompt a discussion of ocean physics.

He dug his cell phone out of his bag, clicked into his surfing forecast app, and handed the device over. "Check it out," he encouraged.

Laney's eyes locked on the screen with interest. She removed her mittens and sat down with the phone on a log. Jason joined Ben in getting a drink, watching her with amusement.

"This is amazing," she said after a moment. "Surf height, swell, wind speed and direction, tide, buoys... and the charts! Who does all this? They must employ meteorologists. This is some pretty sophisticated computer modelling."

"It takes a team of professional forecasters," Jason agreed, sitting down beside her. He couldn't believe he was having this conversation with a female human. He knew women who cared about the surf forecasts, but none had ever given a rip how they were produced. "Meteorologists, for sure, but also experts in ocean physics, geographic data sets, and of course... a thorough understanding of surfing itself..."

He kept talking, because she kept listening. Listening, understanding, and asking questions. It was ranking right up

there as one of the most enjoyable conversations of his life —
academic conversations, anyway — when they were interrupted
by a good-natured snort from Ben.

"And people call *me* a science nerd?" he said with an eye roll.
"You two are unbelievable. Can we get off the diurnal wind
patterns and the tropically influenced pulses and talk about
getting some lunch, please?"

Jason chuckled. "Says the PhD candidate in oceanography?"

"Ocean *chemistry*," Ben corrected. "I don't do physics, at least
not if I can help it. But I could definitely do with a cheeseburger.
Are we done now?"

Laney laughed and rose. She handed Jason his phone back.
Was he imagining it, or did he detect a new sparkle in her
cornflower blue eyes? "Thanks," she said sweetly. "I'll have to
look at it all a little more closely later."

He rose with her. He was about to inform her of just how
much he would enjoy that when they were interrupted. "Hey,
Jason!" a female voice called out cheerfully from down the
beach.

He looked over to see one of the cashiers from the co-op
who'd been flirting with him for a while now. He'd ruled her out
because she was on the rebound from a failed engagement.
Rebound flings, though conveniently short-lived, were too
emotional for his tastes. But she was a nice person, light-hearted
and fun to be around.

He cast a quick glance at Laney, not certain how she was
reacting to the number of women who generally greeted him on
the beaches. He wanted to know if she felt any jealousy... just out
of curiosity. But her reaction, if any, was muted. Her expression
showed nothing.

"Hey, Jessica!" he called back.

He caught Laney's movement out of the corner of his eye. He
swung around to find her eyes glassy, her complexion white. Her
shoulders had drawn up tightly, as if she were flinching from a
blow. In the next second, she swayed on her feet.

"Good God," Ben exclaimed, jumping toward them.

But Jason was closer. He lunged and stretched out his arms.
An unconscious Laney slumped into them.

Chapter 17

Laney opened her eyes to see two handsome male faces staring at her with concern. They were above her, and she was sprawled across Jason's lap leaning against his arm. All of which was strange, because she'd been standing upright not two seconds ago.

"I'm all right," she insisted, knowing nothing of the kind. "I just..." Her voice trailed off. She had no idea how to finish. She struggled to sit up, and Jason helped her right herself. His touch was both strong and gentle, and she'd be tempted to swallow her pride and cuddle right back in if he weren't clad in clammy wet neoprene. "What happened?" she asked finally, perplexed.

"You tell us," Jason replied, his expression disturbingly grave. You just passed out — dropped like a rock for no apparent reason. I think we should take you back to the ER, have them check—"

"Oh, no!" Laney protested. "No way am I racking up more Canadian medical bills! I'm fine now, I'm sure."

Ben's expression was equally concerned. "Laney, you really can't know—"

"What happened, Jase?" asked a third voice. "Is she okay?" Laney looked behind Ben's shoulder to see a woman watching them tentatively. The tall, pretty brunette was wearing a tight-fitting jacket and yoga pants.

"She's good," Jason replied, his eyes still on Laney. "No worries." He didn't sound unworried, but he did sound dismissive.

"Okay," the woman replied unhappily, backing away. "Just checking."

Jason looked up. Seeming to regret his tone, he smiled and called after her. "Thanks, Jess."

Jessica.

Reality hit Laney with a wholesale memory dump. It was all back. It had come back when she'd heard the name.

"Laney!" Ben said with distress, waving a hand before her face. "Are we losing you again?"

Jason swept in with another arm around her back, and it took all her remaining willpower not to lean into his chest like a baby.

"I'm okay," she insisted. But behind Ben's wild hair, the ocean horizon rocked slightly. "At least I will be in a second."

"We're taking you to the ER," Jason proclaimed.

"No, you are not!" Laney said testily. "Please, don't worry about me. It wasn't the head injury. It was just..." Oh, what the hell? "I got my memory back. All at once, actually. It was a little disorienting, that's all."

The men exchanged a look. "You remember why you came here?" Jason asked.

Laney nodded. She didn't want to talk about it.

"Do you remember the accident?" Ben questioned.

She considered a moment. "No. I think... well the last thing I remember is riding on the ferry. From Vancouver." It had been fascinating, watching the car ramp pull up and then feeling the chugging of the engine as the craft floated out to sea. She smiled vaguely. The water had been so blue. She'd never been on that big a boat before. She'd rarely been on any boat before.

But then the smile left her. "My car definitely died in Vancouver. It had been making ominous noises for a while, but then it just jumped and stalled, right in the middle of an intersection. I couldn't get it into gear. It was a nightmare; people honking... I had to have it towed. The mechanic helped me figure out how to get the rest of the way to Tofino using busses and the ferry."

"The ferry ride would have been just a few hours before you hit your head, so that makes sense." Jason stared at her closely again. "Are you sure you're feeling all right? Physically, at least?"

Laney decided to prove the point. She shook herself free of his hold — regrettably — and pulled herself to her feet. The movement wasn't smooth, but she made it. "Tada. All better."

The men looked equally skeptical.

"I do think I might go back to my room and lie down awhile," Laney offered, hoping to appease them. She also wanted — she realized suddenly — to be alone.

Jason and Ben exchanged a glance. "All right," Jason said finally, stepping closer.

Laney looked at the stairs, but the deck was crowded with people. She headed for the path instead.

"Good choice," Ben teased. "If you fall before we can catch you, it'll be softer on your skull."

"Thanks," Laney returned. She wanted to laugh, but her insides were devoid of mirth. She began to walk, with both men following close behind her. They were being so sweet. She wished she could be the same, light-hearted person they'd had dinner with last evening, but with sadness wrapped around her middle like a lead weight, she knew that wasn't possible.

Jessica Nicole Macdonald.

How very convenient that she should forget that name, along with all its horrors. The brain did have amazing powers, did it not? And to think she'd even managed to be happy for a while... to have a little fun!

"Still feeling okay?" Jason asked as the path steepened.

"Stellar," she lied. He had such a nice voice. So smooth and caring... not to mention sexy. Why couldn't her amnesia have lasted a little longer? If she was a real, normal person and not some dead girl's ghost, maybe they could—

No way. Not even then. What's his ex count up to now, anyway?

"You look pale," Jason proclaimed with a grumble.

"It's winter," she returned, embarrassed by her increasing breathlessness. Concussion or no concussion, she was sadly out of shape. The long months spent at her mother's bedside had done her body no favors. After what seemed like an eternity, she reached the main door of the lodge, wiped her shoes dutifully on the mat, and stepped inside.

Jason didn't follow. He and Ben were still wearing full wetsuits, and Ben was toting a cooler. She remembered that the changing area and equipment room were accessed by another entrance. "Thanks for keeping my skull intact," she said, trying hard to exude false cheer.

She was pretty sure neither of them bought it.

"I hope you're feeling better soon," Ben said genuinely. "I'm headed back to Victoria right after lunch to meet Haley at the airport, so this is goodbye. But it's been a delight."

Laney managed a smile. "Likewise. And thank you again."

He gave her a salute and headed off, but Jason stayed in place. "I'm thinking maybe I should come knock on your door in an hour or so," he floated, his brow furrowed.

"There's no need. I promise not to drop dead on your premises," she quipped.

His frown only deepened. "I'm serious. You look terrible. You sound terrible. And I don't believe you passed out just because you got your memory back."

She huffed out a breath, then met his eyes. Those beautiful, intense, gray-green eyes. What was it about the man she found so compelling? In addition to the obvious, of course? Perhaps it was his unusual perceptiveness. Or maybe it was the compassion he'd shown for a woman he had no physical interest in. He was an enigma, that was for sure. As was her own inclination to lean on and to trust him, when she had no logical reason to do either.

She couldn't seem to help herself.

"If you knew *what* I remembered," she answered softly, "you wouldn't say that."

Jason looked taken aback. He glanced at Ben's departing form, then returned his attention to her. "If you want to talk about it—"

"I don't," she answered, more abruptly than intended. Damn her stupid mouth! He wouldn't let it go, now. And she couldn't trust him, not with this. She couldn't trust anybody. "I shouldn't have said anything. I'm fine, really. Take Ben wherever you need to take him. It's not like I'm going anywhere."

Am I? She would be going to Ucluelet. Eventually. As soon as she got her head together and figured out a plan. Never mind that she'd had the whole endless, snowy drive in which to compose a plan, and it had never materialized. She was here on a mission, and near-death experience or no, she would see it through.

Jason studied her another long moment, clearly uncertain how to proceed. "I'll check back with you later," he said finally.

She made a lame attempt to smile again. "Okay," she conceded. "See you then."

His entrancing eyes continued to watch her as she closed the door between them.

Laney's attempt to restore her composure with a brief, cozy nap failed. The wheels in her brain chugged furiously, attempting to marry up her newly returned memory with the present and speculating wildly over her next steps. She soon gave up on evasion and hauled out the dreaded laptop. It was time.

She dimmed the light on her screen and clicked into the file labeled Tremblay, which she now remembered contained the addresses of Jessica's grandparents and uncle. Plugging the former address into her map program, she could see that the grandparents' home was about a half hour's drive away. Jason had guessed correctly about her choice of the surf lodge — she had indeed tried to find a place closer to Ucluelet, but couldn't find anything nearly as affordable.

She closed her eyes and sighed. If the dull ache in the center of her forehead was any indication, her allowable computer time would be short. She needed to plan it well. So, what next? Did she rent a car and drive herself to their house? For what purpose? Was she going to stalk the poor people? Talk to their neighbors? Ask questions around town?

She groaned. She had no idea how to do this. She'd never had any idea. Had she not jumped in her car and started driving largely to avoid figuring it out? Anytime she'd thought about it, she'd run into the same, insurmountable problem. The safe way — getting to know the couple without confessing who she was

— was also the sneaky, underhanded way, and everything about espionage was totally alien to her nature. She was direct and no-nonsense to the bone. She was a lousy liar and an even lousier actress. What chance could she possibly have of pulling off such a crazy con game?

Zero chance, that's what.

What felt the most right would be to walk straight up to their front door, ring the bell, and tell them that their granddaughter wasn't dead after all. But there was a problem with that scenario, too. Convincing these people that their beloved granddaughter was alive would be one thing. Laney thought she could handle that part, with the help of the newspaper articles, as long as everyone spoke of Jessica and Laney both in third person. But what happened when they wanted to find their granddaughter? To know her?

Laney wasn't Jessica. She couldn't *be* Jessica. She was Laney Miller. She didn't want to be anyone else, and nobody was going to make her!

A gentle knock sounded on the door. Her eyes flew open and the computer slid off her lap onto the bed.

"Laney?" a familiar voice said quietly. "It's Jason."

She shut off the computer and pushed it out of the way. Had it been an hour already? "Yeah, hi. Come in."

She knew perfectly well that he would only bring trouble, ask questions she couldn't answer, and offer help she'd have to refuse. But she wanted him here anyway. He represented sanity. And happier thoughts.

"Feeling any better?" he asked, closing the door behind him and leaning comfortably against the sink. His position couldn't possibly be comfortable; he just made it look that way.

Laney moved her computer back onto her lap. "Have a seat," she offered, gesturing at the other end of the bed, which was the only place he could sit in the tiny room.

He sat. "You look," he said tentatively, studying her, "a *little* better."

She smiled. "How terribly honest of you. Thanks. I'm

physically fine, I promise. Mentally, I've had better days."

His eyes continued to study her. "I was thinking about what happened on the beach," he began, sounding as if he'd rehearsed some sort of speech. "I was wondering why you think you got your memory back at that particular time. It seemed to happen pretty suddenly, right when Jessica called out to me. Was there a particular trigger?"

She was really starting to dislike that name. "No idea," she answered with a shrug. "It could have been anything. Or nothing. Who knows?"

Jason raised an eyebrow. Then he chuckled softly. "You're a really bad liar. You know that?"

Laney huffed out a breath. "I'm aware."

"Well, don't strain yourself, then. If you think it's none of my business, just say so."

"It's none of your business."

He sat quietly a moment, considering. "Yeah, that's not going to work. So let's try again. What brought all the negative memories back? Did it have anything to do with me? Something I did, or said?"

Laney smiled at him. "What I can't figure out, you see, is why you even care. We both know I've brought you nothing but trouble since I got here."

He returned a lazy smile of his own. "You're much better at eluding questions than you are at outright lying. You should use that."

"I am."

"What made you remember?"

"Why do you want to know?"

As their eyes met with shared amusement, Laney realized she was feeling better already. The man did have that effect on her.

"Fine," he conceded. "I'll answer if you will. I care because I'm a nice guy, I like you, and I don't want to be making your situation worse without realizing it."

"How would you do that?" Laney asked, confused.

He shrugged. "Maybe your bad memories have something to

do with a man. Maybe somebody I remind you of."

Her eyes widened. He couldn't possibly be farther off the mark. Which was probably a good thing...

"Hmm," he speculated. "That looks like a no."

Dammit. Why did she have to be so easy to read?

"But I have to tell you," he continued uneasily, "that I'm still worried. I can see that you're afraid, Laney. And you don't strike me as a woman who's particularly easy to scare. So I have to ask. Your flight up here... are you running from a particular person? Because if you are—" he sat up and looked at her intently. "We can get you help. Some of my best friends are Mounties. You don't have to deal with something like this alone."

Laney's eyes misted over. He thought she was running from domestic abuse, some psycho-stalker situation. He was willing to stand by her, protect her. How incredibly, unexpectedly sweet.

She could see that her impending tears were confusing him and decided to put him out of his misery. "I appreciate that," she said gratefully. "I really do. But I'm not running from a person. I'm not in any physical danger at all, I swear. If I'm scared, it's only because I'm too big a wimp to deal with a personal matter that's... unpleasant for me. That's all." She smiled at him. "And you know I'm telling the truth because I couldn't possibly lie so well, right?"

His returning smile was slight, at best. He looked like he believed her. But he didn't seem particularly relieved.

"You're not the kind of woman who would pass out over an 'unpleasant' personal matter," he stated. "I don't believe you scare easy, period. You're not going to convince me that this is trivial, so you might as well answer my question. Why did you remember all this when you did?"

Laney rolled her eyes. How could he be so sweet and so tenacious at the same time? "It was the name, okay?" she heard herself say. "That's all. No big mystery!" She tried to keep her tone light, even as she swore internally at her sieve of a mouth filter.

It took a moment for him to understand. "Jessica?" he asked.

"You mean when I called out—"

"Yeah, something like that," she said dismissively. "Not that the name is terribly important, it's just... you know, the brain works in strange ways." She forced another smile. "So, are you happy now? My memory 'attack' had nothing to do with you. Or with your—well, whatever she is to you."

He frowned. "She's just a friend. An acquaintance, really—"

"It doesn't matter," Laney said way too quickly. *Crap.*

He continued to stare at her uneasily.

"Look," she began, thinking hard. What could she say that was truthy enough to be believed but comforting enough to squelch his compulsion to play the hero? "It's like this. I found out something, shortly before I left to come here. It's something personally distressing, but not dangerous. I just have to confirm some facts with some people who live in Ucluelet, and I wanted to see them face to face. Once that's done I can go home and return to my regularly scheduled life. Okay?"

She smiled. That was a pretty darn good generic explanation!

He sat quietly for a long time, saying nothing. She studied him back, trying to find some evidence of relief in his face. She thought maybe she saw a glimmer of it — a slight easing of the tension in his frown lines. But overall, the effect of her words was less than satisfying.

"I hope you know you can trust me," he said finally.

She didn't answer. She hoped the question was rhetorical. Of course she didn't trust him. Why should she? He was friendly, and he'd been kind to her. But she'd known the man for all of three days, only two of which she could remember.

The secret she was keeping was no small, inconsequential thing. It was a horror that risked the undoing of her entire documented life, her very *being*, for God's sake. She hadn't even been able to tell her Aunt June! Entrusting a near-perfect stranger with such a hand grenade would be the stupidest thing she ever did. Once he knew that she wasn't who she professed to be — that her mother was a kidnapper and that she was effectively an undocumented immigrant living off an illegal inheritance — he would *always* know. Maybe they were sort-of friends now, but what about six months from now? What about in ten years? Did she want to spend the rest of her life wondering if he'd ever get personally spiteful enough, or financially desperate enough, to stoop to blackmail?

No way! She could never tell anybody.

Jason's face looked suddenly crestfallen. Then his expression hardened. "You don't need to answer that," he said shortly, rising.

"Wait," Laney protested, rising with him. "Don't take offense, please. I'm just... a really private person."

"I understand," he said more gently, smiling again.

But he didn't understand. He was hurt. *Hurt!* How could that even happen? Weren't players supposed to be immune to such emotions? Why did he even care what she thought?

"My offer stands," he continued. His voice was back to normal, but his eyes still glinted with disappointment. "I'm happy to help if you decide you need anything. Even if it's just a friendly face to hang with. I'll be in the office — have to start my shift now. See you."

Laney tried to think of something to say, but couldn't. She was standing with her mouth gaping as the door closed behind him.

Chapter 18

Jason leaned back in his desk chair and gazed out at the waves, which were decreasing in height now as the swell trended downward. By the time he got off work, they'd barely be rippable. Overnight things would change again, with a new storm system rolling in, promising more wind and weather drama for tomorrow. He loved the winter storms. Their fury might make surfing impossible for a few hours, but their comings and goings were the stuff great waves were made of.

He wondered when Steve might give Laney the go-ahead to get out on the water. The first lesson shouldn't be too taxing. He could tow her board for her, so she wouldn't have to paddle too much, and—

He cut off the thought with a grumble. Why was he wasting his time obsessing over this idea? Laney had expressed no interest whatsoever in learning to surf. She had expressed little enough interest in him, period.

He swiveled around to look at his computer, but his mind remained elsewhere. Laney didn't trust him. Maybe rationally he could understand why, but at a more personal level, her rejection stung. He'd gone over and above for the woman, more than once, and still she seemed suspicious of his motives. He hadn't even hit on her, for God's sake! What was she even suspicious of? Was it so impossible to believe he could just want to be a woman's friend?

He had a sudden image of a few females of his acquaintance laughing hysterically.

He growled beneath his breath. Okay, so maybe friendship wasn't his usual MO, at least not with single women. He either went for it, or — in the case of the forever girls — kept himself at a safe distance. Pursuing a woman over a platonic friendship *was* atypical behavior for him. But that didn't mean there was anything nefarious in it!

He liked Laney. He enjoyed her company. He thought she'd be fun to go surfing with. He thought — no, he *knew* — that once she could surf well, they'd make the perfect team. She'd already taken to surf forecasting like a pro. Her academic understanding of the science behind it was topnotch — well above his own — and once she got that gut-level feel of the ocean beneath her board, the rest of it would come to her instinctively. She'd be poring over the charts, analyzing the data... she'd rise early in the morning and wake him up, all excited because the perfect conditions were pounding at a particular break, and he would throw back the covers and—

Jason shook his head and blinked. *Wait.* How the hell did his imaginary self get in bed with her? That wasn't part of the plan. He wasn't even attracted to her!

Now he imagined himself laughing hysterically.

Okay, fine. He *was* attracted. He was very attracted, and getting more so all the time. She didn't look like the women he usually dated, true, but his body didn't seem to care. She had a cute face with an adorable nose and absolutely amazing clear blue eyes. Her curves were subtle, yes, but she had a firm, healthy earthiness about her that was incredibly sexy. There was nothing artificial or pretentious about Laney Miller. She was all heart, all natural... all woman.

Damn, he wanted her.

The door to the common room popped open suddenly, startling him out of his... regrettable state. *She's a forever girl,* he reminded himself grimly. *Knock it off.*

A blond head appeared. The woman in question smiled at him and walked toward the desk.

Jason pulled himself together.

"Hi," Laney said, with unexpected shyness. He hoped to God she wasn't a mind reader. "I've decided I'd like to go ahead with renting a car. You said I asked you about it when I first showed up, but of course I can't remember what you told me. Do you know where I could get something cheap? Like, really cheap?"

Jason hesitated. He'd been thinking of renting her the Civic, since he could just as easily drive his truck, and the businessman in him was always looking to make an extra buck. But that was before.

"You shouldn't drive, Laney," he reminded. "Remember what your doctor said? About the concussion and brain fog and your reflexes? And that was before you passed out cold."

The cute little face frowned. "I don't remember him saying that. But my time in the hospital is a little fuzzy."

"Which is exactly why you've got no business driving," Jason said firmly. He opened his mouth to offer to drive her himself, then shut it again.

Stop, dude. Just STOP. You're getting in too deep. You need to back the hell off. Now.

"Do you know where I can get a bus schedule, then?" Laney asked lightly.

Jason let out a long, tortured sigh. Was the cosmos out to get him? "There's only one bus that runs this time of year, and it won't help you get around town. It just connects the cities. Theoretically it could get you to Ucluelet in the morning and back in the afternoon, but that would leave you with a whole lot more walking than would fit into your 'no physical exertion' prescription."

Laney's face fell, but her expression quickly changed to determination. "So, do you know a cash-starved teenager I could hire to drive me around on the cheap? Otherwise, I will have to walk."

Jason's jaws clenched. She looked incredibly appealing when she tried to be fierce. "Don't be ridiculous," he replied, thwarting his own voice of reason. "I'd be happy to take you wherever you need to go. It's no big deal. So long as it's not during my office hours — and the waves aren't pumping. You need to do something this afternoon?"

He watched as an interesting progression of emotions flashed across her face. First there was disappointment, then frustration, then a queer sort of hopefulness, followed by resignation.

"I was just thinking about walking around Tofino," she said finally. "I'd like to wander through a few of the shops... you know, typical tourist browsing. Nothing strenuous. Just a chance to get out for a few hours."

Jason considered. She didn't appear to be lying, although she was clearly giving select information. "Well, if that's all, I think I may have a solution for you," he said with a smile. "I happen to know that a few of your fellow lodgers are getting ready to leave for town right now. You could ride in with them, and then I could pick you up as soon as my shift's over. You want me to ask them?"

Her face flushed with pleasure, and the sight warmed him. Way too much. "That would be awesome," she replied brightly. "Would you mind?"

Would he mind? His inner alarm bells were clanging all over the place, but next to her guileless smile his defenses didn't stand a chance. "Of course not. It's nothing." He shook his head at her as he came out from the behind the desk and crossed to the common room door. "Be right back."

Laney paused at the street corner and took in a deep, satisfying breath of the cool, moist air. When cold rain was not pouring onto it, Tofino was an appealing little town. Her head was feeling almost normal, even as the sun shone down over the sweeping green tree tops. And if her goal for the afternoon was to concoct a workable plan for getting to know Gordon and Joan Tremblay... well, wasn't a little window shopping at least as likely to inspire a brainstorm as sitting in her tiny room?

She knew she was deluding herself. But it felt good to be out on her own again, especially now that she knew what she was about and had a reasonably clear head. Was it so wrong to pretend for a little while that she was an ordinary tourist enjoying a vacation? God knew she'd had little enough cheer in her life lately. A touch of frivolity sounded splendid.

She strolled at a leisurely pace through the quaint, festive tourist district. Wooden storefronts, patios, and porches were bedecked with surfing paraphernalia, blooming potted flowers, Christmas lights, and indigenous art. SUVs rolled by with kayaks and canoes strapped to their roof racks; surfboards were carried in various ways by pretty much anything on wheels. The streets were hilly, narrow, and chaotic, and much of the district was perched on a slope leading down to the calmer waters of the Clayoquot Sound.

She passed many businesses that were shuttered for the winter, and she could hardly imagine how bustling the town must become when all the whale watching, charter fishing, bear viewing, and hot springs touring companies were operating at full speed. Even in January, there was no shortage of businesses selling and renting surf equipment, as well as offering lessons, and Laney marveled at how Jason had managed to carve out a place for himself amidst the competition. She passed by his main equipment shop and surf school, which he'd built on the site of the original surfing hostel he'd rehabilitated soon after graduating from college. She admired a good head for business. If her Grandpa Auggie had had a better one, her Gran's future might be more secure...

A heavy weight of sorrow threatened to engulf her, but she managed to beat it back. She would take care of her Gran, no matter what. May Burgdorf's future *was* secure.

Laney passed a colorful shop with a hand-painted sign advertising local crafts and organic espresso. *Sold.* She opened the door to a pleasant tinkling of windchimes decorated with a carved driftwood whale.

"Hello," a woman about her own age called out merrily from behind the register of a small coffee bar to her right. There were a few pub-height tables and chairs inside, but it appeared that most of the cafe business was conducted through the window to visitors enjoying the covered patio. Despite the cool and rainy weather, most every dining place Laney encountered touted an outdoor seating area.

She returned the shopkeeper's greeting and ordered a latte.

So far, she was very much enjoying the Tofino vibe. It was laid back and comfortable, yet so very *alive*. How could it not be, with so many people coming and going, enjoying the ocean and the spectacular scenery? The whole area was like an adult playground.

"You here to surf or to storm watch?" the woman asked pleasantly as the coffee machine whirred.

"Neither exactly," Laney answered without thinking. "But now that I'm here, both are tempting, to be sure."

The woman laughed. "I bet. Where are you staying?"

"The surf lodge." She hadn't intended to gab, but one had to be polite.

"Jason's place?" the barista asked with another smile. Was Laney imagining it, or did this smile pack some extra baggage? "Out on Chesterman Beach?"

Laney nodded.

"Ooh, lucky you," the woman continued, topping off the latte and handing over the steaming cup. "He's a hottie, isn't he?"

The question was light-hearted enough, and given that Laney had grown up in a small town, it shouldn't have been unexpected. So why did she suddenly find herself tongue-tied? Her only reply was a nervous huff of laughter.

She was relieved to find her response drowned out by the laughter of another shopkeeper, who unbeknownst to Laney had been working on the far side of a shelf a few feet away. "You are so bad, Gina," the clerk chastised good-naturedly, moving into view. She also looked to be in her mid-twenties, with a pretty face and long blond hair trailing down her back in a loose pair of braids. "What if Ryan hears you talking like that?"

Gina grinned. "Oh, he knows."

The other woman laughed again. "Well, there's no harm in looking, right?" She threw a smile in Laney's direction. "Don't get us wrong. Jason's a good guy. He's a lot of fun, actually."

"You should know," the barista chided.

The blond smiled crookedly, leaving no doubt as to her relationship with the hostel owner. "Can I help you find anything?" she asked Laney, dismissing the topic.

"No," Laney replied quickly. Perhaps too curtly. "I'm just browsing."

"Well, just let us know," the shopkeeper answered, not seeming offended.

Laney commenced browsing. She found a rack of knitted scarves and fingered through them absently. She was irritated. Why was she irritated? Tofino was a world of young and beautiful people. The fact that Jason had slept with half the women in town should come as no shock.

The clerks had disappeared from view. Laney moved to a display of carved wooden sea creatures, then realized that the women had dodged into a nearby doorway for a private chat. Unfortunately, their voices carried farther than they seemed to think.

"I seriously would do the man if I could get away with it," the barista said. "I mean... Oh. My. God!"

The blond with the braids guffawed.

"Is he worth it?" the barista pressed.

Laney leaned closer, but couldn't hear a response. She suspected a confirming smirk.

"Oh, my God," the barista repeated. "If it weren't for Ryan..."

"I already told you, you're not his type," the clerk said confidently. "You have a boyfriend."

"But if we broke up—"

"It doesn't matter! He knows you *want* a boyfriend."

The barista sucked in a breath of understanding. "Oh."

"Yeah. Did you refill the nutmeg?"

Laney backed away from the doorway. As the shopkeepers returned to their posts, chattering about coffee now, she spent another three minutes pretending interest in handmade tea towels, coasters, and pot holders before smiling her way out the door.

The smile changed into a frown as soon as she stepped outside. She continued down the street, thinking. So, Jason avoided women looking for boyfriends, did he? Clearly, he had no intention of committing himself. To any woman. That figured.

She halted her steps as a squabble broke out a few paces ahead of her. Not between people, but between crows. Two of the ubiquitous black birds were wrestling over what looked like a piece of biscotti, and neither was backing down easily. Laney sidestepped the spectacle, shades of both Edgar Allen Poe and Hitchcock clouding her thoughts as the crows' rooting sections cawed loudly from the trees and rooftops above.

So, how's that master plan for Ucluelet coming along?

Oh, shut up.

She passed a gallery with gorgeous paintings in the windows of stormy skies and breaking waves, but she didn't go inside. She couldn't even afford to *look* at original art. But the next block offered a shop more her speed. It sold everyday clothing and shoes, the practical, weatherproof kind that every Vancouver Islander would need. A selection of rainboots sitting on a portable shelf outside drew her eye. Her sneakers had eventually dried out, but every wiggle of her toes reminded her that the glue binding them together had been compromised. She would wear her snow boots if she could, but like her food cooler and jumper cables, they had been abandoned with her car in Vancouver.

She could see now why everyone around her wore either the lightweight rain boots or — if they were used to the climate — sandals. She located a likely pair of the former and checked the price tag. Then she set the box down and kept walking.

What she needed, she thought with dismay, was a job. Any job she could get, from the moment she returned home until the happy day she could get her fellowship reinstated. Maybe after that, too. At least until the inheritance was settled.

If the truth comes out, it may never be settled.

Laney stopped walking and looked up. Blue skies always calmed her. They might be boring from a meteorological perspective, but they brought her joy. And clarity.

Figure out what you need to do here and just do it, dammit. Then get back home and get to work.

She sighed. The answer was clear enough. She didn't have to like it.

She walked the remainder of the town's business district at a slow, measured pace, then sat down on a bench to finish off her cooling latte. She had come all this way to meet — or at least lay her eyeballs on — Gordon and Joan Tremblay. No matter how ill-conceived her original plan might have been, she intended to see it through, if for no other reason than justifying the funds she'd already spent. The only question was how.

She needed to start by finding out more about them. Where did they go and what did they do all day? If she knew of an event they attended, or a group they belonged to, she could arrange to be in their company in an anonymous fashion. That would be far safer than knocking on their door with some flimsy excuse that would — given her acting ability — likely get her arrested. But how could she find out what she needed to know? She'd exhausted the obvious internet searches already. What she needed was a human connection. Specifically, a local angle. The very thing that she, as an outsider, lacked.

Jason.

A slow smile spread across her lips. Jason knew everybody, and everybody knew him. At least in Tofino. Surely he would have contacts in Ucluelet as well? Other business owners, surfers, suppliers... personal friends. He could open doors for her. He could be indispensable.

Her smile broadened. She didn't like depending on other people. She felt like she had imposed on Jason, in particular, way too much already. The idea of asking him for *more* help should be anathema. But it wasn't. It was highly appealing.

Perhaps she could offer to pay him... not in money, but in labor. She could run the desk for him, give him more time to go surfing. She could work in the equipment shop, answer phones, run the cash register. Her list of minimum-wage job skills was long and comprehensive — she'd pretty much done it all.

Why would he *not* be willing? She would have to protect herself, of course, come up with a plausible reason for needing the information other than the truth. That part could be tricky. Under no circumstances could she let on that she was in legal peril. But surely, she could think up something!

She drained her latte, rose, and threw away the cup. With a jolt of warm caffeine in her veins, she headed downhill to the water's edge to soak up more beautiful views.

She would figure it out, and she would get this thing done. With Jason on board, the whole sordid business was looking... well, much less unpleasant.

Chapter 19

Jason finished checking in his last guest of the day, locked up his office a little early, and headed back to town. He was anxious about Laney, fearful that she had randomly passed out on a street corner and gotten hauled back to the ER. He also worried that she was having a lovely time and would greet him looking healthy and cheerful and so incredibly sexy that he would have to invent a reason to stay away from her.

The second scenario, though obviously better for her, was equally concerning.

It isn't easy to manage a friendship with someone you're attracted to when you're both single... His mind flashed with an image of Ben, smirking at him with that annoying "I know more about women than you do because I'm married" look. Jason's brother Thane did the same thing. Where did they get off, anyway? Jason had more experience with women than the two of them combined!

He ground his teeth as he continued up the Pacific Coast highway. He was perfectly capable of managing a platonic friendship with Laney. All he needed to do was be careful, be sure he wasn't unwittingly giving her the wrong idea. Because if she fell for him, she was bound to get hurt, and he would hate to add to her current trauma.

He would simply pick the woman up, have a few laughs, enjoy her company, drive her wherever she wanted to go, and drop her back off at the lodge. Then he would go out on a real date, with another woman. If Laney knew it was happening, so much the better. It would clarify their relationship, clear up any ambiguity.

Perfect.

He should call the vacationing Aussie surfer. She'd been sending him increasingly suggestive texts over the last twenty-four hours, making clear that both her motives and her expectations were in perfect concert with his own. She had a

beautiful figure, a smashing tan, and beguiling long blond hair...
What color had her eyes been? He thought they were green and
tried to picture them. But the eyes that popped into his head
were a cool, clear blue, set to either side of an adorable, slightly
uptilted button nose...

Dammit!

He could do this. Really, he could. Everything was cool.

He swung into the shopping district, planning to park
somewhere and text Laney to find out her location. But there
was no need. He saw her almost immediately, window-gazing at
the local bookstore while nibbling on what looked like a
chocolate surfboard from the nearby candy shop. He pulled into
a space across the street, rolled down his window, and waved.
"Ready for a lift?" he called out. "Or are you having too much
fun to stop now?"

She smiled at him. Then she pocketed what was left of the
chocolate, checked the traffic, and jaywalked to his car. "Both,"
she answered, getting into the passenger seat. "It's been lovely,
but I do need to get to work now. Thanks for the lift."

She looked considerably more upbeat than when she'd left
the lodge earlier. The near-permanent lines of tension on her
forehead had smoothed, and there was even a ghost of a twinkle
in her eyes. "Work?" he asked, immediately regretting the
question. She'd made it perfectly clear that she didn't trust him,
didn't want him involved with her personal business. But before
he could apologize, she surprised him.

"Yes!" she said cheerfully.

Too cheerfully.

Jason squelched a sigh. She was lying to him again.

"I guess it's obvious that why I came up here is a sensitive
matter," she began. Her tone was almost normal, but
nervousness sped up her delivery. "But I've decided that I need
help, and I have a proposal for you, if you're interested."

Jason seriously couldn't remember ever encountering a worse
liar. Never mind that nothing she'd said so far even seemed
untrue. The motherlode was clearly on its way. "Go on."

She took a breath. "I have a friend back in Oklahoma with a problem. It's a family issue, having to do with a will that's being contested, and some business or other that was supposed to go to one person, but now may go to someone else. My friend thinks his parents are at risk of being taken advantage of by these distant cousins or whatever, but he doesn't have the cash to hire a lawyer or a private detective either one to find out, and neither do they. When he told me about all this, I made a deal with him. I said I'd go up to Canada myself and do some amateur sleuthing for him if he'd comp my rent in one of his sublets. His aunt owns a house in Norman, you see, and she's been letting him stay there and sublet the extra rooms. Well, he jumped on it. So here I am. And I know I don't seem like a likely candidate for this sort of thing, but I *did* have the time on my hands and nothing else to do. The only problem is, since he's not paying me up front, I don't have any cash to spend. The other problem is that since I don't know anybody up here I'm kind of at a loss as to where to start asking questions."

She paused for another breath. Jason said nothing. They were still sitting in his car on the street with the windows rolled down and a cool breeze off the Clayoquot wafting through. He tried hard to keep his face impassive as she added more shovelfuls to the pile.

"So, here's the deal. I may not know anyone around here, but you do. I was thinking that if I gave you these people's names, maybe you could call around and find out some things about them. Ideally, I'd like to run into them somewhere and get a read on them myself, anonymously, of course. And if you'll help me, I can help you by working at one of your businesses. I can cover your shifts at the desk, clean rooms, sort merchandise at the surf shop... whatever. I've done retail. I have references. I know it's a little weird, but what do you say? Am I tempting you at all?"

Jason required a deep breath of his own. Not only was her delivery abysmal, her storyline was ludicrous. As if any sane person would hire her as a private detective! There were other holes in her plot as well, but he saw no need to enumerate them.

He rubbed his face with a hand, hoping to look thoughtful while obscuring any signs of doubt. Calling her out on her lies would be easy, but it would serve no purpose. Whatever had really brought her up here still terrified her. He could see it in her eyes. She was desperate. Her lack of trust in him hurt, but his irritation melted with each glimpse of the frightened fawn that hid behind her mask of stubborn determination. If she couldn't fool him, she would only try to convince someone else to help her. Which would not go well.

Jason wished he could convince her to trust him. But how? He mulled his options carefully before speaking.

"You think you can learn the office spiel quick enough to be of use tomorrow?" he forced himself to ask. The fact that she felt obligated to perform menial tasks as payment for what he would consider a favor was almost as insulting as her distrust. But he recognized mulish pride when he saw it. If it made her feel better to believe he was a mercenary jerk, fine. She was welcome to sit at his desk for a few hours — he could find ways to kill the time.

"Absolutely!" she insisted. "No problem."

"So what is it you want me to do, exactly?" he asked. He didn't sound enthusiastic, but that was okay. He wouldn't be, even if he did believe her. He might be a better actor than she was, but that didn't mean he enjoyed deception.

"The idea is to find out what kind of people they are, without them realizing that anyone is asking about them," she began, the lines of tension gradually returning to her forehead as she spoke. "They're a retired couple, moved to Ucluelet from Toronto about a year ago. What he wants to know is pretty basic, really. Are they good, nice people who lead a happy, peaceful life, or are they litigious money-grubbers who would sue their own relatives to make a buck? You can see why he'd want to know. Are they forgiving or vengeful? How do they feel about family?"

At the last words, her eyes flashed with an emotion he couldn't read. Was it fear? Or perhaps... guilt?

He felt an unwelcome tug at his own heartstrings. Whatever

emotion was driving her, it ran deep. This was important to her. Critically important. So important she'd put everything else in her life on hold and driven thousands of miles to another country to set it right. Who were these people to her? What could possibly be so frightening about a retired couple from Toronto? Why all the cloak and dagger nonsense?

He wanted to be straight with her, just ask her for the truth. But if she didn't trust him, she wouldn't answer anyway. As things stood now, she would only accept his help on her terms, and that meant under false pretenses.

He smothered another sigh and resolved to play along. She would come to trust him, eventually. They just needed a little more time to get to know each other. Then she would tell him the truth on her own.

He was sure of it.

Laney fetched her laptop and emailed a copy of the Tremblay computer file to Jason. By the time she had locked up her room and returned to the lobby, he was pulling a copy from the printer at his desk. "Do you recognize the address?" she asked, then realized she sounded too anxious. "I mean, I'm sure we can find it."

Jason's face was technically smiling, but the eyes she so enjoyed gazing into had developed a new degree of distance. It was possible he didn't fully believe her story about the friend in Oklahoma. But he had agreed to help her, and he wasn't asking any thorny questions. She was grateful for that.

"Oh, I know where it is," he answered. "Ucluelet isn't a big place."

Something in his tone worried her. "What is it?" she asked. "What's wrong with it?"

He offered another empty smile and stashed the paper in a pocket. "Nothing's wrong with it," he insisted. "Would you like to see for yourself? If we head out now, we can do a drive-by while it's still light."

"Yes," she said immediately. "Let's do it."

Within minutes they were cruising down the Pacific Rim Highway again, this time covering new ground to the southeast. Nervous as she was, when they crossed into the national park preserve, Laney once again found her attention drawn out the windows. "It's so beautiful here," she breathed, admiring the tall stands of hemlock, spruce, and cedars that surrounded them. "There's just so much *green*. I wish there were mountains, too. I loved driving through the Cascades, even in the snow."

Jason chuckled. "There *are* mountains here. You would have seen them on the bus ride coming in; it's a shame you don't remember. Rocky peaks, thick forest, babbling brooks, rushing rivers... Vancouver Island has them all."

Laney made no attempt to cover her surprise. "Really? I'd like to see that." A flash of warmth shot through her as the sparkle returned to his eyes.

"You will," he said confidently. "And it is beautiful. When you grow up in a place, you have a tendency to take it for granted. I try not to, but it always helps to see things from someone else's perspective."

Laney remembered the sign at the beach and laughed. "You shouldn't joke about wolves eating dogs, though."

Jason raised an eyebrow. "What joke is that?"

She explained. "Some people are bound to believe it!"

"Laney," he said with amusement. "We do have wolves here. That sign came from the parks staff, and there's no joke about it. We also have black bears and cougars. In fact, Vancouver Island has the highest concentration of cougars in the world."

She opened her mouth to accuse him of teasing her again, but promptly shut it. He wasn't joking. This was serious. Rabid raccoons and bats were one thing, but large predators were not in her repertoire. She could have been killed! "Why was I not informed?" she demanded.

He laughed out loud. "What do you think the sign was for?"

She shut her mouth. Best not to look any more stupid than she already felt.

"Don't worry," he said lightly. "The bears are hibernating and the cougars want nothing to do with humans. I've lived here over twenty years and still haven't seen a live one. As for the wolves, they show up around the lodge occasionally, but you've nothing to fear unless you're small and furry."

Laney turned her gaze back to the window. The dense, moss-draped woods that hugged both sides of the road had taken on a haunting, eerie quality. But that made the scenery even more beautiful; its very wildness both fascinated and excited her.

The view changed again, with signs of civilization increasing as they crossed back out of the reserve and neared the neighboring beach town of Ucluelet. The town's outskirts were studded with a variety of tourist shops and accommodations, much like Tofino, but as they drove into the town proper she noticed several distinctions.

"Ucluelet is different, isn't it?" she asked, breaking a lengthy, companionable silence. It was nice that Jason didn't want to chatter all the time. He seemed to sense that she was fully absorbed with the view, which she appreciated. "The vibe is different. It's not surfing and art galleries so much as—" she looked around thoughtfully. "Fishing. And eating out and spending time with family. It's like a comfortable, downhome nineteen-fifties nostalgia kind of place. As opposed to hippie-chic."

Jason chuckled. "Definitely less bohemian. But it's a great place for fishing or a relaxing family vacation. More ordinary working people live here year round. It's less expensive."

Laney smiled. Her Grandpa Auggie would have loved it here. He'd get a kick out of fishing in something besides a lake. And her Gran would enjoy sitting out on a deck in the sunshine, knitting or quilting while watching the boats on the water.

Jason drove in a little loop around the business district, then headed back out the way they had come. "I wanted you to see the town first," he explained. "Now we'll check out your address."

Laney tensed. She wasn't ready for that part. But she never

would be.

"Are you nervous?" he asked.

She jumped at the question. She should say something like "why would I be?" But she had a strong suspicion it would be pointless. "I wish I wasn't," she said instead.

She tried not to look at him, but she failed. The brief glance she stole made her wonder again whether he was buying her story, seeing as how he appeared to recognize the scrap of truth she'd just delivered for what it was. He looked sympathetic. Perhaps even a little pleased.

Laney kept her face averted. She couldn't deal with his emotions right now. Not when she could barely face the truth herself. She wasn't ready. For any of it.

"It's coming up on the left," he announced.

She swung her head around again, looking past him out the windshield. The narrow lane on which they drove meandered through more thick trees, here and there offering glimpses of the Ucluelet inlet on the other side of the modest houses and occasional B&Bs dotted along it. Laney could see that any of the homes would have an incredible view from its backyard, and she found the whole neighborhood charming until Jason slowed the car to a crawl. Then her breath caught.

The house before them wasn't like the others. It wasn't a house at all. It was an *estate*. A frickin' mansion! Stone pillars flanked either side of a newly paved drive that led through carefully manicured clusters of trees and shrubs. The main residence was some architect's celebration of the Pacific Northwest — a striking blend of wood, native stone, and abundant glass. It was one and a half stories here, two and a half there. Decks and sunrooms abounded. A separate building, half buried in a cluster of woods to the side, had the appearance of a guest house. In the opposite direction was a simpler structure, reminiscent of a barn, that could house anything from prize race horses to a yacht. It was the last dwelling at the end of the road, spanning several acres of lawn and forest, all right on the water.

"Looks pretty sweet," Jason commented. "I bet they've got a

private dock in the back."

Laney said nothing. There was nothing to say.

"Do you want to pull in for a closer look?" he asked.

"No," she said quickly. "No, we're done now. Can we go back?"

Since the car didn't move for a moment, she assumed he was studying her. But she had turned her face away — from both him and the giant house. "Are you a hundred percent sure this is the address I had in the file?" she squeaked.

"Yes," he answered, turning the car around. "The number is posted on the entryway."

To her chagrin, the house was now out her window. She could either look at it or allow him to see her angst. She chose to look at the house. But her eyes were no longer seeing it.

Rich. Gordon and Joan Tremblay were rich. And not just "Now we can retire to Florida" rich. They were "Our next place should have a car elevator" rich! They were *those kind* of people.

"Are you okay?" Jason asked tentatively.

"I will be," she forced out. She didn't want to talk. She couldn't talk. All she wanted was to go someplace and cry.

Why? Why was she so upset? She couldn't seem to answer her own question. She wanted to know that Jessica's grandparents were okay, that they didn't need their granddaughter back, that they didn't need anything. If they were super-freaking rich, they should lack for nothing, so what was the problem? Could she not go home now and consider her obligation met? Should she not be happy that nothing else was required?

But she wasn't happy. She wasn't happy at all, and it must be because she'd been hoping for something else. Some other set of grandparents, people who were kind and folksy and loving and open and normal. People who ate peanut butter straight from the jar and clipped coupons for groceries. People who made casseroles for church potlucks and bought used cars. People who would keep a picture of Elizabeth and Carl and little Jessica on the fireplace mantel, treasuring their faces every day, even after all these years. People who would love her.

Jessica, she corrected herself quickly, her face aflame. People who would love Jessica! People who would be made happy by her news, who would be grateful just to know the truth and would want nothing more. People who would never dream of making Laney's situation any more difficult than it already was. People she could trust with her life!

Jason had said something else, but she didn't know what it was. She put a hand to her cheek to make sure she wasn't crying. She felt no moisture, but she feared it was only a matter of time.

Chapter 20

Laney paid no attention to where Jason was driving. She was too focused on keeping her eyes dry. There was no possible way to explain an explosion of tears on behalf of a school friend's extended family's potential legal squabbles.

The more she thought about the problem presented by Jessica's grandparents' wealth, the more miserable it made her. She hadn't decided whether she would tell them the truth, but even if she wanted to, she couldn't now. These people had money. Lots of it. And apparently no heirs besides one childless middle-aged son. It would be hard enough to approach them with some delusional-sounding story about switched toddlers and stolen identities. But with a substantial inheritance involved, it would be impossible. What else could they possibly think but that she was some unscrupulous grifter? A soulless, contemptible fraud taking advantage of their feelings for their poor, deceased daughter and granddaughter for personal profit?

Of course they would think the worst of her! Why wouldn't they?

She could never tell them the truth. Ever.

Whether they were nice, loving people or not.

"Come on," Jason commanded.

Laney looked around. The car had stopped. His door was open and he had one foot on the ground. But they weren't at the lodge. "Where are we?"

He twisted back around toward her. "Wickaninnish Beach. There's a killer sunset happening even as we speak. By the time we get to Chesterman, it'll be too late to see it. But this'll be gorgeous." He caught her eyes. "Come on. You won't regret the effort. I promise."

"Fine," Laney said mechanically, turning to open her door. She didn't want to go anywhere, with Jason or anyone else, but if she had to look into his empathetic, uncannily all-seeing eyes one more second, she was going to drown his upholstery.

She followed him along a boardwalk that led to an impressive wooden visitor's center with giant storm-watching windows and outdoor viewing decks. The public building appeared to be closed, but Jason clearly had other plans. He stepped off the boardwalk onto the beach and led her to a jumble of logs up near the tree line, well away from the lapping waves. It was only after she had settled onto one of the logs beside him that she even noticed the sunset.

He was right. It was spectacular. The shining golden orb hung low above the water, shedding a cone of light that illuminated layer upon layer of steadily approaching waves. Rocky islands were silhouetted upon the horizon, while above them hung puffy white altocumulus clouds. The sky overhead was calm and still tinted with blue, but down closer to the water it burned with a splash of vibrant orange, red, and yellow.

Laney sat and stared, hugging her coat tightly around her. The sunset was stunning, as were all of her natural surroundings. But the usual joy couldn't reach her. Her body seemed like a cold, empty shell, protecting a center that was nothing but a question mark. She didn't know who she was. She wasn't even sure whom she wanted to be. She didn't know what she wanted, period.

"If you're too cold, we can go back," she heard Jason say. He was sitting beside her, but at too great a distance to offer any warmth. Too bad she wasn't up to his standards — if he found her attractive, she would at least have an arm around her shoulders right now.

"I'm fine," she lied, to no logical end. She was miserable and she was cold. Why bother to pretend otherwise?

"I don't understand what it was about the house that upset you so much," he said quietly.

Laney's eyes remained on the sunset. She shivered. She was certain her trembling was visible, but Jason remained where he was, his hands on the log to either side of him. Damnation, was she not the only female around at the moment? Was she *that* undesirable? "I was hoping they'd be normal people," she answered without thinking.

"People who live in big houses aren't normal?" he questioned.

"They're rich," she tried again, her teeth chattering.

"Rich people aren't normal?" he pressed.

"You don't understand!" she said shortly.

He moved slightly closer. "Make me understand," he pleaded.

Laney fought a strong urge to scream. He had no idea how much raw animal magnetism that husky whisper of his exerted, even to a woman who wasn't freezing. Then again, maybe he did. He probably made use of it quite often. The question was why he was bothering to use it now, on a woman he didn't give a damn about.

She stopped herself. That wasn't fair. Jason might not *want* her, but he did care. He had saved her life out on that rock. He had visited her in the hospital multiple times, hauled her stuff to her bedside, helped her with her computer, taken her out to dinner with a friend, and schlepped her sorry rear end to the grocery store and everywhere else she wanted to go. And he'd never asked for a single thing in return.

Except her trust.

Wow. And she hadn't thought it possible she could feel any lower.

She shifted and looked at him. He was a genuinely nice guy, wasn't he? She'd never known a "man of a million women" to be so, but there was a first time for everything. He looked back at her without flinching, curious, maybe even hopeful. The dim light obscured the color of his eyes, but the subtle rays of sunset still showed off their killer twinkle.

She let out a long, exhausted breath. "Oh, hell. You don't believe a word I've been telling you, do you?"

His full, sensual lips smiled lazily. He shook his head.

"I'm sorry," she apologized. "It's just really hard for me to trust a person I've only known a couple days. And this thing is big. For me it's... potentially dangerous."

She said nothing else, waiting for him to comment. He

seemed deep in thought.

"You don't have to share anything with me that you don't want to," he said finally, his voice mild. "But you should save yourself the effort of lying. You really are incredibly bad at it."

Laney laughed out loud, surprising herself. Nothing had changed with regard to her predicament. Yet she felt better. She treated herself to a lingering look at him. Could he really just want to be her friend?

The thought sent her insides churning, till maddeningly, she was on the brink of tears again. *Will somebody please just shoot me now?* she raged, frustrated. Never before in her life had she been so unable to control her emotions!

But *yes*, dear God, did she ever need a friend. She did have friends already, good friends. Several of her fellow grad students in Norman, as well as college friends from Cape Girardeau and Columbia in Missouri. But over the last horrible months, she had neglected all of them. She'd deleted her social media accounts after college, she was never a big texter, and while she was ordinarily good with Christmas check-ins, she'd made no effort whatsoever this year. None of her friends even knew that her mother had died, much less everything else that had happened, and the thought of trying to bring any of them up to date now — over the phone, no less! — was as guilt-inducing as it was daunting. It was all her fault, not theirs. Either way, none of them were here now.

But Jason was. "I'd like to be your friend, Laney," he suggested softly.

A song played in her mind. It was a television theme song, from her Gran's favorite program. It was ancient, but one of the networks played reruns every night from nine to ten, and Gran had watched them religiously, over and over. Laney had absorbed enough episodes in the last year to recite half the dialogue herself. Four retired women, all living together companionably in a pastel-laden house in sunny Florida. *The Golden Girls.*

Thank you for being a friend...

Everybody needed somebody. And whether it hurt her pride
or not, she needed Jason. It would be easier if he were fat and
bald, but hey — she would manage.

"I'd like that too," she answered. Her voice sounded
surprisingly bright. Or maybe not so surprising, since she really
was feeling better.

He smiled back. "Cool! So if we're officially friends, can I put
a nonthreatening arm around you? You look cold."

"Please!" she laughed, scooting over and cuddling in. "Thank
God, I thought you'd never ask. I'm freezing my butt off over
here."

She felt his deep laughter rumble through his chest as he
rubbed her upper arm briskly for a moment, then held her tight.
"So I noticed. Didn't want to get my face slapped, though."

Laney wasn't sure why he would say that. But the sunset was
beautiful, this gorgeous hunk of a man was now officially her
friend, and having his strong arm around her shoulders was
exquisitely, amazingly comfortable. For now, it was all she could
ask for.

Jason's heart beat entirely too fast as he cradled the still-
shivering Laney to his side. Given that her puffy winter coat was
overkill for the weather, he suspected that her trembling came
more from frayed nerves than cold temperatures. Either way, a
friendly hug was in order. He just hoped she warmed up soon.
Because her proximity was warming him up a little more than
desired.

At least the air had been cleared. They were friends and only
friends, and that was good. He'd never had a meteorologist
friend, and he was greatly looking forward to it. She would make
one incredible surfer someday, too. If the friend thing worked,
he might even be around to see it happen.

He would like that. He would like that very much.

Damn, his jacket was stifling.

"So tell me," he began, distracting himself. "What do you

have against rich people, anyway? You're an American! Aren't you supposed to be all for capitalism and the pursuit of prosperity?"

She huffed out a laugh. Her voice was partly muffled by the fabric of his jacket as she nestled her head alongside his collar bone. She fit to his side perfectly. He wondered if she noticed that. "I'm not opposed to it," she answered. "But super wealthy people *are* different. They value different things in life. That's how they got rich in the first place."

"Not necessarily," he argued. "If you're climbing your way to the top by stepping on other people, then yeah, that's an ethical problem. But you can't convince me that making money and being a nice person are mutually exclusive. I *am* a businessman, you know."

She gave another muffled laugh. "Aren't Canadians supposed to be all about equality? Are you sure you aren't American?"

"I am American, actually," he confessed. "Half, anyway. I was born in Seattle."

Her head lifted abruptly. "You're half American? How does that work?"

"My mother is Canadian and my father is American," he answered, puzzled by her sudden interest in the topic. "We lived in Washington State till I was ten, and then my parents divorced and my mother brought me and my brother back to her hometown in Canada. So I have dual citizenship. Which sounds great, until tax time."

Her blue eyes, which had looked strangely hopeful for a moment, resumed their previous despair. "I see. You have American citizenship because you were born there. You would have even if both your parents had been Canadian."

"That's right." Her head returned to its niche on his chest. He promptly broke out in a sweat. She felt so *right* where she was. He couldn't bring himself to dislodge her.

"Why the interest?" he pressed, trying not to notice the smell of her shampoo. Her hair was pure blond, with no trace of darkness at its roots. Literally everything about Laney was natural. Earthy. Honest. Sensual.

Holding her so close was pure, unmitigated torture.

Holding her at arm's length would be worse.

"No reason," she lied, still snuggling comfortably.

A drop of sweat rolled down Jason's neck. He made the sound of a buzzer. "False. Try again."

She tensed a little. Then she sighed. "Fine." She made a move to straighten up, and Jason promptly set her aside from him and swiveled to face her.

"The Tremblays," she began, her tone wary as she weighed her words carefully. "It's my own family they might be important to. Possibly dangerous to. I came up here with no real plan, just this half-baked idea that I needed to get to know them first. Without them knowing who I was."

Jason contemplated the hard-won information. She was telling him the truth now, and it made sense. Her mother's death must have been the catalyst. Besides the drama of deathbed confessions, the exposure of wills and other private legal documents did sometimes bring nasty surprises. The Tremblays must be relatives. Relatives Laney either didn't know about before, or didn't think mattered. It was the "possibly dangerous" part that troubled him. Her fear was real, and he didn't believe it was based on any disputed inheritance.

He wanted to press for more, but stopped himself. The trust she'd shown in him so far was gratifying, but he knew it had limits. He waited for her to say more, but she remained quiet.

"Thanks for that," he offered finally. "You know I'm happy to help you, if I can. I just have one qualifying question, Ms. Miller. Are you out to do good or evil?"

She smiled at him. "Only good. I promise." She paused a beat, then added, "for everyone involved."

"All right, then," he smiled back. "Both Tofino and Ucluelet are pretty small towns, and I do know plenty of people in both. I should have a decent shot at finding out the kind of information you'd like to know, without the Tremblays realizing that anyone is asking about them — or at least without them having any idea that you're behind it. So how about we come up with a more practical plan of attack? Together?"

Her blue eyes swam with... fondness. She looked almost as if she wanted to be kissed. Did she?

Her head snapped away. She did not.

Dammit! He chastised himself immediately. What was he thinking? He had no business rooting for her to feel something for him — not when he would only break her heart. Nor could he root for sheer physical attraction; forever girls didn't separate the two.

"Thank you," she said, somewhat unsteadily. "I meant what I said about working for you. I'll feel better if I have some way to repay your time."

"You seem to be forgetting that we're officially friends now," he protested. "Friends don't do favors because they expect to be paid."

Her face clouded. She knew he was right, but for whatever reason, she was still uncomfortable. She didn't seem to want to owe him anything.

"Fine," he conceded. "If you want to help me around the lodge, I can try to make you sorry you offered. Good enough?"

She smiled. "Perfect. Thanks. Will I be able to watch you surf from the office window?"

Jason's heart skipped a beat. "You like watching me surf?" He sounded like an adolescent. Women watched him surf all the time. They oohed and aahed and cheered and went to a great deal of effort to puff up his ego every which way possible. But Laney's wanting to watch was different. She didn't give a damn about his ego. What she wanted was to study the art itself, to absorb it, to learn it. Surfing was a passion she was only just discovering for herself.

It was her destiny.

He sprang up from the log and offered her a hand. "If I'm out, I'll do my best to surf within viewing range," he promised. "Let's head back now, shall we?"

She reached up toward him, still smiling, and as their hands clasped he was able to picture his own destiny quite clearly. Both involved large amounts of cold water.

Chapter 21

Jason stood in the doorway of Laney's small room, reluctant to move any closer. His attraction to her was a problem, and he needed to address it, pronto. She was suffering enough emotional pain already, and though he still didn't know its source, he was determined not to add to it. Whether he wanted to jump the woman's bones or not — and there was no more fooling himself about that; he absolutely, definitely did — he could not let her see it. If she had any gushy romantic feelings about him, his attraction would only encourage her. If all she felt for him was raw, animal lust — the mere thought of which induced another sweat — well, that would only encourage *him*, potentially beyond endurance. He couldn't let it get to that. Even if she claimed that a temporary hookup was enough for her, even if she actually believed it at the time, he knew better. Experience showed it would all end badly.

Perhaps he was getting ahead of himself. Perhaps she felt nothing for him either way. But he refused to take that chance. He cleared his throat. "I only have about an hour to strategize tonight, then I've got to get to town. I have a date. But we can start putting a plan into action first thing tomorrow morning. Okay?"

Laney looked up from where she was sitting on her bed, booting up the computer on her lap. She appeared startled. That was bad. But to her credit, she recovered quickly. "Sure," she agreed. "So what is the plan? What do you need to get started? I had more info on Gordon, but I'm afraid I didn't save it. I was..." A flash of annoyance crossed her face. "I clearly wasn't thinking straight before I left Peck. But I can find it all again, I'm sure. I had to sign up for—"

She uttered a four-letter word he hadn't heard her use before. "The free trials!" she lamented. "I forgot to unsubscribe!" She swore again. "My card will get charged for all the— Oh, I'm so stupid!"

"You had a concussion," Jason reminded softly, trying not to grin. She was cute when she was angry, but he knew better than to tell any woman *that*. "It's okay to give yourself a break for forgetting something."

She was not appeased. "Well, this is going to take a while. If I can't remember the passwords I'll have to change them all and *then* cancel." She looked up, her face reddened with both embarrassment and frustration. "I'm sorry, but this is going to take forever. You might as well go on. I'll copy everything I find into a file and we can go over it tomorrow."

Jason had been dismissed. It was what he wanted, but he didn't like it. What he'd like to do was make them both a cup of hot chocolate, nestle into the loveseat in his office, and let nature take its course. "Okay," he replied. "Sounds good."

"Have a good night," she said, rather stiffly.

He tensed. "I will. See you tomorrow."

"Bye."

He stepped outside and shut her door. He was doing the right and decent thing, he reminded himself. He was no good for her. She was no good for him. Their lifestyles and values were incompatible.

He walked to his office, then pulled out his phone. The Aussie would be only too happy to hear from him. They could meet up at Wolf in the Mist, have dinner and a few drinks, then head back to his place. He stared at her last emoji-laden, unmistakably lascivious text.

He stood, staring, for a very long time. Then he put the phone back in his pocket, collected his stuff, and drove home.

There was nothing wrong with him, he told himself. He just wasn't in the mood. His mind was too embroiled in the tasks ahead. He could easily look up a little more about Gordon and Joan Tremblay on his own computer, maybe get started with a few phone calls tonight. If he found out anything good, he could greet Laney with it first thing tomorrow. She'd like that.

He microwaved two hot dogs and a cup of rice, washed them down with cola straight from a two-liter, then settled onto his sectional couch with his laptop. It didn't take him long to discover Gordon's preretirement line of work. When he saw the name of the investment banking firm in question, he knew which contact would be first on his list.

"Hey, Grandpa," he greeted a few moments later. "It's Jason. How's everything going?"

Joe Grant, a kindly but stoic man who had spent his entire working life as a banker, gave his usual rundown of happenings in the small north island town where Jason and his brother had spent their teen years. Jason listened to his grandfather's discourse on the weather, the state of his grandmother's arthritis, and the perils of the national economy before asking his primary question. "By the way, I came across the name Gordon Tremblay today, and I was thinking about when Whitney Mayer did their buyout. That was before you retired, right?"

"Oh, yes, about eighteen months before," the banker replied, displaying his still-sharp memory. "Whitney Mayer brought in a lot of changes. Not all good ones, either, in my opinion. But it pleased your grandma, at least, since she was finally able to convince me to retire."

"Do you remember anything about Gordon Tremblay specifically?" Jason asked. "Like what kind of reputation he had as a CEO?"

Joe cleared his throat, signaling that his grandson was in for another lengthy discourse. "Tremblay had a good reputation within the industry itself. He was known to be ethical and fair-minded. Big philanthropist, too. But his philanthropy was part of the problem. He was an environmentalist, back when not too many businessmen were, and he was outspoken about it. He ruffled a lot of feathers in the logging industry, and I don't need to tell you how that went over with our clientele. The pulp mills were already hurting."

"I see the problem," Jason agreed, even as his personal respect for Gordon ticked up a notch.

"The bank did well enough under him, though," Joe conceded. "And he did donate to other causes, like the universities. He had an interest in Vancouver Island, for sure. I don't know if he vacationed here or what, but it was his run-ins with the local loggers that made him unpopular at the bank."

Jason smiled to himself. Figuring out where Gordon spent his money could be helpful. Not only would it tell Laney something about his character, but it could lead to closer personal contacts. He thanked his grandfather for the information, chatted a while longer about business and economics — subjects on which Jason was the only family member willing to indulge him — and said goodbye.

Jason's next round of computer searches proved more frustrating. If Gordon had donated to any of the environmental charities associated with his new home base, he had done so anonymously. Another credit to his character, perhaps, but inconvenient for Jason. Still, he had no intention of giving up. He picked up his phone and made another call. His friend Chaz answered on the second ring.

"Jason! My man! Whuzzup?"

He grinned at the greeting. Chaz was the volunteer head of the Pacific Rim chapter of SurfersAct, a national charity aimed at cleaning up the crapload of plastic littering the world's beaches and oceans. He was also an excellent surfer, and a really nice guy. "Hey. Listen, I've got a quick question for you. You've got Gordon Tremblay down as one of our donors already, don't you?"

Jason felt a pang of guilt at the deception. Tremblay wasn't on the official list of donors, and if he'd given anonymously, Chaz wasn't supposed to say so. But he might if he thought Jason already knew.

"Yeah, man, he's like platinum league. Why, you're not planning to hit him up again, are you?"

Jason smirked. "Well I was thinking about it, but I won't now. Thanks."

"No problem."

"He gives to a lot of local stuff, right?"

"Aw, hell yeah," Chaz elaborated. "He's awesome. Crazy-ass rich, but he shares the love. He started up one of the first salmon societies — you know, the big one in Port Alberni? He fishes himself. Used to surf, too, did you know that?"

Jason did not. But it pleased him immensely. "Does he still?"

"Nah, he's got bad knees or something. But he used to surf Tofino. Back before our time. He's got a place in Ucluelet now."

"Yeah, I've seen it," Jason admitted conveniently. "It's massive." He chatted with his friend a bit more, renewed his promise to show up at the next beach cleanup, and rang off. Feeling pleased with himself, he threw a packet of popcorn in the microwave and then typed the new info into his file. He was two for two, and each lead was conveniently creating another. He envisioned Laney smiling as he presented her with exactly what she desired...

He smelled something burning.

Crap! He jumped up, grabbed a pot holder, and tossed the smoking, blackened bag of popcorn into the sink. Grumbling at his sudden, disturbing inability to control his own brain, he threw another bag into the microwave and stood over it until it was done. Then he poured the popped corn into a bowl, sat back down, and picked up his phone. Two texts had just come in, both from women, both asking him what he was up to. *Perfect,* he told himself. There was still time to go out; he would answer one or the other and see if she was available. He'd gotten far too distracted with Laney. He hadn't been with another woman for *days* now!

Yes. That was what he would do.

He threw back a fistful of popcorn and chewed it thoughtfully. He wondered if Laney liked the gourmet variety, and if she preferred white cheddar or caramel-coated. Then he pulled up his voice call app and clicked on the picture of a shaggy-bearded mountain man.

His older brother picked up immediately. "Jason, are you psychic, or what?" Thane's booming voice called out merrily. "I was just about to call you! Wait..." His tone turned to dismay. "Mom didn't get to you already, did she?"

"No, Mom didn't get to me," Jason assured, glad of it. He loved his mother, but if she didn't give up on the "You're old enough to start thinking about dating a *nice* girl" campaign she'd unveiled over Christmas, he was going to start sending her calls straight to voicemail. "What's up?"

"Good news!" Thane proclaimed, his voice cheerful again. "Mei Lin is pregnant!"

Jason put down his popcorn. A sly grin spread across his face. "Seriously? Bro, that's awesome!"

"Thanks," Thane replied. "We're pretty happy about it."

Jason kept smiling. His sister-in-law was a sweetheart, and he loved that the two of them were so happy. Never mind that his bumbling brother had fallen into the perfect relationship ass-backward. Thane was a great guy, and he deserved his happiness. But... already? "Dude," Jason teased, "how long have you been married? Like, five minutes?"

"Shut up," Thane returned affectionately. "You'll be an uncle by summer. Get used to it."

An uncle. Jason liked that idea. He liked it a lot, actually. "Another generation of Buchanans taming the Alaskan wilderness! That is too cool. Has Dad bought him or her a pair of boots yet?"

"Well, somebody's got to," Thane remarked. "But there's time, yet. So hey, why'd you call?"

Jason had almost forgotten. For some odd reason, he was picturing himself carrying the little bundle of joy in a backpack around the forests of Gustavus. A plausible scenario, except that the tow-headed tot he envisioned was an unlikely fantasy child for his dark-complexioned brother and raven-haired sister-in-law. He shook himself back to reality. "Yeah, I've got a question for you. I'm trying to find out more about a philanthropist named Gordon Tremblay. Word has it he was a part of getting the Forest Society going. You know anything about him?"

The Forest Society was a group of fishermen, scientists, and industry people who worked with the provincial government to protect salmon habitats, and although Thane lived in Alaska now, he used to work for the BC Fish and Wildlife department in Port Alberni. "I've heard of him," Thane confirmed. "Never met the guy, but his name got thrown around a lot, both on the job and at the university. He was a big fisherman himself, very dedicated. He gave a lot of money to a lot of causes, but he ticked off some people in the forestry department because he set up an endowment for Earth, Ocean and Atmospheric instead." He chuckled to himself. "That was decades ago, but those academic types can be cutthroat, and memories are long."

Jason was aware. He'd heard his brother complain about ivory-tower politics the whole time Thane was working on his grad degree. "Why would Tremblay give to EOA when he was so invested in forest restoration?"

"I'm pretty sure he did make donations to Forestry, too," Thane replied. "But the endowment was a special lump sum thing he set up as a memorial to his daughter. The story I heard was that she died in a weather-related accident, which motivated him to throw some serious cash at better early warning systems. Unfortunately for him — and what still ticks off Forestry — is that UBC isn't really doing much with forecasting anymore. But the University of Victoria is, as you probably know, and they got their own endowment. Tremblay set them up at a half-dozen grad schools, not just UBC. You've got to admire the guy for trying to make a difference."

Jason's interest was piqued. A weather-related accident? His mind leapt immediately to Laney's tornado, and he tried to remember what he'd read in her newspaper clippings. But he couldn't make a connection. The only family members of Laney's mentioned were her and her mother, both of whom had survived. Who exactly was Gordon's daughter?

"You don't remember the name of the daughter, do you?" Jason asked.

"Not hardly," Thane replied. "You're lucky I remember that much. Did I mention that I'm going to be a father?"

Jason laughed. "You did." He thanked his brother for the info, sent congratulations and well wishes to his sister-in-law, and hung up with a smile on his face.

Thane and Mei Lin were having a baby. *Wow.* The whole family would be over the moon. His mother in particular had been hinting about grandchildren for years now, long before Thane had even met his wife. Jason thought his mother had given up on her younger son's prospects, but Christmas seemed to have renewed her optimism. Which was unfortunate, since Jason had no plans to change anything about his perfectly satisfactory personal life.

Another blond head popped into his imagination, this one fully mature and unquestionably female.

He growled beneath his breath. Then he stuffed his mouth with another fistful of popcorn and got back to work.

Chapter 22

Laney sat alone on a recliner on the lodge deck the next morning, her head tilted backward. A storm was coming in, and she was enjoying the feel of the wind and the cool splash of mist on her face. She watched the swirl of clouds in the sky, attuned to their density and pattern of movement. Coastal storms weren't like the inland beasts she knew, and that alone made them exciting. Between her rain jacket and the torn plastic poncho she'd rescued from the trash bin in the common room earlier, she was able to stay relatively dry. Not that she would care, if it weren't for the cold. Splashing about in the rain on a warm spring day — much to her mother's chagrin — had always been a favored pastime.

The smile slipped from Laney's face as reality returned. *My mother.* Christi Miller would always be her mother. But was it wrong to continue to think of her as the only one? Was it wrong to hide the truth from Jessica Macdonald's family?

Laney didn't know.

She had been raised to believe in right *or* wrong. Trying to put wiggle room between the two, so the reasoning went, was faithless and cowardly. But what if right and wrong looked the same? What if no matter her course of action, a mix of good and bad would result? How could she weigh the relative merits of each option, deciding which was to the greater good, when she couldn't predict either outcome?

Follow your conscience, Gran had always said confidently. But on the critical issue at hand, Laney's conscience remained stubbornly silent. *Honesty is the best policy,* another platitude advised. But what about *let sleeping dogs lie?*

Her mind rocked with an image of Jason, curled up under a heavy brown comforter with one bare, muscular shoulder exposed. He was deeply asleep, his hair tousled, his long lashes quivering slightly as he dreamed. The mental picture filled her with warmth, until the camera panned over to the nude, artificially tanned, fake-bosomed bombshell lying next to him.

She huffed with annoyance and tried to refocus on the clouds. Jason was her *friend.* She shouldn't care who he slept with. Since when did she care about her male friends' sex lives? It was none of her business.

Deny, redirect, repeat. She'd been following the same mantra all night long. It hadn't worked. But she had yet to think of a better solution.

While Jason had spent last evening out on the town having a fabulous time, she'd spent hers alone with her laptop feeling aggravated. Getting back into her accounts with the newspaper archive and the address registries had taken forever, thanks to her absurd tendency to pretend she would remember such things and thus didn't need to record them. Eventually, she had relocated the information she'd found before and forced herself to copy it all into a file. She'd even dug a little deeper into the Toronto paper and found a mention of Joan Tremblay in conjunction with a charity event. But she could find nothing useful anywhere regarding Carl or Elizabeth Macdonald. The usual online hits that marked school achievements and job history, allowing a public view into the life of any millennial or Gen Z, didn't exist for their generation. The two had died before social media even became a thing.

She turned to the small table beside her and reached for the once-steaming mug of coffee that a friendly pair of surfers from Australia had insisted she try. She doubted that any coffee could completely eliminate the cobwebs from her restless night. But James and John had assured her that a "long black" was the cure for what ailed her, and as her insides warmed and her brain began to buzz, she saluted their cultural wisdom. The lodge had no espresso machine, but the Aussies had located a grinder and something called an AeroPress and apparently made do.

She would have to thank them effusively later. In the meantime, she would enjoy the storm. She lowered her gaze to watch the waves, reveling in the complex interplay of wind and water, sky and sea. There was little else she could do to further her mission until Jason reappeared. Most of the surfers at the lodge were still sleeping, and despite the steadily increasing waves, none were out on the water. Thanks to the fascinating discussion she and Jason had had yesterday, she now understood why. The height of the waves might be steadily rising, but both the wind and swell direction were unfavorable for surfing at Chesterman Beach. As the storm drew closer, conditions would only worsen.

Not for the first time, Laney wondered what riding on a surfboard would feel like. It must be amazing to experience the power and movement of a wave beneath one's feet! Gambling the risk of a cold dunking against the reward of a thrilling ride would be an added bonus. She pictured herself standing tall next to Jason, the two of them shredding one gnarly wave in perfect harmony—

"So if you had nothing else to do," an amused voice asked from behind her, "would you stay out here through the whole storm?"

Laney smiled at Jason as he walked up. "I've done it before. But in this case, I'd probably cry uncle when the wind blew away my poncho, seeing as how these are my only shoes."

"Seriously?" Jason replied, his tone leaving no doubt what he thought of her decrepit sneakers. He was wearing waterproof boots himself, along with a rugged, waterproof jacket with the hood thrown back. Misty rain clung to his brown curls, flattening some and accentuating others. The look was unkempt, raw, and incredibly sexy.

Deny, redirect, repeat.

"Don't diss the sneakers," she replied. "They've been through a lot."

He grinned at her and sat down. "Speaking of uncles, I found out last night I'm going to be one! My sister-in-law is pregnant, due next summer. How cool is that?"

"Very cool," Laney replied with a smile. She liked the way

Jason spoke so fondly of his brother. As a child she had pined for siblings. She still did. "You'll make a great uncle."

He smiled back at her, but too soon the glint of unfettered joy in his eyes morphed back into concerned sympathy. "Did you have any breakthroughs in your research last night?"

She sat up and turned toward him, adjusting the poncho as she moved. The wind wasn't bad yet, but the rain was getting heavier. "Not really. I learned that Joan Tremblay was involved with the Children's Aid Foundation in Toronto twenty years ago. The rest I knew already." Her mouth formed the next words despite direct orders from her brain to stifle them. "So how was your date?"

He looked back at her with a blank expression. Had he actually flinched a little, or was that her imagination? "Fine," he answered. Was he studying her as intently as she was studying him? She averted her eyes. None of her thoughts were safe for him to see.

"That's good," she replied. "If you want to see what I found, we can go back inside now."

For a long moment, he made no comment. Then he lifted his hood onto his head and sat forward. "I did a little research on my own last night. And I found a couple things that should help us."

Laney's heart beat faster. Whatever he was about to say, she was afraid of it, and she hated herself for being afraid. She tried to say something nonchalant but wound up saying nothing.

He noticed her angst. For a moment he looked like he was going to press her about it, but he didn't. Instead he told her of Gordon Tremblay's history as an environmental philanthropist. She listened with conflicting emotions. Even as she approved of Gordon's values, she found herself wishing the man had some secret vice. Something that would render him unsympathetic. Unworthy.

Jason's next words felt like a sucker punch. "Gordon also set up large endowments at a half dozen universities as memorials to his daughter. She died in some sort of storm, and he earmarked his donations for research into better early warning systems. I don't know her name or any details about what happened to her, but I asked Ben to see if he could find out more from UVic about their endowment. Once we know her name, we—"

Laney wasn't looking at Jason anymore. Her focus had returned to the ocean, a churning tempest that mirrored her own insides. *So.* Gordon had been affected by his daughter's death. He had responded to his grief and helplessness by taking concrete, practical action.

She could identify with that.

Gordon must be a good man. He must have loved Elizabeth. Would he not have loved Jessica, also?

"Laney," Jason said gently. "I didn't tell you this to make you sad. You've got me at a disadvantage. I'm missing something."

"I know," she heard herself say vaguely. "I'm sorry."

"Don't be sorry," he shot back. "Just level with me. Please?"

Laney turned her gaze back to his face. To his kind, sensitive gray-green eyes. Sharing her secret with anyone was risky, but so was continuing this farce of a mission alone. She needed someone to talk to. Someone to help her gain a wider perspective, to make sure that, going forward, she wasn't operating purely on emotion.

Besides which, Jason wasn't stupid. If he continued to help her it would only be a matter of time before the nature of her connection to the Tremblays was obvious. She had neither the will nor the energy to continue concealing it.

The rain was coming down harder. Cool drips had started to run down her neck. She pulled up her own hood and adjusted the poncho more carefully over her legs and feet.

"Do you want to go in?" Jason asked.

"No," she answered, casting a quick glance over her shoulder. Unsurprisingly, they were alone. "No one can overhear us out here. What I have to say could get me in a lot of trouble. Legally. Financially." Her gaze held his. "I need to have your word it will go no further. Are you sure you're okay with that?"

His eyes were puzzled, and anxious. But his expression was resolute. "Of course."

Laney believed him. It was another emotional choice on her part, but so be it. Sometimes the gut did know best. She took in a deep, embarrassingly ragged breath.

She started talking.

It was all Jason could do to keep his hands to himself as Laney sat, mere inches away, and started trembling again. The 'officially friends" thing gave him cover to be affectionate, but a sixth sense told him that right now, she didn't want coddling. She was obviously used to being independent, to feeling strong and capable. All she wanted was for him to shut up and listen.

"It started with the tornado that hit Peck when I was a toddler," she began, her tone dry and her tempo quick. "Did you tell me you saw the articles I brought? I can't... I'm a little fuzzy on what happened in the hospital."

Jason nodded, feeling slightly guilty again. He suspected at the time that she wasn't fully grasping his apology. "I was trying to find an emergency contact for you. I couldn't help but read the articles. It was an amazing story."

She nodded, her expression grim. "It was. I grew up surrounded by people who called me a 'miracle baby.' No one could believe I had really been lifted up inside a funnel cloud and set safely back down again, but they had to believe it because there was no other explanation." She swallowed hard. "But that day wasn't a miracle for everybody. Four people died."

She went quiet. After a moment, Jason tried to help. "An elderly man and a family from out of town," he supplied, remembering the articles.

Laney's blue eyes turned to look at him, their clear depths wracked with pain. "The family who was killed was named Macdonald. Carl, Elizabeth, and Jessica Macdonald. Elizabeth was Gordon and Joan Tremblay's daughter."

Jason's breath caught. So this was the connection: the

daughter who died in a storm. But... hadn't Laney said that the Tremblays were family? "So the article was wrong? About them merely passing through Peck on the highway?"

She shook her head, loosening drops of rain from the edge of her hood. "They didn't know anyone in Peck. They were Canadians living temporarily in Nashville. The articles were right about that, but wrong about something else. The child they brought with them wasn't a baby. She was sixteen months old. A toddler."

Laney's voice quavered. Jason inched closer to her, confused. "Why is that important?"

She drew back from him and stood. A gust of wind picked up her poncho, but she caught it in a hand and stuffed it partway inside her raincoat pocket. Then she stepped to the banister and cast her gaze out at the waves again. Jason moved to stand beside her. He said nothing else. He just waited. She took another deep breath.

"Jessica's body was never found. Elizabeth and Carl's bodies were far-flung, so there was no question that the three of them had been airborne." Her eyes turned disturbingly glassy. "I sometimes imagine what it must have felt like, being spun around in circles high above the ground, with the three of them all spinning around with me. I don't remember any of it, of course. But can you imagine if I had been older? What I might have seen and remembered?"

"No," he said honestly. "I can't. It must have been very traumatic for you."

She turned to him. "More than anyone knew. Because afterwards every face I looked into was a stranger to me."

He was confused again. "Amnesia?"

She shook her head. "No. Two little girls were pulled up into that god-awful tornado that day, Jason. Two blond-haired, blue-eyed toddlers. Only one came down alive again." Her shaking increased. "That little girl was me."

A streak of cold raced up his spine. The dead child. The Tremblays' granddaughter.

"Laney Miller died that day, you see," she continued in a hoarse whisper. "It was Jessica Macdonald who survived."

Jason's heart skipped a beat. What she was saying was incredible. "Your..." He faltered, wanting to choose his words carefully. "The woman who raised you, she—"

"She lied," Laney said flatly. "They told her they'd found me and she went to pick me up, but when she saw I was the wrong girl she just... lied."

Jason listened, feeling increasingly numb, as Laney told the story of a grieving, desperate widow who had claimed an orphan child as her own. Of the well-meaning but uninformed town who had taken a mother's word as gospel and never looked back. Of a great-grandmother, tortured by guilt and fear of hellfire, who had broken her oath only when robbed of her full faculties.

There was no malice in Laney's tone. She seemed not to blame the woman who raised her, calling her "my mother" without hesitation. Nor did she blame the complicit grandparents who had helped keep the devastating secret. But though she didn't seem to blame anyone else, her own face was writ large with guilt.

"The Tremblays don't know," she finished finally, her voice sounding strained and weak. "They have no idea."

Jason moved closer. He couldn't help himself. Keeping a polite distance was impossible when the woman so obviously needed to be held. "It's not your fault, Laney," he said firmly, reacting not to her words, but to what he saw in her face. "None of it is your fault. The Tremblays will see that."

She winced. "Will they?" Her eyes flooded with tears. "And how would they feel if they knew I might not tell them at all?"

Jason got it, then. The whole ugly, brutally unfair dilemma into which fate had placed her. Her predicament was beyond unfair. It was plain damned cruel.

"Oh, Laney, I'm so sorry." He pulled her to him, their slippery wet raincoats squeaking against each other as he gathered her to his chest. Both their hoods fell back, but the rain wasn't important. Her head nestled obediently into the crook of his neck, and his hands stroked her back. As her quivering form melted into his solid one a certain transfusion took place; he could feel some of the tension flow out of her, replaced by a dose of his own strength. She seemed comforted, and comfortable. At least for the first few seconds.

Then something changed. The turning point was difficult to define, but for him, what started out as a compulsion to comfort turned into a rapidly kindling core of flame. He wanted her. He wanted all of her. *Now.* He wanted to turn her face to his and kiss her until she forgot every word she'd just spoken. He wanted to replace her sorrow and angst and guilt with joy and warmth and pleasure... to transport her to another realm of reality where all that mattered was the two of them and how absolutely fantastic they could make each other feel—

Laney pushed him away.

He was startled. He tried replaying the last few seconds in his mind. Had the tape skipped somewhere? Had he actually kissed her? *No,* he had not. His lips were cold with rain, not warm with the feel of her. His hands had stayed on her back; they hadn't traveled. And they had touched her only through her raincoat, at that! Never mind what the hell he'd been thinking. He hadn't done anything!

"I'm sorry," she apologized, flustered. "I didn't mean... It's just that..."

He had the feeling he should apologize himself, but this time the words "I'm sorry" didn't roll so easily off his tongue. He wasn't sorry in the slightest. How could he regret three of the most intense seconds of his life?

Seriously, dude? I mean you didn't even—

It didn't matter. Laney had just ignited something in him that he'd never felt before. Its novelty alone made it exhilarating.

She was talking again. "I didn't mean to be so abrupt. But I don't need your sympathy. I need your help!"

Her words struck like a cup of ice sliding down his collar. *Pull yourself together, dude.* "Of course," he said gruffly, taking another half step back. He tried hard to refocus his thoughts. How could he help her?

No, besides that!

"Don't you see?" she said with frustration. "Everything about me is fake! My birth certificate, my social security number, my passport... it's all invalid. I'm not even an American citizen! If I reveal the truth to the Tremblays, or to anyone, everything I have is at risk! How can I take care of my great-grandmother if I'm not her next of kin? If I can't access my mother's money to support her?"

Jason's mind cleared. She was right. The peril in which she found herself was real. The consequences of revealing what she knew would go well beyond emotional upheaval. "I get it," he confirmed, ashamed he hadn't seen it sooner. No wonder she cared so much whether the Tremblays were "good" people! If she gave them the power, they could ruin her.

"From all we know of Gordon so far," he said tentatively, "we have no reason to believe he isn't honest. And fair."

"Maybe," Laney retorted. Her voice was stronger now, but the wind had picked up, as had the crashing of the nearby waves. Jason had to move closer to hear her. "He seems like a nice enough man. But what do we really know? Being a philanthropist is easy when you're loaded. His daughter's death clearly affected him, but we don't know how, not really. What if he's the type who throws his money around to control people?"

Her eyes sparked with fear again, and her voice quavered. "What if he tries to control *me?* To force me to be someone I'm not?"

A streak of lightning split the sky. Both Jason and Laney turned their attention to the horizon, and after another moment, they heard and felt a rumble of thunder.

"Isn't lightning unusual on the coast?" Laney asked, her voice suddenly steadier.

"Yes," Jason answered. "I've never seen it fork quite like that before. Not here anyway." *And what fortunate timing it had.* One more second of watching her chin tremble, and he would have earned another shove.

"Listen to me, Laney," he urged, turning her to face him. He intended to continue holding her arms, gently, but found he couldn't do it. Her wet raincoat wasn't enough to buffer the strange, searing heat that shot through him at their touch. He dropped his hands, not trusting himself.

"I see what you're up against," he continued earnestly. "I get it. But you don't have to deal with this alone. *Nobody* should have to deal with something like this alone. I'm no private detective, but I'm sure I can help you figure out what the Tremblays are really like. I have at least one more call to make, I've just been waiting till a decent hour. Why don't we go back inside and I'll get started?"

Her clear blue eyes studied his thoroughly, searching for something. He wasn't sure if she found it or not. He wasn't sure what he was feeling himself.

"You can go inside if you like," she said quietly. More distantly. "I appreciate your help very much. But I'd like to stay out here a while longer. Maybe take a walk down by the beach."

The rain was pelting now, and both the skies and seas were angry. Jason didn't know if she was crazy or if this was just a meteorologist thing.

Amazingly, she smiled at him. "Don't worry. I won't go anywhere near the water this time. I've learned my lesson about waves. And the tide is going out. I checked."

Jason tried to smile back. But he wasn't feeling it. The imprint of her hands on his shoulders, pushing him away, still stung. He wasn't used to being pushed away. He couldn't remember it ever happening before. He was too careful, too conscientious. Hell, he was the one pushing women away from him!

A rush of anger threatened. He hadn't crossed the line with her physically; he knew he hadn't. And she couldn't read his mind. So why? If she trusted him enough to share her deepest secret, why was the thought of being more than friends so violently disagreeable to her?

"Suit yourself," he replied, more stiffly than intended. He faked a smile as penance, then turned back toward the lodge. "I'll get started on those calls."

Chapter 23

Laney felt something cold and looked down at her feet. She had stepped in a sandy puddle of rain or seawater — probably both. Her shoes were soaked through again, and she should chastise herself appropriately. But she was already too angry — and felt like too much of a fool — for one more act of stupidity to matter. She stepped out of the puddle, moved higher up the beach, and continued her aggressive stomp through slightly drier sand.

She didn't know what had happened. She thought a good walk in the rain would help her figure it out, but so far it wasn't working. One second she'd been holding herself together just fine, forcing out the last details of her sorry story. Then Jason had given her a friendly hug. She suspected that he could see her trembling, which would have fired off his protective male instincts. Her tendency to shake when she was cold or uptight was a nervous habit of longstanding; it didn't mean that she was falling apart. Nevertheless, she had accepted Jason's gesture in the spirit it was intended: a hug between friends.

Then all hell had broken loose. From where her head rested on his shoulder, her lips were inches from the warm, smooth skin that stretched over his collarbone. All of a sudden she could think of nothing but closing that distance — pressing her lips to that tantalizing triangle of flesh, sampling the smell and the feel and the taste of him. She imagined her mouth moving farther, kissing his neck, his jawbone, his cheek. Then her lips would meet his, and she would realize he was kissing her back, his desire just as mad, just as hot, just as insanely all-consuming as her own. He wanted her too, right there, right then. Absolutely nothing could stop it from happening...

And then she'd shoved him away. Yes, *shoved* him! She hadn't intended to push him away, certainly not as forcefully as she did. He hadn't done anything wrong, hadn't encouraged her sudden attack of lust in any way. What she had done was rude, uncalled for, and unforgivable!

It was also impossible to explain. *Excuse me, Jason, I know you were only trying to be nice, but it's just that I had this weird, overwhelming urge to totally do you right there on the deck and I really wasn't sure I could control myself.* Oh, yeah. That would go over great. Particularly with the cringeworthy "I'm really flattered, but I think we should just be friends" speech he would have to force out afterwards.

She turned her face to the wind and groaned out loud. As if she didn't have enough problems without thoroughly embarrassing herself! Jason had been crystal clear in his messaging. He wanted to be her *friend.* He had a *date* with somebody else, *last night.* She knew better than to fantasize about a man who wasn't interested. More galling still, even if he was interested in her, she wasn't interested in him! He was a player, for God's sake. He would be nobody's boyfriend, not for long anyway.

Her steps slowed slightly. Her previous relationships had all been exclusive and long term, and they'd all been failures. Could she not do the standard millennial thing and just dabble with a man for a while, no strings attached? She tossed the idea around in her mind. Then she grudgingly discarded it. Maybe she could consider such a thing with some man, someday, but not with Jason. He had been with another woman just *hours* ago, for God's sake! She couldn't and wouldn't take that. Some women didn't care, but she wasn't one of them.

As if it matters anyway, she thought with new anger at herself. *When he doesn't want you.* Not for a serious relationship *or* a one-time hookup!

Her steps halted. She had reached a rocky outcropping where the boulders met the sea. She could either forge a path all the way up into the forest to get around the rocks, or she could do the intelligent thing and turn around now. She chose the intelligent thing.

Avoiding Jason any longer would accomplish nothing. She'd needed some time to get her head together, and she'd had it.

There would be no further apology from her; forgetting her freakout had ever happened would be less awkward for both of them. There could be no backtracking on accepting his help, either; she was already in too deep. Besides which, she couldn't bear the thought of losing his friendship. She enjoyed his company far too much for that, never mind needing his help.

She just had to stop thinking about him *that* way. Which meant no touching. No matter the intent, if her sex-starved body couldn't handle any kind of contact — which it clearly couldn't — then there would be none. If tempted, she would simply start thinking about his other women. That would help.

She trudged back to the beach below the lodge, barely cognizant of the storm's rising intensity. As she mounted the steps she could see Jason sitting on the deck above, looking perfectly at ease in his hooded jacket, newly acquired rain pants, and wellington boots. She mounted the stairs and walked toward him, conscious of moving neither too fast nor too slow.

Keep it cool, idiot.

When she reached the deck, he put a hand under his chair and pulled out a second pair of boots and a folded pair of rain pants. "Here," he offered. "If you're going to storm-watch like a local, you're going to need the proper gear."

Laney accepted the offering. "Where did this come from?"

He shrugged. "They're loaners from the storeroom. I keep a variety of raingear around, for guests who don't know better." His lips curved into a smirk. "And for meteorologists."

She smirked back. "Thanks. I'm already wet now, but I'll put them on next time I go out." She stowed the gear under her own chair and sat down.

Neither of them said anything for a moment. She was tense. He seemed as though he were about to speak, and she couldn't decide which she wanted to hear less. A gentle lecture about how selfish she was being in not rushing over to tell the poor, decent Tremblays the truth? Or his polite assurance that her shove was unnecessary because he thought of her as a little sister?

She wished she could crawl under her chair with the rain

boots.

"I've found out something else," he said finally. "About Gordon and Joan."

Laney released a pent-up breath. More data sharing, she could deal with. "Thank you," she praised. "I'd love to hear it."

He sat up and moved his head closer to hers. The wind was gusting; if he didn't move he would have to shout. "You said that Joan had been involved with Children's Aid in the past, so I thought there might be a chance she was involved in a similar charity locally. I know a woman who does child advocacy; she's the one who got me started running free surf lessons for kids in foster care. She's familiar with all the children's charities around here, so I asked her if—"

"You do free surf lessons for foster kids?" Laney exclaimed. She hadn't meant to interrupt, certainly not to sound so surprised. But she was.

"Sure," he replied. "It's not all me — it's a team effort. I coordinate and provide the gear. The volunteers aren't professional instructors, but they're all skilled surfers and they're great with the kids. One guy even brings his dog to ride along on the board. They love that."

"I bet," Laney replied, noting the sparkle in his eye. He enjoyed working with kids. She wouldn't have guessed that. She supposed there was a lot she didn't know about him.

"Anyway," he continued. "Becky *has* heard of Joan Tremblay. Apparently Joan has a long history of volunteer work with children's causes, both here and in Toronto. Becky hasn't met her, but she knows people who have, and they all speak highly of her. Apparently, she's a real dynamo."

Laney's emotional reaction to this information was as confused as it had been with Gordon. Charity work of any kind was admirable. But in and of itself, it was no proof that a person was *nice*. Executive wives of Joan's generation were expected to perform noble deeds just to keep up appearances. She could still be a total shrew.

"Becky said something else, too," Jason added. "She

remembered reading an article about the Tremblays recently, something that was printed in the newsletter of one of the charities she works with. She didn't save her copy of it, and they're not published online, but she was pretty sure the library kept such things on file in the community archive. She said it was a story about Gordon and Joan taking a bunch of kids out for the day on their fishing boat last summer. And she said it had pictures."

Laney swallowed. She had yet to see a picture of any of Jessica's relatives besides her uncle. Not even the Macdonalds' obituary had included one. She suspected that if she invested enough time, she might eventually find a black and white of Gordon standing in the midst of a bunch other suits at some board meeting or other. But she hadn't dug that deep.

Accumulating biographical data was one thing. Looking into a human face was another.

"What are you afraid of, Laney?" Jason asked gently, leaning closer still.

Stop that. Please. His empathy, his kindness, his newly revealed fondness for unclehood and foster children — how could she keep him at a safe distance when the more she knew about him, the more she liked?

"I mean, I know what you have to be afraid of legally," he continued. "But how do you feel about the truth coming out? I can't tell if you're looking for assurance that the Tremblays won't make your life more difficult, or if you're hoping to find some justification not to tell them."

She chuckled ruefully. "That's because I don't know myself."

Jason let out a breath. "That's understandable. But listen. I—" He made a move as if to touch her, but stopped himself. He wouldn't want to give poor, pathetic her the wrong idea, would he? "You've had to deal with an incredible amount of truly soul-wrenching stuff, here. And all in a very short time. Maybe it would be better if you slowed—"

Laney didn't want his sympathy. She couldn't take it. In the last few, horrific months she'd had enough sympathy from enough people to last a lifetime.

"I came here to figure out the right thing to do and get it over with," she broke in defensively. "And that's what I'm going to do. Taking a week to sob on your shoulder, wrap myself in a fuzzy blanket, and drink warm soup won't help a thing. It will only delay the inevitable." Her mind cast a beguiling image of Jason wrapped up in the same blanket, but she squelched it.

She attempted a smile. "I know you're concerned about my mental health, and I appreciate that. I'm well aware that I look and act and sound like a total wreck. But I promise you, I'm fine." She pulled the rain gear out from under her chair and stood. "Would you be willing to drive me to the library? If we hurry, we can be back in time for me to take over your afternoon shift at the desk."

The look he returned was all over the place. Sympathy, understanding, aggravation. At one point she was sure he was about to argue with her, but in the end his expression calmed. "Fine," he replied, standing.

They walked back into the building, and Laney excused herself to make a quick change of clothes. She wouldn't have balked at jumping straight in his car, wet sneakers and all, but she felt a need to demonstrate some capacity for self-care. She put on several layers of warm, dry clothes, topped them off with the rain pants and jacket, then pulled on the boots. They fit perfectly, which gave her pause. Jason must have paid attention to the size of her feet.

She wasn't sure how she felt about that.

She shrugged it off and headed back out to meet him. They were in his car and pulling back out onto the highway when her phone alarm sounded. "Oh," she remarked as she dug into her bag. "That means it's time to call my great-grandmother. Midafternoon is best for her, but I keep forgetting about the time change. Do you mind?"

"Of course not," he answered, seeming distracted by his own thoughts.

Laney located the phone and turned off the alarm, then

noticed that she'd missed a call. Aunt June had tried her earlier, then left a text instead, asking Laney to call her back. "I, uh... better call my aunt first, actually," she revised. She dialed the number with a renewed sense of panic. Something was almost certainly wrong.

June answered on the second ring. "Oh, hi honey. Thanks for calling me back."

Laney knew that fake happy voice. "What is it? What's wrong?"

"Now, take it easy, sweetie, it's nothing terrible. Your Gran's all right, health-wise. She's just been having a tough time the last day or two, and I've talked to her care manager and they've asked me to speak with you about something."

Laney's bad feeling got worse. She'd been trying to call her Gran regularly, but she'd only managed to connect with her twice since the accident, and neither conversation had gone well. Gran didn't seem to understand who she was, and Laney's attempts to explain only agitated her. "What's that?"

June exhaled heavily. "Now, I don't want you to take this personally, honey, because we all know you aren't the problem. It's the disease. But the truth is that for whatever reason, talking to you on the phone seems to upset your Gran. They say she gets all anxious and starts wringing her hands and pacing and spouting off all that hellfire nonsense that she started with at the funeral. It has something to do with Christi and her confusing the two of you... they can't make sense of it, and they can't talk sense into her either. Yesterday it got so bad, with her crying and carrying on, that they had to sedate her — they were afraid she might try to hurt herself."

Laney's blood ran cold. No one else might understand what May was thinking, but she did. Gran felt guilty. Guilty for her own role in the deception, and guilty that she hadn't been able to save Christi from an eternity of fire and brimstone. How tormented Gran's poor mind must be!

And any mention of Laney only made her feel worse.

"So, what they've suggested," Aunt June continued miserably, "is that you might not want to call her for a while. Just for a few days, to see if she calms down a little. Then we'll see. I'm so sorry, honey."

"Don't be sorry," Laney insisted. "It's not your fault. I understand. I won't call until you tell me otherwise." She forced herself to change the subject, to keep her aunt talking about grandsons and snowfall and television before drawing the conversation to a close. Her diversion had the desired effect: June forgot to ask if Laney remembered why she drove to Canada.

She hung up the phone, returned it to her purse, and stared at the rhythmic motion of the wipers on the windshield. No sooner had one layer of drops been swept away than another replaced it, creating successive ripples across the glass. The storm must have been raging throughout her call, but she hadn't been aware of it. Jason said nothing to her and she didn't look at him. Her eyes filled with tears.

She didn't want him to see.

Chapter 24

Jason drove along the hilly streets of Tofino, grateful that his familiarity with the town precluded the need to read road signs. The rain was pelting so heavily he could barely see three feet before the bumper, and driving took all his concentration.

Laney said nothing. She hadn't said a word since ending the phone conversation with her aunt, and he had no need to ask her why. June was a loud talker. Even with the rain, he'd heard nearly every word. And although he wanted very much to pull the car over and take Laney into his arms, he resisted the urge. Partly because, after the incredible sensation he'd experienced the last time, he was wary of his own response. But also because, when she was fighting so hard to keep herself together and appeared to be winning the battle, he was loath to interfere.

He maneuvered his car to the far side of town and pulled up beside the square, blue-painted wooden building that housed the town's modest library. "This is it," he announced, seeing her make no reaction to the car's being parked. "Would you like to go in with me, or just wait here? I can make a copy for you."

Laney woke up. "No, of course I'll go in. And we'll make a copy, too."

He smiled, having to give her credit. Her voice sounded perfectly normal, and aside from a mild redness around the lids, her eyes showed no evidence of the tears she'd been fighting. They dashed through the rain to the door, which Jason swung open. Then they stomped and shook the excess water off themselves over the doormat. "I'm afraid it's a pretty small library," he explained. "It's underfunded; the town's been waiting on a new building forever. But the staff do a good job, especially with the local stuff, and that's all we need."

He approached the small counter and was pleased to see Ned Wu, the retired schoolteacher who served as the main librarian.

His younger assistant wasn't someone Jason cared to run into with Laney along. Not that he was self-conscious about his exes. He worked hard to make sure that his relationships ended cordially, with no misunderstandings or hard feelings. Still, there was no point in rubbing Laney's nose in his history, was there?

"Hello, Mr. Buchanan," the librarian greeted him formally. "How might I help you folks today?"

Jason grinned. Ned reminded him of a cartoon superhero. At work he wore thick glasses and cardigan sweaters and spoke with perfect grammar. But in a wetsuit out on the ocean, he was a total badass. Jason explained what they were looking for.

"The fall newsletter," Ned said confidently, withdrawing a plain manilla folder from a metal file cabinet. He thumbed through it and pulled out a stapled set of pale yellow papers, once folded down the middle. "Here you are."

Jason thanked him effusively, then turned to Laney. The article they sought was on the first page. They stepped to the other side of the room and, since he could see Laney shaking again, he held out the paper himself where both could see it. The article was illustrated with a black and white photograph of the retired couple and three children standing on the deck of a fishing boat. Gordon was a large man, imposing in both height and posture, with a full head of what was probably snow-white hair, light eyes, and a practiced smile. Joan, who looked like a midget beside him, had slightly darker hair pulled back tight. She wore large round sunglasses that obscured her eyes, and she wasn't smiling. She had one arm wrapped protectively around a child of about five who clung to her leg and was attempting — successfully — to hide his or her face from the camera. Two elementary-age boys stood to either side of the couple, each holding a decent-sized fish and beaming from ear to ear. *A Day to Remember* the headline read. Jason scanned through the caption, which named the couple but not the children, and the first page of the article, which described a number of summer outings but offered no new information on the Tremblays.

He looked at Laney. She was absorbed in the picture, her

brow furrowed in concentration. She said nothing, but she continued to tremble. He waited another few moments. "I think there's more inside," he suggested, lifting the bottom corner. She nodded, and he flipped two pages to the story's conclusion. Another smaller picture showed the boat's bridge, where a smiling boat captain looked on as a grinning girl of eight or nine brandished the wheel. Jason scanned the remainder of the article, which described the Tremblays only as "longtime volunteers" with the organization. Evidently, the couple had been living or vacationing in Ucluelet for a while now.

He turned back to Laney and found her staring thoughtfully into space. "I'll make a copy," he announced, and then did so. After returning the article to the Clark Kent version of Ned, he led a zombified Laney back outside to the car.

Mercifully, the rain was easing up. "So, what did you think?" he asked before turning the key in the ignition. It was a lame question, but he felt a strong need to reassure himself that she was still alive.

She snapped to attention and cleared her throat. "I couldn't tell much," she offered, her voice nearly normal. "Their faces were so small and grainy. But the kids looked happy."

"Yes, they did, didn't they?" Jason agreed.

"It didn't help," Laney said abruptly. She turned toward him. "I still don't know what I should do. And I'm beginning to think that nothing I hear or see or read about them is going to be enough. That I'm going to have to meet them."

He smiled at her encouragingly. He could see that she found the prospect terrifying. But she wouldn't let that stop her. "Well, I have good news on that score. I know the captain who was with them. His name is Max Tollison, and he owns the boat shop down by the harbor in Ucluelet. He does sales, charters, repairs — you name it. Been in business forever. I'm willing to bet he and Gordon know each other."

Laney's face was pale, but she appeared encouraged. "You know Max pretty well?"

He felt a flush of warmth. It felt good to be useful to her. "I do. Well enough, anyway."

"You think he could help us set up some kind of covert meeting?"

"I can try." Jason would make it happen if it was the last thing he did. Looking in her eyes now, so fearful and optimistic at the same time, made his chest ache. He understood where she was coming from. If she found out that her grandparents were good people, she would feel obligated to return their granddaughter, at the cost of losing herself. If they were not good people, she would feel a whole different kind of hurt. She might keep her legal identity, but her unwelcome knowledge would be a heavy burden to carry... forever.

Jason checked his watch and started up the car. She didn't ask where they were going and he didn't explain. He just drove to one of his favorite hangouts and opened the door.

"Why are we here?" Laney asked, looking up at the craftsman style wooden inn on the corner.

"Because it's lunchtime," Jason replied. He jogged around the car and opened her door, chivalry backlash be damned. "A bowl of warm soup may not solve a problem, but it does make a person feel better. Particularly when it's Tofino chowder. Come on. My treat."

She frowned at him. "I have canned soup at the lodge."

"Well, I don't," he insisted. "Indulge me. Please? If you like, I can add your portion of the bill to your lodge tab."

To his surprise, she smiled crookedly and got out of the car. "No, you won't. Liar."

He grinned back at her. "Busted."

The rustic restaurant and bar was famous for its brunch, and they settled into a cozy table on the second level with an impressive view of the Clayoquot Sound. A gas fireplace flickered nearby, and Laney watched with interest as the rain slowed and a patch of brighter sky opened up over the water. "It's beautiful here," she said dreamily. "Even when it's wet."

Jason's heart beat entirely too fast. Her words excited him. For whatever reason, he wanted her to love Tofino as much as he did. He wanted her to come back when she was healed and learn to surf. He wanted to be the one to teach her. He wanted— "Are you guys ready to order?" a cheerful male voice asked.

Jason looked up at their waiter, a younger surfer he knew well. Half the wait staff in town were surfers eking out a living for the sake of their next ride. It was a scene he'd been a part of himself once. "Almost. What'll it be?" he asked Laney.

She surveyed the menu skeptically, which amused him. Dungeness crab, charred octopus, and fried squid were probably not on the menus of her usual midwestern haunts. But when she raised her cute little chin, she had an adventurous sparkle in her eye. "I'll take whatever's the most uniquely local."

Jason's body temperature edged up another degree. He really, *really* liked this woman. "The lady will have the seaweed salad," he said loftily, smiling. "And a bowl of Tofino chowder. Same for me."

Much to his delight, Laney seemed both willing and able to take a temporary break from her weightier thoughts. As they waited for their food, they talked of other things. Of college past and friends present, islands and plains, burgers and streaming movies, and of course — surfing. She seemed fascinated, not just with the sport or the intricacies of its forecasting, but with the entire culture built up around it. Nearly everything about Tofino was foreign to her, but rather than being intimidated by its differences, she seemed energized by them. Listening to her describe her previous, unsatisfied longing to see the ocean, he realized that the shell-shocked woman he'd come to know in the last few days was only a dim reflection of her usual self.

He wanted to see her whole again.

"Here you go!" the waiter announced cheerfully, setting their food before them. As soon as he'd left, Laney inspected her first course as if it were a lab specimen.

"I've been noticing the seaweed on the beaches," she said. "It varies in appearance at different places, but all of it looks like some gourmet salad to me. It's not bright green and stringy like you'd think, but so... leafy. And all the colors! Deep greens, reds, purples, even orange. I couldn't help thinking it looked edible, or at least it should be. But this—" she pierced a bumpy, brownish-green leaf with her fork "—this doesn't look familiar."

"It's bull kelp," Jason advised.

Her eyes widened. "You mean those giant rod things with the big balls on the ends?"

Jason laughed. "Yep. It's made from the blades."

Laney stuffed a forkful into her mouth, savored a moment, and grinned. "I like it," she announced. "The seasoning makes it, don't you think?"

Jason did. They moved on to the soup. Laney seemed to find the chowder, with its combination of fish, clams, potatoes, and leeks, equally appetizing, and by the end of the meal, Jason realized he couldn't remember ever enjoying a woman's dinner company more. It hadn't been a date, nor had it felt like one. There had been no superficial, overly happy chitchat. No forced, nervous giggles. There was plenty of laughter, but all of it had been genuine. Laney had made no effort whatsoever to impress him. The contrast with his usual dates was beyond refreshing. Besides which, she was not only interesting to talk to, she was just plain *fun*.

Unfortunately, the meal had to end. And no sooner had the two of them returned to the car than she appeared to lift own her temporary reprieve. "We're late," she said worriedly, looking at her phone. "I was supposed to start working the desk for you at noon."

Jason sighed. He wasn't sure where she got that idea, since his hours varied depending on the scheduled check-ins. He explained that his first new lodger wasn't expected until two, but she did not seem mollified. As they rode out of town and back to Chesterman Beach, he could feel the weight of her worries descending on her like a fog.

"When do you think you might be able to contact the boat captain?" she asked.

"I'll call him this afternoon," Jason promised. As much as he wanted to help end her torture, he dearly wished she'd called a longer timeout.

He had just parked the car back at the lodge when his phone rang with the low moan of a whale song. He got text alerts almost constantly, but he'd assigned this particular ringtone to Ben's number so he wouldn't miss it. "Wait a minute," he said as Laney placed her hand on the door handle.

He scrolled through a series of incoming texts. "Ben's found out something about the endowment. He says it was actually made in the names of all three of them: Gordon's daughter, son-in-law, and granddaughter. The funds were earmarked for research into early warning systems, specifically on the 'detecting, monitoring, and forecasting of tornadoes and hurricanes through improvements in radar technology and computer modelling.'"

"Computer modelling," Laney repeated. "That's what I do."

"It sounds like you and Gordon had similar reactions to the same tragedy," Jason observed.

For a moment she seemed lost in thought. "Jason," she said quietly. "Have you ever heard about the tornado in Joplin, Missouri?"

He looked up from his phone. "Yes, but I don't know much about it, except that a lot of people died."

"A hundred and fifty-eight people," she said heavily. "It was an EF5 multiple vortex, nearly a mile wide, and it destroyed almost a quarter of the city. The sirens went off twenty minutes before it struck, but not enough people paid attention. There was confusion over what the sound meant: Was a tornado imminent or just possible? How close was it, really? So people went about their business and hoped for the best. Just like they did in Peck." She paused, then inhaled deeply. "You asked me once why I went into meteorology, but I didn't really explain. The day the tornado hit Joplin was their high school graduation day. A couple hours away, it was also my graduation day. We learned what had happened just after the ceremony. Several of my classmates had friends or family there. One girl lost her aunt, her grandfather, and a baby cousin. I'd always been fascinated with tornados and weather, but that day cemented my career goal. I was going to fix the system. I was going to figure out how to keep people safer."

Jason drew in a breath. He'd never considered that Laney might have lived through other tornados in her youth, much less had any connection to the horror in Joplin. "That's an admirable goal."

She smiled a little. "Well, they fixed the warning system without waiting for me, thank goodness. The meaning of the sirens is communicated more clearly now, including a new designation for a 'tornado emergency' that tells people to take cover right away, in no uncertain terms. But prediction can always be improved. In fact, there's some research coming out of UVic right now — a professor there has been making great strides with stochastic models. I was just thinking that maybe Gordon's money has been partly responsible for that." She looked up suddenly. "Sorry, too much information."

"No. Not at—" Jason's phone made the whale song again. He looked down. Ben had sent an image. It looked like the cover of a program or leaflet announcing the endowment, and it featured a full-color photograph of the family being honored. "Laney," he whispered roughly. "I think you should see this."

He handed her the phone.

Chapter 25

Laney stared at the image on Jason's phone for a very long time. She felt vacant. Drained. Bloodless. Yet at the same time, somewhere painfully deep within her chest, a queer heat had begun to kindle.

Three people had sat for the studio picture. A man and woman in their late twenties and a baby a few months old. The baby, lying on her mother's lap, wore a beautiful white dress covered with delicate pink rosebuds. Her head was capped with a fuzz of indeterminate brown; her eyes were squinched nearly shut. To Laney, she looked like any baby. No recognition stirred. She felt no sense of connection.

The man was standing with one arm curled possessively about his wife's shoulders. He was of average height, lean, and dressed in a style Laney thought of as "ivy league preppy." Bookishly handsome, he had straight dark-blond hair, kind brown eyes, and a winning smile. Laney let her eyes linger on his pleasing features, studiously avoiding a more direct examination of the woman seated beside him.

Eventually, she drew in a breath and forced her eyes toward the face in question. Elizabeth Tremblay Macdonald was smiling. More accurately, she was beaming. Her bright blue eyes and rosy apple cheeks radiated pure joy. She looked as happy as any wife and young mother could be.

She also looked like Laney. They had the same light-blond hair, the same scant eyebrows, the same high cheekbones and pert, slightly upturned nose. Elizabeth had a cleft in her chin, which Laney did not. She also looked older, in an undefinable, accumulated wisdom sort of way. And she was dressed not in jeans and a sweatshirt but in a tailored dark-green dress that had probably cost as much as Laney's entire wardrobe.

The resemblance was, nevertheless, remarkable. One might

even say uncanny.

Laney had no idea how long she sat and stared. How long her mind chugged with racing, contradicting, agonizing thoughts. But at some point, she handed the phone back to Jason. "Maybe trying to meet with Gordon and Joan isn't such a good idea after all. They might notice..." The quaver in her voice was maddening, as was the moisture once again building behind her eyes.

"Oh, who am I kidding?" she said with a strangled laugh. "We both know that all I've really been doing since I got here is looking for an excuse to turn around and go back home! I don't want to tell them. I don't want to give up my life. I don't want to be vulnerable to them, dependent on them. I never want to be dependent on anyone! But nothing we've found out gives me any excuse *not* to tell them. They seem like perfectly nice people who loved their daughter very much. Why would they not want to know the granddaughter who looks just like her? Their only grandchild?"

"They would," Jason said softly, sympathetically. He was sitting on the other side of the car and made no move to touch her. That was her fault, too. They had agreed to be friends, but after she'd shoved him away for no reason, why should he risk offering comfort again?

"I have to tell them the truth," she continued, still struggling to stanch her emotions. "I just do. It's only fair to them, and I won't be able to live with myself if I don't. So I should get it over with. Whatever happens afterward, I'll just have to take it one step at a time."

Jason was quiet for a moment. "That's very brave of you," he said finally, his voice a husky whisper. "I know what you're risking, and it's no small thing. Don't you dare beat yourself up feeling like it's trivial, like you've been selfish even to consider keeping the status quo. None of what happened was your fault; you're as much a victim of circumstances as the Tremblays are. If anything, your position is worse because you're the one who's being forced to make this decision. And if it matters, I... well, I think you've handled all this amazingly well, Laney. You're a strong woman. I admire that."

She wanted desperately to look at him. To take comfort from the compliment, to accept a nourishing, friendly hug in the spirit intended. But she couldn't move her head. Looking into those gorgeous gray-green eyes of his would undo her.

"Thank you," she replied, putting a hand on the car door. "Now I really should get to work at the desk. Could you call Max, please? See about setting up a meeting? I have no idea how to do this. Maybe we should have him tell them that I'm... someone who knew their daughter when she lived in Tennessee. It's true, technically. Then when they arrive, maybe you—"

She looked at him, accidentally. But she held it together. Being in action mode always helped her feel stronger. "I'm sorry. I didn't mean to presume. Would you be willing to go in first, maybe break the news in stages? Seeing me might be a bit of a shock, and I... well, I don't want to make this any harder on them than it needs to be."

His smile was warm. "Of course. I'd be happy to. I'll call Max as soon as you're settled in at the desk."

"Thanks," Laney repeated. She opened her car door, got out, and was overwhelmed by yet another fierce, infuriating desire to cry — exceeded only by an even fiercer desire to scream out loud. Would she never be rid of these insufferable attacks of raw emotion? Why did Jason's kindness to her only seem to make them worse?

With a mighty effort, she steeled herself against both impulses and stomped away toward the lodge. The sooner this unreal chapter of her life was concluded, the better off she would be. The tears would stop as soon as her life got stable again. Predictable. Safe. Controlled.

Jason-less.

A flat, familiar landscape of brown and gray.

Jason gave Laney a brief tutorial on the lodge's check-in

procedure, installed her in his office, and stepped into an empty guest room. She didn't need to cover the desk for him, since no new arrivals were expected for at least another half hour. But since having something concrete to do seemed to make her feel better, he was willing to oblige. He picked up his cell phone and dialed Max Tollison's number.

Twenty minutes later, he hung up the phone with a sigh. Why could nothing about Laney's wretched situation be easy?

He walked back to the lobby with his feet dragging. There was no easy way to tell her. She would be upset and there wouldn't be a damn thing he could do about it — as usual. If they could just be clear on their status as friends, he could at least hold the woman when she needed him to. But no, despite their last discussion on the topic, things between them had only gotten more muddled. She was developing feelings for him, he could see it in her eyes. That meant she was vulnerable to being hurt by him, and adding more pain to her life was the absolute last thing he wanted. She wouldn't settle for a time-limited hookup, nor should she. And he couldn't promise anything else. Hell, he couldn't even promise to behave himself as a friend — not with the memory of her body clasped against him still searing his every thought. So what did that leave them with?

Nothing. That's what.

He reached his office door. He had no answers for their predicament, no plans for how to move forward. But he couldn't put off what he had to tell her. He opened the door to find her standing at the window, gazing out at the sea. The rain had abated, but the wind was still brisk. The trees bowed and swayed under its pressure, and impressive waves continued to crash against the rocks below, sending up plumes of frothy spray.

"No one's come in," she reported. "I swept some sand off the floor, though."

"Thanks," he replied. His voice sounded as down as he felt.

She noticed. Her eyes widened as she turned fully toward him. "What is it? What did he say?"

"Nothing terrible," Jason answered, attempting to lighten his tone. "It's just going to be a little complicated." He sat down on the wicker loveseat opposite the counter and gestured for her to join him.

"Just tell me," she demanded.

"Not until you sit down."

She didn't move.

"I've had to catch you in a dead faint twice now," he said wryly, changing tactics. "Can you give my back a break, please?"

She huffed out a breath and dropped down beside him. Their shoulders bumped only briefly before she straightened and pulled away, but the sensation still affected him. He wanted her closer. He'd desired many different women at many different times, but the effect Laney had on him was painful. Maybe it was because she was so different from his norm. Maybe it was because he knew he couldn't have her. Either way, he questioned how much more he could take.

"First, let me give you the good news," he began. "Max was happy to tell me all about the Tremblays. He and Gordon have been friends for nearly a decade, as I suspected. Back when Gordon was busy working and making money hand over fist, his favorite pastime was fishing on Lake Ontario. As a getaway, he and Joan would rent a place in Ucluelet, and he'd charter boats from Max to fish for chinook and halibut. The two men even made a few trips up to the Northwest Territories together. A couple years ago Joan decided she'd had it with the snow and cold, so they decided to leave Toronto altogether. They bought property on the harbor and built the house we saw yesterday."

He stopped and took a breath. Laney was watching him intently, drinking in every word. "Max had nothing but nice things to say about both of them. He said Gordon is smart as a whip, and though he can be autocratic, he has a reputation for being fair and aboveboard. He also, according to Max, has a real soft spot for kids. Joan has a long history of doing volunteer work with children's charities, and she and Gordon do a lot of that work together. He loves taking groups of kids out fishing on his boat, like we saw in the article. He's had a bunch of surgeries on his knees and has trouble walking long distances, but he's otherwise in good health. Joan has some lung issues that made winters in Toronto hard, but as far as I could tell, she's in reasonably good health, too. They're both around eighty, Max thought. He's met their son Richard, too, but only once. You were right about them having no grandchildren. He said..."

Jason paused. The hard part was coming. "Max knew about the tornado. He said that Gordon and Joan both had been greatly affected. After Richard was born, Joan had been told she couldn't conceive again, so Elizabeth's birth had seemed like a miracle. They absolutely doted on their daughter, her whole life. They were very pleased with her choice of husband, and when their granddaughter was born" — he looked at Laney and was relieved to see she still had color in her cheeks — "they doted on her, too. Max couldn't tell me much more because he said it was hard for Gordon to talk about. But Max did say that there were pictures of the family all over the couple's house. And that they usually took a cruise at Christmas, because Joan couldn't bear to be home around the holidays."

Laney made a sharp intake of breath, and her eyes began to water. Jason hated upsetting her, but he was too close to the end to stop now. "I told Max what we'd discussed, that I'd met a woman who'd known Elizabeth and wondered if she could speak with them. He wasn't sure if they'd want to meet with you or not. But he told me he couldn't help me right now, anyway." Jason braced himself. "Because the Tremblays aren't in Ucluelet. They live here most of the year, but in the winter Joan prefers a warmer climate. They left the beginning of December, and he isn't expecting them back until March."

Now Laney's face lost all color. "March?" she repeated weakly.

"I'm afraid so," Jason answered.

"Are they... in Florida?" she asked. "California?"

He shook his head. "Hawaii."

"Hawaii!" Laney exclaimed, jumping up from the loveseat. Jason had expected such a reaction. But although he hated to see

TOFINO STORM

her angry, at least her blood was pumping again. "I can't go to Hawaii! I couldn't afford to come here!"

"I know," he commiserated. "I'm sorry."

"Till *March?*" she continued to exclaim. "What am I going to do? This isn't something I can handle over the phone! I just... I can't! If I don't manage this right, if there's some miscommunication or something... they'll either think I'm a fraud and have me prosecuted or..." The anger left her as suddenly as it came. Her voice dropped to a croak. "If they say anything, make anything public, I could lose everything. If only I could meet with them face to face, talk to them, I'm sure that wouldn't happen. I'm sure I could make them understand."

"I think you're right," Jason agreed, rising also. "You should wait until you can talk to them in person. There's no chance they'll think you're a fraud then. I'm sure of it."

She stepped back to the window and began to pace. "If only I could convince them to come back here, just for a little while. Then I could—" She blew out a breath. "No. Nothing short of the truth would get them to do that, and I have to be with them when I tell them."

"Maybe it's best to wait, then," Jason offered, even as he questioned the statement. Having this hanging over her head for months would be torture.

Laney shook her head at him. "How can I wait? Right now, like you said, I'm legally an innocent victim. I didn't create the problem; I didn't know I was living with a false identity. But I know *now*. How can I go on signing checks as Laney Miller? Signing legal documents to probate the will of a woman I'm not even related to? Reentering the US on a falsified passport? If I keep quiet and do all those things for another three months, it will make me a part of the fraud!"

Jason swallowed. She was right. He was no lawyer, but it certainly seemed like it would complicate her case if she waited until after inheriting her mother's estate to admit she was somebody else. "Then you'll have to go to Hawaii," he decided. "Forget about the money. You can borrow it from me."

She let out a groan. "Thank you for that, Jason, but I can't borrow something I can't pay back. The reality is I may never get the inheritance, or the money from the house, or even my mom's car. God only knows how many thousands I'll wind up owing the hospital, on top of what I've already spent to get here. There's no money and Hawaii is crazy expensive! Not to mention I'd be all on my own breaking the news to them... they'd keel over with the shock." She sank back down onto the love seat and rubbed her face with both hands. "I'm sorry. I just need to think."

Jason had already been thinking. The idea came to him like a Christmas present, all wrapped up with a shiny red bow. He didn't know why he hadn't thought of it before.

"Laney," he said earnestly, sitting beside her again. "It might not be so impossible after all. Max didn't know where they were staying, but he did say they were on Maui. And I happen to know a place on Maui that we could stay for free. Ben already offered me his and Haley's condo — it's empty now, while they're in Victoria, and he said I could stay there anytime. As for food, well, you have to eat something wherever you are. The only cost to you would be the plane fare. And that's what credit cards are for." He pulled her hands away from her face. "You need to do this, Laney. There's no other way."

Her hands felt like ice. She looked at him incredulously. "We?"

Jason replayed the speech he'd just given. He supposed he had said that. He supposed he meant it. "Yes, *we*," he confirmed. "I've been wanting to surf in Hawaii for ages. As soon as Ben offered I knew I would make it happen, I just didn't know when. But this is perfect. He said the condo has two guestrooms and an extra bath and they let friends stay there all the time. They have some little cabins in Alaska they loan out to friends, too. That's the kind of people they are. You met Ben — if you told him the truth, you know he'd be happy to help you. He's captained whale-watching tours on Maui for years; I bet he knows every boat captain and charter business on the island. It really is perfect, Laney, don't you see?"

His heart was beating wildly. He and Laney together... on Maui. He could see that hot little body of hers in a bikini, sipping from half a coconut with a carefree smile on her face. He would love—

Wait. Was he crazy?

"Are you crazy?" Laney parroted. Her eyes were bright, her cheeks aflame. "You... You don't have to go with me. What—"

"I want to," Jason interrupted. "And yes, maybe I am a little crazy. But you know what? So are you. And don't deny it." He waited. He was making a leap of faith, but his confidence was absolute. There was the Laney he'd met, and there was the Laney who lurked beneath that trembling exterior. The real Laney was afraid of nothing, he knew it in his gut. She was headstrong, obstinate, thrill-seeking, and beautifully, fantastically impulsive... just like him. He was not imagining the ghost of a smile that flitted at the corners of her lips.

"Let's do this thing," he pressured shamelessly. "Hang the consequences. It's destiny."

Her perfect lips twitched once more. Then suddenly, amazingly, he was rewarded with a smile.

"Oh, hell," she whispered with a sigh. "Why not?"

Chapter 26

Laney fidgeted in her middle seat, wishing that the sleeping woman by the airplane window hadn't closed the blind, preventing her from studying the clouds. She hadn't flown very often, and never over the ocean. She also wished that the businessman in the aisle seat didn't have his earphones turned up so loud that she jumped every time something exploded in the idiotic movie he was watching. She couldn't concentrate well enough to watch a movie herself, much less read; nor could she talk to Jason, who was stuck in another middle seat four rows back. She had nothing to do but stare at the seatback in front of her and wrestle with her thoughts.

She still couldn't believe she was here, now, on a plane to Hawaii. It had all happened ridiculously fast, once Jason had explained her situation to Ben. Laney understood that the oceanographer/boat captain had no small amount of experience crisscrossing the Pacific on a budget, but still, he proved amazingly helpful — insisting they stay at his condo, vowing to find out exactly which boat Gordon fished on, and even finding an incredible last-minute deal on two one-way fares from Victoria to Maui. Laney had barely had time to decide what to pack and what to leave — much less what to think or how to feel — before she and Jason were throwing their bags in his car and heading off to the airport in the dark before dawn.

She regretted the timing, as the darkness had obscured her view of the wild mountains and old-growth forests in the center of the island through which they traveled first. The sun hadn't risen until they reached the island's more populated eastern shore, and none of the more picturesque areas of Victoria had been on their way to the airport. But how could she complain? She was going to Maui! Her debt would increase, but she truly didn't feel she had another choice. She'd just have to live off peanut butter and pineapple and pray for an equally cheap flight home.

She twisted in her seat to glance backward. She could not see Jason, and didn't know why she kept trying. He was there somewhere. Eventually, they would get a chance to talk. He had played loud music to keep himself awake while he was driving, then fallen asleep during their layover in Calgary. Apparently he had been up most of their already short night trying to work out staffing coverage for his various businesses. She hadn't wanted to bother him, but there were things she wanted to say. Again. She was determined that he not feel obligated to babysit her. He had wanted to go to Maui to surf, and she was determined that he should do that. He should enjoy a vacation worth his money, not waste his time on her problems.

Her head ached slightly, but she chose to ignore it. She'd been told that flying so soon after a concussion wasn't the greatest idea, but she'd been free of symptoms for two days now, and she'd done far stupider things. Like let herself fall for a man like Jason Buchanan and then consent to cohabitate with him in a condo in paradise.

She sighed with frustration. Being so close to him and not even touching would be sheer, raving torture, but she could see no better course of action. Her feelings for Jason ran deep already, never mind that all they'd ever done was hug. As tempting as it was for her to throw all caution to the wind and indulge in a mind-blowing, once-in-a-lifetime tropical sexcation, she knew how much she would suffer for it later. Her feelings for Jason would become even more intense, making it that much more painful for her to walk away from him.

And she would absolutely have to walk away. Because he wasn't offering her anything else. He hadn't even offered her a mind-blowing, once-in-a-lifetime tropical sexcation. Although a few times, lately, she'd gotten the feeling he might not mind...

After another highly counterproductive mental trip to la-la land, Laney gave herself a shake and forced her attention back to greater problems. Getting herself within hailing distance of

Gordon and Joan was only the first step in the mission before
her. She still had to reason out how a meeting could be arranged.
She and Jason had already decided that involving his friend Max
any further would be a bad move, because if Gordon's first
perception of her was that she had pursued him across an ocean,
it would make her motives seem nefarious. Far better for him to
think that Laney and her traveling companion had run into him
accidently while on vacation. She could explain the whole story
later, after she'd revealed her true intent.

Assuming they're still listening, rather than calling 911...

Laney clenched her teeth, determined to bury her negativity
and do this thing right. So, how could she manage it? Assuming
that Ben could find out where and how Gordon went fishing,
and perhaps identify a mutual friend to serve as a go-between,
what would Laney's message to the Tremblays be? How could
she convince them to meet with her?

She pondered the question for some time, considering and
then dismissing the idea she'd had before, of using Jason as a
front man. If a middle-aged friend of Elizabeth's really wanted
to meet the Tremblays, why would she send some young surfer
hunk to run interference? Even the slightest hint of deception
on her part would set the stage all wrong. Laney didn't want to
lie to or trick them. What she wanted was to tell them some part
of the truth. Enough to make them want to meet her, but
without any suggestion that their granddaughter could still be
alive. If they suspected anything near the truth, seeing her face
would be too much, too soon. She had to handle this
intelligently. Because if they thought she was out to get their
money, that she was trying to manipulate them emotionally—

Positive thoughts, she reminded herself as her pulse rate climbed.
Only positive thoughts! There had to be a way to do this. *Think,
Laney. Think!*

She thought. Then she thought some more. Eventually, she
smiled. She pulled her phone from the seatback pocket and
clicked into a notebook app. She would write them a letter.
Calling Gordon would be too intrusive, too personal. Sending an

email wouldn't be personal enough, and they might not even read it — the couple were pushing eighty, after all. But a handwritten letter they would respect. They would read it, and they would respond. They would have to.

Her thumbs flew as she composed her message. She would buy some decent paper at the airport and then recopy it in her best script.

Dear Mr. and Mrs. Tremblay,

Writing this letter is awkward for me, as I'm sure it will be for you to receive it. But my name is Laney Miller, and I grew up in the town of Peck, Missouri. Right now I'm staying with a friend here on Maui, and when I heard someone say you were here too, I knew I had to try and see you. I've tried to look you up before, because I wanted to contact the next of kin of the family from Tennessee who died so tragically in the Peck tornado. I'm sorry to say I wasn't able to follow through with contacting you then, but I hope to make up for it now.

I'm very sorry about what happened to your daughter, son-in-law, and granddaughter. I know it must have been terrible for you. I am guessing it was especially difficult for you that no one ever located your little granddaughter. The reason I'm writing is that I have some information about your granddaughter's possible resting place that I imagine you might want to know.

If it's possible, I would very much like to meet with you both in person while I am here. I promise I will not take up much of your time, but would appreciate having the opportunity to unburden myself of this information, which again, I apologize for not bringing to you sooner.

Thank you very much,

Sincerely,

Laney Miller

She would add a postscript to the bottom with the address of the Parkers' condo and her cell phone number. For good measure, she would add her home address in Peck as well. Using her real name would be essential to her letter passing the smell test, as the Tremblays might very well check her background before agreeing to meet with her. There was a chance they would connect her name to the "miracle baby" newspaper articles, but that was a chance she was willing to take. As she had discovered herself, local newspaper articles from the nineties were only discoverable through paid databases, not a simple internet search. Even if Gordon and Joan did go there, they'd have no reason to make the next fantastic leap. In fact, by alluding to information about Jessica's remains, she hoped to assure they would not. The far more plausible conclusion would be that she had grown up with a personal interest in the tornado and its victims, and was thus acutely aware of any local rumors or lore surrounding them.

She saved the document, put away her phone, and breathed out heavily. *Positive thoughts,* she reminded herself.

Everything will work out fine.

The plane bumped down onto the tarmac, jolting Jason awake. His heart began to race. Was he really on Maui? With Laney? He had been afraid it was all just a dream. But no… through the sliver of window available to him, he could just see the distant outline of jagged peaks in the moonlight. *Amazing.*

He turned on his phone and was immediately besieged by five hours' worth of accumulated texts. He scrolled past the various messages from acquaintance-women, quickly addressed those related to his businesses, and then opened up an impressive string from Ben. As announcements from the flight attendants boomed over the speakers, he read through the thread, his grin broadening as he went.

Ben Parker was worth his weight in gold. By making "a few calls," he had learned that Gordon Tremblay had leased a small, but well-appointed fishing boat for the duration of the winter from a local company owned by a man named Paul Kimball. Ben had known 'Pauley' for many years, and after being assured that Laney was a personal friend with no evil intent, Pauley had said he'd be happy to meet her and help her get in touch with Gordon. Ben added that Pauley was a fixture at the marina in Ma'alaea and could easily be found either on the docks or the nearby bar, depending on the hour.

Jason checked the local time. It was early evening. They'd have to drive through Ma'alaea to get to the condo anyway. Why not stop and look him up at the local watering hole? Laney would be pleased to have a game plan and a starting point.

He continued to smile to himself. He still couldn't believe he was here. He had always considered himself a lucky guy, but providence in this case was extraordinary. Had he reacted entirely on impulse, with no thought whatsoever to the pitfalls of traveling across an ocean with a woman he was insanely attracted to but couldn't possibly sleep with? He had. Did he regret it? Not a chance. He was happy to be here and happier still to be here with Laney. Tomorrow could take care of its own damn self.

He waited anxiously for his chance to deplane and caught up with Laney staring out the windows just past the jetway. "Look inviting?" he asked.

She turned to him with sparkling eyes and a gorgeous flush to her face. "I couldn't see anything out the plane windows, and it's too dark to see much now either, but it still looks amazing!"

Jason took in the sight of lighted taxiways and outbuildings, towered over in the distance by silhouetted volcanic peaks. "I have a feeling we'll see far better views than this," he said cheerfully. "Want to go find some?"

"Absolutely," she agreed, her eyes still shining with excitement. As they walked through the terminal toward baggage claim, he filled her in on Ben's news and she described the letter she'd written to the Tremblays. Her plan was inspired, and he was impressed with her cleverness. Every flash of the non-concussed, non-traumatized Laney he managed to see was more fascinating than the last, and he couldn't wait for the next surprise.

Once outside in the open air, they stopped at the same point beside a flowering bush and set down their bags. They laughed as each had the same idea: stretching out their arms to the warmth and breathing deeply of the moist, floral-scented air. Jason had changed into a fitted tee and shorts already, but Laney looked ridiculously uncomfortable in jeans and a long-sleeved thermal rolled up to her elbows.

Jason kept his eye roll to himself. She had remarked before they left that she had no summer clothes with her, but she refused to spend money buying anything new, even if they'd been able to find what she needed in Tofino in January. It was all he could do to get her to "borrow" a few things from the lodge's lost and found box, which was a sorry assortment indeed. Secretly, he planned to sneak off and buy her a few things at the first opportunity. If the weather stayed this hot, he might even convince her to wear them.

After a brief argument about how she was *not* paying for half the car he would have rented if he came by himself anyway, they were back to laughing over nothing, tooling through the lighted streets of Kahului with the windows down. They made a quick stop at a drugstore for Laney's letter writing supplies, but he could tell she was as eager as he was to leave the city behind. Both of them were anxious to get to the ocean, and neither could wait until the sun came up tomorrow, revealing the full spectrum of natural beauty that surrounded them.

When they reached Ma'alaea they turned towards the harbor, located the bar Ben had mentioned, and parked nearby. While Laney worked on her letter, Jason stepped outside and attempted to reach Pauley with the number Ben had provided. The phone went unanswered, but after Jason sent a brief explanatory text, he received a friendly invitation to walk right up. A few minutes later, he and Laney found themselves sitting at a small table outside the crowded bar and grill, listening to the chatty boatman expound on himself, Ben Parker, invasive fish, idiotic tourists, high taxes, and Gordon Tremblay, in that order. Pauley, who appeared to be around sixty, had the weather-beaten look of a man who'd spent half his life in the sun and would never regret a minute of it, no matter how many skin cancers he had removed.

"Yeah, Gordon's got one of the penthouse units, over that way," Pauley said, pointing vaguely down the beach from the marina. "Gorgeous place. Easy walk down to the slip. Gordon can't walk too far, you know. On account of his knees. But he's out on the *Journey* pretty much every day the weather's good. His wife goes with him too, a lot of days."

"Do you think he'll be out tomorrow?" Laney asked eagerly. "How does the weather look? I mean, for boating? I noticed the surf report's not great," she added to Jason as an aside.

Jason's heart warmed. So, she was checking out surf reports now, was she?

"Good enough," Pauley answered. "I'd imagine Gordon will be out, yes. He'll be leaving long before dawn though, hoping for a Bigeye. You said you had something you wanted me to give him? I'm sure I'll see him when he gets back, if not before."

Laney handed him her envelope. "That would be fabulous. Thank you."

Jason bought the man another drink, listened to a few more stories about the infamous Ben Parker and his 'brilliant lawyer wife,' and deflected several sales pitches before he and Laney headed back to the car for the final leg of their drive. Laney, having accomplished the first step in her mission in record speed, soon grew quiet and began to yawn. It was past midnight in Tofino time, and they'd had a very long day. By the time they reached the resort area on the western shore of the island, secured the key from the caretaker, and stepped inside the Parkers' condo, she seemed exhausted. But after turning on the lights and looking around, she quickly rallied.

"Oh, wow," she said breathlessly. "This place is... are we

seriously staying here for free?"

"We are," Jason confirmed, equally impressed. The condo was open and airy, set on the corner of a high-rise with floor to ceiling windows and a wrap-around lanai. When the sun came up, they would almost certainly have a spectacular view of the ocean in one direction and the mountains in the other. The furniture was modern, new, and high quality — far beyond the usual wicker beach vibe, and the whole unit featured a carefully coordinated palette of colors and was decorated with original art.

"All done to Ben's specifications, I'm sure," Laney teased.

Jason laughed. "Clearly." They both knew that Ben would be perfectly happy living in a tent on the beach, provided of course that his wife was there with him. The refined taste in evidence here would be Haley's.

"I'm almost afraid to touch anything," Laney murmured as she explored, finally setting her things in the extra bedroom with the feminine-looking sitting area. Jason put his stuff in the third bedroom, which was darker in tone, had more comfortable chairs, and looked like it doubled as a man-cave. "It was really nice of them to let us stay here," she said as she returned to the living room.

"Well, I did let Ben stay at my duplex for a weekend, you know," Jason replied. "I figure this is the least he can do."

Laney chuckled. "Right."

They smiled at each other, but after a moment, things grew awkward. It was quiet, and they were alone. Laney's previously shining face clouded, and she let her gaze drop. "We need to talk," she announced. "We should have talked before, but this trip just came about so fast." She sat down on one of the couches, tacitly inviting him to do the same.

Jason tensed. He didn't know what she was about to say, but he was certain he wouldn't like it. Not when she looked so unhappy. He picked out an armchair opposite her and sat down.

She made a lame attempt to smile. "It's just that, as much as I appreciate your making all this happen for me, I don't want you to feel like you owe me anything. You've never owed me anything — I'm the one who owes you. So please don't feel like you have to babysit me this whole time, no matter how much of a wreck I might be. I want you to enjoy this trip as if it were a solo vacation. I want you to go surfing and do whatever else you would do if I wasn't even here. Okay?"

Jason's jaw tightened. He respected her sense of pride and understood that she disliked feeling beholden. But her insistence on trying to turn their every interaction into some kind of business deal was maddening. "I thought we decided to be friends," he said, more stiffly than intended.

Her blue eyes widened. "We are," she said uncertainly. "But..."

"But what, Laney?" he interrupted. His tone still sounded sharp, but he couldn't seem to help it. "Don't friends do nice things for each other? Why is it so hard for you to accept a friendly gesture from me for what it is?"

Now her jaw tightened. She met his gaze levelly. "Because I don't know what it is, Jason. Your actions don't make any sense to me. Why would you even want to be my friend? I mean, don't get me wrong — I'm not down on who I am... normally. But, come on! The whole time you've known me I've been a friggin' hot mess! You're not interested in me romantically and you could get sex from any number of other women anytime. So, seriously," she threw up her hands. "Why? What are you getting out of this? What do you want?"

Her outburst left him speechless. He sat there, blinking back at her, for an awkwardly long time. She'd taken the most burning question in his chest — which he'd been doing a stellar job of avoiding — and thrown it right out in front of him. What *did* he want? All he knew was that he was here now, with her, because he wanted to be. He wanted her, period, exactly as she was. Stubborn, combative, constantly on the verge of falling apart, brave, trembling, whip-smart with ocean weather patterns, witty, secretly athletic, dressed in ridiculous-looking completely inappropriate clothes, wise to his tricks, loyal, and brutally honest. He wanted her by his side and he wanted her in his bed.

It didn't seem that complicated. Why did she have to make it that way? Could they not just roll along and see what happened without all the messy introspection?

He stood up. "I enjoy your company," he said brusquely, avoiding her eyes. "I don't see what's so surprising about that. We have a lot in common."

She stood up with him. "We do," she said more softly. "It's just that it feels one-sided. I get a chauffeur and a free condo and a shoulder to cry on, and you get the pleasure of my company. Woohoo. I just want to do something nice for you for once. Like making sure my problems don't totally bring down your vacation. Okay?"

"Sure," he said, still sounding miffed. What was wrong with him? More to the point, what was wrong with her? What made her so damn sure he wasn't interested in her physically or romantically, anyway? So he hadn't technically made a move on her. Okay. But she hadn't encouraged him either, and that didn't stop him from wanting her.

Why was he fighting so hard against his attraction anyway?

Oh, right. The forever girl thing.

Silently, he swore a blue streak.

"Listen, Laney," he said finally, managing at last to control his voice. "I think we both know what the problem is, here. We're coming from different places; we have different values. We want different things out of life. We're not compatible for anything besides friendship. So let's just focus on that. Okay?" He caught her eyes, but they were studying him so intensely he dropped the contact.

"Of course," she replied. Her own voice sounded resolute. "I agree completely. I'm glad that's settled."

"Me too." He walked into his bedroom, retrieved his wallet and keys, and returned with a totally fake smile on his face. "And now if you'll excuse me," he announced, "I'm going to indulge your request and do what I would do if I was here by myself. I'm going to take a walk, maybe check out the local bars. You need anything while I'm out?"

"Oh," she with surprise. He glanced at her just long enough to see that she looked hurt. Maybe a little angry. "No, I don't need anything. I'll probably just go to bed. That's good though. I'm glad you're getting out. Have a nice time."

"Thanks. I will." He made his way to the door. "Sleep tight." He stepped out and closed the door without looking behind him. There were other people waiting at the elevator, so he took the steps down. Eight flights later he still needed to move. He found a road and walked down it. He passed a half dozen other resorts and at least as many bars. A couple women flirted with him as they walked past. He wondered what would happen if he brought one of them back to the condo.

He could absolutely do that. The terms of his relationship with Laney were clear. They were friends sharing a space. She could be a guy friend or his sister. Who he brought back to his own room and what went on inside of it were his business. Laney shouldn't care. She wouldn't care. Nor would he care if she went out and brought back some—

Oh, hell no. That wasn't happening!

He reached the end of the sidewalk by the string of resorts and turned towards the water. At the beach he slipped off his sandals and walked barefoot in the sand.

Maybe Laney *would* care if he brought another woman home. He could have sworn she looked miffed when he'd said he was off to the bars. At a minimum, she'd looked hurt.

He felt a wave of remorse, but squelched it. She'd practically ordered him to do it! She was the one acting irrationally, not him.

A thirty-something woman was standing on the beach admiring the night sky. She was wearing a flesh-colored bikini whose outline was barely visible underneath a completely transparent sarong. She turned to him with a smile that dripped of invitation. Jason smiled back, then walked on past.

He was losing his mind. He could think of a hundred good reasons why he should follow up on the tacit offer and not a single reason he shouldn't. Except that he didn't want the woman. He wasn't sure why. He just didn't.

Laney *would* be upset if he brought a lover home. He knew it in his gut, logical or not. And if they were both going to be jealous of each other's paramours, what the hell kind of friendship did they have?

At the entrance to a complex full of shops and restaurants, he brushed the sand off his feet and slipped his sandals back on. Bright lights and loud voices drew him up the boardwalk. He saw a bar ahead and began walking toward it, but stopped short in front of a shop window. The mannequin in the display was wearing a sleeveless Hawaiian dress and sexy sandals. In his mind, Laney was wearing them. He had to supply certain details from his imagination, since the frumpy clothes she wore hid her assets. Luckily, Jason had an excellent imagination.

He would give anything to see her in that dress. Better yet, in a bikini of his choosing. His blood heated as he dwelt on the thought. How could he want a woman so badly when he'd seen virtually nothing of her body?

Jason didn't know. He didn't understand anything that was happening with Laney. But he was tired of overthinking. He was on *Maui*, dammit, and he intended to enjoy himself. He cast another glance toward the bar ahead.

He turned and walked into the store.

Chapter 27

Laney brushed her hair the next morning, resisting the urge to scratch at the annoying staples in her scalp. At least they only itched now, rather than ached, and her bruises were fading nicely. If it weren't for her pending hospital bills, she could almost forget that six days ago, she'd nearly died.

But she wouldn't forget. Not ever. Jason and Ben had saved her life, and now they were good friends. She would focus on that. *Friends.*

She stared at her reflection. The dark rings under her eyes were pathetic. She would conceal them if she could, but she had no makeup handy. Maybe Jason wouldn't notice, or at least wouldn't ask. Under no circumstances would she confess how many hours she'd lain awake, listening for him to return, telling herself it didn't matter if he brought another woman home. Wondering if he would sleep somewhere else altogether. Imagining exactly what was going on with him, every ticking second. She doubted she would have slept at all if the front door hadn't finally opened and closed with no noises indicative of female company. It seemed as though Jason had puttered about in the kitchen a minute, then gone straight to bed. But she had continued to toss and turn, regardless.

Now, she had a new day to face. And she was going to do that, sleep deficit or no. She opened the door to her room and crept out. There was no sign of life from Jason's room. If her shower and blow dryer had awakened him, he must have gone back to sleep. Relaxing a little, she headed for the kitchen. She had only taken a few steps before stopping in her tracks.

There, flung over the back of the couch, was a woman's dress. A pair of sandals sat on the floor beneath. She felt sick to her stomach. *So.* There was a woman in there with him. Right now. A very quiet woman, but a woman. Laney had been right to think the worst of Jason. He had actually gone out and picked up the first—

Her heart skipped. Was that... a price tag? She moved stiffly forward, extended a hand. Yes. The dress still had tags on it. So did the shoes. They were new. Brand new. And there was a sticky note attached.

Merry Christmas, Laney!

This is your belated gift. I'll get mine when you put it on and shut the hell up about it.

Fondly, Jason

Laney was glad she hadn't bothered with eye makeup, since whatever she had applied would now be smeared. The sounds of someone stirring filtered out from Jason's room, and she snatched up the dress and shoes and bolted back into her own.

Jason hadn't brought back a sex partner. He'd brought back a present. For *her!*

She heard the door to his room open. She froze in silence, feeling like a guilty child as she stifled a strong desire to sniffle. After a moment the door to the bathroom opened and closed. She released a breath, wiped the tears from her cheeks, and checked herself in the mirror. Good God, she looked horrible. Her eyes now had rings underneath them *and* were puffy and red! She had to get herself together. She took another look at the dress, then held it up in the mirror. It pretty much screamed "Hawaii." Spaghetti straps, a shapely, form-fitting top, and a flowy skirt, all in a beautifully understated floral pattern of bright hibiscus contrasting with a subtle dark background.

Could she wear it? She pulled it aside again to reveal what she was currently wearing. It was the best the lost and found box had to offer: a pair of navy women's track shorts and a promotional tee from a 2013 car cruise in Spokane. She huffed out a laugh. Jason was right. Not even a guy friend would want to stroll around a vacation paradise with a woman looking like that! Nor would a real friend refuse a gift that came from the heart.

When Jason emerged from the shower sometime later, Laney was standing out on the lanai with a freshly brewed cup of coffee in her hand. She heard him walking towards her and turned around with a smile. "Good morning! I made a whole pot," she said cheerfully. "The view from here is even more amazing than we imagined. I may never want to leave!"

Jason said nothing. He stood in the center of the room, wearing a stylish pair of shorts and a soft, bright-colored shirt that hugged his muscles to maximum effect. His adorably curly hair was still damp. His eyes were wide. His mouth — if not exactly hanging open — was not completely closed, either. After a long moment, he swallowed. "Merry Christmas," he said, a devilish smile playing on his lips. "To me."

Laney laughed, hoping she wasn't also blushing. He hadn't looked at her like that before. She shouldn't enjoy it so much now. But she *so* did. She raised her coffee cup, as if in a toast. "Merry Christmas to us both. And thank you."

"Thank you," he grinned back at her. She stepped to the railing, expecting him to join her on the lanai, where they could ooh and ahh together over the Parkers' unbelievable everyday view of white sand; dark blue, whale-filled waters; and striking islands on the horizon. But unexpectedly, he pivoted and disappeared back into his room.

When he reappeared a few minutes later, his eyes glanced over her only briefly before he poured himself a cup of coffee and then joined her at the lanai's patio table. "I have a text from Pauley," he informed her. "He says he saw Gordon early this morning and handed him the note."

Laney's happy mood crashed. The news wasn't bad; in fact, it was good. But she'd been doing a stunning job this morning of forgetting why she was here. It was easy enough to do when one's hair was blowing in a warm trade wind, with the sounds of fluttering palm trees and happy beachgoers echoing up from below. The sky was as blue as the ocean, with bright white cumulus clouds drifting high and harmless over the rippling waters and green mountains beneath. With the balmy air bathing her bare arms and shoulders, and the memory of the look in Jason's eyes warming up her insides, she was feeling like she'd stepped into heaven.

Now she was back. "I suppose Gordon could contact me any time after he gets back to shore then," she remarked. "If I'm lucky he'll want to meet soon. I don't want... I mean, it would be better for everyone if we can just get this thing resolved."

"Your letter was compelling," Jason encouraged. He still didn't seem to want to look at her. "I doubt you'll have to wait long. In the meantime, how would you feel about finding some breakfast? The coffee's great, but I'm starving. Besides, a little sightseeing would be a nice distraction while you wait, don't you think?"

Laney had no problem with that plan. She did have a problem with the continued awkwardness between them. At least now, the problem at hand was clearer to her. She might be a relative ignoramus where relationships were concerned, but she knew raw animal lust when she saw it. Jason *did* want her. The revelation both excited and further confused her. They had agreed that their values were incompatible. She assumed that was because he wasn't looking for a serious relationship, and he presumed that she was. But if he liked her as friend *and* he was attracted to her, why exactly was the prospect of a real relationship so daunting to him?

"I'd love to go sightseeing. And get breakfast," she said agreeably. "Whatever you'd like to do."

"Okay, then," he said, rising. "Let's do it."

She rose also. The sliding glass door onto the lanai wasn't open wide enough for both of them to pass through at once. Being closer to it, Jason could have gone through, but since he seemed to be waiting for her to go first, Laney — who was feeling unusually feminine in the Hawaiian dress — decided to indulge him. But somehow they got their signals crossed. Just as she moved forward, Jason stretched out a hand to open the door wider, the result of which was a bumbling collision of his arm with her chin. In reaction, she teetered backward and he swiftly took hold of her upper arms to steady her.

"Sorry," they said simultaneously, erupting in nervous laughter.

Laney could have stepped back then, but she didn't. Her bare arms tingled at his touch. Did he feel that? She wanted to know. Her eyes sought out his, and she was not disappointed. The gray-green orbs practically crackled with electricity. There was no doubt. He felt it, too.

She stepped closer, still keeping eye contact. Not quite touching. The air between them felt like an open flame.

Laney didn't think anymore. She closed the irritating distance, her arms clutching his waist, her lips pressing his. He resisted for all of two seconds before his own muscular arms pulled her tighter against him, deepened the kiss. The sensations he evoked were like nothing she'd ever experienced before. His touch was possessive, all-consuming, exhilarating. She lost track of anything and everything else in the world; she lost her friggin' mind. She had his shirt up his back and halfway off one shoulder before some tiny kernel of intelligent thought managed to weasel its way into her brain.

She stopped. With an audible groan of frustration, she tugged his shirt back down and pulled away.

He let her go immediately. For a long moment they stood still, only a few inches apart, staring at each other and breathing hard.

"Not a good idea," Laney whispered hoarsely.

"Not at all," he agreed. He stepped back and turned his head.

Laney couldn't seem to catch her breath. She appreciated his stopping when she did. But couldn't he at least try to talk her out of it? "So, why isn't it a good idea?" she asked. "I mean, from your perspective?"

Jason turned back to her. His face was flushed and sweaty. He looked impossibly gorgeous. "You know why, Laney. Because you're the kind of woman who plays for keeps. Casual hookups aren't your thing."

Anger sparked. "And what makes you so sure of that?" she

demanded.

"Am I wrong?"

Her cheeks pulsed with heat. How she would love to show him just how wrong he was! But she couldn't, dammit, because he wasn't wrong. "No, you're not," she said instead, her anger igniting. "I'm not interested in casual hookups, recreational sex, friends with benefits, or whatever else you choose to call it. How unfortunate for us both that that's the only thing you *are* into!"

Now his face reddened. "You don't know that!" he protested hotly.

"Am I wrong?" she shot back.

He made a move as if to answer, but stopped himself. He was breathing as heavily as she was. He also appeared just as angry.

"I thought not," she answered for him. "I knew you were a player the first time I laid eyes on you."

He had the audacity to look startled. "Now, wait a minute!" he fired back. "I am *not* a player!"

"Well, what do you call it then?"

His jaws clenched as he struggled to compose himself. "A player is a man who deceives women by making them think they're the only one, when they're not. I don't do that. I've never done that. Any woman I get involved with knows exactly what I'm offering. And what I'm not."

Laney was not appeased. "How noble of you."

"I'm telling you the truth!" he insisted. "Ask anyone in Tofino if you don't believe me!" He went quiet a moment. "Not that it matters," he finished gruffly.

As quickly as his anger had flared, it seemed to drain out of him. And as Laney reflected on his words for the first time, her own anger followed suit. He wasn't lying to her. Hadn't his ex at the coffee shop already said as much herself? *You're not his type... He knows you want a boyfriend.*

Laney wasn't being fair to him. He might not want what she wanted, but that didn't make him an unethical, insensitive jerk. Which is what she had effectively called him.

"I'm sorry," she said genuinely. "I do believe you. And you're right. You're not a player and I shouldn't have used that term. In any event, I've got no right criticizing your lifestyle. I apologize."

"It's all right," he said softly, his ready forgiveness only making her feel worse. "Your nerves have got to be on edge right now. We shouldn't—" He shook his head. "Any way you look at it, this is a bad time. Can we just go out and... well, see Maui?"

When he smiled at her again, the sight of her old friend Jason nearly crumpled her heart. If she didn't stop pushing, she would lose him altogether. She couldn't deal with that. She cared about him too much. Needed him too much.

"How about we forget the last half hour ever happened?" she suggested, her voice painfully weak. *Buck up, woman!*

His eyes were twinkling again. "Forgetting would be difficult," he said softly, leaving no doubt as to which part of the last half hour he was referring to. His voice dropped lower. "Impossible, actually. How about pretending to forget instead?"

Laney knew she hadn't a prayer at accomplishing either. But she could see no other way forward.

She nodded and walked back into the condo.

Chapter 28

Jason had expected Maui to be gorgeous. But the sheer number of jaw-droppingly beautiful vistas they encountered on a leisurely drive up the western coast of the island surprised even him. The ocean was striking enough, with its deep blue color — which he had to admit, even Tofino on a clear day couldn't compare to — and with the rocky cliffs of Lana'i and Moloka'i rising from its depths in the distance. But the farther north they drove, the more lush and verdant Maui became, with jagged green peaks straddling jungle-like valleys whose tumbling brooks carried mountain rain out to sea. They made a stop on the cliff above Honolua Bay, where he admired the breaking waves at its base, fiercely jealous of the small band of surfers who were practiced enough to take on the break even with the unfavorable wind. Laney kept telling him he should surf whenever and wherever he wanted, but he knew that this morning was not the time. He suspected that she would hear from Gordon soon, and he wanted to be there when she did.

After rounding the northern tip of West Maui, they stopped to get a view of the famous Nakalele blowhole. Laney hopped out of the car and stepped up beside him, and as had been happening all morning, he was unable to keep his eyes off her. She looked so lovely. The wind tossed her blond hair carelessly about her pretty face and ruffled her flowing skirt. And her bare shoulders — which had started out pale but were turning more golden brown by the hour — were beyond tantalizing. He truly couldn't understand how he'd ever thought she wasn't beautiful.

Perhaps his view had been colored by the enigma of her — by the gradual but steady reveal of the fun-loving sprite that recent fate and hardship had managed to all but obliterate. He saw more of the real woman every day, every time her mind was sufficiently distracted from her worries. And the more he saw of her, the more he wanted to see.

"Why aren't you getting a sunburn?" he teased good-naturedly as they neared the overlook. "I mean, seriously... your hair is so light! How can you possibly tan like that?"

Her lips lifted into a fetching — and uncharacteristically shy — smile. "I don't know," she answered, giving a shrug to the delectable shoulders in question. "I've always tanned really easily." Her smile turned sly. "Other women hate that."

Jason laughed out loud. "I'll bet they do."

All morning they had maintained, by unspoken mutual agreement, a safe physical distance between them. There were no accidental shoulder bumps, no guiding hands on arms or backs. Just casual conversation and increasingly easy laughter. He was proud of the awesome job he'd been doing pretending that their explosive kiss on the lanai had never happened. But he was under no delusions about how long he could last. Once Laney's whole impossible situation with her family was resolved, they were absolutely going to revisit that kiss. How they would get there from here he didn't know. All he knew was that the promise of more was the only thing keeping him sane.

A sound like a giant wet cough, followed by a torrential spit, rent the air. It was coming from the next outcropping of cliff over, a few hundred yards away. They stopped and stared as a towering plume of frothy white water rose from a basin of black volcanic rock, sailed into the air, slowed, then crashed back down, draining away through rocky crevices to return to the sea.

"That is *so* cool," Laney said with delight. "But it doesn't look safe for those people to stand there."

Jason grinned at her unintended irony. Several people in bathing suits were standing on the wet rocks near the blowhole's opening. He'd heard that tourists sometimes perished here, swept off their feet and sucked down into the hole along with the returning water. Warning signs were ample, but routinely ignored. "Yes," he said with obvious sarcasm. "How presumptuous of a tourist to think they know better than the locals what's safe."

Laney's expression of wonder didn't alter as she jabbed him playfully in the ribs. "Oh, shut up."

Jason feigned a painful grunt with a smile. He knew she was fantasizing about how much fun it would be to be down there herself. Her lust for adventure was strong, if still largely untapped, and he longed to help her discover it. He wondered what had managed to suppress her inner adrenaline junkie this long, and suspected that chronic financial stress had certainly had something to do with it. But beyond that, her own positive character traits seemed to be at odds with each other. What was a thrill-seeking personality to do when it was also loyal, responsible, hard-working, and self-sacrificing?

Almost as if she could read his mind, Laney broke her gaze away from the intermittently erupting blowhole in order to check her phone. She'd been doing so all morning, though more frequently as time went on. He watched as her eyes flashed with disappointment. She dropped the phone in her bag and looked up again. But new worry lines remained on her forehead.

"He'll call," Jason assured.

Her blue eyes flickered his direction, but only briefly. She'd been unwilling to meet his gaze for any length of time since their argument.

The words she'd said to him then still stung. If she truly thought so little of him, why would she even want to be his friend? Her use of the words "the first time I laid eyes on you" had only added insult to injury, because unbeknownst to her, she'd actually rushed to judgment of him *twice*. Before the concussion she had dismissed him at a glance. At the hospital later she was polite but still wary. She'd known nothing about him then; he'd done nothing to deserve her censure. But as much as he'd like to write the whole thing off as her fault for being too judgy, he knew she wasn't the only one. As careful as he was not to misrepresent himself to the women he dated, people on the outside saw only one thing — a man who slept with a lot of women. Could he really expect Laney, or anyone else who didn't yet know him, to assume he *wasn't* a player?

But I never hit on her! He told himself, knowing the defense was bogus even as he floated it. On no planet would Laney assume that he was keeping his hands to himself because he was a nice guy who could read women well enough to know she wasn't into hookups. What she would assume was that he wasn't attracted to *her.* Women were idiotic like that.

His mind replayed their kiss, and he smiled to himself. At least there could be no more confusion on that score.

The sun was glinting off her newly bronzed shoulders. His lips were mere inches away from her smooth, supple skin. All he had to do was lower his head...

Laney jumped. Jason sprang back. He was an instant away from apologizing when he realized he hadn't touched her. He hadn't even moved.

Laney dropped her bag from her shoulder, dug around in it, and produced a vibrating phone. "Hello?" she said nervously, stepping toward their car.

Jason followed, keeping a polite distance behind, until a frantic gesture of her hand assured him she wanted him closer. As he neared, she held out the phone from her ear, enabling him to listen.

"Yes," she said unsteadily. "This is Laney Miller. Thank you for getting back to me."

"I understand you'd like to schedule a meeting," a stern male voice boomed through the phone. "But as you can imagine, this is a rather difficult topic for us. It would be better if you could give me a little more information over the phone first."

Jason watched with admiration as Laney drew in a breath and straightened her spine. Her next words were clear and direct. "I understand the delicacy of the situation. And I do sympathize. But no, I'm afraid there's nothing else I can say right now. Speaking about something like this over the phone doesn't feel right. But I'm happy to meet with you and your wife wherever and whenever you like, and I promise to be brief. I don't want to upset you. I'm hoping that what I have to say, you'll find comforting."

There was a pause. Laney shot a glance at Jason, and he gave an encouraging nod.

"Well, if that's the way it has to be," Gordon replied finally, sounding disgruntled. "Needless to say, my wife is anxious to meet with you. Let's meet at the Hula Beans coffee shop by Ma'alaea Harbor. Four o'clock."

Laney's shoulders slumped with relief. "That sounds perfect. I'll be there. Thank you."

"Yes. Four o'clock," he repeated curtly. The line went dead.

Laney stood still a moment, breathing heavily. "Not exactly the warm, fuzzy type is he?"

"He was a CEO. I'm sure that's the way he talks to everybody," Jason assured. "Except the kids he takes out on his fishing boat. One dose of that voice and they'd probably jump overboard." He kept his tone light, understanding her concern. Gordon Tremblay might be a loving family man. But he sounded like he could also be a formidable enemy.

Laney said nothing. When Jason saw her shaking, he didn't think twice. He swept his arms around her and pulled her into a hug. For the first time all morning, the kiss and its aftermath fled his conscious mind, replaced with a fierce protectiveness. "Don't worry," he whispered in her ear, his heart warming as she clung to him without protest. "Everything's going to be all right."

Laney held her head high, determined not to tremble, as she swung open the door of the coffee shop at 3:55PM. The ambience was light, bright, and casual; the seating area nearly deserted. Gordon and Joan were already there, seated at a table for four in the far corner, two steaming but untouched mugs of coffee sitting in front of them.

Laney felt the comforting touch of Jason's hand on the small of her back. She steeled herself. *No cowering. You've done nothing wrong.*

The reminder was necessary. Whatever she might be feeling or thinking about this moment, she knew that the Tremblays' experience was in no way equivalent to her own. Whereas she was laying eyes for the first time on biological relatives, they were expecting to hear grim details about the body of a beloved family member, possibly preceded by a shameless attempt at extortion.

They looked the part. Gordon rose as they entered and placed one hand protectively — or commandingly? — on his wife's shoulder, as if to say, "Don't get up. I'll handle this." As Laney walked toward them, with Jason a step behind, Gordon's cool blue eyes darted from one to the other, assessing them. His jaws were clenched, his forehead deeply lined. His whole countenance spoke of unquestioned authority.

The woman beside him seemed small and shriveled in comparison. She sat motionlessly, her face nearly white, her mouth drawn into a thin line. The only sign of life she emitted was the stare of the small, dark eyes behind her glasses, which fixed on Laney immediately and followed her every movement.

Laney kept walking. Never in her life had she felt a stronger desire to turn tail and run. But she had to do this thing. She smiled. "Mr. and Mrs. Tremblay. Hello. I'm Laney Miller." She extended a hand. *Don't tremble!*

Her hand trembled. It was also freezing cold. But if Gordon noticed, her distress had no effect on him. He reached out his own massive paw, gave her hand one firm shake, then quickly dropped it. His sharp eyes turned to the man beside her.

"Jason Buchanan," Jason introduced, extending his own hand. The men shook.

"Pauley says you're from Tofino," Gordon remarked, making the comment sound like an accusation.

"Yes, sir," Jason replied easily. "I own the Pacific Rim Surf Lodge at Chesterman Beach, and the Pacific Rim equipment rental in town."

Gordon nodded, his face granting a modicum of respect. "I've heard of them. Pretty ambitious undertaking for a man your age."

Jason smiled. "We're doing well enough."

Laney looked back at Joan. The woman sat motionless, saying

nothing. She had not been introduced. The gaze she fixed on Laney was so penetrating that Laney averted her eyes. *Did she know? Could she see it?*

"Sit down," Gordon ordered, rather than invited. He sat, and Jason and Laney followed. There was no mention of the newcomers ordering coffee. The Tremblays seemed not to notice their own.

Laney set down her bag, breathed deeply, and sat up straight. Emotional wreck though she might be, she would not allow Gordon Tremblay or anyone else to bully her. His hostile suspicion might be justifiable, but it was counterproductive to both her purpose and his own best interests. Besides which, no matter how rich, powerful, and intimidating he might be, as her Grandpa Auggie used to say, *the man still puts his pants on one leg at a time.*

"Before we go any further," she proclaimed, keeping her voice soft even as she forced herself to make unflinching eye contact with Gordon. "I want both of you to know that I don't want anything from you. Nothing at all. I only ask that you listen to what I have to say. Because for both our families' sakes, it needs to be said. Then I'll go. All right?"

Perhaps she was imagining the slight softening of the lines on Gordon's forehead, the hint of human feeling that sparked deep within his otherwise cold eyes. She decided to assume the best. "I have no personal memory of the tornado that hit Peck in the spring of 1994," she began. "I was too young. We'd only just moved there a couple days before it happened. My father had died in a military accident, and my mom, who'd grown up in Peck, wanted to move nearer to her parents. But all she could afford to rent was a mobile home, and it was no match for the tornado. It tipped over and was largely destroyed. We were lucky to survive with minor injuries."

Laney turned to Joan. "I'm sorry that your daughter's family wasn't so lucky. From what I know of the tornado it sounds like there wasn't anything they could have done that would have changed the outcome. Everyone in Peck felt horrible for them.

I've heard that volunteers were out for days, looking everywhere for your granddaughter's remains."

Joan still looked like a wax figure. No emotion whatsoever made its way to her face, and her eyes were difficult to read. She seemed frozen, petrified.

Laney felt a painful wave of sympathy. She knew what Joan expected her to say next. That some kids playing in a creek had found a skeleton, or that somebody's dog had brought back a suspicious bone. But it was time now to rock the poor woman's world — for better or worse. "I hadn't spent much time in Peck before then, so people in town didn't know me, but everyone knew my mother. When the trailer tipped, she was knocked unconscious, and when she woke up she found herself in her worst nightmare. She couldn't find me, or our dog."

"How old were you?" Joan murmured, her thin lips quivering. They were the first words she had spoken. Her face could not appear more bloodless.

"Twenty months," Laney answered. "You can imagine how terrified my mother was. How frantic. All the neighbors dropped everything to help her look for me, even people whose own houses were torn apart. No one had any idea if I'd wandered off on my own while she was unconscious, if I was dead and buried somewhere under a pile of rubble, or even if—"

"*Jessica!*" Joan bolted upright, bumping the table and sloshing coffee out of the mugs. She clutched at her husband's shoulder. "Gordon, it's Jessica!" Her dark eyes burned with intensity and her sharp cheeks flared a ruddy color.

Gordon sprang up and threw a restraining arm around her shoulders. "Joan!" he rebuked, his voice sympathetic and chastising at the same time.

"*Look at her!*" his wife said emphatically, taking her eyes off Laney just long enough to glare at her husband. "Just look at her! She's Elizabeth's daughter, Gordon! Can't you see it?"

Laney could neither move nor speak. She couldn't even breathe.

Gordon's countenance weakened, but only slightly. His gaze

slid smoothly over Laney's features before he turned his
attention back to his wife. His words to her were warm,
concerned. "Sweetheart, don't do this. People look alike. You
can't jump to conclusions. Please, sit back down."

Joan's eyes flooded with tears. She dropped into her chair, her
eyes still locked on Laney.

"This isn't what we were expecting," Gordon said gruffly.
"Are you claiming to be our deceased granddaughter? Is that
what this is about?"

Laney drew in a ragged breath, determined to keep her
composure. She hadn't said anything of the kind, and she would
not let Gordon put words in her mouth. "I came here to tell you
what I know," she said softly, but firmly. "You're free to draw
your own conclusions. Until a few weeks ago I didn't see
anything strange in the tornado story I grew up with, other than
the improbability of any toddler being lifted up into a funnel
cloud and surviving. Everyone said it was a miracle. I had no
reason to believe that any deception was involved until my
mother—" her voice cracked. Guilt pummeled her at the implied
accusation, but she reined it in. "My mother died of cancer
shortly before Christmas. She was raised by her grandmother,
my great-grandmother May, who is eighty-seven now and has
dementia. Gran had been getting worse for years, but my mom's
death accelerated her decline, and after the funeral she started
saying things that disturbed me. Like how I wasn't *their* Laney.
How I was 'the other one.'"

Joan, who had been sitting with her husband's arm around
her shoulders, grasped his free hand tightly with both of hers.
She turned her mouth to his ear and murmured something Laney
couldn't hear.

Gordon shook his head. He looked thoroughly miserable.
"Please don't do this, Joan. I told you that you shouldn't come.
You know what happened the last time!"

The last time? Laney's stomach roiled. Had they been the
targets of a fraud in the past?

"Listen, young lady," Gordon said to her, sternly. "Stop

dancing all around this. If you want to claim to be Jessica Macdonald, let's see your proof right now. Otherwise, we're done here. My wife has suffered enough. And frankly," his eyes glinted ever so slightly with sadness, "so have I."

Laney felt a new, crushing weight of guilt. Maybe she shouldn't have put them through this. Maybe she'd only made everything worse. "I don't have any proof," she admitted. "I don't know the truth myself. I didn't ask for any of this; when I started having suspicions I set out to *dis*prove them. But I couldn't. Instead, I kept finding little things that made the impossible seem even more likely. And then when I saw a picture of your daughter—"

She stopped. She was getting ahead of herself. "I don't want to upset anybody, or disrupt anyone's life, including my own. That's why I did everything I could think of to get answers myself, before involving you. I even sent off a DNA test, a maternity test with hair from my mother's hairbrush. But lab results take weeks, and when I found the pictures—"

The pictures! She reached for her bag, but Jason was ahead of her. He had already fished out the stack of photos and was holding them out to her. Laney flashed him a small smile of gratitude as she accepted them.

"The first thing I did was go to our family photo album," she continued. "So that I could prove to myself that I was *me*. But what I found was a gap. Between about six months and nearly two, there were no photographs of me at all. My mother had always said they were lost at the developers. But then I found the negatives, which she'd kept and hidden. The toddler in the negatives didn't look like me. But these pictures did. They were taken after the tornado."

She laid four pictures on the table, fanned out for the Tremblays to see. Pictures of a smiling two-year-old with her mother and her grandparents. The moan that escaped Joan's lips was painful to hear. "Oh, Gordon," she choked. "Look. *Look!*"

Gordon looked. And for a brief moment, he seemed nearly broken. His shoulders slumped, his jaw went slack, and his eyes widened. But in the next moment, everything changed again. He swept up the photos in his hand. "May we borrow these?" he asked, his tone less hostile, but still distant. "We'll need to have them examined by a professional. Let's go, Joan."

She looked up at her husband disbelievingly. "But—"

"Photographs can be doctored," he said to her tenderly, but firmly, helping her to her feet. "Please. You promised."

Joan's dark eyes, now watering profusely, rested on Laney apologetically. Longingly. "I'm sorry," she said softly. "But we've been through this before. And it was very hard."

"I'm sure it was," Laney said genuinely. "I'm sorry."

Joan almost smiled, but then averted her eyes. "Let's go, then," she said to her husband.

"Give us twenty-four hours to check this out," Gordon ordered. "Then we'll see where we stand. We'll meet here again, tomorrow. Same time."

"That's... fine." Laney felt a sudden spurt of terror. She rose with them. "But... please! Before you go, I need you to understand something!"

The Tremblays stopped moving and looked at her. "What's that?" Gordon demanded suspiciously.

"Please, try to understand my position," Laney pleaded. "I'm a graduate student. I have my great-grandmother to take care of. Only Laney Miller can do that. If something gets out that... that I've been living under a false identity, that my passport isn't valid, that I'm not really my great-grandmother's legal guardian..." The Tremblays were staring at her blankly. She began to panic. "Don't you see? I have to trust *you*, right now. What I've told you could put me in serious legal jeopardy!"

Joan shot a warning look up at Gordon, who for once kept his mouth shut. Joan stepped forward and put out a hand to press Laney's arm. "We do understand," she said mildly, although her voice was still strained. "Don't worry, honey. We'll... well, we'll talk more tomorrow, all right?"

Laney didn't see that she had a choice. With no more than quiet, sharp nods all around, the Tremblays took her pictures and walked out the door. Their mugs of coffee remained on the table. Untouched.

Laney dropped back into her chair, exhausted.

"You handled that brilliantly," Jason praised.

She blew out a breath. "It didn't feel that way." She had ruined everything. She hadn't known what to expect, but she'd never thought the encounter would end like this — would *feel* like this. Gordon had acted as though he hated her. Joan had seemed more open minded, but sooner or later he would convince her that Laney was a fraud — a lookalike that some scammer had recruited to play the part. They'd hardly even asked her any questions! Now she'd lost her baby pictures. Never mind that she hadn't looked at them for years — she felt like a chunk of her life had been stolen.

"You can't expect to be objective," Jason said.

Laney could hear him, but his voice seemed disembodied. Her eyes stayed fixed on the puddles of coffee that had sloshed out on the table. The air around her was frigid.

"From my perspective, your approach was perfect," he continued. "You didn't make any demands on them, you didn't claim anything you couldn't prove. You were upfront and honest; you were even sympathetic to their position. They could have been a hell of a lot more sympathetic to yours, in my opinion, but I'll make allowances for their being blindsided. Their reaction was normal and expected. You have to remember, this meeting was just the first step."

Laney turned to him, feeling slightly more hopeful. "You think so?"

"Of course. You have to give them time to digest the information, to process the shock." He rose and offered her a hand. "Now let's get out of this insane air conditioning and back into the sun. You could use a little more Maui right now, don't you think?"

Laney smiled weakly, put her hand in his, and stood. He looked so alive, so solid, so dependable. He had said almost nothing, yet his quiet presence at her side had been priceless.

He'd felt no need to butt in or take charge. He'd just been there. For her.

"Would you mind terribly if we just go back to the condo?" she asked. "It's already evening in Tofino time, and I'm beat."

"What about dinner?" he asked, sounding disappointed.

"We bought groceries this morning, remember? I can just nuke something." Laney wondered if she should tell him that all she really wanted to do was curl up on the couch with her head on his shoulder, eat popcorn, watch a movie, and forget that anyone named Tremblay ever existed. But she wasn't sure how he would take that suggestion. It sounded pretty relationship-y.

He shrugged and nodded. "Fine. Back to the condo, then."

They drove back to West Maui in near silence. The sun was already dropping low in the sky, and despite the beauty of the ocean on one side and a dormant volcano on the other, she had trouble keeping her eyes open. Only after they had returned to the condo and she had shoved her dinner into the microwave did either of them speak of the meeting again. She wanted to put the Tremblays out of her mind, but her brain wouldn't stop replaying the conversation. "Jason?" she asked uncertainly, leaning out over the kitchen counter toward where he stood, gazing out the windows at the lowering sun. "Do you think there's any chance Gordon is really... a nice person?"

He walked toward her. "I don't know, Laney, but I do know that the man we met today wasn't Jessica Macdonald's grandfather."

"What?" she asked, distressed.

He shook his head with a smile, then leaned over the counter. "The man we met was Gordon Tremblay, CEO. The businessman. The hard-nosed intimidator. It's a role he plays; all executives do. It's like a poker face. At home with his wife, with his son, even out on his fishing boat — he could be completely different. You saw hints of that in the way he talked to Joan, didn't you? He was trying to be a hardass with you and comfort his wife at the same time — that's why he didn't want her to be there. My guess is she was with him this morning when he got the letter, and she insisted on coming."

Laney wanted to be hopeful. But she was afraid to be. "He seemed domineering. He could have made her come."

"Why would he? Nah. I'll bet you anything Joan has that man wrapped around her little finger."

Laney smiled. Jason was being so sweet to her. He seemed to know just what to say. But she wanted more than words. She walked around the counter, and he straightened as she approached. "I don't know what to do with myself now," she confessed. "I don't even know what to hope for. What do you think they'll do?" As she'd hoped, his arm slid naturally around her shoulders, and she leaned into his side.

"I think they'll hire a private detective," he answered, giving her a brotherly sideways hug. "I think that by four o'clock tomorrow, they'll know everything there is to know about Laney Miller, and probably about Jason Buchanan, too. And every bit of it will back up your story. You have nothing to worry about. They'll know you're not a fraud."

A sudden chill crept down her spine. She had other fears. Deeper fears. Fears she hadn't managed to voice yet, even to herself. "But what is the truth, Jason?" she forced out finally, her voice a rough whisper. "Who am I, really? Am I still Laney, or... am I Jessica?"

He turned; his eyes found hers. "You're the same person you've always been, and always will be," he said with emphasis. "It's not your fault if people called you by different names at different points in your life. You are *you*. The reality you've lived is the only reality." He broke off his gaze and pulled her to his chest, then rubbed her back gently. "Call yourself whatever you like. Let others make the adjustment. I have to confess, though, I like the name Laney. It's cute and sassy, just like you."

She chuckled into his shoulder. This felt good; he felt good. But she wanted more. What would it matter if he broke her heart later? That organ had been nothing but a quivering mass of pulp since her mother died, anyway. What was one more blow?

She raised her head. She smiled and leaned her lips toward

his...

Suddenly, they were apart. Jason was holding her away from him. "No," he said softly. "Not now."

"Now is good," she argued.

"No, it's not." He dropped his hands from her arms and stepped away. "You're vulnerable as hell right now, and despite first impressions, I am not a jerk." He picked up his keys from the counter. "We've had this conversation twice already. We're friends. Period."

"Where are you going?" she asked with horror. She couldn't deal with another night like the last one. She just couldn't!

He stopped. His gray-green eyes studied her a moment, their depths fraught with conflicting emotions. Frustration. Lust. Resignation. Hopefulness. But what finally rose to the surface was pity. "I'm only going out to grab something to eat," he said mildly. "I'll come back." His lips curved into the faintest of smiles. "Alone."

Chapter 29

Jason threw away the wrapper from a ridiculously overpriced burger and headed to the beach to catch the sunset. He felt bad leaving Laney in the condo by herself, but if she insisted on tempting him to take advantage of her she was eventually going to get what she wanted. Except that it wouldn't be what she wanted. *He* wasn't what she wanted.

No woman who cared about marriage and a family would want him. He'd never had the faintest desire to get married, or even to date one woman exclusively for any length of time. He wasn't jealous or possessive of the women he dated, and he studiously avoided any who refused to offer him the same leeway. He had a system. It had been working great for a long time now.

Laney was screwing up everything. The woman was possessive as all get out — she'd practically cried when she thought he was heading out to the bars again. Never mind that she kept saying they should only be friends! But instead of having the reaction he should have had, which was to be annoyed and set her straight, he'd actually *liked* it. He was *glad* she was jealous. What the hell was that about?

Even worse, he felt possessive of her! The idea of her being with another man drove him batcrap crazy.

He picked up a hunk of coral from the sand, drew back his arm, and sent it sailing over the ocean. The beach was crowded with happy people, which was irritating. Spooning couples, cavorting kids, intergenerational families... all were oohing and aahing over the magnificent sunset.

There was nothing wrong with his chosen lifestyle. He tried to make women happy, they made him happy, and nobody got hurt. He *was* happy!

Except when he started thinking about something he never

used to think about: the distant future. His own middle age.
Would the lifestyle he enjoyed so much now still work for him
then? When he was in his fifties, would he be hooking up with
single forty- and fifty-year-old women? He frowned. Not too
many women in that category came to Tofino to surf. And the
image of his middle-aged self trolling the beaches for twenty-
somethings was disturbing. He knew men like that. He
considered them pathetic.

The sunset was brilliant, with vibrant oranges and reds and
almost-purples reflecting off the low-lying clouds over the water.
He turned away from it and headed for one of the alleyways
between the resorts.

Was his chosen lifestyle a legitimate, socially evolved choice...
or was it just immature?

No, he argued with himself. Marriage wasn't for everyone, and
it wasn't for him. Age was irrelevant. His dad was in his seventies,
and — aside from the brief, otherwise disastrous marriage that
had produced Jason and Thane — he had always been happily
single. Jason was like his dad in many ways. Stanley Buchanan
insisted that he was better off single because he could never
make any woman happy, which made perfect sense to Jason.
Stanley had certainly hurt Jason's mother enough. But that didn't
mean he wasn't a good father to—

Jason huffed out a growl. He liked kids and wouldn't mind
having a few of his own, but the idea was a non-starter. Kids
didn't fit into the big picture, and that was that. Mei Lin and
Thane would have a baby soon; being an uncle would be stellar.

He emerged into a lighted parking lot. He stopped. His
muscles were tense, his heart was beating fast, and he felt like
crap. What was wrong with him?

Laney was wrong with him.

He had to do something about it. He pulled out his phone
and clicked into his contacts. His call rang several times before it
was answered.

"Jason!" his brother's hearty voice greeted. "What's up?"

"Hey, bro," Jason returned, leaning against a lamppost.

"Listen, I need some advice."

"Oh? You got a wolf problem?"

Jason *wished*. "No. Woman problem."

Silence followed.

"Thane?"

"Yeah, man, I'm here," his brother said finally. "Just looking for someplace to sit down."

Jason's eyes rolled. His brother would milk this occasion for all it was worth. When it came to women and sex, Jason had always been the one *giving* the advice. Never mind that he was nearly three years younger.

"Okay," Thane boomed happily. "You've got the guru of love, here. What seems to be the problem?"

Jason gritted his teeth a moment, then proceeded. "I just want to ask you a question. When you first met Mei Lin, what exactly was different about her? I mean, compared to the others." Jason wasn't sure how to put the question. His brother hadn't had many others; where women were concerned, he'd always been like a bull in a china shop. Women were attracted to Thane; he just never knew quite what to do with them. But still, he'd managed a few relationships before his wife had come along. He must know something.

"Well now," Thane said thoughtfully. "That's pretty easy. For one thing, I thought about her constantly. Even before anything physical happened between us. I just wanted to be around her, you know?"

Jason knew. He sighed. "What else?"

Thane thought a moment. "Well, the better I got to know her, the worse it got. I felt like I'd lost control of my own mind. And then there was this thing... I kept catching myself obsessing over what was best for her. You know, rather than just thinking about what I wanted. Makes me sound bad, I know, but when you first start seeing somebody you don't always really care what—"

"Yeah, I get that," Jason interrupted impatiently. He was two for two, damn it. "But isn't all that just infatuation?" he argued. "I mean, I've only known the woman for six days!"

Thane scoffed. "Hell, bro, you think I wasn't infatuated with Mei Lin after six days? We didn't use the L word then. That came later. But the crazy, mind-altering stuff was definitely the first step."

Jason considered. "Infatuation doesn't always lead to love."

"Course not," Thane said matter of factly. "But you can't know where it's going until you give it a try. So who's the unlucky lady?"

Jason's face felt hot. "I have no desire to get married. You know—"

"Who said anything about marriage?" Thane shot back, his tone full of mirth. "Did I say anything about marriage? There *is* a middle ground between hooking up once and having three kids and a minivan, you know. There's this other thing — it's called a relationship. See, that's where you say 'no' to all the other women—"

"I know what a relationship is!" Jason snapped.

"So what have you got to lose?" Thane pressed. "Except the other women?"

"I don't want any other women!"

Crap. Jason hadn't intended to say that. Had he meant it? The other end of the line went silent. "Thane?"

His brother chuckled merrily. "Oh, yeah. You got it bad."

Jason swore under his breath. Then he sighed, loud and long. "I know. But this isn't just about what I have to lose. What if she gets hurt?"

"You really do care, don't you?" Thane returned, his voice softening. "It's true, she could get hurt. So could you. That's the way it works. Aren't you supposed to be the risk taker in the family?"

Jason had no good response to that. He *was* a risk taker. He was still scared. "Dad never fell in love," he blurted. "With anybody. His whole life. He told me so."

Thane was quiet for a beat. "You're not him, Jason. Do you want his life?"

No, Jason thought emphatically. *No, I don't.* What kind of life he did want, he still wasn't sure. But how was he supposed to figure it out if he didn't at least explore his options?

Maybe giving a real relationship a try was the best thing to do.

A heavy weight seemed to slip from his shoulders. He heaved out a sigh of relief. "Thanks, Bro," he said sincerely. "Listen, I'll, uh... talk to you later, okay?"

"Did I mention that I'm going to be a father?"

Jason laughed out loud. It felt good to laugh. He felt good, period. "Yeah," he said fondly, grinning. "I think you did."

Laney leaned back in her beach chair and let out yet another unintentional sigh. She loved watching Jason surf. He was gorgeous enough in a form-fitting wetsuit, but watching him catch a warm blue wave bare-chested in board shorts was really too much. Still, she was glad she'd insisted he surf this morning. It was going to be a very long day waiting for her next meeting with the Tremblays, and she would be hopelessly uptight every minute of it. Why shouldn't one of them enjoy themselves, at least? She owed him that much.

Her behavior last evening had been wretched. Unforgivable. She'd practically thrown herself at the man, *again*. Never mind how many agreements they made, she'd gone and done whatever she felt like. Being rejected had stung, but she knew he'd been right. She had been an emotional mess, and no matter how much she would have enjoyed a reckless night of mad passion — and make no mistake, she would have enjoyed it very much — the end result would be dreadful.

She couldn't be with Jason unless she was the only one. Not the only one forever, maybe, but the only one for now. It wasn't a point on which she could compromise.

In short, their situation was hopeless.

But she still loved watching him surf.

She looked out over the azure water toward where the reef break termed Rainbows had been firing off surfable waves all morning, straight out from the perfectly groomed beaches of

West Maui's resort district. The lineup was crowded, and Jason had had to wait a very long time to catch his first wave, but once he'd had a chance to show his stuff his opportunities had come more regularly. Rainbows was a fickle break that needed a precise set of conditions to be at its finest, and Jason's being here this morning was no accident. Laney had gotten up before dawn to research the best spots for intermediate and advanced surfers, then analyzed the forecast on her surfing app before making the suggestion.

Jason had seemed delighted. She figured it was the least she could do. He had returned to the condo at a reasonable time last night, alone, just as he'd said he would. But she'd been too embarrassed to face him. After he'd left she had indulged herself in another good, long, cathartic cry, then crawled into bed with her laptop and watched mindless sitcoms until she fell asleep. It hadn't taken long. She'd been wiped out both physically and emotionally.

This morning, she was still a wreck. But curiously, Jason seemed happier. They'd eaten breakfast together on the lanai, chatting about nothing important. They'd even laughed a little. She wondered if Haley and Ben spent every morning like that. How nice it must be to share something so mundane, yet so deeply enjoyable, with someone that you loved.

An overwhelming wave of sadness swamped her. She sucked in a breath and tilted her closed eyes into the sun. *Stop it. You'll be fine. You've made a good guy friend — two, counting Ben — and after today, your responsibility to the Tremblays will be absolved. Namaste.*

She breathed out again, slowly. She couldn't tell herself that her life would soon get back to normal. It would never be the same without her mother and the Gran she used to know. But it could still be good. Jason or no Jason. Money or no money. Legally alive or legally nonexistent. She would make it so.

"Excuse us," a soft female voice said tentatively. "Laney?"

Her eyes flew open.

Standing beside her beach chair were Gordon and Joan Tremblay.

Chapter 30

Laney nearly knocked her chair over backward. "Oh!" she exclaimed, rising clumsily to face them. "Hello. I... Are we late?" She glanced worriedly at the time. It wasn't even noon yet. "I thought you said four o'clock. At the coffee shop?"

"We did, honey," Joan said, smiling. "I'm sorry. I just, well... we couldn't wait. I hope you don't mind."

"Of course not, but—" Laney's confusion was near complete. "But how did you even know I was here?"

The man behind Joan gave a chuckle. Laney stared at both of them, disbelieving. Their resemblance to the couple she'd met yesterday was superficial at best. This Joan's cheeks were flushed, her dark eyes shone with pleasure and her mouth crinkled into a constant smile. Gordon's previously cold eyes were dancing with some inner light, his smile was genuine, and his whole bearing was subdued and relaxed. "Well," the new man explained, "We did check the address you gave us first, but when you weren't there we got creative. Pauley said your friend was a surfer, and I figured if I were his age and Rainbows was pumping, this is where I'd be. And here you are."

Laney blinked. Was she imagining these people?

"We should have called and warned you first, I know," Joan said apologetically. "But I'll confess, I wanted to see you in person and we couldn't wait till four. We have all the information we need already. Not that I didn't have everything I needed the moment I saw your sweet little face in those pictures!" She tossed her head toward her husband with a good-natured eye roll. "But the great skeptic here had to do his due diligence."

Gordon added nothing to that. He just stood there and smiled.

"You... called a private detective or something?" Laney inquired, not sure what she should be asking first. They seemed to think their purpose in being here was obvious, but her mind reeled with questions.

"Oh, he called several," Joan said offhandedly. "Had the poor people working all night." She removed a wicker mat from beneath her arm, unrolled it with a snap, and laid it out on the sand. "How about if we all sit down?"

"Oh, please, take my chair," Laney offered, gesturing to it.

But Joan, who had already plopped herself down on the mat, waved the offer away. "Oh, we're fine, dear. You take it." She looked up at Gordon, who was fidgeting beside her. "Sit down, you old fusspot. I'll haul you back up later."

Gordon gave a lame snort of protest, then eased his long legs down onto the mat beside his wife. Feeling awkward, Laney pushed her chair to the side and dropped down to sit level with them on the sand.

"Now," Joan said excitedly, her brown eyes twinkling. "I think it's time we properly introduced ourselves. I'm your grandmother, Laney. And this is your grandfather. And while I know all this must be hard for you, I want you to know that this is one of the happiest days of our lives."

Laney's eyes burned. They seemed too dry for tears. Everything that was happening felt too unreal. "You believe that I'm Jessica Macdonald," she said roughly.

Joan smiled gently. "We do, honey. We *know* you are. Even though I'm sure you have a hard time believing it, yourself. I have something to show you." She reached down into her bag. "Here. Look at this. This is you on your first birthday, just four months before the tornado. With your biological mother, Elizabeth."

Laney looked. When her eyes connected with the faces in the picture, tears did come. Plenty of them. The little girl wearing the purple and yellow Barney hat was *her*. The young mother holding her close, kissing her on the cheek, was the same woman in the family portrait on the endowment flyer.

"We can arrange a DNA test if you'd like," Gordon said softly. "But you don't have to. We know you're Elizabeth's daughter."

"And we know that you're also Laney Miller," Joan said firmly. She caught Laney's eyes. "We would never ask you to give up any part of who you are, honey. You have a family who loves you, and they raised you beautifully. Your grandfather and I promise not to interfere with that. I won't say we haven't had our moments of anger over losing you, and I'm sure we'll keep on having them. But none of that is your concern."

A flash of worry intruded into Laney's otherwise easing mind. "My mother didn't— I mean, I know what she did was wrong, but my father had just died, and—"

"You don't need to explain anything to us," Gordon insisted. "You couldn't anyway; you were only a child. Nothing that's happened has been your fault."

Joan reached out a tentative hand and laid it on Laney's arm. "We know you loved your mother, honey. I promise you, we'd never do anything to hurt her memory, not when it would hurt you, too." She looked up at her husband. "We've been talking about it all night, and we've agreed that the best thing for all of us is to let the past stay in the past. What's done is done, and there's been good that's come out of it as well as the bad. We just need to figure out how to move forward."

Laney looked from one of her grandparents to the other, their images blurring through her tears. They *were* good people. Very good people. Both of them!

"Thank you," she said, her voice choked. "You have no idea what that means to me."

"We have some," Gordon said jovially. "You were wise to be so concerned about your legal status. I'm afraid it's quite a quagmire."

"I know," Laney said with a gulp, fear taking hold of her again. "But until I can afford a lawyer to—"

"Why on earth should you pay an attorney?" Gordon interrupted, sounding a bit more like a CEO. "You didn't create the problem. But your grandmother and I do bear some responsibility, for being so consumed with our own grief that we didn't properly investigate the situation. We could have searched harder and longer for Jessica's remains. We could have done our own due diligence, instead of blindly relying on what the police told us. If we'd realized that another little girl was involved, we could have demanded that the authorities do their job and confirm that child's identity." He calmed himself with a sigh. "But we didn't do any of that. We failed our daughter, and we failed you. It's our job now to fix it. Not yours."

"However *you* want us to handle it," Joan added quickly. "If you want to remain as Laney Miller, we'll respect that. From what I understand, establishing American citizenship might be difficult, but I promise you, we'll do everything we can to try and make your identity legal. If you'd like to keep your name, but accept your Canadian birthright, we'll go that route. It all sounds very complicated, but that's the sort of thing lawyers live for, isn't it? So please, don't you give that another thought."

Laney was overwhelmed. They weren't asking her to take the name Jessica, they weren't even calling her that. And if they were willing to help her straighten out her documentation, without defaming her mother or interfering with her relationship with Gran...

"There's only one thing we ask of you, sweetheart," Joan continued softly, her voice pleading. "And that's to give us the chance to get to know you again. Please... stay awhile. If your time at the condo runs out, we can find another place for you to stay on Maui. Or, if your young man needs to get back to Tofino and you want to go with him, we'll go back to Ucluelet. That's fine, too."

"We know that your house in Peck is up for sale," Gordon chimed in. "And that your great-grandmother is in Sikeston, and we'll be happy to fly you down to visit her as often as you like. I'm sure you plan to go back to graduate school at some point, but until then, please consider staying near us. We'll do everything we can to make it work, to make your life easier, if you'll just give us... some more time with our granddaughter."

Joan's eyes had moistened. Her chin quivered even as she smiled. Gordon looked as eager and vulnerable as a small boy.

Laney's heart felt ready to burst. "Of course," she exclaimed, wiping away the senseless tears. "Of course, I will. I... I want to get to know you, too!"

Hugs seemed absolutely necessary. But they were too awkward sitting down, so Joan stood up and pulled Gordon after her. When she opened her arms, Laney fell into them. Or rather, Joan fell into Laney's arms. Either way, the women's hug was warm and heartfelt. And when Laney turned to Gordon, she realized the real man was the one she saw now. The loving father, husband, and grandfather — who just happened to be a kickass business mogul. He hugged her tenderly, then Joan hugged Laney again, then Gordon hugged Joan, and when at last they all pulled apart, none of their eyes were dry.

"Will you join us for dinner tonight?" Joan asked happily. "You and your young man?"

"We've got amberjack and snapper both, fresh-caught just yesterday, and your grandmother makes a mean fish taco," Gordon added.

"We'd love to," Laney laughed, even as a stray thread of sadness flitted through her. "But he's not my young man. Jason and I are just good friends."

The Tremblays exchanged a brief, but obviously amused glance. "Oh?" Joan said wryly. "You don't say. Well, you're both welcome to come in any event."

They worked through the details as Laney walked with the couple back around the resort to where their car was parked. Not until after she'd waved their departing vehicle goodbye and returned to the beach did she notice Jason walking toward her, his surfboard tucked under his arm. He was dripping wet, with his slick, bare shoulders gleaming in the sun and his curly brown ringlets weighted down with drops of seawater.

Laney felt like singing. Or dancing. Or flying. But she wound up running and jumping instead. She ran across the beach and flung herself at Jason, giving him precious little time to drop his surfboard before catching her in midair.

"Did you see them?" she asked in the middle of her launch.

"They were here!"

"I saw," he said with a grunt as her weight fell upon his chest. "I didn't want to interfere. I'm guessing they brought you good news?"

He lowered her feet back to the ground, and she stared happily up at him, her arms still locked around his neck. "The best news possible," she exclaimed. "They were wonderful. It's all wonderful!"

Jason smiled at her. "I'm so glad, Laney," he said softly. "I love seeing you this happy."

She kissed him. Or maybe he kissed her. It happened so quickly, so spontaneously, so naturally, she felt no need to think about it. All she knew was that she was *happy*. Wonderfully, gloriously, happy. At peace with the past, optimistic about the future, and absolutely, fantastically excited about the sensations Jason was making her feel right now. Touching him, holding him, kissing him like this was amazing... it was better than before, even... it was...

Bound to end. Her bubble of happiness deflated slightly as she began to anticipate his drawing back, pushing her away. Just knowing it was coming was like a physical pain. Why the hell did she keep doing this to herself?

He stopped the kiss and pulled back. She groaned aloud, a new spate of bittersweet tears threatening. "I hate it when you do that!" she said childishly.

But he was laughing. "I have something to ask you," he chuckled, his eyes shining at her. "I didn't want to mess with your head earlier, when so much was going on, but now I think..."

Laney held her breath. If it was bad news, she was going to scream. No negativity was allowed on this otherwise perfect day.

"The friends thing isn't working," he announced. "It's not enough for me. I feel... differently about you, Laney. And I want to try the real thing." His confidence seemed to waver suddenly. "You know, a relationship. Where we're exclusive. Doing the couple thing. Officially."

Laney stared. She didn't realize how long she'd gone without breathing until her lungs expelled with an audible huff.

"I mean, only if you want to," he added, for once misreading her completely. "Maybe it's not the best—"

Laney shut him up with a kiss even smokier than the last one. When they parted some time later, it was only due to lack of oxygen.

And certain public ordinances.

"Does that answer your question?" Laney asked breathlessly.

"It does," Jason whispered, his voice rough. "Now let's go."

She grinned. "Back to the condo?"

"Not yet," he said cryptically, releasing her to pick up his board again. He took her hand in his and began leading her back towards the car. "First, we're going shopping."

Laney stopped walking. "*Shopping?* Are you kidding?"

He raised an eyebrow.

Laney looked down at her outfit. The Hawaiian dress was in the wash; all she'd had to put on this morning was more from the lost and found bin. Some saggy, ill-fitting Bermuda shorts and a misshapen tank advertising a pizza shop in Vancouver. She sighed. As much time as she spent admiring his appearance, she really should step up her own a bit. "I suppose I could afford a few decent things," she conceded, walking again.

"I couldn't care less about decent," Jason replied. "I'm buying you a bikini."

She stopped again. "A bikini?" she protested. "I've never worn a bikini in my life! And anyway, you can't—"

"Sure I can," Jason interrupted with a grin. "A man's entitled to buy nice things for his girlfriend, isn't he?"

Laney closed her mouth. After a long, rather pleasurable moment of reflection, she reached a hand up to his face. She traced a finger along his perfect jawbone, then down his neck and across one muscular shoulder. She'd been wanting to do that for a while now. She'd been wanting to do a lot of things.

"Yes," she agreed, grinning back. "Yes, he can."

Epilogue

Laney laughed out loud as the tallest surfer on the lineup made a lame attempt at an alley-oop, separated from his board completely, then fell back into the ocean with an entirely unnecessary show of flailing and splashing.

"That's very good, dear!" the woman sitting on the log next to Laney called out to her husband sarcastically, favoring him with a grin and a thumbs up as soon as he resurfaced. "He's such a ham," she said to Laney as an aside, her eyes full of affection. "I don't know why he enjoys surfing so much when he's obviously so bad at it. Still, I have to say, he's gotten a lot better lately. Jason is a very good teacher."

"Yes he is, isn't he?" Laney's face glowed with pride as she smiled back at her friend. Ben and Haley had been spending a lot of weekends in Tofino over the spring, which was only fair, since Laney and Jason had spent at least as much time at their condo on Maui. This weekend was a parting celebration, of sorts, since the lawyer and her husband would be spending their summer on the move. Ben's research required the collection of ocean samples from all over the world, which should make for an exciting few months for them.

Laney was envious of the opportunity, but only a little. Though she fully intended to travel the world someday, for now she was content with her lot. The Tremblays' guest house in Ucluelet was sufficiently private, yet allowed for plenty of family time, which she was enjoying every bit as much as her grandparents were. Gordon and Joan had been true to their word, not forcing her to assume Jessica Macdonald's identity, but supporting whatever identity she chose to forge for herself. She was a Canadian citizen now, legally known as Laney Jessica

Miller, which everyone involved seemed to think a fair compromise. US citizenship would take much longer to establish, if she was successful at all, but as time went on she found it mattered less.

Gordon and Joan were indeed good people, and she had quickly learned to love them, much as — she knew with certainty — her toddler self had done before. She was equally certain she had always loved her Uncle Richard, who despite his dour-looking picture in the art magazine was both kind and hysterically funny. Laney adored every member of her new family, even as she stayed close to her existing one.

No one on either side contested the facts. The DNA test had proved that she was not Christi Miller's child, and no further testing seemed necessary. When June and Amy had been told the story, they'd been frankly horrified, dispelling any doubts Laney might have had about her aunt's complicity in the fraud. Instead, June had confirmed that she had not seen Christi and Jimbo's child for nearly a year at the time of the tornado, that all she'd ever heard about the Macdonalds' child was that it was a baby, and that no hint of suspicion had ever crossed her mind. Perhaps if the couple who'd found Laney had turned her over to the police first, or if the missing child's remains had ever been found, the whole scenario might have played out differently. But Laney had no desire to look back anymore. And neither, thankfully, did anyone else.

The Tremblays' attorneys had handled the whole affair with both brilliance and discretion, and although it was too much to hope that no one in Peck would ever find out what Christi had done, they appeared none the wiser yet. Perhaps, Laney reasoned, the passing of time would render the revelation less sensational anyway. In any event, the big brick house had been sold to a nonprofit for use as a group home, and Laney felt little need to return to the town, except for an occasional, brief trip to check in with old neighbors and visit the cemetery. From now on, though, any such trips would be made in conjunction with a visit to Jimbo Miller's family plot in Dade County, where she had made a tribute of her own. The Ontario tombstone bearing Jessica Macdonald's name had been removed, but Laney couldn't bear for the daughter of Christi and Jimbo to be forgotten. Though the lost child's existence couldn't be trumpeted in Peck, Laney Carole Miller did at last have a pink granite memorial of her own — right next to her biological father and grandmother.

Laney still worried about her Gran. On her first visit after returning from Maui, she had made a point of reassuring May that the truth was out now, that Jessica's family had been notified, and that everything was okay. Sometimes May seemed to understand this, and sometimes she didn't, but Laney chose to believe the knowledge helped her. Whenever May began fretting over hell and damnation, the staff were instructed to repeat that mantra, and it did seem to calm her down. Gran hadn't mentioned the issue in a couple months now, even when Laney was present. And while Gran didn't always recognize Laney by sight or voice, when reminded who was visiting her, May smiled and spoke to her great-granddaughter in the same loving way she always had.

"You know," Haley said confidentially, jolting Laney from her thoughts. "Ben takes personal credit for you and Jason getting together. He says he could see the sparks between you from a mile away, even though you both worked so hard to fight it. He was sure Jason would cave eventually, if the two of you could just spend enough time together."

Laney chuckled as she watched the two men riding a wave together toward the shore. "Well, he was right, wasn't he? He can take all the credit he wants." She let her eyes linger on the pleasing lines of Jason's wetsuit. He was all hers now, and she fully intended to keep him. Looking back on the first few days of their acquaintance, all their confusion and deliberation seemed ridiculous. How could they have seemed so different, when they were really so much alike? Adrenaline-junkies, both of them. Lovers of life. Adventurers. She hadn't recognized those qualities in herself until she met him. And he hadn't known what love was. Not till it smacked him upside the head.

Now it all seemed crystal clear, even the niggling discontent she'd felt while living in Missouri and Oklahoma. The whole time she'd been pining for the ocean, unwittingly and involuntarily, because it was a part of her. Maybe in a past life she'd been a fisherman or a sea captain or a narwhal... she didn't really know how it was possible. But the sea flowed through her veins now, and she knew she could never bear to be parted from it again. When she picked up her graduate studies, it would be at the University of Victoria. She was still determined to apply her passion for the weather toward more accurate computer storm modelling. She could hardly help it if her thesis turned out to be applicable to surf forecasting as well.

"Yo!" Jason called out as the men trudged up the beach in their surf boots. "It's your turn, Laney." He closed the distance between them and grinned at her. "No more lounging around."

Ben made a show of collapsing next to Haley, spattering sand all over her. "I'm exhausted," he complained. "It's tough to be great. But yes, go on, Laney. You can have all the master's attention now. Who knows? A few more lessons, and you may be almost as good as me."

Everyone laughed. They all knew that Laney's skills had surpassed Ben's ages ago. Jason insisted she was a natural, and Laney didn't argue. Surfing was the single most fun activity she'd ever experienced.

Jason held out his hand, and Laney, clad in a wetsuit nearly identical to his own, took it. As they touched, his eyes gleamed with anticipation.

Correction: Surfing was the second most fun.

About the Author

USA-Today bestselling novelist and playwright Edie Claire was first published in mystery in 1999 by the New American Library division of Penguin Putnam. In 2002 she began publishing award-winning contemporary romances with Warner Books, and in 2008 two of her comedies for the stage were published by Baker's Plays (now Samuel French). In 2009 she began publishing independently, continuing her original Leigh Koslow Mystery series and adding new works of romantic women's fiction, young adult fiction, and humor.

Under the banner of Stackhouse Press, Edie has now published over 25 titles including digital, print, audio, and foreign translations. Her works are distributed worldwide, with her first contemporary romance, *Long Time Coming*, exceeding two million downloads. She has received multiple "Top Pick" designations from *Romantic Times Magazine* and received both the "Reader's Choice Award" from *Road To Romance* and the "Perfect 10 Award" from *Romance Reviews Today*.

A former veterinarian and childbirth educator, Edie is a happily married mother of three who currently resides in Pennsylvania. She enjoys gardening and wildlife-watching and dreams of becoming a snowbird.

Books & Plays by Edie Claire

Romantic Fiction

Pacific Horizons

Alaskan Dawn
Leaving Lana'i
Maui Winds
Glacier Blooming
Tofino Storm

Fated Loves

Long Time Coming
Meant To Be
Borrowed Time

Hawaiian Shadows

Wraith
Empath
Lokahi
The Warning

Leigh Koslow Mysteries

Never Buried
Never Sorry
Never Preach Past Noon
Never Kissed Goodnight
Never Tease a Siamese
Never Con a Corgi

Never Haunt a Historian
Never Thwart a Thespian
Never Steal a Cockatiel
Never Mess With Mistletoe
Never Murder a Birder
Never Nag Your Neighbor

Women's Fiction

The Mud Sisters

Humor

Corporately Blonde

Comedic Stage Plays

Scary Drama I
See You in Bells

CPSIA information can be obtained
at www.ICGtesting.com
Printed in the USA
BVHW032312160120
569740BV00001B/53

9 781946 343048